A GOOD WOMAN

A GOOD WOMAN

A Good Woman

by

LOUIS BROMFIELD

Author of

"THE GREEN BAY TREE"
"POSSESSION"
"EARLY AUTUMN"

GROSSET & DUNLAP, *Publishers*

by arrangement with
FREDERICK A. STOKES COMPANY

Printed in the United States of America

To

STUART P. SHERMAN

TAKEN BY DEATH AT THE MOMENT
WHEN THE AMERICAN WRITING TO WHICH
HE GAVE HIMSELF WITH SO MUCH
DEVOTION, NEEDED HIM MOST SORELY.

FOREWORD

"A Good Woman" is the last of a series of four novels dealing from various angles with a strongly marked phase of American life. The book was planned, without being in any sense a sequel, as part of a picture which includes three other sections—"The Green Bay Tree," "Possession" and "Early Autumn." Taken together the four might be considered as a single novel with the all-encompassing title "Escape."

LOUIS BROMFIELD.

Paris, June 15, 1927.

CONTENTS

PART ONE
THE JUNGLE

A GOOD WOMAN

1

She found the letter when she returned to the slate-colored house from the regular monthly meeting of the Augusta Simpson Branch of the Woman's Christian Temperance Union. It was eleven o'clock at night and this letter lay, like any quite ordinary and usual letter, on the dining-room table in the dim radiance of gaslight turned economically low in the dome hand-painted in a design of wild-roses. Her first thought as she took off her sealskin tippet was that it must have arrived by the last post, which came at four, and so could have been in her hands seven hours earlier if the slattern Essie had not forgotten to give it to her. But what, she reflected as she removed her hat and jacket, could you expect of a girl of unknown parentage taken from the county poor farm to help around the house in return for her clothing, her board and two dollars a month pocket money? What could you expect from a girl who was boy-crazy? How was such a creature to understand what a letter from Philip meant to her? What could a slut like Essie know of a mother's feelings for her only son?

She knew it was from Philip by the round, boyish handwriting and by the outlandish stamp of Zanzibar. (It would be another for the collection of her brother Elmer.)

Mrs. Downes approached the table with the majestic step of a woman conscious of her dignity and importance in the community; the knowledge of these things lay like a shadow across the sweep of her deep bosom, in the carriage of her head, in the defiant rustle of her poplin bustle and leg-o'-mutton sleeves. It was so easy to see that, in her not too far-distant youth, she had been an opulent beauty in the style of Rubens, less yielding and voluptuous, perhaps, than his Venuses, but of a figure which inclined to overflow. And this beauty in its flowering had not gone unnoticed, for in that far-off day she had been courted by half the eligible, and all the ineligible, men of the town. In the brief moments of depression so rare with a person of such abundant vitality, she comforted herself by thinking, "In any case, I could have been the wife of a county judge, or a bank president, or even of a superintendent of the Mills." But the truth was that she was not the wife of any of them (in fact she had no husband at all) because, by a unique error of judgment forever inexplicable, she had chosen to marry one of the ineligibles, the giddiest but the most fascinating of all her suitors. Now, at forty-eight, she had come to believe that it was better so, that she was more content with the position she had made for herself, single-handed, than as a protected wife who was a mere nobody. The memory of her ancient beauty, hardened long ago into roughly chiseled lines by the struggle to succeed, she had put aside as a negligible affair in comparison to the virtues with which time and trouble had endowed her.

Her sense of satisfaction flowed from many springs, not the least of which was the knowledge that when Mr. Downes saw fit to desert her (she always phrased it thus to herself) he had not left behind a bereft and wilting female. She took satisfaction in the knowledge that she had calmly burnt his note explaining that it was impossible for any man to continue living with so much virtue, and then with equal calm told the world that Mr. Downes had gone away to China on business. Rolling up her sleeves, she had embarked fearlessly upon establishing a bakery to support herself and the two-year-old son who remained, the sole souvenir of her derelict mate.

Indeed, she had not even asked help of her brother, Elmer Niman, the pump manufacturer, who could have helped her easily enough, because she could not bear the thought of giving him an opportunity to say, "I told you so," with regard to Mr. Downes, and because she knew well enough that his penurious nature would never provide her with enough to live upon decently. These were the reasons she set down in her conscious mind; the ones which she did not consider were different—that hers was a spirit not to be chained, and possessed of an energy which could not have been soothed by rocking-chairs and mere housekeeping.

And so, almost at once, the bakery had flourished, and as the Mills brought prosperity and hordes of new citizens to the town, it turned presently into the Peerless Bakery and Lunch Room, and quite recently it had become the Peerless Restaurant, occupying an entire ground-floor at the corner of Maple and Main Streets. She was now known in the town as "an independent woman," which meant that she had no debts, owned her own house, and possessed a flourishing business.

All this she had wrought out of nothing, by her own

energy, and far from harboring thoughts of retire-
ment, she still went every day to survey the cooking and
to sit near the cash-register during the full stream of
noon and evening patronage.

But Mr. Downes, it seemed, fancied himself well out
of a bad bargain, for he never returned; and when a
year had passed, during which she constantly spoke of
his letters and his doings in China, she went to the
mausoleum which her brother called his home and told
him that she had had no news of Mr. Downes for some
months and that she feared something had happened
to him in the Orient, which was, as he (Elmer) knew, a
sinister place at best. So Elmer Niman, hopeful that
some fatal catastrophe had befallen a brother-in-law
of whom he disapproved, and to whom he had never
spoken, took up the matter with the Government. The
ensuing investigation dragged into light two or three
stray, light-fingered gentlemen whose last desire was
to be unearthed, but found no trace of the missing
Mr. Downes—a mystery explained perhaps in Emma's
mind by the fact that he had never been in China at all
and that she had never received any letters from him.

In due time Mrs. Downes put on mourning and the
derelict husband became enveloped in the haze of romance which surrounds one who apparently has met
his death among the bandits of the Manchurian mountains. From then on she never spoke of him save as
"Poor Mr. Downes!" or "My poor husband!" or to
friends as "Poor Jason!" She alluded to a fatally
adventurous nature which she had never been able to
subdue and which had always filled her with foreboding.
And now, twenty-four years later, she had come, herself, to believe that his body had long ago turned to

dust in the Gobi Desert. (She had always been rather vague about geography and from time to time distributed his remains over half of Asia.) At the time the affair aggravated her brother's nervous dyspepsia by causing him much fury and agitation, and it cost the Government a large amount of money, but it fixed the legend of Mr. Downes' business trip to China, and so left her with more dignity and prestige than are the lot of a deserted wife.

The sedative effect of more than twenty years had dimmed the fascination of Mr. Downes to a point where it was possible for her to believe that he was, after all, only a scamp who had trifled with her affections and one whom she had never really loved at all—or at least only enough to make the presence of a son respectable in the eyes of the Lord. If he had "lived," she told herself, he would have gone his waggish, improvident way, leaving her and her son somewhat at the mercy of the dyspeptic Elmer; as things stood, she was successful and well off. Her once passionate and rather shameful desire to have him back seemed very remote now; she no longer wanted him to return; her only fear was that he might rise from the grave in which she had placed him with such thoroughness. For years the thought had raised an uneasy feeling in her bosom; but when years passed without a word from him she decided that he must really be dead. There were still moments, however, when she came close to betraying herself by saying, "When Mr. Downes went away"—which could, of course, pass for meaning anything at all.

Each night she thanked God that her son—their son, she was forced to admit—would never know that his father was a scamp. He was a half-orphan to whom she had been both mother and father, and her training (she thanked God again) had left its mark. Her son was a fine young man with no bad habits, smoking, drinking or otherwise, who, married to Naomi Potts (known throughout the churchgoing world as "the youngest missionary of God"), was himself spreading the light among the heathen of that newly discovered land between Victoria-Nyanza and the Indian Ocean. He and Naomi and a third missionary were the first in the field. "In blackest Africa" was the way she expressed it. "My son," she would say proudly, "who is head of a mission in blackest Africa."

No, she reflected frequently, it was impossible to think of Philip, so handsome, so clean, so pure, so virtuous, so molded by her own hand, as the son of Jason Downes. She had succeeded in everything save changing his appearance: he had the same rather feline good looks which had ruined his father by inducing women to fling themselves at his head. (It was a thing she could never understand—how any woman could fling herself at the head of a man, even a man as handsome as Jason had been.)

2

The sight of the letter, so carelessly tossed aside by Essie, filled her with a sense of disappointment: if she had only received it at the proper time, she could have read it to the ladies of the Augusta Simpson Branch. Only an hour before she had "craved the indulgence" of the ladies while she read "one of my son's interesting letters about the work they are doing in blackest Africa." The letter still crackled in her reticule, filling her with an immense pride, for was not the career of Philip, and Philip himself, simply another evidence of her sterling character? If Essie hadn't been a slut she would have had two letters to read.

She drew her solid body up to the table and, clamping on her pince-nez (which for a moment exasperated her by becoming entangled in the white badge of her temperance) she tore open the battered letter and holding it at arm's length because of her far-sightedness, began to read.

At first glance she was disturbed by the brevity of it and by the fact that there was no enclosure from Naomi. Usually Philip wrote pages.

"Dear Ma:

"I write this in great haste to tell you that by the time this reaches you we will be on our way home.

"I don't know whether the news has reached you, but there has been an uprising among the tribes to the north of Megambo. They attacked the mission and we narrowly escaped with our lives. I was wounded, but not badly. Naomi is all right. There was a strange Englishwoman who got caught with us. She wasn't a missionary but middle-aged and the sister of a British general. She was seeing the country and doing some shooting.

"We sail from Capetown in ten days and ought to be home in time for Christmas. I ought to tell you that I've made a mistake in my calling. I'm not going to be a missionary any longer. That's why I'm coming

*home. Naomi is against it, but when she saw I was in
earnest she came, too.*

"*I will try to send you a letter from Capetown, but
can't promise. I am very upset and feel sick. Meanwhile love from your devoted son.*

"*Philip.*"

For a moment she simply stared at the letter, incapable of any logical thought. Her hand, which
never shook, was shaking. She was for a moment, but
only a moment, a broken woman. And then, slowly,
she read it again to make certain that she had not read
it wrongly. On reflection, she saw clearly that he was
upset. The letter was hasty and disorderly in composition; the very handwriting had changed, losing
its round, precise curves, here and there, in sudden
jagged and passionate downstrokes. And at the end
he did not write, as he always did, "We pray for you
every night."

Beneath the shower of light from the wild-rose dome
she tried to fathom the meaning of the letter, struggling
meanwhile with a sudden sense of loneliness such as she
hadn't experienced since she sat in the same spot years
before reading Jason's last letter. Coming home, giving
up the work of the Lord in blackest Africa! (Just
after she had read aloud before all those women one of
his interesting letters.) Philip, who had always placed
his hopes unfalteringly in the hope of the Lord. *I've
made a mistake in my calling.* What could he mean by
that? How could one mistake a call from the Lord?

He was, she saw, in earnest. He had not even
waited for a letter from her. If she could only have
written she would have changed everything. And there

was that hint, so ominous, that he would have left
Naomi behind if she chose not to follow him. Something strange, something terrifying, she felt, had
happened, for nothing else could explain this sudden
deterioration of character. There was no hint of what
had caused it, nothing (and her suspicions were
bristling) unless it had to do with that Englishwoman.
For a moment she felt that she was dealing with some
intangible mystery and so was frightened.

After she had grown more calm, it occurred to her
that this strange, inexplicable letter might have been
caused by the fever that had attacked him twice, that
it was a result of the wound he wrote of, or perhaps
merely a passing wild idea—only Philip had never had
any wild ideas, for you couldn't properly call his
ecstatic devotion to God a wild emotion. Once, as a
boy, he had had a sudden desire to become an artist,
but she had changed him quickly and easily. No, he
had always been a good boy who obeyed her. He did
not have silly ideas.

During an hour shaken with doubts and fears, one
terror raised its head above the others—the terror that
after twenty-four years of careful training and control,
twenty-four years spent in making him as perfect as his
father had been imperfect, the blood of Jason Downes
was coming into its own to claim the son which she
had come long ago to think of only as her own.

The return of Philip seemed almost as great a
calamity as the flight of his father. For the second
time in her existence a life carefully and neatly arranged appeared to fall into ruin. How was she to
explain this shameful change of Philip's heart to the
Reverend Castor, the members of the church, the

women who had listened to his letters? It was, she saw, an astonishing, scandalous thing. What missionary had ever turned back from the path shown him by God? What was Philip to do if he was not to be a missionary?

She tried to imagine the confusion and trouble the affair must be causing Naomi, who was the child of missionaries. She had never *really* liked Naomi, but she felt sorry for her now, as sorry as it was possible for a mother to feel for the wife of her son. But Naomi, she thought, almost at once, was quite able to look out for herself, and she must be working on Philip, even now, to turn him back to God. Suddenly she had an unaccustomed feeling of warmth for Naomi. After all, Naomi had had a great success four years ago at the tent meetings. She had converted scores of people then; certainly she could do much to turn Philip from his colossal error and sin.

Her first impulse to take the letter to Elmer died abruptly, as a similar impulse had died twenty-four years earlier. For the present she would say simply that Philip and Naomi were on their way home to rest from their hardships, from the fevers and the wound which Philip had received during a native uprising. She regretted that Philip had not written some details of the affair, because it would have made a most fascinating story. The ladies would have been so interested in it. . . .

3

Rising, she removed the stamp for Elmer and then thrust the letter itself boldly into the blue flames of the anthracite stove. Then she turned out the gas and with a firm step made her way up the creaking stairs of the house which she owned, free of all mortgage and encumbrance, made so by her own efforts. She had decided upon a course of action. She would say nothing and perhaps by the day Philip arrived he would have been made to see the light by Naomi. Meanwhile his return could be explained by his hardships, his illness and his wound. The poor boy was a hero.

On the way up she remembered that she must reprove Essie about the letter, though, as it turned out, it was perhaps just as well that she hadn't seen it until after the meeting, for she could scarcely have read one of Philip's letters with a whole heart knowing all the while that he was already on his way home, fleeing from the hardships the Lord saw fit to impose. Still Essie must be reproved: she had committed an error.

Again she fell to racking her brain for some explanation of what had happened to Philip. He had never been unruly, undutiful or ungrateful save during that period when he had been friends with Mary Conyngham and it couldn't, of course, be Mary Conyngham's bad influence, since she hadn't seen him in years and was a woman now with two children and a husband buried only the day before yesterday.

While she undressed she reflected that she had had a hard day full of cares, and she thanked God for that immense vitality which never allowed weariness to take possession of her. She had fought before, and now, with God's help, she would fight again, this time to save her boy from the heritage of his father's blood. When she had brushed her short, thin hair and donned a nightgown of pink outing-flannel with high neck and long sleeves, she knelt in the darkness by the side of the vast walnut bed and prayed. She was a devout woman and she prayed every night, never carelessly or through mere force of habit. Although she did not discount her own efforts, she looked upon prayer as one of the elements which had made of her life a success. Religion to Emma Downes was not tainted with ecstasy and mysticism; in her hands it became a practical, businesslike instrument of success. To-night she prayed with greater passion than she had known since those far-off days (whose memory now filled her with shame) when she had prayed in the fervor of an un-balanced and frightening passion for Mr. Downes, that the worthless scamp might be returned to her, for her to protect and spoil.

She prayed passionately that the Lord might guide the feet of her strayed boy back in the consecrated paths on which she had placed him; and as she prayed it occurred to her in another part of her mind that with Philip as the first in the field she might one day be the mother of the Bishop of East Africa. And when at last she lay in bed the awful sense of loneliness re-turned to claim possession of her. For the first time in years she felt an aching desire for the missing Jason Downes. She wanted him lying there beside her as he had once done, so that she could share with him this new burden that the Lord had seen fit to impose upon her.

4

The mission, a little cluster of huts, two built of mud and logs and the others no more than flimsy affairs of thatched reeds, stood at the edge of a tangled forest, on a low hill above the marshy borders of the tepid lake. All about it there rose a primeval world, where the vegetation was alternately lush and riotous or burned to a cinder, and the earth at one season lay soaked with water and gave off a hot mist and at another turned so dry that the fantastic birds and animals for hundreds of miles gathered about the life-giving lake to drink and kill and leave the border strewn with bleaching bones. Once, a dozen years earlier, the mission had been a post for Portuguese slave-traders, but with the end of the trade the jungle had once more taken possession, thrusting whole trees through the decaying thatch and overrunning barricade and huts with a tangle of writhing vines. It was thus they had come upon it, young Philip Downes and his pale wife, Naomi, and the strange Swede, Swanson, who by some odd circumstance felt that he was called by God from the state of hospital porter to save the heathen from their sin. Of the three, only Naomi, the daughter of missionaries, knew anything of the hostility of such a world. Philip was a boy of twenty-three who had never been outside his own state and Swanson only an enormous, stupid, tow-headed man with the strength of a bull.

It was a world of the most fantastic exaggeration, where the very reeds that bordered the lake were tall as trees and the beasts which trampled them down—the lumbering leviathans of the Old Testament—were, it seemed, designed upon a similar scale. In the moonlight the beasts thrust their way by sheer bulk to break great paths to the feeding-grounds along the shore. At times, during the rainy season, whole acres of the shore broke loose and drifted away, each island a floating jungle filled with beasts and birds, to some remote, unseen part of the greenish, yellow sea. One could watch them in the distance, fantastic, unreal ships, alive like the shore with ibis and wild ducks, herons and the rosy paradisical flamingoes whose color sometimes touched the borders of the lake with the glory of the sunrise.

It was here in this world that Philip, with an aching head and a body raw with the bites of insects, found the first glow of that romance with which Naomi, despite her poverty of words, her clumsiness of expression and her unseeing eyes, had managed to invest all Africa. In the beginning, during those first terrible nights, Philip felt the unearthly beauty of the place was dimmed by a kind of horror that seemed to touch all the primeval world about him. It excited him but it also roused an odd, indescribable loathing. It seemed naked, cruel and too opulent. But in the beginning there had been no time to ponder in morbidity over such things; there was only time for work, endless work—the chopping away of the stubborn vines and saplings, the strengthening of roofs, the filling-in of gaps in the stockade against thieving natives and prowling animals. For him the work beneath the blazing sun was a ceaseless agony; he had not the slow, oxlike patience nor the clumsy, skillful carpenter's hands of Swanson. There was only work, work, work, with no prospect of conquering the heat, the rains and the horrible vegetation which, possessed of an animal intelligence, sprang up alive where it had been slaughtered only the day before. It seemed to him in moments of blank discouragement that all which remained of their lives must be sacrificed simply in a struggle to exist at all. There would be no time to spread the Word among the black people who watched them, alternately shy as gazelles or hilarious as hyenas, from the borders of the forest or the marshes.

He was not a large man—Philip—and his hair was dark, curling close against his small head. His skin, olive-colored like his father's, framed blue eyes that seemed to burn with a consuming, inward fire, the eyes of one who would never be happy. And he was neatly made with light, supple muscles. One would have said that of the three he was the one most fitted to survive in the fantastic, cruel world of Megambo.

And yet (he sometimes pondered it himself) the great blond Swanson, with his pale, northern skin and thin yellow hair, and Naomi with her thin, anemic body and white, freckled skin, seemed not to suffer in the least. They worked after he had fallen with exhaustion, his nerves so raw that he would wander off along the lake lest the seething irritation that consumed him should get the better of his temper. Swanson and Naomi went hopefully on, talking of the day when these rotting huts over which they toiled would give way to houses of brick where sons of negro children would sit learning the words that were to lift them from the sloughs of sin to the blessings of their white brethren. Naomi was even more clever than Swanson. Her courage never flagged and the strange, happy, luminous look in her eyes was never dimmed. She knew, too, the tricks of living in such a world, since, except for two voyages to America to raise money for missions, she had never lived in any other.

They could even sleep, Swanson and Naomi, lost

in an abysmal unconsciousness, unmindful of the dreadful sounds that came from the forest, never hearing the ominous rustling of the reeds along the shore, nor the startled, half-human cry of a dying monkey and the steady crunch-crunch of the leviathans pasturing in the brilliant moonlight. They did not hear the roaring of the beasts driven in by the drouth and burning heat from the distant, barren plains. Nothing seemed to touch them, no fear, save that they might fail in their great mission. There were times in those first months when, unable to bear it longer, he burst out to Naomi with the belief that Swanson was only a stupid lout no better than the natives.

And Naomi, taking his hand, would always say, "We must pray, Philip. We must ask God for strength. He will understand and reward our sufferings."

Sometimes he knelt with her while they prayed together for strength. She possessed a sweetness and a calm assurance that at moments made the whole thing all the more unbearable to him.

But no good came of her prayers, not even of the savage remorse which claimed him on such occasions. He was tormented, not alone by a sense of his own weakness, but also by a shameful sense of disloyalty; in that savage world the three of them must cling to each other and to God, even though the place made for them a prison from which there was no escape, wherein their nerves grew frayed from the mere constant association with one another. If they fell asunder, only horror and destruction faced them.

"God," Naomi would say, with the odd, unearthly certainty which colored all her fearless character, "will reward you, Philip. He will reward us all in proportion to our sufferings."

But he found presently, to his horror, that he could not believe what she believed. He felt that he could believe, perhaps, if his sufferings and his reward were both less grandiose. It was harder, too, because there were moments when Naomi and Swanson seemed to him complete strangers who understood nothing of his torments. How could they, whose faith knew no doubts, whose nerves were never worn?

And so, during these first two years, he slipped more and more from a dependence upon God to one upon his mother, who in that smoky mill town on the opposite side of the earth seemed as remote as the Deity Himself. But he could at least write to her, and so ease his soul. He felt that she, who was always right, understood him in a way that was forever closed to Naomi. His mother had suffered and made great sacrifices for his sake. There were no limits to the debt he owed her. In moments when his faith and courage failed, moved more by a desire to please her than to please God, he fancied her, in sudden nostalgic moments, standing near him watching and approving his struggle, always ready to smile and praise. It was that which he needed more than anything—the sympathy which seemed not to exist in Swanson's oxlike body nor in Naomi's consecrated heart. And so he came to pour out his heart to her in long, passionate letters of a dozen pages and she sent him in return the strength he needed.

It was as if the image of Emma Downes hung perpetually above himself and Naomi. From Emma's letters he could see that she never ceased to think of them. She prayed constantly. He could see the pride she had in him to whom she had been both father and mother, teaching him all that he knew of life. He saw that for her sake he must make of this fearsome venture a brilliant, resplendent success, not alone by bringing hundreds of poor, benighted, black souls to Christ, but by rising to the very heights of the church. She had allowed him, her only son, to go out of her widowed tragic life whither he had chosen to go, sending him on his way with words only of hope and encouragement. At times it was less his faith in God than his faith in his mother which gave him the courage to go on.

As if the presence of Naomi broke in upon that bond between them, he took the letters off to the borders of the forest to read them again and again in solitude. In waves of homesickness the tears sometimes came into his eyes. He thought of her in a series of odd detached pictures—bending over his crib when he was a little boy, baking him special rolls of pie-crust flavored with cinnamon, working over the ovens until morning in order to have the toys he wanted at Christmas. He owed her everything.

5

He was, at twenty-three, a boy singularly innocent of life, and since there were, save for his own sufferings, no realities in his existence, he lost himself with all the passion of adolescence in God and Heaven and Hell. Of love (save for that pure flame which burned for his mother) he knew nothing, nor did he understand, for all the agonies of a sensitive nature, such things

as suffering and beauty and splendor. For him, as
for Naomi, the flame of faith engulfed all else, but
for him the flame sometimes flickered and came near
to going out.

He did not know whether he loved Naomi or not,
nor what the emotion of love toward her should be.
They were brother and sister in Christ and so bound
together in Heavenly love. She was his wife by some
divine arrangement which slowly began to be clear to
him.

It had happened during those months when Naomi,
on leave from her father's post, near Lake Tchad, had
come to stay as guest in his mother's house, and in
that zealous atmosphere, she had seemed a creature
bathed in the rosy glow of Heavenly glamour. In the
church and at those tent meetings where she spoke
from the same platforms as the great evangelist, Homer
Quackenbrush, people honored her as something akin
to a saint. She was a real missionary, only twenty-
three, who had been born in a mission and had never
known any other life. He had listened while she
spoke in her curious, loud flat voice of her experiences
in Africa and slowly she had worked a sort of enchantment upon him. He became fascinated, enthralled,
filled by a fire to follow her in her work, to seize the
torch (as she described it) and carry it on, unconscious all the while that it was not the faith but something of the mystery and romance of Africa that
captured him. He had gone home one night after the
singing to tell his mother that instead of seeking a
church he meant to become a missionary. Together
they had knelt and prayed while Emma Downes, with

tears pouring down her face, thanked God for sending the call to her boy.

And then, somehow, he had married Naomi, never understanding that he had consented to the marriage, and even desired it, not because he was in love with Naomi Potts, but with the mystery and color of Africa which clung to her thin, pale figure and her dowdy clothes. The marriage had filled his mother with happiness, and she was always right; she had been right ever since he could remember.

He never knew that he had married without ever having known youth. He had been a boy of an oddly mystical and passionate nature and then, suddenly caught by a wave of wild emotion, he had become overnight a married man. Yet there came to him at odd times the queerest feeling of strangeness and amazement toward Naomi; there were moments when, rousing himself as if from a dream, he found that he was watching her as she went about her work, wondering what she was and how it had come about that at twenty-three he found himself married to her—this stranger who seemed at times so much nearer to Swanson than to himself.

It was difficult to confide in Naomi or even to think of her as an ally. She worked like a man and slept too peacefully; she never had any doubts. Even when she nursed himself and Swanson through the fever (which miraculously passed her by that they might be saved to carry on their work) she went about tirelessly with the expression of a saint on her plain, freckled face. In moments when the chills left his miserable and shaking body for a time, he fancied (watching her) that the Christian martyrs must have had the same serene look in their eyes. You could not look at her without feeling your faith growing stronger. It was better than reading God's Word. . . .

And yet she never seemed quite real, quite human. There was no bond between them save their work.

6

It was not prayer that brought them in the end a certain rest and peace, but the coming of the dry season, when for a time Nature changed her plan of torment and gave them a respite. At about the same time there began to steal over Philip the sense of peace that comes of growing used to suffering. They learned how to protect themselves from the insects and how to keep a fire burning all night to frighten away prowling animals, how to outwit the porcupines that attacked their yams and the armies of voracious ants which had twice marched through the compound bent upon devouring the very dwellings over their heads. They succeeded in persuading the natives that they were neither gods nor slave-traders, but only fellowmen come to save them from a vague and awful destiny.

And again it was Naomi who succeeded where Philip failed. It was as if the naked blacks possessed some instinct which told them that he lacked the fire that burned in the heart of Naomi. She had a way of reassuring the black girls who, giggling and slapping one another, hung about the enclosure. With an immeasurable perseverance she drew them into the stockade, where she gave them gaudy trinkets out of her own pitiful stock. And at last one morning Philip returned from shooting ducks to find her telling them stories out of the Bible in a queer jargon made up of signs and Bantu words and the savage, guttural sounds she had picked up somehow from contact with the natives. Swanson, with all the handicap of a stupid brain, followed in her steps.

It was at the end of the second year when the natives, bored, began to slip away and all their efforts seemed to come to nothing, that Philip became aware of an awful doubt. It seemed to him in the agony of worn nerves that there was a vague and irresistible force which kept drawing Naomi and Swanson nearer and nearer to each other, into an alliance, horribly treasonable in a world of three people, against himself. It was a torturing sensation, not even of honest jealousy which would at least have been clear and definite, but only an inexplicable, perhaps unjustified, feeling of being thrust aside from the currents of understanding which bound them together. Naomi was *his* wife and she obeyed him, as did Swanson, because he was the active defender of their little world; yet even this seemed to draw them together. Sometimes in a kind of madness he fancied that they plotted against him almost without knowing it, by some secret, unspoken understanding.

It never occurred to him that there was any question of infidelity, for such a thing had no place in their scheme of things. He knew, as he knew that the sun rose each morning, that she was as virginal as the dew which fell on cold nights. Except as they appeared embarrassingly in their contact with the natives such things as lust and love and birth did not exist. Yet there were moments when he seemed to grow dizzy and the whole universe appeared to tremble about him, when he was like a tree shaken in a tempest. He became prey to a vague sense of misery from which he found rest only by tramping for hours along the borders of the lake. At such times it seemed that there lay before him only bafflement and frustration. Once he came to his senses in horror to find himself at the edge of the lake ready to commit the greatest of sins, that of murdering himself, a servant of God.

From then on he suffered a new horror—that he might be going mad.

Sometimes in the night he lay restless and tormented, scarcely knowing what it was that gave him no peace save that it was in some way concerned with Naomi lying in the hut opposite him in the glow of the fire. She slept like a child, her face lighted with the familiar look of bland satisfaction—Naomi whom he had never approached, whom he had never kissed since the day of the wedding years and years ago, it seemed now, in that black and sooty town on the other side of the world. To touch her, to attempt the horrible thing he could not put from his mind, would, he knew, turn their tiny, intense world into a hell and so destroy all they had built up with so much agony and terror.

He was afraid of her for some profound, unnamable reason. In the long, still nights, when every sound took on the violence of an explosion, he had at times a sinister feeling that he stood at the edge of a yawning chasm into which he might precipitate the three of them by so much as crossing the room.

For it had been arranged long ago in the darkened parlor of his mother's house that he and Naomi were never to live together as man and wife, never so long as their minds and bodies were occupied in their consecration to Christ. It was Emma Downes who arranged everything, standing in the parlor on the day of the wedding, talking to a Philip dressed in black and newly ordained both as missionary and bridegroom.

When he thought of his mother it was always as he had seen her on that day—wise, powerful, good and filled with joy and faith, in her purple merino dress with the gold chain attached to Aunt Maria's watch— a woman to whom he owed everything.

He could hear her saying with a strange translucent clarity, "Of course, now that you and Naomi have given yourselves to God, you must sacrifice everything to your work—pleasure, temptations, even" (and here her voice dropped a little) "even the hope of children. Because it is impossible to think of Naomi having a child in the midst of Africa. And any other way would be the blackest of sins. Of course it wouldn't be right for a young girl like Naomi to go to a post with a man she wasn't married to—so you must just act as if you weren't married to her. . . . Some day, perhaps when you have a year's leave from the post, you might have a child. I could take care of it, of course, when you went back."

And then looking aside, she had added, "Naomi asked me to speak to you about it. She's so shy and pure, she couldn't bring herself to do it. I promised her I would."

Sitting on the edge of the narrow sofa, he had promised because life was still very hazy to him and the promise seemed a small and unimportant thing.

Indeed he had only a hazy knowledge of what she meant and he blushed at his mother's mention of such "things."

7

It was during the third year that the image of his mother began to grow a little blurred. At times the figure on the opposite side of the world seemed less awe-inspiring, less indomitable, less invincible. He wasn't a boy any longer. He had knowledge of life gained from the crude, primitive world about him, and of the intimations born of his own sufferings. It was impossible to exist unchanged amid such hardships, among black people who lived with the simplicity of animals and held obscene festivals dedicated to unmentionable gods of fertility.

He had come to Africa, one might have said, without a face—with only a soft, embryonic boyish countenance upon which life had left no mark; but now, at twenty-six, his features were hardened and sharpened—the straight, rather snub nose, the firm but sensual mouth, the blue eyes in which a flame seemed forever to be burning. The fevers left their mark. There were times when, dead with exhaustion, he had the look of a man of forty. Behind the burning eyes, there was forming slowly a restless, inquiring intelligence, blended oddly of a heritage from the shrewd woman who was always right and of the larky cleverness of a father he could not remember.

Naomi had noticed the change, wondering that he could have grown so old while she and Swanson remained unchanged. There were even little patches of gray at his temples—gray at twenty-six. For days she would not notice him at all, for she was endlessly busy, and then she would come upon him suddenly sitting on a log or emerging from the forest with a queer dazed look in his eyes, and she would say, "Come, Philip, you're tired. We'll pray together."

Prayer, she was certain, would help him.

Once, when she found him lying face down on the earth, she had touched his head with her hand, only to have him spring up crying out, "For God's sake, leave me in peace!" in a voice so terrible that she had gone away again.

The look came more and more often into his eyes. She watched him for days and at last she said, "Philip, you ought to go down to the coast. If you stay on you'll be having the fever."

She was plaiting grass at the moment to make a hat for herself. Standing above her, he looked down, wondering at her contentment.

"But you'll go too?" he asked.

"No . . . I couldn't do that, Philip . . . not just now—in the very midst of our work, at a time like this, Swanson couldn't manage alone and we'd lose all we'd gained. I'm strong enough, but you must go."

"I won't go . . . alone."

She went on plaiting without answering him, and he said at last, "It doesn't make any difference. I'm no good here. I'm only a failure. I'm better off dead."

She still did not cease her plaiting.

"That's cowardly, Philip, and wicked. God hears what you say."

He turned away dully. "I'd go to the coast if you'd go."

"I can't go, Philip. . . . God means us to stay."

The dazed look vanished suddenly in a blaze of fire. "God doesn't care what happens to us!"

Then for the first time she stopped her work. Her hands lay motionless and her face grew white. "You must pray God to forgive you. He hears everything." And then flinging herself down on her knees, she began to pray in her loud, flat voice. She prayed long after he had disappeared into the forest, now running, now walking, scarcely knowing what he did.

He had wanted desperately to go to the coast, partly because he felt tired and ill, but more because it would have been a change from the monotony, a lark, a pitiful groping toward what he had heard people call "a good time." And he couldn't go alone, for staying alone in some filthy town on the Indian Ocean where he knew no one was no better than staying at Megambo. Yet the thought of the coast, however bad it might be, stirred him with a new hunger simply to escape: it was not the coast itself, but the thing for which it stood as a symbol—the great world which lay beyond the barrier that shut in the three of them there on the low hill between the forest and the lake. . . .

In the end he was afraid to go lest he might never come back.

He did not fall ill again with the fever and so give Naomi another proof of her infallibility and her intimacy with God's intentions; and presently he plunged savagely into the ungrateful work among those childish black people whom he loathed, not because God had refilled the springs of his faith, but because it seemed the only way to save himself.

But something queer had happened to him as he watched Naomi fling herself into the dust to pray for him, something which in a way brought him peace, for the night no longer brought with it a cloud of confused and vague desires. It was not actual hatred that took the place of the torments, but only an indifference which closed him in once and forever from Naomi and Swanson. His life became a solitary thing which did not touch the lives of the others.

For as he plunged into the forest a great light burst upon him and he saw that Naomi, rather than leave Megambo, would have let him stay, without a thought, to die in that malarial hole.

8

It was the same dry season that marked the beginning of a new life in which he saw things which remained hidden to the others. It had been going on for a long time before he noticed any change beyond the fact that there were occasions when the lake, the distant mountains, and the flamingo-tinted marshes seemed more beautiful than they had been before. He noticed strange colors in the forest and the sound of bees and the curious throb of tom-toms in the village. Things which once he had felt only with the rawness of frayed nerves, he discovered in a new way. It was as if what had been a nightmare was turning into a pleasant, fantastic dream.

And then one day it came upon him suddenly as a sort of second sight, in a flash of revelation which the Prophets would have said descended to him from God; it was a kind of inspired madness which changed the very contours of the world about him, altered its colors and revealed meanings that lay beneath. For a time the lake, the low hills, the forest, all seemed illuminated by a supernatural light.

He had been tramping the borders of the muddy lake since dawn and as the sun, risen now, began to scald away the scant dew, he threw himself down to rest in the precarious shadow of a stunted acacia. Lying on his back he watched the wild bees and the tiny, glittering gnats weaving their crazy patterns through the checkered light and shadow, until presently there swept over him a strange, unearthly sense of peace, in which he seemed to exist no longer as an individual set apart, but only as a part of all the world of bees and gnats and animals and birds all about him. All at once the fears and torments of his mind became no more substantial than the shadows of the parched acacia-leaves. He seemed suddenly to fit into some grand scheme of things in which he occupied but a tiny, insignificant place, yet one in which he knew an odd, luxurious sense of freedom and solitude, cut off from Naomi and Swanson, and from all the things for which they stood as symbols. Dimly he experienced a desire to remain thus forever, half-enchanted, bathed as in a bath of clean cold water, in a feeling of senses satisfied and at peace.

He never knew how long he lay thus, but he was aware, after a long time, of music drifting toward him through the hot, pungent air from somewhere near the borders of the lake. It was a weird, unearthly sound which resolved itself slowly into a pattern of melody sung by high-pitched, whining voices—a melody cast in a minor key, haunting and beautiful in its simplicity, tragic in the insinuation of its haunting echoes. It was brief, too, scarcely a dozen bars in the notation of civilized music, but repeated over and over again until it became a long, monotonous chant. Its few notes belonged to that bare, savage world as the flamingoes and the hippopotami belonged to it.

Sitting up with his brown hands clasped about his knees, he listened, permitting the sound to flow over his tired nerves; and straining his feeble knowledge of the savage tongue, he discovered what it was they were singing. Their reed-like voices repeated over and over again:

> *Go down to the water, little monkey,*
> *To the life of lives, the beginning of all things.*
> *Go down to the water, little monkey,*
> *To the life of lives, the beginning of all things.*

Slowly he raised himself to his knees and discovered whence the music came. Through a wide gap in the reeds, trampled down by the great beasts of the lake, he caught a distant view of a procession of black women, slim and straight, all of them, as the papyrus that bordered the water. They wore the amulets and the wire ornaments of virgins and carried earthen jars balanced on their heads. At the edge of the water they stooped to fill the jars and raising them to their heads rose and moved up the banks. They were bringing life to the yam plantations, carrying the water from the lake to the parching earth on the high banks.

He knew them; they belonged to a remote village where the activities of Naomi and Swanson had not yet penetrated. Once or twice he had discovered them, perhaps these same black virgins, peering at him from the shelter of the thick forest. But they were different now, touched by a savage dignity that arose from a confidence in their own solitude. One line moved up the bank and the other down, passing and repassing each other in a perfection of repeated contours. They marched to the rhythm of their endless chant, their high-pointed, virginal breasts and slim bodies glistening like black marble in the sun.

Go down to the water, little monkey,
To the life of lives, the beginning of all things.

Creeping forward on his hands and knees, he came to an opening which revealed the goal of their march. It was a yam plantation and set in the midst was a grotesque figure, half-man, half-beast, carved of wood and painted in brilliant colors, a monstrous image such as he had seen once at the orgiastic festivals in the village at Megambo. One by one as they passed it, each virgin put down her jar and prostrated herself. Each third one emptied the water over the belly of the obscene god. He knew what it was. By chance, he witnessed a rite not meant for his profane eyes, a religious ceremony which none ever witnessed save the virgins who performed it. There was a black man at Megambo whose eyes had been pierced for having watched the adoration of the god of fertility.

Watching the thing, Philip was seized by a sudden passionate desire to set down in some fashion the beauty of the weird procession, to capture and fix the flow of the repeated contours and the sad splendor of the moaning chant. He wanted passionately to make the world—that great world which lay beyond the ragged coast towns—see the wild beauty which he found in the scene. His brown, thin, young hands felt a fierce hunger for some instrument with which he might draw the scene. The desire struck down, down deep into the past, into the hazy, half-forgotten childhood, when he had made pictures for Mary Conyngham, trying all the while to make her see what he saw in the world about him.

Then, abruptly, while he lay there on his stomach watching, the chanting ceased and the figures of black ivory slipped away like shadows into the dark forest, leaving him alone in a world that had suddenly become translated into something that lay beyond reality, in which every color seemed to have grown brilliant and every leaf and tree-trunk seemed outlined by light. The stagnant lake, lying like brass beneath a flaming sun, took on a beauty he had not seen there before.

It was a strange, new world in which he was still lonely, but in a different way. It no longer held any terror for him. He seemed in a miraculous fashion to understand things which before had been hidden from him.

9

It was noon and the air was filled with a scalding heat when he came at last within sight of the mission. Long before he saw it, there came toward him, on the hot breeze, the familiar sound that was like the droning of a hive of bees, and as he drew nearer he caught sight of Naomi seated beneath the thatched portico of the main hut, on a little platform built for her by Swanson to keep her long skirts out of the dust. Before her on the parched earth sat nine girls shrouded in shapeless sacks of magenta and white calico; they were repeating after her in droning voices the story of the visit of the Queen of Sheba to the court of Solomon. They repeated it in a version translated clumsily by Naomi herself, but out of it they managed somehow to wring an irresistible and monotonous rhythm which caused their supple bodies to sway backward and forward.

She was shrewd, Naomi! She had chosen the story of a black queen.

And then he saw that the performance was being watched by another person, a stranger, white like themselves. It was a woman, dressed like a man save that in place of trousers she wore an extremely short skirt that barely reached the tops of her strong boots. She was tall and thin with a long horse face burned and leathery from exposure to the weather. She stood like a man, with her legs rather well apart, her hands in the pockets of an extremely worn and soiled jacket, watching the spectacle out of a pair of bright blue eyes that were kindled with the light of a great intelligence. She might have been forty-five or sixty: it was impossible to say.

The forest behind her, he suddenly discovered, was alive with negroes who moved about cooking over the coals of a fire, their activities directed by a nervous, yellow man with the hooked nose of an Arab. They were niggers from the North, from somewhere near Lake Tchad.

As he approached, the woman turned sharply and after giving him a searching look, resumed her absorption in the spectacle, saying at the same time in a low voice as if he had entered in the midst of a service that was not to be interrupted, "I am Lady Millicent Wimbrooke. I am on my way south. I asked hospitality for a few hours, as good water is difficult to find."

It was a flat, metallic voice, without color, and after she had spoken, she took no more notice of him. She appeared to be fascinated by the spectacle of Naomi and the black girls repeating their lessons. About the hard mouth there flickered the merest shadow of mockery.

There was something menacing in the presence of the Englishwoman, something which seemed to fill the hot air with an electric tension. It was like having a fragment of some powerful explosive suddenly placed in their midst for a few hours, something which they might regard without touching. Also she was extremely hard and disagreeable.

She ate with them at the crude table fashioned by Swanson, having herself contributed the meat—the tenderest portion of a young antelope shot early that morning on the plains by her own hand. She talked of the country with a sort of harassed intensity as if she hated and despised it and yet was powerless to resist its fascination.

"They're no earthly good, these damned niggers," she said, "they'd all leave me at the clap of a hand to die of starvation and thirst. It's only the Arab's whip that keeps them in order."

Philip felt himself hating her for her arrogance and for the contempt she had for all this world, including themselves, but he sometimes felt as she did about the "damned niggers." He saw Naomi recoil as the words fell from the stranger's thin, hard lips. It was blasphemy to speak thus of their black brothers, of God's children.

But Lady Millicent did give them much valuable information about the Lake tribes and their fierce neighbors in the North. She knew, it appeared, an immense amount about this wild country. She was, she said scornfully, an old maid and she had first come out to this malignant country five years earlier with her brother who had promptly died of fever. She was now making this trip because she had to see the country where only Livingstone and one or two others had been before her.

The Lake tribes, she said, were peaceful black people, who lived by herding a few thin cattle and innumerable scraggy goats brought thither in some time which may well have been as remote as the Deluge. It was fertile land when there was rain and the people were comparatively rich and good-natured. Probably missionaries would find them easy to convert, as they had a childlike curiosity about new stories, and of course the Bible was filled with all sorts of fairy tales. (Again Philip saw Naomi wince and Swanson raise his stupid blue eyes in astonishment and horror.) The Lake people were not warlike; when their fierce neighbors of the North, who lived by robbery and war, came on a raid, the Lake people simply vanished into the bush, taking with them all their possessions, leaving behind only huts which might be burned but could be rebuilt again with little effort. Since the end of the Slave Trade, they had had a long period of peace.

Once Naomi interrupted her by saying, "Our experience with these people has been different. We've used only kindness and it's worked wonders. Of course, they thieve and they lie, but we've only been here three years and in the end we'll make them see that these things are sin."

Lady Millicent laid down her fork. "My dear

woman," she said firmly, "niggers haven't any sense of sin. They don't know what you are talking about. My brother used to say the only good nigger is a dead nigger, and the longer I live the more I'm certain of it."

After that a painful silence descended on the table, for it appeared that this stranger seemed intent not only upon disagreeing with them, but even upon insulting them; Naomi and Swanson, his earnest baby's face streaming with perspiration, took it all mildly, even when Lady Millicent observed that "missionaries often made a lot of trouble. In the Northeast where the niggers have given up polygamy, all the extra women have become whores. Instead of sleeping with one man a dozen times a year, they sleep with three hundred and sixty-five different ones. That's what you have done for them up there."

Swanson suddenly burst out in his funny, incoherent fashion, "If I could talk I'd argue . . . but I'm not good at words." Poor Swanson, who could only work for the Lord with his big, sausage-like hands.

But for a moment, when it seemed possible that she was to have a battle, the face of the Englishwoman softened a bit. She looked almost as if she could be fond of Swanson. For Naomi she had only a nostril-quivering contempt.

As for Philip, he sat all the while watching her like a bird fascinated by a snake. Naomi saw that also.

He seemed scarcely able to think in any sensible fashion; he, who had once believed so profoundly, found himself tossed this way and that by conflicting emotions. She made him feel insignificant and sick. It was as if she had the power of destroying all the satisfaction that should have come from their work.

He had heard of people like this—unbelieving, wicked scoffers who felt no need for turning to God in search of strength; but he could not quite believe in her, this gaunt, fearless old maid. No one had ever disagreed with them before; no one had ever doubted the holy sanctity of their mission; all the world they had known believed in them and covered them with glory, as Naomi had been covered during the tent meeting in the smoky Town. She had the power of making him ashamed that he was such a fool as to believe he could help the "damned niggers." She made him feel in a disgusting way ashamed of Naomi and poor, stupid Swanson. And then immediately he was ashamed of being ashamed. He had, too, a sudden flash of consciousness that the three of them were helpless, silly babes, facing a terrifying mystery. They were like insects attacking feebly a mountain of granite. To succeed one needed to be as hard as Lady Millicent Wimbrooke.

She disturbed him, too, as an intimation of that world which lay beyond, awaiting him.

After the meal she rose abruptly and summoned two bearers, who set up a collapsible canvas bathtub in one of the huts. When they had filled it with water and she had bathed, she slept for an hour, and then, summoning the Arab, Ali, set the train of bearers in order with the air of a field-marshal, and thanking her hosts, started her caravan on its way through the forest, herself at the head, walking strongly, her short skirt slipping about her bony knees.

When she had gone, the three of them—Swanson, Naomi and Philip—stood at the gate of the enclosure looking after the procession until the last of the bearers was swallowed up in the thick shadows of the forest.

Then in silence they returned to their work, disturbed and puzzled by the odd feeling of suspense she left in passing.

Late that afternoon Naomi observed suddenly, "She oughtn't to have stopped here. She is a wicked woman."

10

It was long after midnight when Philip was awakened out of a deep sleep by a sound like thunder. Sitting up in his bunk (for he always wakened quickly and sharply) he experienced a feeling of delight that it would rain soon, putting an end to the long, baking drouth. And then slowly he understood that there could be no thunder at this season, and that it was not the sound of thunder; it was too small and sharp and ordered. It was a sound made by man lacking in the grandiosity of the preposterous Nature that dominated Megambo.

Sitting on the edge of the rough bed, he saw the familiar outlines of the mission take form in the darkness—the hut with the eternal insects and animals rustling in the thatch, the bunk opposite where Naomi lay sleeping quietly, all her dislike of Lady Millicent effaced now by the blank look of contentment. He saw the storeroom and Swanson's hut, and last of all the great, lumpy figure of Swanson himself, sitting by a fire that was almost dead. He was asleep with his head sunk between his knees, his great hands hanging like clusters of sausages. (He always fell asleep, careless of danger, certain that God was watching over him.)

It was a clear night, but moonless, when the mon·strous trees showed black against the star-powdered sky, and save for the reverberant, thumping sound, silent, as if the unnatural thunder had frightened the very animals to take cover, to listening with hair and ears bristling. Fascinated by the sound, Philip rose and walked out into the enclosure; he wore, in the hut, only a cloth wrapped about his waist, and standing there beside the dying fire he looked and felt a part of all that untamed wild. He was not a big man, but a singularly well-built one, with muscles hard yet supple —a man such as his father must have been when he aroused such turbulent emotions in a breast so chaste as that of Emma Downes.

Listening to the unearthly sound, Philip extended his arms, watching the muscles flex beneath the tanned smooth skin, and suddenly there swept over him a vivid and poignant sense of delight in being alive. He felt the warm life sweeping through him and a sudden fierce pride in a body of which he had never before been conscious. He had a wild desire to leap the flimsy barricade and running, running in the light of the stars, to lose himself in the sable shadows of the forest.

He thought, "I am alive! I am alive!"

He was aware of the things that exist only in the night, of the demons worshiped by the witch-doctor of Megambo, of unearthly creatures that hovered in the shadows of the forest. The scene by the lake returned to him . . . the procession of virgins pouring the fertile waters of the lake over the belly of a repulsive idol.

He thought, "We are bewitched—Swanson and Naomi and I. We will die prisoners without ever having broken the spell."

In the heat of the still night death seemed all about on every side.

"I am awake and yet asleep. I am the only one who sees. . . ."

The strange thunder kept on and on, now near at hand, now far away, rising and falling in volume.

Again the odd, voluptuous feeling of power lying in his own supple body swept over him. Leaning down he touched Swanson's soft, heavy shoulder. "Swanson," he said, and there was no answer. He shook the man savagely, and Swanson, coming out of a deep sleep, stared up at him.

"Yes, I fell asleep again. . . . I can't help it."

"Listen!" Philip commanded.

After a silence, Swanson said, "It's thunder . . . it's going to rain."

"It's not thunder—look at the sky—what is it? You ought to know."

Swanson was humble with that childlike humbleness that always put Philip to shame, as if he said, "I won't be presumptuous. You're much more clever than I am."

"I don't know," he said; "maybe we'd better ask Naomi."

She wakened quickly, catching at once their vague sense of alarm, for Swanson appeared now to be frightened and uneasy for the first time. She, too, listened and said, "I don't know. I never heard it up North in Pa's country. It sounds like drums—like tom-toms. I've heard that sometimes they signal that-a-away."

The three of them—Philip and Swanson still half-naked (for they had forgotten even decency) and Naomi in a long, shapeless calico nightgown—went out again to stand under the open sky by the fire to listen.

After a long time Naomi said, "Yes, it's drums all right. It must mean some kind of trouble."

They slept no more that night and toward morning as the sky beyond the burnished, black surface of the lake began to turn the color of a flamingo's breast, the sound seemed to die away a little, bit by bit, as if it were a long piece of cane being broken off, a morsel at a time. At daylight it died altogether, leaving only a hot, empty stillness, and far away, near the place where Philip had seen the black virgins, the glow which they had mistaken for the rising dawn turned to the gray smoke of a burning village. The gray column spread fan-wise against the horizon until all the bush for miles lay covered by a thick blanket of gray rising above an angry red line. On the surface of the lake the fragile, black silhouette of a canoe jumped for a moment like a water-spider against the horizon, and disappeared.

The sun, dimmed and red, flooded the basin of the lake and the marshes with dull, yellow light, and revealed the village below them—their own village, Megambo—standing silent and deserted. There was no echo of loud, carefree banter, no crowing of cocks, no sound of women screaming at one another over the morning fires. It was silent like a village stricken with a plague wherein all were dead.

As the day advanced it seemed to Philip that they, too, were dead. In that empty world, he could not bring himself to go off alone into a menacing silence where the sound of a rifle-shot might rouse all the forest into life. It was as if thousands of eyes watched them from out of the shadows. He went as far as the

village and found there not so much as an earthen pot.
A whole people had disappeared, with everything they
possessed, as if the earth had swallowed them up.

The hours dragged one into the next while they
waited; there was no work, for there were no black
people. It was impossible to leave when one did not
even know what there was to flee from. Swanson pot-
tered about with his clumsy hands, suffering less than
Philip or Naomi. He tried vainly to fill in the silence.

As for Naomi, she seemed to have grown suddenly
helpless and dependent, now that the very foundation
of her existence, her reason for living was withdrawn.
Philip, watching her, found a shameful satisfaction in
the sight of Naomi, rudderless and the prey of a nameless terror. Her pale complacence melted into uneasiness. She retired now and then into the hut to
pray. She prayed to the Lord to send them some
sign by which to interpret the silence and the emptiness. He would, she was certain, perform some miracle
as he had done in guiding the Children of Israel out of
the Wilderness. He would not abandon them, his
chosen servants. She abased herself before God, groveling in the dust as the black women had done before
the monstrous idol.

As they watched the distant fire, driven by the
changing wind, eating its way toward them, the terror
mounted, gnawing at their tired nerves.

The faith of Naomi was rewarded, for at last there
came a sign, although it was not in the least religious
and came from the most profane and unmystical of all
sources. At noon Philip, standing in the gateway,
saw emerging from the forest the weather-beaten figure

of Lady Millicent Wimbrooke. Across her arm with an air of easy repose lay a rifle. Across her thin back was slung a second gun, and across her flat breast were slung bandolier after bandolier of cartridges. The pockets of her weather-beaten skirt and jacket bulged with more ammunition. She gave the effect of a walking arsenal. Before her, carrying the collapsible bathtub, walked the Arab, Ali, the muzzle of a third rifle pressed into his back.

Watching her, Philip wished that she had not returned, and Naomi, instead of feeling relief at the sight of a white woman, was frightened, more frightened and more resentful than she had been of the silence. It was a nameless fear, but because of that all the more dreadful. Naomi, who believed that all people were the children of God, hated Lady Millicent Wimbrooke.

The invincible spinster appeared to believe that they knew what was taking place in the forest and on the distant plain. She did not speak of the silence. Without greeting them she said, "I must have a bath now, but I can't leave Ali unguarded." She glanced at the three of them and then quickly, with the air of conferring an honor, she handed her rifle to Philip. "Here," she said. "You watch him. If he gets away, he'll make trouble and without him we're lost. He knows the way to the coast. He used to come here in the days of the slave-traders."

She explained briefly that the sound of drums had wakened her in the night and that when she rose to look about, she discovered that not one of her bearers remained. They had vanished into the bush. "They're like that, these damned niggers." She had caught Ali in the act of robbing her and since then she had not left him out of range of her rifle. She finished by saying, "How soon will you be ready to leave?"

It was Naomi who asked, "Leave? Why are we leaving?"

"You can't stay here unless you *want* to die."

The return of the Englishwoman had an amazing effect upon Naomi. The terror seemed to have left her, giving way to a sudden, resentful stubbornness, tinged by hatred.

"God means us to stick to our post," she said. "He will care for us."

Lady Millicent laughed. It was a short, vicious, ugly sound. "You can trust to God if you like. I intend to leave within an hour. I shan't argue it with you, but I mean to take Ali, and without him you'll be lost."

"But why?" Philip asked suddenly. "Is it necessary?"

She gave him a look of utter scorn. "Do you know anything about this country? Do you know what's happened?"

"No," said Philip, meek as a lamb, "I don't."

"Well, they've come down for blood—from the North, and they aren't afraid of any white man and they never heard of God. Besides, before night the fire will be here."

She turned suddenly and poured out a torrent of guttural sounds on the miserable Arab, who turned and entered Swanson's hut.

"If he tries to escape," she told Philip, "just shoot him, and remember I know what I'm talking about . . . I've lived among 'em."

Taking her canvas bathtub, she left them, going down to the Lake.

They knew now what they had to fear, and with the knowledge Naomi seemed once more to gain control of her flagging spirit. There was even color in her cheeks and a new light in her pale eyes. To Philip she seemed almost pretty.

After the Englishwoman had disappeared, she called Philip and Swanson and said, "I am not going to leave. God means us to stay. He has refreshed my spirit."

Philip argued with her. "The Englishwoman knows best; she has lived here."

"She is sent by the Devil to tempt us," said Naomi in a strangely hysterical voice. "She's an evil woman . . . I've prayed and God has answered me." It was difficult to know whether she was stubborn because of faith or because she hated Lady Millicent Wimbrooke.

When Philip didn't answer her, she turned to Swanson. "You'll stay, won't you?"

"If God means us to stay," he answered weakly. "I don't know."

A kind of scorn suddenly colored her voice. "And you, Philip . . . will you stay or will you go off with your friend?"

"What friend?" asked Philip.

"Her," said Naomi, who could not bring herself to say "Lady Millicent."

"Friend?" he echoed. "Why friend?"

"Oh, you know why. You seem to agree with her. You never said a word in our defense."

This was a new Naomi who stood looking at him, a woman excited and hysterical, and desperate, whom he did not recognize. This new Naomi was the martyr prepared to die for a Heavenly crown, moved by some inward fire that was terrifying and quite beyond control and reason. Between them, husband and wife, the chasm had opened again. He saw her suddenly as he had seen her when she was indifferent to the danger of his staying at Megambo—a woman to whom he was less than nothing, who would sacrifice him for the mad faith he no longer shared.

He looked away because he suddenly found her face hard and repulsive, saying, "You're crazy, Naomi. I don't know what you're talking about."

"Oh, yes, I'm crazy, but I know what I mean and you do, too. You've abandoned God and faith. You're like her now."

She was growing more and more excited. It struck him suddenly that she was jealous of Lady Millicent —that strange, battered, weather-beaten old maid; but the idea was too fantastic. He put it away. She might, perhaps, be jealous because the Englishwoman had picked him as the one who was most sane, but it couldn't be more than that. Before he was able to answer, he saw Lady Millicent herself entering the gate and barring it behind her. She looked in at the door of Swanson's hut. "He's pretending to be asleep," she said. "I know the Arab tricks."

Then wiping the sweat from her face, she said, "We may have to fight for it. There's a band of them painted like heathen images coming along the lake." Again she addressed Philip. "Do you know how to use a gun?"

"Yes."

"The others," she asked, indicating Naomi and Swanson, "are they any good?"

"No."

Naomi came forward. "Philip, I forbid you to kill." She placed herself suddenly between him and Lady Millicent, but the Englishwoman pushed her aside.

"This is no time for rot!" She gave such a snort that it seemed to him sparks must fly from her nostrils. "I can't defend all of you . . . with two able-bodied, strong men."

"We're missionaries," said Philip. "We didn't come to kill the poor heathen but to save."

"Well, I mean to kill as many as possible."

Suddenly there was the cannon-like report of an old-fashioned musket, and a bullet sang past them, embedding itself in the thatch of Swanson's hut. Philip saw Lady Millicent thrusting a rifle on Swanson to guard the wily Arab—Swanson who couldn't bear to kill a rat. There was another report and the slow whistle of a bullet. Then he found himself suddenly on the forest side of the stockade, beside the Englishwoman. There was a rifle in his hands and he heard her saying, "Don't fire till they get clear of the forest—then they'll have no shelter."

She was crouching behind the barricade like an elderly leopard, peering toward the forest. The bath-tub lay where she had tossed it aside. Through a gap in the wall he saw seven black men, hideously painted and decorated with feathers, running toward them. He raised the rifle and some one seized his arm. It was Naomi, screaming, "Don't! Don't! Thou shalt not kill!"

He heard the hoarse voice of Lady Millicent calling out, "If you want to live, fire! Fire *now!*"

He struck Naomi savagely, pushing her into the

dust. She lay there praying hysterically. He fired. He heard Lady Millicent firing. He saw one black man after another pitch forward and fall. She was (he thought) an excellent shot. The voice of Naomi praying wildly rose above the noise, the shots and the wild cries of the attacking niggers. Then all at once, those who remained alive turned and ran for the forest. He took careful aim, and one of them fell, kicking grotesquely. There was another report beside him, and the second fell on the edge of the forest. He saw the last of them turn and fire his musket. Then something struck him on the head like the blow of a club.

He heard a great voice calling, "I want to *live!* I want to *live!*" and all the world about him exploded with a great flash of light.

11

He wakened with the acrid tang of smoke in his nostrils, conscious of a slow, gliding motion, to find himself being carried on the back of Swanson. They were moving along a narrow path bordered by tall dry grass. At the head marched Ali followed by Lady Millicent, her rifle pressed against his trembling spine, her salvaged bathtub slung across her flat shoulders; and close behind came Naomi, still in her wide hat of thatched grass, her long, grotesque calico skirts muddy and wet to the waist from wading some stream. They had escaped with Lady Millicent's arsenal of ammunition and the clothes on their backs. The sun had slipped below the distant mountains and they walked through a twilight dimmed by the clouds of smoke borne toward them by a rising wind.

He got down at once and set out to follow them, feeling weak and shaky, until Lady Millicent (whom Naomi watched with the expression of one observing the source of all evil) provided a drink from the flask which she carried on her hip.

They marched in silence, racing against the fire and the rising wind, in the knowledge that if they reached the river before dark they were safe; and Philip, his bandaged head filled with a sickening ache, managed slowly to reconstruct what had happened since he was wakened by the thunderous echo of tom-toms. It all returned to him slowly, bit by bit, with an increasing vividness which reached its climax in the image of a hideously painted black man kicking grotesquely as he lay on his face by the edge of the forest.

The image somehow cleared his head and he was conscious slowly of a new and thrilling sensation of freedom. Presently he understood what it was: he had killed the men he had come to turn to God and he was never going back to that inferno beside the brassy lake. It was all over now. He hadn't even any faith. He was free and fearless. He had killed a man— perhaps three or four men. (He would never know whether he or Lady Millicent was the better shot.) But it did not matter. He was free and he was alive. Even the ache in his sick body seemed to fade into silence.

The little column before him had halted suddenly and as he moved up he found them standing about the body of a black girl that lay on its face full in the middle of the path. Swanson, bending down, turned the naked body over and they saw that she was young, straight, and beautiful in her savage way. By the wire ornaments Philip recognized her as one of the virgins from the village near the lake—perhaps one of those he had watched pouring water over the belly of the idol. There was no mark on her; they could not tell how she died. And they left her lying there because there was no time. The leopards would come to bury what was left of her after the cruel fire had passed. There would be a fête for the leopards with all those black men who lay outside the barricade.

As they turned to hurry on, the Englishwoman pointed behind them to a great column of flame and smoke. "Look," she said. "There's the mission."

With a little sigh, Naomi sank down in the middle of the path and began to weep hysterically. It was Philip who knelt beside her and lifted her up, trying to comfort her. They hurried on, his arm about her waist. She only addressed him once and then it was to say, "I can't help it, because it's the end of me—the end of everything." He had never seen her like this—broken, trembling and frightened.

At that moment he felt toward her for the first time as he supposed husbands must feel toward their wives. He pitied her, but his pity could not stifle the fierce wave of delight that welled up deep inside him. He turned to look for the last time at the columns of flame and smoke and was seized by a savage joy in the spectacle. He found it wildly beautiful, for he saw it with that new vision which had come to him by the lake; but that was not the reason why he felt this intoxicating happiness.

He was free. He meant to live, to have his youth. He meant never to go back.

PART TWO

THE SLATE-COLORED HOUSE

LONG ago Mrs. Downes had followed the example of
other thrifty householders and painted her dwelling
that peculiar slate-gray which gave the whole town so
depressing an aspect. It was a color which did not
show the marks of the soot that rose from the blast-
furnaces and chimneys to fall and fall again over the
community. The color, however, in the case of Emma's
house, seemed to extend to the inside, to lie in some
peculiar fashion in the very warp and woof of the
place. Being a woman of affairs she was seldom at
home save when she returned to sleep and so the breath
of conviviality scarcely touched its walls. The nearest
approach occurred on the occasion, once each year,
when she opened the place to entertain the Minerva
Circle. Then she flung open the massive oak doors
which separated the dining-room from the parlor and
had in bleak rows of collapsible chairs, hired from
McTavish, the undertaker, to support the varying
weights of her fellow club members.

The refreshments were provided from the kitchens
of her own restaurant—an assortment of salads, sandwiches and ice creams familiar enough to the regular
patrons, but exciting and worldly novelties to ladies
who did their own cooking or at best had only rather
incompetent hired girls. But even this occasion was
not one which left behind those ghosts of gayety which
haunt the pleasant houses of the blessed; it was at best

a gathering of tired, middle-aged women seated on hard chairs who wrestled with worries over children and husbands, while one or another of their fellow-members read from a rustling paper the painfully prepared account of her trip to the Yellowstone, or if the occasion was an intensely exciting one, of her voyage to Europe. Sometimes, it is true, Emma Downes rose to announce that she would read one of the interesting letters from her son, for these letters came vaguely under the head of geography and foreign travel, just as at the meetings of the Woman's Christian Temperance Union, they came hazily under the classification of temperance. And as many of the members belonged to both organizations and were also friends of Emma, they sometimes heard the same letter several times.

No one ever dined or lunched with Emma. She had no meals at home, as she took no holidays save Sunday, when it was the tradition to lunch with Elmer, who, she sometimes reflected, was certainly rich enough from the profits of his pump works to set a better table. In Emma there was a streak of sensuality which set her apart from her brother—she liked a comfortable house and good food (it was really this in the end which made the Peerless Restaurant a triumphant success). But there was evidence of even deeper fleshliness, for the brief interlude of Mr. Downes—that butterfly of passion—had shaken her life for a time and filled it with a horrid and awful uneasiness.

In the parlor, above the tiled mantelpiece, there hung an enlarged photograph of the derelict husband from which he looked out as wooden and impassive as it was possible for a photographer to make him. Yet life had not been altogether extinguished, for there was in the cocky tilt of the head and the set of a twinkling eye which could not be extinguished, in the curve of the lip beneath the voluminous dragoon mustaches, something which gave a hint of his character. He was, one could see, a swaggering little man, cock-of-the-walk, who had a way with women, even with such game as the invincible Emma—a man who was, perhaps, an odd combination of helplessness and bravado, a liar doubtless and a braggart. On the occasions of Minerva Circle meetings a vase of flowers always stood beneath the picture, a gesture touching and appropriate, since all that remained of Mr. Downes lay, as every one knew, somewhere in China and not in a well-ordered grave among the dead of his wife's family.

2

It was to this bleak and cheerless house that Philip and Naomi returned one winter night in the midst of a blizzard which buried all the town in snow and hid even the flames of the blast-furnaces which were always creeping distressingly nearer to Emma Downes' property.

All the way from Baltimore during two days and a night of traveling in one dreary day-coach after another they had sat sullenly side by side, rarely speaking to each other, for Philip, driven beyond endurance, had suddenly lost his temper and forbidden her to speak again of going back to Megambo. For a time she had wept while he sat stubbornly staring out of the window, conscious of the stares of the two old women opposite, and troubled by suspicions that Naomi was using her tears to shame him before their fellow-passengers. When there were no more tears left she did not speak to him again, but she began to pray in a voice just loud enough for him to hear. This he could not forbid her to do, lest she should begin to weep once more, more violently than ever, but he preferred her prayers for his salvation to her weeping, for tears made him feel that he had abused her and sometimes brought him perilously near to surrender. He tried to harden his heart by telling himself that her tears and prayers were really bogus and produced only to affect him, but the plan did not succeed because it was impossible to know when she was really suffering and when she was not. Since that moment when he pushed her aside into the dust and fired at the painted niggers, a new Naomi seemed to have been born whom he had never known before. It was a Naomi who wept like Niobe and, turning viciously feminine, used weakness as a horrible weapon. There were moments when he felt that she would have suffered less if he had beaten her daily.

She had been, as Emma hoped, "working over him" without interruption since the moment at Zanzibar when Lady Millicent bade them a curt good-by and Philip told her that he meant never to return to Megambo nor even be a missionary again. She was still praying in a voice just loud enough for him to hear when she was interrupted by his saying, "There's Ma, now—standing under the light by the baggage-truck."

Emma stood in the flying snow, wrapped warmly in a worn sealskin coat with leg-o'-mutton sleeves, peering up at the frosted windows of the train. At first sight of her a wave of the old pleasure swept

Philip, and then gradually it died away, giving place to a disturbing uneasiness. It was as if the sight of her paralyzed his very will, reducing the stubbornness which had resisted Naomi so valiantly, to a mere shadow. He felt his new-born independence slipping from him. He was a little boy again, obeying a mother who always knew best.

It was not that he was afraid of her; it lay deeper than fear, a part of his very marrow. He was troubled, too, because he knew that he was about to hurt her, whom he wanted to hurt less than any person in the world. Naomi did not matter by the side of his mother; what happened to Naomi was of no importance.

She saw them at once, almost as if some instinct had led her to the exact spot where they got down. Naomi she ignored, but Philip she seized in her arms (she was much bigger than he, as she had been bigger than his father). The tears poured down her face.

"Philip," she cried. "My boy! Philip!"

From the shadow of a great pile of trunks a drunken baggage hustler watched the scene with a wicked light of amusement in his eye.

Then she noticed Naomi, who stood by, shivering in her thin clothes. For a moment there was a flash of hostility in her eye, but it passed quickly, perhaps because it was impossible to feel enmity for any one who looked so pale and pitiful and frightened. Philip, noticing her, too, suspected that it was not the cold alone that made her tremble. He knew suddenly that she was terrified by something, by his mother, by the sound of the pounding mills, of the red glow in the sky—more terrified than she had been in all the adventure by the burning lake. And all at once he felt inexplicably sorry for her. She had a way of affecting him thus when he least expected it.

"Come," said Emma, composed and efficient once more. "You're both shivering."

The transfer to a smelly, broken-down cab was accomplished quickly, since missionaries have little need for worldly goods and Philip and Naomi had only what they had bought in Capetown.

On the way up the hill, the snow blew in at the cracks of the cab windows, and from time to time Emma, talking all the while, leaned forward and patted Philip's knees, her large face beaming. Philip sat back in his corner, speaking only to answer "Yes" or "No." No one paid any heed to Naomi.

Elmer Niman was waiting for them at the slate-colored house, seated gloomily in the parlor before the gas-logs by the side of his wife, a fat, rather silly woman, who was expecting hourly her second child, conceived, it seemed, almost miraculously after an hiatus of ten years and conscientious effort in that direction. Emma held her in contempt, not only because she was the wife of her brother, but because she was a bad housekeeper and lazy, who sat all day in a rocking-chair looking out from behind the Boston fern in her bow-window, or reading sentimental stories in the women's magazines. Moreover, Emma felt that she should have accomplished much sooner the only purpose for which her brother had married—an heir to inherit his pump works. And when she gave the matter thought, she decided, too, that Mabelle had deliberately trapped her brother into matrimony.

But there was no feeling of hostility between them,

at least not on Mabelle's side, for it might have been said that Mabelle was not quite bright and so never felt the weight of her sister-in-law's contempt. At the moment she simply sat rocking mildly and remarking, "I won't get up—it's such an effort in my condition"— a remark which brought a faint blush into Naomi's freckled cheeks.

As soon as Philip saw his uncle—thin, bilious and forbidding—standing before the gas-logs—he knew that they all meant to have it out if possible at once, without delay. Uncle Elmer looked so severe, so near to malice, as he stood beneath the enlarged photograph of Philip's jaunty father. There was no doubt about his purpose. He greeted his nephew by saying, "Well, Philip, I hadn't expected to see you home so soon."

For a second the boy wondered whether his mother had told Uncle Elmer that he had come back for good, never to return to Africa, but he knew almost at once that she had. There was a look in his cold eyes which, as Philip knew well, came into them when he fancied he had caught some one escaping from duty.

He and Naomi were thrust forward to the fire and he heard his mother saying, "I'll have Essie bring in some hot coffee and sandwiches," dimly, as in a nightmare, for he was seized again with a wild surge of the fantastic unreality which had possessed him since the moment when he fell unconscious beside the barricade. The very snow outside seemed unreal after the hot, brassy lake at Megambo.

He thought, "Why am I here? What have I done? Am I dreaming, and really lie asleep in the hut at Megambo?" He even thought, "Perhaps I am two persons, two bodies—in two places at the same time.

Perhaps I have gone insane." Of only one thing was
he certain and that was of a strange, intangible hostility that surrounded him in the persons of all of them,
save perhaps of Aunt Mabelle, who sat rocking stu-
pidly, unconscious of what they were set upon doing
to him. He knew the hostility that was there in the
cold eyes of Uncle Elmer, and he knew the hostility
that was in Naomi, and it occurred to him suddenly
that there was hostility even in the way his mother
had patted his knees as they rode through the blizzard.

They talked of this and that, of the voyage, the
weather, the prodigious growth of the town and the
danger of strikes in the Mills (for every one in the
town lived under the shadow of the pounding mills),
and presently Emma said, "But you haven't told us
about the uprising. That must be a good story."

Philip said, "Let Naomi tell it. She can do it better
than I."

So Naomi told the story haltingly in the strong
voice which always seemed strange in so fragile a body.
She told it flatly, so that it sounded like a rather bad
newspaper account made up from fragments of man-
gled cables. Once or twice Philip felt a sudden passionate desire to interrupt her, but he held his peace.
It was the first time that he had heard her talking of
it, and she didn't see it at all. He wanted to cry out,
"But you've forgotten the sound of the drums in the
night! And the sight of the fire on the plains!" He
thought his mother might understand what he saw
in it, but Uncle Elmer wouldn't. He decided to save
it to tell his mother when they were alone. It was *his*
story, *his* experience; Naomi had never shared it at
all.

He heard Naomi saying, "And then we came to the coast—and—and that's all there is to it."

"But what about the Englishwoman?" his mother was asking.

"Oh, she went away north again—right away—I must say we were glad to be rid of her. I didn't care for her at all—or Swanson either. She was hard and cruel—she didn't like us and treated us like fools, like the dirt under her feet, all except Philip. I think she —well, she liked him very much."

At the end her voice dropped a little and took on a faint edge of malice. It was a trick Philip had only noticed lately, for the first time during the long voyage from Capetown. It hung, quivering with implications, until Philip burst out:

"Well, if it hadn't been for her we'd all be dead now. I don't know about you, but I'm glad I'm alive. Maybe you'd rather be dead."

Naomi made no answer. She only bowed her head a little as if he had struck her, and Uncle Elmer said, "What about Swanson? What's happened to him?"

Naomi's head, heavy with its mass of sandy hair, raised again. "Oh," she said, "*he* went back to Megambo. *He* didn't want to desert the post. He thought all the natives were depending on him."

"Alone?"

"Yes, all alone."

For a moment the silence hung heavy and unpleasant; Philip, miserable and tortured, sat with his head bowed, staring at the Brussels carpet. It was his mother who spoke.

"I must say it was courageous of him. When I saw

him before you all left I didn't think much of him. He seemed stupid. . . ."

"But he has faith," said Naomi, "and courage. He was for not raising a hand during the attack. He didn't want to kill, you see."

Sitting there, Philip felt them beating in upon him, mercilessly, relentlessly, and he was afraid, not of any one of them but because all of them together with the familiar sight of the room, the veneered mahogany furniture, the red wallpaper, even his father's photograph with the flowers beneath it, made him feel small and weak, and horribly lonely as he had sometimes felt as a little boy. He kept saying to himself, "I'm a man now. I won't give in—I won't. They can't make me."

And then Uncle Elmer launched the attack. His method aimed, as if by some uncanny knowledge, at Philip's weakest part. He began by treating him as a little boy, humoring him. He even smiled, an act so rare with Uncle Elmer that it always seemed laden with foreboding.

"And what's this I hear about your not going back, Philip—about your changing your mind?"

Philip only nodded his head without speaking.

"You mustn't think of it too much just now. Just forget about it and when you're rested and better everything will come out all right."

Then Philip spoke. "I'm not going back."

But Uncle Elmer pondered this, still humoring him as if he were delirious or mad.

"Of course, it's a matter of time and rest. I've always felt toward you as I would toward my own son —if I had one." (Here Aunt Mabelle bridled and preened herself as if flattered by being noticed at last, even by implication.) "I'm thinking only of your own good."

"I'm not going back," repeated Philip dully.

The singsong voice of Uncle Elmer went on: "Of course, once you've had the call—there's no mistake. You can't turn back from the Lord once you've heard the call."

"I never had the call."

"What do you mean? You can't imagine a thing like that. Nobody ever imagined he heard the Lord calling him."

"It's true, though—I must have imagined it."

He couldn't say, somehow, what he wanted to say, because it wasn't clear in his own mind. He *had* thought he had heard the call, but now he saw it wasn't really so at all. He felt vaguely that his mother was somehow responsible for the feeling.

Uncle Elmer waited for a time, as if to lend weight to his words.

"Do you understand that it is a great sin—to abandon the Lord's work—the greatest sin of which a human creature can be guilty?"

Philip was trembling now like a man under torture. He couldn't fight back, somehow, because he was all confused, inside, deep down in his soul. It was as if his brain were all in knots.

"I don't know what is sin and what isn't. I've been thinking about it—I used to think of it for hours at a time at Megambo, I couldn't do my work for thinking of it—I don't know what is sin and what isn't, and you don't either. None of us know."

"We all know, Philip. The Bible tells us."

(Yes, that was true. The Bible had it all written down. You couldn't answer a thing like that.)

"He's lost his faith," said Naomi.

"You must pray, Philip. I pray when I'm in doubt —when I'm in trouble. I've prayed when I've been worried over the factory, and help always came."

"I can't explain it, Uncle Elmer. It's a spiritual thing that's happened to me . . . I couldn't go back— not now!"

Uncle Elmer's eyebrows raised a little, superciliously, shocked.

"A spiritual thing? To turn your back on God!"

"I haven't said that—" How could he explain when "spiritual" meant to them only Uncle Elmer's idea of "Biblical"? "I mean it is something that's happened to my spirit—deep inside me."

How could he explain what had happened to him as he lay in the rushes watching the procession of black girls? Or what had happened as he stood half-naked by the dying fire listening to the drums beating against the dome of the night? How could he explain when he did not know himself? Yet it was an experience of the spirit. It had happened to his soul.

He kept repeating to himself, "I won't—I won't. They can't make me." He saw his mother watching him with sad eyes, and he had to look away in order not to weaken and surrender.

Then Naomi's flat voice, "I've prayed—I've pled with him. I never cease to pray." She had begun to weep.

Philip's jaw, lean from illness and dark from want of shaving, set with a sudden click. His mother saw it, with a sudden sickening feeling that the enlarged photograph above his head had come to life. She knew that jaw. She knew what it meant when it clicked in that sudden fashion.

"It's no use talking about it—I won't go back—not if I burn in Hell."

Uncle Elmer interrupted him, all the smoothness gone suddenly from his voice. "Which you will as sure as there's a God above!"

The thin, yellow, middle-aged man was transformed suddenly into the likeness of one of the more disagreeable Prophets of the Old Testament. He was cruel, savage, intolerant. Emma Downes knew the signs; she saw that Elmer was losing his temper and beginning to roll about in the righteousness that made him hard and cruel. If he went on against that set, swarthy jaw of Philip, only disaster could come of it. They would lose everything.

"We'd all better go to bed; it's late and we're all worn out—Philip and Naomi most of all. There's no hurry about deciding. When Philip's well again—"

They meant to postpone the struggle, but not to abandon it. They bade each other good-night and Aunt Mabelle, rising from her rocking-chair with difficulty, smiled and insisted on kissing Philip, who submitted sullenly. Secretly she was pleased with him as she was always pleased when she saw some one get the better of Elmer.

As the door closed beneath the horrid glare of the green-glass gas-jet, Uncle Elmer turned.

"And what will you do, Philip, if you don't go back? You'll have to start life all over again."

"I don't know," Philip answered dully. But he did know, almost, without knowing it. He knew deep down within the very marrow of his bones. There was only one thing he wanted to do. It was a fierce desire that had been born as he lay beneath the acacia-tree watching the procession of singing women.

3

When Uncle Elmer and Aunt Mabelle, walking very carefully on account of Aunt Mabelle's "condition," had gone down the path into the flying snow, Emma said, "We'll all go to bed now. You're to have the spare-room, Philip, Naomi will sleep with me."

"No, I can't sleep yet. I'm going to sit up a while."

"Then put out the gas when you come to bed. It gets low toward morning and sometimes goes out by itself."

Naomi went off without a word, still enveloped in the aura of silent and insinuating injury, and Philip flung himself down on the floor before the gas-log, as he had always done as a boy, lying on his stomach, with the friendly smell of dust and carpet in his nostrils, while he pored over a book. Only to-night he didn't read: he simply lay on his back staring at the ceiling or at the enlarged photograph of his father, wondering what sort of man he had been and whether, if he were alive now, he would have helped his son or ranged himself with the others. There was a look in the eye which must have baffled a man like Uncle Elmer.

Upstairs, directly overhead, Naomi and Emma prepared for bed in silence. Only once did either of them speak. It happened when Emma burst out with admiration as Naomi let down the heavy mass of dull reddish hair. They both undressed prudishly, slipping on their outing-flannel nightgowns before removing their underwear, and hastily, because the room was filled with damp chill air. Emma lent her daughter-in-law one of her nightgowns, for Naomi had no use for outing-flannel in East Africa, and possessed only a sort of shapeless trousseau of patterned calico. The borrowed garment gave her the air of a woman drowning in an ocean of cotton-flannel.

After the gas was extinguished, they both knelt down and prayed earnestly, and toward the same end—that the Lord might open Philip's eyes once more and lead him back to his duty.

The moment the blankets were drawn about their chins, they began to talk of it, at first warily, feeling their way toward each other until it became certain that they both wanted the same thing, passionately and without division of purpose. Naomi told her mother-in-law the whole story—how she had worked over him, how she had even made the inarticulate Swanson summon courage to speak, how she had prayed both privately and in public, as it were, before Philip's eyes. And nothing had been of any use. She thought perhaps the wound had injured his brain in some way, for certainly he was not the same Philip she had married; but once when she had suggested such a thing to him, he had only attacked her savagely, saying, "I'm just as sane as you are—wanting to go back to those dirty niggers."

"Dirty niggers," Naomi said, was an expression that he had undoubtedly picked up from the Englishwoman. She always spoke of the natives thus, or even in terms of profanity. She smoked cigars. She used a whip on her bearers. In fact, Naomi believed that perhaps she was the Devil himself come to ruin Philip and in the end to drag him off to Hell.

"I would have gone back without Philip," she said, "but I couldn't go alone with Swanson, and I felt that the Lord meant me to cleave to Philip and reclaim him. That would be a greater victory than the other."

Emma patted her daughter-in-law's thin hand. "That's right, my dear. He'll go back in the end, and a wife ought to cleave to her husband." But there was in the gesture something of hostility, as there had been in her touching Philip a little while before. It was as if she said, "All the same, while he's here, he belongs to me."

And then Emma, listening, said, "Sh! There he comes now up the stairs."

They both fell silent, as if conscious that he must not know they lay there in the darkness plotting (not plotting, that was a word which held evil implications) but planning his future, arranging what would be best for him body and soul—a thing, they knew, which he could not decide in his present distracted state of mind. They both fell silent, listening, listening, listening to the approaching tread of his feet as they climbed the creaking stairs, now at the turn, now in the upper hall, now passing their door. He had passed it now and they heard him turning the white china knob of the door into the dismal spare-room.

He would think they were both asleep long ago.

They talked for a while longer, until Naomi, worn by the wretched journey in a day-coach and lulled by the warmth with which the great vigorous body of Emma invested the walnut bed, fell asleep, her mouth a little open, for there had never been a surgeon anywhere near her father's mission to remove her adenoids. But she did not sleep until Emma had learned beyond all doubt that in this matter Naomi was completely on her side; and that there was no possibility of children to complicate matters. Naomi was still a virgin, and somehow, in some way, that was a condition which might be made use of in the battle. She was not certain of the manner, but she felt the value of Naomi's virginity as a pawn.

Nor did she fall asleep at once. She suffered from a vague, undefined sense of alarm, which she had not known in more than twenty years of life wherein men played no rôle. She had not suffered thus since the disappearance of her husband. He seemed to have returned to her now with the return of her son. Philip, she saw, was a child no longer, but a man, with a little gray already in his black hair, terrifyingly like his father in appearance.

It was more, too, than appearance, for he had upon her the same effect that his father had had before him —of making her feel a strange desire to humor, to coddle him, to go down on her knees and do his bidding. He was that sort of man. Even Naomi seemed at moments to succumb to the queer, unconscious power. Lying there in the darkness Emma determined resolutely to resist this disarming glamour, for she had lost his father by not resisting it. She must make the resistance for her own and for Philip's good, though it would have been a warmer and more pleasant, even a voluptuous feeling to have yielded to him at once.

One thing, she saw, was clear—that Philip did not mean to run away as his father had done. He had returned to fight it out, with his dark jaw set stubbornly, because there was in him something of herself, which his father had lacked, something which, though she could not define it, filled her with uneasiness. She, the invincible Emma, was a little frightened by her own son.

And it touched her that he seemed so old, more, at times, like a man of forty than a boy of twenty-six: his face was lined, and his mouth touched by bitterness. He was no longer her little boy, so soft and good-looking, with that odd, blurred haze of faith in his blue eyes. He had a face now and the fact disturbed her, she could not tell why. He had been a little boy, and then, all at once, a man, with nothing in between.

At last—even after Philip, lying tormented in the spare bedroom, had fallen asleep, she dropped into an uneasy slumber, filled with vague alarms and excursions in which she seemed to have, from time to time, odd disturbing glimpses of a Philip she had never known, who seemed to be neither boy nor man, but something in between, remarkably like his worthless scamp of a father, who lived always to the full.

4

The Town stood built like Rome upon Seven Hills, which were great monuments of earth and stone left by the last great glacier, and on these seven hills and in the valleys which surrounded them a whole city, created within the space of less than a century, had raised houses and shops, monstrous furnaces spouting flame and smoke and cavernous sheds black and vast as the haunts of legendary monsters, where all day and night iron and steel drawn from the hot bellies of the furnaces was beaten into rails and girders, so that other towns like it might spring into existence almost overnight. The Mills and furnaces could not, it seemed, work fast enough, so there were always new ones building, spreading out and out, along the borders of the railroad which touched the Atlantic Ocean on one side and the Pacific on the other.

It was not a pretty town. The sun rarely rose unobscured by clouds of hanging black smoke: the air was never still day or night from the vibrations of that gigantic beating and pounding. There was no house nor building unstained by long streaks made by the soot which fell like black manna from the skies. But it was a rich town, fabulously rich and busy as an ant-hill overturned carelessly by the foot of man. People were always crawling in and out of the Mills, up the long hill to the Main Street that was bordered by hundreds of little shops which sold cheap clothing and furniture, swarming over the bright steel threads of the railroads and through the streets in the dark region known as the Flats, which was given over to the slave ants brought in from foreign countries to work day and night without light or air. On the hills, at a little distance, dwelt those who in a way subsisted upon the work of the slave ants—all the little merchants, the lawyers, the bankers who were rich because the world about them was rich, because the little world was a hive of activity where men and women were born, and toiled, and lived and died endlessly. For them it was not a struggle to exist. It was scarcely possible not to succeed.

It had made even Emma Downes rich in a small way. The money seemed forever pouring out, rolling off: one had only to find a clear spot and stand there waiting to catch what rolled towards it.

On the seven hills the ants had their social life, divided into caste upon caste. In the Flats the slave ants had no existence at all. They seldom climbed the hills. One never saw them. But on the hills there were ants of all sorts, and odd reasons determined why they were what they were: sometimes it was money, sometimes ambition, sometimes clothes, sometimes the part of the ant-hill which they occupied, sometimes the temple in which they worshiped. They fussed over these things and scurried about a great deal in their agitation.

At the bottom of the heap were the slave ants who had no existence and at the top was an old woman who occupied a whole hill to herself and was content to live there surrounded on all sides by the black, dark mills and the workers. She was a sort of queen ant, for she was a disagreeable, scornful old woman, and she made no effort. She was immensely rich and lived somberly in a grand manner unknown elsewhere in the Town; but it was, too, more than this. She was scornful and she inspired awe. Her name was Julia Shane. She had been born a queen ant.

Emma Downes did not know her. It is true that she had seen the old woman often enough in a mulberry victoria drawn by high-stepping black horses, as she passed the Peerless Restaurant; she had seen her sitting very straight and grim, dressed in mauve and black, or wrapped comfortably in sables. Sometimes her daughters rode with her—the one who was religious and worked among the people of the Flats, and the one who lived in Paris and was said to be fast.

There were reasons, of course, why they did not know each other—antlike reasons. Emma lived in the wrong part of the Town. She was the sister of Elmer Niman, who was a pious man with a reputation for being a sharp dealer. Emma and Elmer cared nothing for the things on which the old woman spent insanely great sums of money, such things as pictures and carpets and chairs. To Emma, a chair was a chair; the fancier it was, the prettier and more tasteful it must be. And Emma went to a church that was attended by none of the fashionable ants, and the old woman went to no church at all. Emma was President of the Woman's Christian Temperance Union, which the old lady considered not only as great nonsense, but as an impertinent effort to fly in the face of Nature. Emma had a missionary son, and to Julia Shane missionaries were usually self-righteous meddlers. (The old lady had never even heard of Naomi Potts, "the youngest missionary of the Lord in darkest Africa.") There was reason upon reason why they never met. Emma thought her a wicked old thing, who ought to be reformed, and Julia Shane didn't know that Emma existed.

It was immensely complicated—that antlike world.

For Philip it was no more complicated now than it had been in his childhood, when he had gone his own shy, solitary way. He had been lonely as a child, with the loneliness which all children know at moments when they are bruised and hurt: only with him it seemed always to have been so. It may have been the domination, even the very presence, of a woman so insensitive and crushing as Emma Downes that bruised and hurt him ceaselessly and without consciousness of relief. It was worse, too, when she was your mother and you adored her.

He had been happiest in moments when, escaping from his mother and the slate-colored house, he had gone off to wander through the fields beyond the Town or along the railway tracks among the locomotives. It was the great engines which he liked best, monsters that breathed fire and smoke, or sat still and silent in the cavernous roundhouse, waiting patiently to have bolts tightened, or leaks soldered, so that they might go on with their work. They did not frighten him as they might have frightened some children: they seemed ferocious but friendly, like great ungainly dogs. They terrified him less than Uncle Elmer or the preacher, Mr. Temple. (Mr. Temple was gone now and another younger, more flowery man named Castor had taken his place.)

By some miracle he had been able to keep his secret from his mother and continued, even when he was grown, to wander about for hours among the clanging wheels and screaming whistles during his holidays from the theological seminary. Some childish cunning had made him understand that she must never know of these strange expeditions, lest she forbid them. She was always so terrified lest something happen to him.

In all his childhood he could remember having had only two friends—one of them, McTavish, the undertaker, was kept as much a secret as the friendly locomotives had been; for Philip, even as a child, understood that there was something about the fat, jovial man which Emma detested with a wild, unreasonable fury.

The other was the black-haired, blue-eyed, tomboyish

Mary Watts, who lived a dozen blocks away in a more fashionable part of Town where each house had its big stables and its negro coachmen and stable boys. She was older than he by nearly two years, and much stronger: she detested girls as poor weak things who liked starched skirts and dickies of white duck that were instruments of torture to any one who liked climbing and snowball fights. So she had recruited Philip to play on the tin roof of the carriage shed and build the house high up in the branches of the crabapple tree. He always felt sorry for her because she had no mother, but he saw, too, with a childish clarity, that it was an advantage to be able to do exactly as you pleased, and build the tree-house as high in the air as you liked, far up among the shiny little red apples where it made you thrillingly sick to look over the edge.

But this friendship was throttled suddenly on the day (it was Philip's twelfth birthday) they went to play in the hay-loft. They had been digging in the fragrant hay and building tunnels, and feeling suddenly tired and hot, they lay down side by side, near the open door. In the heat, Philip, feeling drowsy, closed his eyes and listened to the whirring of the pigeons that haunted the old stable, happy, contented and pleased in a warm, vague way to be lying there beside his friend Mary, when suddenly he heard his mother's hearty voice, and, opening his eyes, saw her standing at the top of the stairs. He could see that she was angry. She said, "Philip, come home at once —and you, Mary, go right in to your aunt. You ought to be ashamed of yourself!"

She swept him off without another word and at

home she shut him in the storeroom, where she talked to him for an hour. She told him he had done a shameful thing, that boys who behaved like that got a disease and turned black. She said that he was never to go again to Mary Watts' house or even to speak to her. She told him that because he had no father she must be both father and mother to him, and that she must be able to trust him in the hours when she was forced to be at the bakery earning money to feed and clothe them both.

When she had finished, Philip was trembling, though he did not cry, because men didn't behave like babies. He told her he was sorry and promised never to speak to Mary Watts again.

And then she locked him in for an hour to ponder what she had said. He didn't know what it was he had done: he only felt shameful and dirty in a way he had never felt before, and terrified by a fear of turning black like those nigger boys who lived in the filthy houses along the creek by the Mills.

When Emma came back to release him from the storeroom prison, she forgave him and, taking him in her arms, kissed and fondled him for a long time, saying, "And when you're a big boy and grown up, your mother will always be your girl, won't she?"

She seemed so pleasant and so happy, it was almost worth the blind pain to be able to repent and make promises. But he never had the fun of playing again with Mary Watts. He went back to his beloved engines. Sometimes he played ball, and he played well when he chose, for he was a smallish, muscular boy, all nerves, who was good at games; but they never interested him. It was as if he wanted always to be alone. He had had friends, but the friendships had ended quickly, as if he had come to the bottom of them too soon. As a little boy there was always an odd, quizzical, affectionate look in his eye, and there were times when, dreaming, he would wander away into mazes of thought with a perpetual air of searching for something. He, himself, never knew what it was.

And then at seventeen, taciturn, lonely and confused, he had stumbled upon God. The rest was easy for Emma, especially when Naomi came unexpectedly into their lives. Sometimes, in bitter moments, she had thought of Philip as a symbol of vengeance upon his errant father: she had kept him pure and uncontaminated by the world. She had made of him a model for all the world to observe.

5

When, on the morning after his return, Philip went out of the door of the slate-colored house, and down the walk through the drifted snow, he knew suddenly that he was more lonely, more aimless than he had ever been. The blizzard was over, and the sky lay cold and gray above the curtain of everlasting smoke. At the gate he hesitated for a moment, wondering which way he would turn; and then abruptly he knew that it made no difference; there was no one that he wanted to see, no one with whom he could talk. He knew that in the house behind him there were two women who thought it shameful for him to be seen at all in the streets. They had even hoped, no doubt, that he would not show himself so soon. Even people who knew the story Emma had told of illness and wounds and a holiday, would think that he ought to have stuck at his post and fought it out there.

People, he knew—at least the people of their sort who were church-goers—were like that: they were willing to pile glory upon visiting missionaries, but they gave money grudgingly and expected missionaries to stick to their tasks. The money they gave warmed their hearts with a wicked Roman Catholic sense of comforts bought in Heaven. They would think he ought not to have returned until he had earned a proper holiday. For himself he did not care, especially since he knew he was far more wicked than they imagined, but with his mother and Naomi it was different. At the sight of Naomi, sitting pale and miserable across the table from him at breakfast, he had been stricken suddenly with one of those odd twinges of pity which sometimes delivered him into her hands, bound and helpless. When he thought of it now—how near he had been to yielding—he was frightened. Such odd, small things could turn a whole life upon a new path.

He closed the gate and turned towards the left, without thinking why he had chosen that direction until he found himself turning down the long hill to the Flats. He was going towards his beloved locomotives exactly as he had done a dozen years earlier when he could think of no one he wanted to see in all the Town; and suddenly he was almost happy, as if he were a boy of twelve once more, and not a man of twenty-six who had lost more than ten precious years of life.

It struck him, as he waded through heaps of snow already blackened by soot, that the Town had changed: it was not, in some subtle way, the same place. Where once it had seemed a dull, ugly Town, friendly because it was so familiar, it now seemed rather exciting and lively, and even thrilling. It was so alive, so busy, so filled with energy. As he descended the hill the impression grew in intensity. The pounding of the Mills, the leaping red flames above the furnace chimneys, the rumbling, half-muffled clamor of the great locomotives—all these things gave him a sudden, tremendous feeling of life. He saw for the first time, though he had passed them a thousand times in his life, those long rows of black houses where the mill-workers lived huddled together in squalor. He saw one or two sickly geraniums behind the glass, a crimson featherbed hung from a window, a line of bright clothes all dancing frozen and stiff as dead men in the cold wind.

For a moment he halted on the bridge that crossed Toby's Run and, standing there, he watched the great cranes at work lifting, with a weird animal intelligence, their tons of metal, picking up a burden in one place and setting it down in another. The air smelled of hot metal and the pungent tang of coal-smoke. Beneath him the stream, no longer water, but a flowing mass of oil and acids and corrosion, moved smoothly along: in a stream so polluted even ice could not freeze along the banks. Beyond the mills and piled low on the top of its patrician hill the mass of Shane's Castle showed itself against the leaden sky. It had been red brick once, but long ago it had turned black. There were only dead trees in the park surrounding it.

It all stood out sharp and clear—the houses, the river, the furnaces, the great engines, the lonely, quiet homes on the hills; and suddenly he knew what it was that made the difference. The Town seemed a new, strange place because of that queer thing which had happened to him at Megambo. The scales had fallen from his eyes. He remembered how suddenly he had seen the lake, the forest, the birds, in a new way, as if outlined by light; and that odd, sensual feeling of strength, of vigor, of life, overwhelmed him again, as it had done while he stood naked in the moonlight listening to the ominous drums. For a moment he fancied that he heard them once more, but it was only the pounding of the Mills. It was new to him after having been away for so long; the sound hadn't yet come to be a part of the silence which one did not hear because it was always there.

As he turned away he caught a glimpse of a pale, tall figure all in gray turning a corner down one of the sodden streets of the mill-workers. After a moment he recognized it slowly: it was Irene Shane, the daughter of Old Julia—the daughter who had given all her life and her money to work among the poor of the Flats. He remembered her then—she was the one who had started a club-house and a school where the foreigners, the Hunkies and Dagoes, might learn to speak English and their wives might learn to save the babies who died like flies. She carried it on herself, with only the aid of a Russian mill-hand, because people in the Town wouldn't give money. He remembered his mother's having mentioned it in a letter. "The Church was against it," she wrote, "because it took time and money away from foreign missions."

He looked after the thin figure until it disappeared into one of the houses, and then turned away. As he walked he found himself thinking of Mary Watts. His mother had written that Mary Watts had something to do with the club-house, until she married the new superintendent of the mills. He must ask his mother what had become of Mary Watts. Of course, she was Mary Conyngham now. . . . It was odd, but she was the only person in the Town that he wanted to see. At last he had thought of some one.

On his way up the hill once more, he passed, near the establishment of McTavish, the undertaker, the tall, powerful, middle-aged figure of the Reverend Castor bound upon some errand. He was a rather handsome man, a little pompous but with a kind face, who was quite bald and wore the hair which the Lord had spared him very long and wound about his head, in a way calculated to conceal his baldness. People said he was a good man, and a fiery preacher with a wife who had been a complaining invalid for fifteen years and rarely left her bed. Philip scarcely knew him, though it was he who had married himself and Naomi and blessed them when they left for Africa. The clergyman did not see him now and Philip slipped by unnoticed.

From behind the glass of the Funeral Parlor, he knew that McTavish and his cronies had seen him. They sat in there hugging the stove, a group of middle-aged and elderly men who played checkers or rummy and gossiped all day. It was a great place for news, since most deaths were reported at once to the fat, good-natured McTavish. Every one was buried by McTavish; he was the one who laid the hill-ants to rest deep in the gravel of the seventh of these glacial hills. McTavish never went to church and the big iron stove was known, even on Sunday, as the nucleus of a band of shocking atheists and mockers. McTavish seemed to understand at once whether the one he had come to bury was loved or whether it was simply a relative from whom you were likely to inherit. He was a bachelor who had no life save that which centered about the iron stove; yet he knew the Town in a way that no one else knew it because he was always near to the root of all things.

Philip knew that the group about the stove were saying, "There goes Emma Downes' boy who went to Africa for a missionary. He was always a queer one—not a bit like Emma."

And then they would launch into talk about the old story of Jason Downes and his fantastic disappearance into the depths of China, where he had escaped in the end the last ministrations of McTavish. They knew everything, those old men. Each one was a walking history of the Town.

Philip, half a block off now, began to feel that sense of life which somehow sustained them. He began to feel people, ambitions, jealousies, loves and hatreds, stirring all about him in a strange, complicated maze.

Naomi was waiting for him, dressed to go out. She had put on a thick blue veil because, Philip suspected, she did not want to be recognized.

"Your Ma wants us to eat at the restaurant," she said, and together they set out in silence.

Miraculously they met no one on the way, and once inside the big, white, clean restaurant, Emma led them to the table where, shielded by a screen from draughts, she always ate. The restaurant began to fill with customers—clerks, lawyers, mill-employees, shopkeepers, farmers and their wives in from the country for the day—all lured by the excellent food supplied by Emma. After a time the tables were all filled and people stood

waiting their turn. It was marvelous, the success of
Emma. Dishes clattered, orders were shouted, the
cash-register clanked and banged unceasingly. She
was proud of the place and happy there: it was clear
that she could not imagine living away from such a
hubbub and din.

While they were eating the stewed dried corn which
she gave her customers in place of the usual insipid
canned variety, she asked, "What did you do this morning, Philip?"

"I went for a walk."

"Where?"

"In the Flats."

"You might have chosen a handsomer part of the
Town. You might have gone out to see the new Park."

He didn't tell her about the locomotives. Once he
had kept it a secret because she would have forbidden
him to return to them. Now, he kept his secret for
some other reason: he did not know quite what it was.
He only knew that Emma and Naomi must not know
of it. It would only make them believe that he was
completely crazy.

Presently, when they had reached the squash pie,
he asked, "What's become of Mary Watts?" And at
the same moment he felt himself blushing horribly, for
in some way the memory of the imprisonment in the
storeroom returned to claim him unawares, and make
him feel a shameful little boy unable to look his mother
in the eye. Only he understood now: he knew what lay
beneath the ancient, veiled accusations. . . .

"Oh, she's had a sad time," said Emma. "You know
she married the superintendent of the Mills—John
Conyngham—a man fifteen years older than she was,

and every one thought it was a good match. But he died—three weeks ago—while you were on the ocean, leaving her with two small children. They've some money, but not very much. The Watts house was sold when old Watts died—to pay his debts. She's living with Conyngham's sister, who's quite well off. They're in the old Stuart house in Park Avenue. Old Stuart lost all his money hanging on to too much land, so they bought the house off him. I guess Conyngham wasn't a very good husband—I used to see his bicycle sitting in front of Mamie Rhodes' house. There couldn't have been much good in that—men like Mamie Rhodes too well."

She knew it all, the story in all its details, even to Mamie Rhodes, at whose name women in the Town were wont to bristle. No one *knew* anything about Mamie: it was just that she was much too young for her years, and did something to men—nobody knew just what it was—that made her very popular.

"And what was he like?" asked Philip.

"Conyngham," said Emma, "John Conyngham? He was handsome, but I never liked his looks. I'd never trust a man that looked like that."

What she meant was that there was something about John Conyngham that reminded her of the derelict Mr. Downes, and that the sight of him had always disturbed her in a terrifying way. She couldn't bear to look at him.

"He died of pneumonia," she said above the clatter of the dishes and the prosperous banging of the cash-register. "They say he caught it coming home in the rain from Mamie Rhodes' on Thanksgiving night."

Philip listened and the dull red still burned under

the dark skin. He was aware that the two women were watching him, secretly, as they might watch a man who was a little unbalanced: they had been doing so without cessation since his return. They were a little like two purring cats watching prey all innocent of their intentions.

6

It was impossible, of course, for the three of them to continue playing the game of hide-and-seek, pretending that Philip and Naomi had not returned or that Philip was too ill to go out; it was impossible for Naomi to go about forever disguised by a thick veil. Even Emma's eternal policy of allowing things to work themselves out appeared after a month to be productive of no result, for Philip's "mental condition" showed no signs of improvement. He remained, rocklike, in his determination, while the two women watched, stricken with uneasy fears because the Philip whom they had once known so well that they could anticipate and control his every impulse, now seemed a creature filled with vague and mysterious moods and ideas that lay quite beyond the borders of their understanding.

Their watching became at times unbearable to him, for it gave him the suffocating sense of being a maniac who was not to be trusted alone. He took to spending more and more time away from the house, either walking the country roads or wandering through the black Flats where he was safe from encountering any one or anything, save the gray figure of Irene Shane, going her tireless rounds. Once he had a glimpse of the old lady herself—Irene's mother—riding by wrapped in sables on the last ride she was ever to take.

A sense of waiting, more definite, more intense, than the tension of the long day at Megambo, settled over the slate-colored house. It was broken on the fourth Sunday after Philip's return when the three of them lunched, as usual on boiled mutton, at Uncle Elmer's. It was a gloomy lunch, tainted by the sense of Philip's sin. The gloom enveloped all of them, save Aunt Mabelle and her ten-year-old daughter, Ethel, who showed already signs of resembling her mother in feebleness of character and inertia of mind. The room was, through a lack of windows, dark, and under the fog of smoke that enveloped the Town it became even more cavernous and dreary; but Elmer Niman never permitted his wife to waste gas in illumination. One groped for food in the dark, while Elmer talked of the low pressure occasioned by the sad waste of gas in the Town.

The break came only after considerable preparation on the part of Emma. She said, quite casually, "I saw Reverend Castor yesterday. He came into the restaurant to see me."

"He's not looking as well," put in Aunt Mabelle. "It must be a strain to have an invalid wife. It's not natural for a man to live like that."

Elmer interrupted her, feeling perhaps that she was bound toward one of those physiological observations which she sometimes uttered blandly and to the consternation of all her world.

"He is a good man. We are fortunate in having him."

"God will reward him for his patience," observed Emma.

"I talked to him day before yesterday," said Naomi. "I think I may go to sing in the choir while we are on our holiday."

Vaguely Philip began to sense the existence of a plot, conceived and carried out with the express purpose of forcing him to do something he had no desire to do. It seemed to him that they had rehearsed the affair.

"There is an empty place on the alto side," observed Emma. "They could use a good strong voice like yours."

"Of course," said Naomi, "it's so long since I've sung—not since I used to lead the singing at the revival meetings."

"And Philip—he used to sing."

"He never does now. He wouldn't help me teach the natives at Megambo."

Philip, listening, fancied that he caught a sympathetic glance from Aunt Mabelle. She was silly and stupid, but sometimes it seemed to him that she had flashes of uncanny intuition: she had, after all, had great experience with the tactics of Elmer and his sister. She sat opposite Philip, eating far too much, lost in cowlike tranquillity. She was still bearing patiently the burden which by some error in calculation had been expected hourly for more than a month. Only yesterday she had said, "I expect little Jimmy will have all his teeth and be two years old when he is born!"—a remark that was followed by an awkward silence. Married to another man she would undoubtedly have had ten or fifteen children, for she was born to such a rôle.

"That's how I met Elmer," she said brightly, "singing in the choir. I used to sing alto, and he sang bass. He sat right behind me and his foot. . . ."

"Mabelle!" said Elmer.

She veered aside from the history of a courtship which always engaged her with a passionate interest. "Well, I've always noticed that lots of things begin in church choirs. There was that Bunsen woman who ran off with. . . ."

Emma trod upon her, once more throttling her flow of reminiscences.

"That's right, Naomi," she said, "it'll help pass the time while you're waiting." And then, polishing her spoon with her napkin (an action which she always performed ostentatiously as an implication upon the character of Mabelle's housekeeping) she said, "By the way, he's planned a Sunday night service which is to be given over entirely to you and Naomi—Philip. Think of that. It's quite an honor." (She would sit well down in front that night where she could breathe in all the glory.) "I told him, of course, that you'd be delighted to do it."

"Yes," said Naomi, "he spoke to me about it. We'll tell our experiences." The prospect of so much glory kindled a light in the pale eyes—the light of memories of revival meetings when she had been the great moving force.

Then Philip spoke for the first time. "I won't do it—I'm through with all that."

There was a horrible silence, broken only by the clatter of a fork dropped by little Ethel on her plate.

"What do you mean?"

"I told you all that before. I thought you must

have understood by now. I can't go on saying it forever."

"But, Philip . . . you can't refuse a good man like the Reverend Castor. You can't when he's been so kind. He always prayed for you and Naomi every Sunday, publicly, as if you were our special missionaries."

There was only silence from Philip. The dark jaw had hardened suddenly.

"When we were all looking forward to it so much," added Emma.

Then suddenly there came to him a faint suspicion—shadowy and somewhat shameful—of what it was all about. They were looking forward to an orgy of public notice and glory, to sitting bathed in the reflected light while he talked about Africa to a congregation of faithful admirers. He even suspected that this was the reason they were so determined to ship him back to Africa. They would find glory in his sufferings. He was angry suddenly, even hostile.

"You can tell him I won't do it."

"But, Philip, you must tell him yourself."

"I don't want to see him."

Here Uncle Elmer took a hand, using the familiar tactics. "Of course, I can understand that—Philip's not wanting to see him." He grimaced suddenly at Emma to let him manage it. "I'll speak to Reverend Castor myself. I'll explain about Philip's condition."

For a second Philip grew hot with anger; he even pushed back his chair from the table as if to rise and leave. It was, oddly enough, Aunt Mabelle who restrained him. He fancied he caught a sudden twinkle in her round eyes, and the anger subsided.

Another painful silence followed, in which Rose, the negro maid-of-all-work, placed the Floating Island violently before Aunt Mabelle to be served. The room grew darker and darker, and presently Uncle Elmer said, "I suppose, Philip, if you intend to stay here you'll be looking for some sort of work. It will mean, of course, starting life all over again."

"Yes."

"Of course you could teach—a young man with a good education like yours. It cost your mother a lot of work and trouble to educate you."

"Yes."

"But if you can't get such work right away, I could make a place in the factory for you. Of course," and here Uncle Elmer smiled his most condescending smile, "of course, with your kind of training you wouldn't be much good at first. You'd have to learn the business from the ground up. You could begin in the shipping department."

It was the first time any of them had admitted even a chance of his not returning to Africa; but they did not mean to yield, for Emma said, "That perhaps would help him over this nervous trouble."

And then Philip shattered everything with an unexpected announcement. It was as if a bomb had exploded in the dust and shadows beneath the table.

"I've already got a job," said Philip. "I'm going to work to-night at midnight."

"To-night—at midnight?" asked Emma. "What on earth do you mean?"

"I'm going to work in the Mills. I've got a job."

"The Mills! You're crazy. What do you mean—the Mills?"

"I mean the Mills," said Philip, looking at his plate. "It's all been settled."

Suddenly Naomi began to cry, at first silently, and then more and more noisily, as if all the dammed emotions of months had given way. Emma rose to comfort her, and Aunt Mabelle, murmuring, "Oh, dear! Oh, dear!" helplessly pushed the water-pitcher across the table. Little Ethel, conscious of the strain of the whole meal, and frightened by the outburst of hysterics, began to cry too, so that Aunt Mabelle became occupied in comforting her.

Philip, able to stand it no longer, rose and, flinging back his chair, said, "Damn!" in a loud voice, and walked out of the house. His swearing moved Naomi to new outbursts. She began to cry about the Englishwoman—the source of all her troubles.

It was all horrible, and it was the last time that Philip ever entered his uncle's house.

When he returned late that night he found them all waiting for him in the parlor, ready to attack once more, but they accomplished nothing. He went upstairs and changed his clothes. When he came down, he was dressed for the Mills in an old pair of trousers, an old coat and a flannel shirt. Aunt Mabelle, round and sloppy, was standing in the ghoulish light of the green lamp. The others were all seated in the parlor gloomily, as if brooding over the problem of a daughter gone astray.

From the shadows, Aunt Mabelle seized his arm, "Is it true? Is Naomi going to have a little baby?"

Philip looked at her with a sudden astonishment. "No," he said savagely. "Who gave you such an idea?"

Aunt Mabelle seemed to shrink into herself, all softness and apology. "I didn't know . . . I just couldn't
understand a woman carrying on like that if she
wasn't."

7

It was more than an hour before the midnight shift
began at the Mills, and during that hour Philip walked,
sometimes running, along the empty streets, through
the falling snow, all unconscious of the cold. He was
for a time like a madman living in an unreal world,
where all values were confused, all emotions fantastic
and without base: in his tired brain everything was
confused—his love for his mother, his hatred for his
uncle, his pity for Naomi, and his resentment at all
three of them for the thing they were trying to do.
He wanted to run away where he might never see any
of them again, yet to run away seemed to him a
cowardly thing which solved nothing. Besides, if he
ran away, he would never see Mary Conyngham, and
Mary had in some odd fashion become fixed in his mind,
an unescapable part of the whole confusion. He *must*
see Mary Conyngham, sometime, in some way.

He was afraid to stay, depressed by the feeling that
whenever he returned to the house, he was certain to
find them there—waiting, watching him. Why, a man
could be driven to insanity by people like that who
treated him always as if he were mad.

But worst of all, he had no longer any faith in
God: there was nothing of that miraculous essence
which seemed to take from one's shoulders all the burden of doubt and responsibility. He couldn't say any
longer, "I will leave it to God. He will devise a way.

Whatever happens, He will be right. I must accept His way." He knew, sharply, completely, for the first time, that a faith must be born in himself, that he had taken up his own life to mold in his own fashion: there was no longer that easy refuge in a God, Who would arrange everything. If he had trusted to God now he would have been on his way to Africa, disposed of, not by God, but by the hands of his mother and Naomi and Uncle Elmer.

He could be a coward and weak no longer.

After he had gone a long way he found himself on a height that seemed strange to him, in that part of the Town which lay just above the Flats. It was not strange, of course, for he had stood on the same spot a hundred times before. It was strange only because he was in an odd fashion a new person, born again, a different Philip from the one who had stood there as a boy.

The sight that lay spread out below him suddenly brought a kind of peace: he stopped running, and grew calm and, watching it, he succumbed slowly to its spell. By night, the hard, angular lines of that smoky world melted into a blue mystery, pierced and spotted here and there by lights—the great blue-white lights of the arc-lights in the Mill yards, the leaping scarlet flames that crowned the black furnaces, the yellow lights plumed with steam of the great locomotives moving backward and forward like shuttles weaving a vast carpet with the little signal-lights, red and yellow and mauve and green, set like jewels in a complicated design. In the darkness the grim blacks and grays took on color. Color and light lay reflected from the canopy of smoke and steam that hung above the whole spectacle. Piercing the glow of light, rose the black columns of the chimneys and furnaces.

Above it all rose the endless sound of pounding, like the distant booming of a gigantic surf, pierced now and again by the raucous, barbaric squeals of a locomotive.

Halted and given poise by the sight, he stood for a long time looking down into the very center of the roaring hive, forgetting himself suddenly and all his fantastic troubles; and slowly an odd thing happened to him. He felt strong: he wasn't any longer puzzled and afraid. It was as if there lay in the turbulent scene some intoxicating sense of power which took the place of his missing faith. The spectacle beneath him became alive with a tremendous sense of vitality and force that he had not found in all his mystical groping toward God. This thing that lay below him was real, he knew, real in a solid, earthly fashion, created by men in the face of hostile Nature, free of any weak dependence upon a Power which at best had only a doubtful existence. Yet the awful power of this world created by the feeble hand of man was in an odd fashion like the power of the lake, the forest, the sounds of life on the hill at Megambo.

Hazily there came to him the feeling that here lay his salvation, and presently he was overcome by an intense desire to plunge deep into the very midst of the whirling maelstrom of noise and heat and light and power.

Hurrying, he descended the hill, crossing the little river of oil and corruption, passing a great open space covered with cinders, beneath the white glare of lights hanging high above him, until he came at last to a high fence and a gate where he explained who he was and showed his card. He had an odd feeling that he should have said simply, "I have come here to save myself," as if the Italian gatekeeper would have known what he meant.

Inside this barrier the sound of pounding grew more and more violent. He went past one cavernous shed and another and another until he came to the one marked with a gigantic number in white paint—17. The yard, the shed, all the world about him was swarming with men—big, raw-boned men with high cheekbones, little, swarthy men, black men, men with flat, Kalmuck noses, some going towards the sheds, some moving away from them. Those who moved homeward were so black with sweat and soot that one could not tell which were negroes and which were white.

Stepping through a doorway, he found himself in a vast cavern echoing with sound, that reached up and up until its height became lost in smoke and shadows. High up, near the top, great cranes with white lights like piercing eyes, and tiny, black figures like ants climbing over them, moved ceaselessly back and forth, picking up tons of metal and putting it down again with a tremendous clatter. Here and there along the sides stood furnaces out of which men were drawing from time to time great piles of metal all rosy-white with heat. Flames leaped out of the ovens, licking the sides and casting fantastic shadows over the powerful, half-naked figures of the workers. The gigantic sound of hammering reverberated through the black cavern.

After a moment Philip addressed a thin, swarthy man with burning eyes. "Where is Krylenko?" he asked. But the man understood no English. "Krylenko," he repeated, shouting, above the din, "Krylenko."

The thin man grinned. "Oh, Krylenko," and, pointing, indicated the figure of a powerful, blond man, who stood leaning on a crowbar before an oven a little way off. He was, like the others, naked to the waist, and his white skin was already streaked with soot and sweat. When he turned, Philip saw that he was young, younger even than himself, and that his eyes were blue beneath a great mop of hair so yellow that it had the appearance of having been bleached. The eyes were intelligent.

In English with only a shadow of an accent he told Philip to strip off his coat and shirt and take up a crowbar. In a moment he was standing there with the others, indistinguishable among so many workers. He was half-naked, as he had been beside the fire at Megambo, and the same voluptuous sense of power swept through him. It was oddly terrifying, this cavern filled with flame and smoke and sweating men. It was oddly like the jungle.

8

Behind him in the slate-colored house Aunt Mabelle waited, yawning and wishing for bed, while Elmer and Emma and Naomi sat in silence, pondering whether their battle had been completely lost. They sat in silence, and Naomi sometimes dried her red-rimmed eyes and sobbed, because there was nothing to say, nothing to do. It was all so much worse than they had expected. With Philip living, as one might have said, in hiding, life could still be endured, and one

could go on pretending, pretending, pretending, that
he was merely ill, and one day would go back to
Megambo to the glory and justification of them all.
No one of them really believed any longer in the pre-
tense of Philip's illness. Tacitly they would pretend to
believe it because it was a good weapon: they would
not even admit their doubts to each other. But from
the moment he sprang up from Uncle Elmer's table
they knew that he was quite in his right mind, and
knew exactly what he meant to do. He was in his
right mind, but he was a strange, unmanageable
Philip.

And now he had disgraced them in a new and shame-
ful way by going to work, not in an office over columns
of figures, or even into a polite business such as Uncle
Elmer's pump works, but by plunging straight into the
Flats, into the Mills to work with the Hunkies and
Dagoes. It was a thing no American had ever done.
It was almost as if he had committed theft or murder.

After they had sat thus for more than hour, always
beneath the larky gaze of the "late" Mr. Downes,
Uncle Elmer rose at last and making himself very
thin and stiff as a poker, he said, "Well, Em, I've
decided one thing. If Philip doesn't come to his senses
within two weeks, I'm through with him forever. You
can tell him that—tell him I give him just two weeks,
not an hour more—and then I'm through with him.
After that I never want to see him again, or hear his
name spoken. And when he gets into trouble from his
wicked ways, tell him not to come to me for help."

He expected a response of some sort from his sister,
but there was only silence, while she sat grimly regarding the carpet. It seemed that he felt a sudden

need for an answer, even though he must strike at her unchivalrously upon a wound which he must have believed cured long ago.

"You see," he said, "all this comes of making a marriage long ago that I was against. I knew what I was talking about when I warned you against Jason Downes."

For a moment she did not answer him, but when she spoke it was to upset him, horribly, by one of those caprices to which women are prey. It may have been because of the strain of the day, but it was more probable that there still was left the embers of her old, inexplicable passion for the worthless Mr. Downes, embers fanned into flame by the return of Philip.

She said, "Very well, Elmer. I'll tell him, but you can consider everything over between you and me, too. I don't want to see you again. If you can't speak to Philip, you needn't speak to me either. I should never have told you. You haven't done anything at all but make things worse."

For a time he only stared at her out of round eyes that were like blue marbles. "Well!" he said, coughing. "Well! I've done my duty. Don't say that I haven't."

"A lot of good it's done," said Emma with bitterness, "a lot of good. . . ."

She seemed, the indomitable Emma, very near to tears. In her corner Naomi snuffled so that they would take some notice of her.

He had meant to make his exit with a cold dignity, and a sense of injury, but Aunt Mabelle stood across his path. Unable any longer to keep up the battle against sleep, she was dozing peacefully in her rocking-chair, unconscious even of the scene that had taken place. She had to be prodded and spoken to sharply, and at last she wakened slowly to profuse apologies, and a walk home with a husband who never addressed her.

Her child was born the following day. Early in the evening before Elmer came home from the factory, she came to see Naomi, to discover what had happened on the night before, during her nap. (She had a way of "running in" on Naomi. They liked each other.) While she was talking the pain began, and Naomi went at once to fetch a cab. It arrived quickly, and Mabelle bustled into it, was driven home at top speed. But haste was of no use; she was carried upstairs by the cab driver and the butcher's boy, and before the doctor arrived the child was born. Naomi had never seen anything like it: the whole business took less time than with the native women at Megambo.

"I'm like that," Mabelle told her; "it only takes a minute."

The child was small and rather puny, to have been born of such an amiable mountain as Mabelle. It was a boy, and they called him James after his grandfather.

Emma called on her sister-in-law and sent broths and jellies from the restaurant, but she did not speak to her brother.

She told the news to Philip when he wakened to go to work, and he looked at the floor for a long time before he said, in a low voice, "Yes—that's fine. He wanted a boy, didn't he?"

Something in his eye as he turned away made Emma lay a hand on his arm.

"Philip," she said in a low voice, "if you're *really*

never going back to Africa, I mean *really* not going back—you might have a child of your own."

"Yes," he answered, "I might."

That was all he said, but Emma in all her bluntness had divined the thought that came to him so quickly. He wanted a child with all the hunger of a deeply emotional nature; what she did not divine was that he did not want a child with Naomi for the mother. He couldn't bear to think of it, and he went to work that night sick at heart, plunging into the work like a man leaping from an unbearable heat into a deep pool of cool water. In that fiercely masculine world, he found pleasure in the soreness of his muscles, in the very knowledge that he would, when the day was finished, fall into a deep slumber, wearied to death, to find a world in which would be no troubles.

9

Naomi, too, had suffered in her own complaining fashion. After a life passed in a fierce activity, the empty days began to hang upon her spirits like leaden weights. As far back as she could remember her life had been a part, as the daughter and then the wife of a missionary, of a struggle against heat and disease and ignorance, her soul always warmed by the knowledge that she was doing God's work, that the pain and discomforts of the body were as nothing in comparison to the ecstasies of the soul. Save for a few weeks, she had never known life in the civilized world, and now in the midst of it there seemed to be no place for her. She tried dusting and cleaning the slate-colored house (there was no cooking to do, for

they ate always at the restaurant), but there was no
satisfaction in it. She came in a few days to hate it.
She tried making garments to be shipped to the missions, long nightgowns with which to clothe the nakedness of savages, but her fingers were clumsy, and she
found herself as indifferent a seamstress as she was a
housekeeper. The tomblike silence of the house depressed her, and in these first weeks she dreaded going
out, lest she should meet women who would ask after
her plans. After a time she found herself seated like
Aunt Mabelle for hours at a time, staring out of the
windows at the passers-by.

After the scene at Uncle Elmer's there seemed for
a time no solution of their troubles. She plunged into
choir singing, where her loud, flat voice filled a much-
needed place; and she went without Philip to talk at
the Sunday Evening Service of her experiences in
Africa. Emma was there and Uncle Elmer, treating
the congregation to the spectacle of a brother and
sister who occupied the same pew without speaking
to each other. But somehow everything was changed,
and different from those glorious days so short a time
before when the sound of her voice had moved whole
congregations to a frantic fervor. The assembly-
room now showed great gaps of empty seats, like missing teeth, along the sides and at the back. Naomi
wasn't any longer a great attraction as "the youngest
missionary of the Lord in darkest Africa": she was a
woman now, a missionary like any other missionary.
And there were, too, strange rumors circulating
through the flock of the quarrel between Emma and
her brother and other rumors that Naomi and Philip
weren't really missionaries at all any longer, but had

both deserted the cause forever. There were a hundred petty bits of gossip, all magnified and sped on their way by friends of Emma who resented the reflected glory in which she bathed herself.

No, something had gone wrong, and the whole affair seemed stale and flat, even the little reception afterward. Emma, of course, stood with the Reverend Castor and Naomi, while members of the congregation filed past. Some congratulated Naomi on her work and wished her fresh successes; one or two asked questions which interested them specially—"was it true that a nigger king had as many as eighty wives?" and, "did they actually eat each other, and if so how was the cooking done?" Emma was always there, beaming with pride, and answering questions before Naomi had time to speak. The Reverend Castor from time to time took Naomi's hand in his and patted it quite publicly, as if she were a child who had recited her first piece without forgetting a line. He kept saying, between fatherly pats, "Yes, the Lord has brought our little girl safely home once more. He has spared her for more work."

But it was a failure: it had none of the zest of those earlier meetings, none of the hysterics and the wild singing of *Throw Out the Life Line* and *The Ninety and Nine*, and other hymns that acted as powerful purges to the emotions. The occasion was dampened, too, by the curiosity of various old ladies regarding the absence of Philip; they kept asking question upon question, which Emma, with much practice, learned to parry skilfully. "He didn't feel well enough to make the effort. You see, the fever clings on—that's the worst part of it."

For she was squeezing the last drop of triumph before the débâcle; and of course she always believed in the depths of her soul that Philip *would* go back to Africa some day. She meant, in the end, to accomplish it as she had already accomplished the things she desired—all save the recovery of Mr. Downes.

But it was Naomi who suffered most, for behind the mild and timid exterior there lurked an ironclad egotism which demanded much of the world. It demanded more attention and enthusiasm than had been her share at the Sunday Evening Service; it demanded respect and, curiously enough, evidence of affection (it was this last rather pitiful hunger that drew her close to Aunt Mabelle). She understood well enough that Emma had no affection: what capacity for love Emma possessed was all directed toward Philip. And before many weeks had passed Naomi knew bitterly that although she lived in the same house with her husband and his mother she really occupied no more of a place in it than Essie, the poor-house slavey. But Aunt Mabelle was kind to her, and would come and sit for hours rocking and gossiping, occasions when the only interruption was the periodic cry of the pallid baby, which Mabelle stifled at once by opening the straining bombazine of her bosom and releasing the fountain of life.

This last was a spectacle which Naomi came to regard with a faint and squeamish distaste. She grew to have a passionate dislike for the pallid infant that lay gorged with milk in Mabelle's ample lap. Even the frank and open manner of the black women had never accustomed her to the exposé in which Mabelle indulged with such an air of satisfied pride.

"I've always had plenty of milk," Mabelle would say, as she settled back comfortably. "The doctors say I've enough for any three normal children."

Naomi, indeed, had spent half her life in an effort to conceal black nudity in yards of cheap calico.

But deeper than any of these flurried emotions lay the shadowy knowledge that the pallid child was in a way a reproach to herself, and a vague symbol of all the distasteful things that lay before her, for she felt that sooner or later the tangle would end in bringing her to the state of a wife in reality, of facing even perhaps the business which Mabelle managed with such proud composure. In the midst of the wilderness at Megambo she was still safe, protected by the fantastic sense of honor that lay in Philip; but here in this complicated world of which she knew nothing, when each day she felt her security, her fame, her glory, slipping from under her feet, the thing drew constantly nearer and nearer. If she could not force Philip to return, the day would come when with all her glory and prestige faded and bedraggled, she would no longer be a missionary, but only Philip's wife.

There were moments when, on the verge of hysteria, she thought of leaving them all and going back alone to Africa; but when the moments passed, she found herself strangely weak and incapable of action. For a strange and frightening thing had begun to happen. At Megambo when Philip had always been gentle and submissive, it was herself who dominated and planned. They were comrades in the work of the Lord, and Philip rarely reached the point of being irritable. In those days he had meant no more to her than the clumsy Swanson. Save that he was tied to her by law, he might have been only another worker in the mission. And now it was changed somehow; and Philip ignored her. There were whole days when he never spoke to her at all—days and nights spent in working in the black Mills and sleeping like a dead man to recover from the profound weariness that attacked him.

This new Philip frightened her in a way she had never been frightened before. She found herself, without thinking, doing little things to please him, even to attract his notice. There were still moments when, wrapping herself in the shroud of martyrdom, she flung herself, the apotheosis of injured womanhood, before him to be trampled upon; but they were not profitable moments, for they no longer had any effect upon him; and so, slowly they came to be abandoned, since it seemed silly thus to abase herself only to find that she had no audience. It frightened her, for it seemed that she was losing slowly all control of a life which had once been so neatly and thoroughly organized. She wanted desperately to regain her ancient hold over him, and in the lonely moments when Mabelle was not there she sometimes awakened in horror to find herself sitting before the gigantic walnut mirror letting down the masses of her long, straight, reddish hair, trying it in new ways, attempting to discover in what position her face seemed prettiest. And then, filled with disgust at her own wickedness, she would fling herself on the walnut bed and burst into a passion of tears and prayer, to arise at last strangely calm and comforted. Surely God would not abandon her—Naomi Potts, who had given all her life to God. Sometimes she fancied that she, instead of Philip, was the one whose brain was weak; for no sane woman could do the things she had done.

Slowly, imperceptibly, the curious power of the Mills had begun to make itself felt. It was as if Philip, returning from the Flats at noon each day, brought with him, clinging to his very clothes, traces of the fascination which they held for him. It was not that she herself felt any of the fascination, for she regarded the Mills with a growing hatred: it was only that they fixed upon Philip himself some new and tantalizing quality. She liked to see him come home at noon, hard and unshaven, blackened by soot and sweat. Sitting in her rocking-chair by the window, the sight of him as he swung along, his head bowed a little, filled her with odd flutterings of pleasant emotion. She felt at times that strange weakness which so often attacked Emma unawares—of wanting to yield and spoil him by caresses and attention. She had strange desires to fling herself down and let him trample upon her, not in the old, dramatic sense, but in a new way, which seemed to warm her whole body.

This new Philip, hard and thin, returning from the Mills with his flannel shirt open upon his bare chest, disgusted and fascinated her. And then when the knob turned and the door opened, all the little speeches she had planned, all the little friendly gestures, seemed to wither and die before his polite coldness.

He would say, "I'll wash up and we can go right away to eat," or "Tell Essie to bring some hot water."

There was nothing more than that. Sometimes it seemed to her that he treated her as a servant whom he scarcely knew.

It came, at length, to the point when she spoke of it, timidly and with hot blushes, to Aunt Mabelle. She said she wanted to be kind to Philip, she wanted to be friendly with him, but somehow she couldn't. He was so changed and cold and hard. If she could only get him back to Africa everything would be all right: they had been happy there, at least she had been, and as for Philip, he didn't seem any happier now that he was doing what he wanted to do. He never seemed happy anywhere, not since the day they had arrived at Megambo.

Mabelle, rocking little Jimmy, listened with the passionate interest of a woman who found such a conversation fascinating. She led Naomi deeper and deeper into the mire and at last, when she had considered all the facts, she said, "Well, Naomi, it's my opinion that you ought to have a child. Philip would like a baby. He's that kind. I know them when I see them. Now, my Elmer hates children. They get in his way and I think they make him feel foolish and awkward, God alone knows why. But Philip's different. He ought to have a lot of children. He'd love 'em, and it would be a tie between you."

Naomi raised the old difficulty. "But if we go back to Africa—we can't take a little baby there."

"Well, you'd have to work that out, of course. Em would take care of it. She'd find time somehow. She can do anything she sets her mind to." Naomi, it seemed, wouldn't meet her eye and Aunt Mabelle pushed on, with the tact and grace of a walrus. "Did you ever see a doctor to find out why you hadn't had one? A doctor can help sometimes."

Naomi was suddenly pale and shaking. Without

looking at Mabelle she said in a low voice, "I don't have to see the doctor to find out why."

Mabelle's rocking-chair paused in its monotonous bobbing. "You don't mean to say you've been doing sinful things to prevent it—you, Naomi Downes, a missionary!"

Naomi, wringing her hands, said, "No, I don't know what you mean. I haven't been doing sinful things. . . . I . . . we couldn't have had a baby . . . we've —we've never lived together."

The rocking-chair still remained quiescent, a posed symbol of Mabelle's shocked astonishment. "Well, I don't know what you mean. But it seems sinful to me if a man and wife don't live together. What does the Bible say? Take unto yourself a wife and multiply. Look at all the begats."

Naomi burst out, "We meant to . . . some day. Only we couldn't out there in Africa."

"Well, you ought to have taken a chance." Mabelle seemed outraged and angry for the first time in all Naomi's friendship with her, and it was only after a long time that the rocking-chair began once more its unending motion. The baby, startled by a sudden cessation of the soothing motion, set up a cry and Mabelle, loosening ten of the twenty-one buttons that held together her straining basque, quieted it at once.

"What do you expect?" asked Mabelle rhetorically. "What do you expect? A man isn't going on courting forever for nothing—especially after he's married to a woman. He'll get tired after a while. Philip's a man like any other man. He's not going on forever like this. He isn't that kind. Any woman can tell in a glance—and he's the kind that can wrap a woman

around his thumb." Then, being a woman whose whole
philosophy was based upon her own experience, she
said, "Why, even my Elmer wouldn't stand it, like as
not. He's not much at things like that and he's always
ashamed of himself afterwards. I guess it was a kind
of duty with him—still he's a man." And turning
back again to the subject at hand, she asked, "Did you
ever know about Philip's father? Why, that man was
like a rabbit. You'd better look out or you'll lose
him altogether."

It was the longest single speech Mabelle had made
in years, and after it she sat rocking herself for a
long time in profound meditation. Naomi cried a little
and dried her eyes, and the baby fell back into a state
of coma. The chair creaked and creaked. At last
Mabelle got up heavily, deposited the sleeping child
on the sofa, and put on her jacket and hat.

"Take my advice, Naomi," she said. "It can't go on
like this. If you don't want to lose him, you'll do
what I say. I'm a good judge of men and Philip is
worth keeping. He's better than his Ma, Pa, Uncle
Elmer, or any of 'em. I wish I was married to such a
man."

10

Emma in these days found relief in a vast activity.
The restaurant business kept growing and growing
until at last she secured a long lease on the shoe store
next door and undertook the necessary alterations.
She was in and out of the place a score of times a
day, watching the carpenters, the plumbers and the
painters, quarreling with the contractor and insisting
that pipes should be placed where it was impossible

to place them and pillars spaced so that there would be a permanent danger of the roof falling in upon her customers.

She was active, too, in her church work and contributed half a wagon load of cakes and pies to the annual June church fair. The Minerva Circle met at her house and Naomi was introduced to those members whom she did not know already, and so launched in a series of sewing parties which she attended in a kind of misery because on account of Philip she could not answer honestly the persistent questions of her new women "friends." And Emma kept up as well her fervent activities as President of the Woman's Christian Temperance Union, carrying war into the enemy's country, trying to drive whisky from a country of mills and furnaces where every other corner was occupied by a saloon. She even called upon Moses Slade, Congressman of the district, and lately become a widower, in his great boxlike house set back among the trees on Park Avenue. It was an odd call which began with open hostility when she urged him to wear a white ribbon and declare himself at once on the side of God and Purity.

But Slade, being a politician, felt that Fortune had not yet sided with God and Purity, and declined the honor with a great flow of eloquence for which he was famed. There was much talk of his being chosen to represent the majority of the people, and as yet the majority seemed unfortunately ("the human race is naturally wicked and must be educated to goodness— we must not forget that, Mrs. Downes") still on the side of gin.

He was a man of fifty, with a great stomach and

massive feet and hands, who had a round, flat face and a broad, flat nose, with odd little shifty eyes. He was bald in front, but what remained of the once luxuriant black locks was now worn, loose and free, bobbed in a style which women came, shockingly, to adopt years afterward.

He received Emma in his study, a room with red walls, set round with mastodon furniture in mahogany and red leather. In the beginning he was taken aback by the vigor and power of Emma's handsome figure.

She said to him, "The day will come, Mr. Slade, when you will have to vote on the side of purity if you wish to survive—you and all your fellow-members."

And he replied, "That, Mrs. Downes, is what I am waiting for—a sign from the people. You may tell your members that my heart is with them but that I must not lose my head. A sign is all I'm waiting for, Mrs. Downes—only a sign."

Emma, feeling that she had gained at least half a victory, turned the conversation to other things. They discussed the Republican chances at the coming election, and the lateness of the summer, the question, as it was called, of "smoke abatement" and, of course, the amazing growth and prosperity of the Town. They found presently that they saw eye to eye on every subject, for Emma was in her own way a born politician. Congressman Slade observed that since the death of his wife (here a deep sigh interrupted his observation) life had not been the same. To lose a woman after thirty years! Well, it made a gap that could never be filled, or at least, it was extremely unlikely that it would be filled. And now his house-keeper had left, leaving him helpless.

Emma, in her turn, sighed and murmured a few words of condolence. She knew what it was to be alone in the world. Hadn't she been alone for more than twenty years? Ever since Mr. Downes, going to China to make a fortune for himself and his son, had been killed there. They hadn't even found his body, so that she hadn't even the consolation of visiting his grave. That, of course, was a great deal. Congressman Slade ought to be thankful that he had his wife's grave. It helped. In a way, it made the thing definite. It was not like the torturing hope in which she had lived for twenty years. . . . Yes, more than twenty years, hoping all the while that he might not be really dead. Oh, she understood. She sympathized.

"But as to the housekeeper, Mr. Slade, don't let that trouble you. Come and take your meals at the restaurant. I'd be delighted to have you. It would be an honor to have you eat there."

"I'll take up your offer," he said, slapping his knee almost jovially. "I've heard how excellent it is. But, of course, I'll pay for it. I couldn't think of it otherwise."

For a moment, there appeared in the manner of Emma the faintest hint of an ancient coquetry, long forgotten and grown a little stale. It was a mere shadow, something that lurked in the suspicious bobbing of the black ostrich plumes in her hat.

"Oh, don't think of that," she said. "It would be a pleasure—an honor."

She rose and shook his hand. "Good-by, Mr. Slade, and thank you for letting me waste so much of your time."

"It was a pleasure, madam, a pleasure," and going to the door, he bowed her out of his widowed house.

When she had gone, Moses Slade returned to his study and before going back to his work he sat for a long time lost in thought. The shadow of a smile encircled the rather hard, virtuous lips. He smiled because he was thinking of Emma, of her fine figure and healthy, rosy face, of the curve of the full bosom, and the hips from which her dress flowed away like the waters of a fountain.

From the very moment of Minnie's death—indeed, even long before, during the dragging, heavy-footed years of her invalidism—he had been thinking, with a deep sense of guilt, of a second marriage. The guilt had faded away by now, for Minnie had been in her grave for two summers and he could turn his thoughts in such a direction, freely and with a clear conscience. After all, he was a fine, vigorous man, in his prime. People talked about fifty-five as old age—a time when a man should begin to think of other things; but people didn't know until they *were* fifty-five. He had talked like that himself once a long while ago. And now, look at him, as good a man as ever he was, and better, when it came to brains and head. Why, with all the experience he had had. . . .

As he sat there, talking to himself, his earnestness became so great that his lips began to move, forming the words as if he were holding a conversation, even arguing, with another Moses Slade, who sat just across from him in the monstrous chair on the opposite side of the desk. He must, he felt, convince that other Moses Slade.

He went on talking. Look at Mrs. Downes! What a fine woman! With such noble—(yes, noble was the only word)—such noble curves and such a fine, high color. She, too, was in her prime, a fine figure of a woman, handsomer now than she had been as a skinny young thing of eighteen. There was a woman who would make a wife for a man like himself. And she had sense, too, running a business with such success. She'd be a great help to a man in politics.

He began prodding his memory about her. He remembered the story of her long widowhood, of Mr. Downes' mysterious death. Yes, and he even remembered Downes himself, a whipper-snapper, who was no good, and had a devastating way with women. (Memories of a hot-blooded youth began to rise and torment him.) Well, she was better off without him, a no-good fellow like that. And what a brave fight she'd made! She was a fine woman. She had a son, too, a son who was a missionary, and—and— Why, come to think of it, hadn't the son given it up and come home? That didn't sound so good, but you could keep the son out of the way.

The truth was that Moses Slade really wanted a skinny young thing of twenty, but a Congressman who wrote "Honorable" before his name couldn't afford to make a fool of himself. He couldn't afford to marry a silly young thing, or ever get "mixed up" with a woman. A man of fifty-five who kept wanting to pinch arms and hips had to be careful. If he could only pinch, just one pinch, some one like—well, some one as plump as Mrs. Downes, he'd feel like a boy again.

He felt that youth would flow back again into him
through the very tips of the pinching fingers. It
wasn't much—just wanting to pinch a girl. Why did
people make such a fuss about it?

He almost convinced himself that a full-blown rose
like Emma Downes was far better than a skinny young
thing. There was, too, of course, the Widow Barnes,
who lived next door, still in her prime, and with a large
fortune as well.

He took up the Congressional Record, and tried to
lose himself in its mountains and valleys of bombast
and boredom, but in a little while the book lay unnoticed on his heavy thighs and he was arguing with
the other Moses Slade across the desk.

Suddenly, as if he had been roused from a deep sleep,
he again found himself talking aloud. "Well," he
thought, "something has got to be done about this."

11

Meanwhile Emma, walking briskly along beneath the
maples of Park Avenue, found her mind all aglitter
with interesting projects. She often said that she always felt on the crest of the wave, but to-day it was
even better than that; she felt almost girlish. Something had happened to her, while she sat with Moses
Slade, consoling him and accepting his consolations.
He had noticed her. She marked the look in his eye
and noticed the fingers that drummed impatiently the
fine edge of his black serge mourning trousers. A man
behaved like that only when a woman made him nervous
and uneasy. And as she walked, there kept coming
back to her in a series of pictures all the adventures

of a far distant youth, memories of sleighrides and church suppers, of games of Truth and Forfeits. There was a whole gallery of young men concerned in the flow of memories—young men, tragically enough, whom she might have married. They were middle-aged or oldish now, most of them as rich and distinguished as Moses Slade himself. Somehow she had picked the poorest of the lot, and so missed all the security that came of a sound husband like Slade.

Well (she thought), she wasn't sorry in a way, for she had been happy, and it wasn't too late even now to have the other thing—wealth, security. She'd made a success of her business, and could quit it now with the honest satisfaction of knowing it hadn't defeated her—quit it, or, better still, pass it on to Philip and Naomi, if he were still sure that he wouldn't go back to Megambo. Perhaps that was the way out—to let him take it off her shoulders, and so bring him out of those filthy mills where he was disgracing them all. But then (she thought), what would she do with no work, nothing on which to center her life? It wasn't as if she were tired: she'd never felt as well in her life as in this moment moving along under the slightly sooty maples. No, she couldn't settle down to doing nothing, sitting at home rocking like Naomi and Mabelle. (She fairly snorted at the thought of Mabelle.) Of course, if she married again, married some one like Moses Slade—not Moses Slade, of course (she scarcely knew him), but some one like him. Such a thing wasn't impossible, and with a husband of his age marriage couldn't be very unpleasant. She could go to Washington and do much good for such causes as temperance and woman suffrage.

And then, abruptly, her thoughts were interrupted by the voice of some one speaking to her.

"How do you do, Mrs. Downes?" Looking up, she saw it was Mary Watts . . . now Mary Conyngham . . . looking pale and rather handsome in her widow's clothes.

"Why, Mary Watts, I haven't seen you in ever so long."

There was a certain gush in Emma's manner that was too violent. The cordiality of Mary Watts had, too, the note of one who disliked the object of her politeness. (Emma thought, "She usually pretends not to see me. She's only stopped me because she wants to ask about Philip.")

"I've been away," said Mary; "I had the children in the South. That's why you haven't seen me."

"Yes, now that you speak of it, I do remember reading it in the paper."

And Mary, who never possessed any subtlety, went straight to the point. "I hear," she said, "that Philip has come home."

"Yes, he's been home for some time."

"Is it true that he's working in the Mills . . . as a day laborer?"

("What business is it of yours?" thought Emma.)

"Yes, it's a notion he had. I think he wants to find out what it's like. He thinks a missionary ought to know about such things."

"I suppose he'll be going back to Africa soon?"

"Oh, yes. I think he's impatient to be back."

"His wife's here, too?"

"Yes, she's here."

"I've never met her. Perhaps I'd better call."

"Yes, she's always there. She doesn't go out much."

There was an awkward pause and Mary, looking away suddenly, said, "Well, good-by, Mrs. Downes. Remember me to Philip."

"Of course," said Emma. "Good-by."

Once after they had parted, Emma looked back to watch Mary. She looked handsome (Emma thought), but sad and tired. Perhaps it was the trouble she had had with Conyngham and Mamie Rhodes . . . carrying on so. Still, she didn't feel sorry for Mary: you couldn't feel sorry for a girl who had such superior airs. She was always stuck-up—Mary Watts; and she'd better not try any of her tricks on Philip.

Her thoughts flew back to Philip. Something had to be done about him. He'd been home for nine months now, and people were beginning to talk; they were even beginning to find out about the Mills. (Why, Mary Watts knew it already.) Being so busy with the new addition to the restaurant and the church and the Union affairs, she hadn't done her best by him these last few weeks; she'd been neglecting her duty in a way. It wasn't too late for him to go back to Megambo— why, he might still become Bishop of East Africa. If he didn't, it would go to that numbskull, Swanson, as first in the field.

And instead of that, he was working like a common Dago in the Mills.

And Naomi, she wasn't any help at all. Funny, too, when she'd always thought Naomi could look out for herself and manage Philip. Instead, she seemed to grow more spineless every day—almost as if she were siding with Philip. She was getting just like Mabelle, sitting around all day in a trance, rocking. Something had to be done.

Then, for no reason at all, unless it happened through that train of memories fired by the behavior of Moses Slade, which led back to her youth, she thought of Naomi's preciously guarded virginity.

Perhaps (she thought) if they had a child, if Philip and Naomi lived together as man and wife, they would all have a greater hold upon him. A man with a *real* wife and children wasn't as free as a man like Philip, who had no responsibilities (now that he'd become so strange), save those imposed by the law. Perhaps he would come to love Naomi and do things to please her. He'd come in time to want things from her. A thing like that did give you a hold over a man: it was a precarious hold, and you had to be very clever about it, but it was something, after all. If there was a child, she (Emma) could take charge of it when Philip and Naomi went back to the place God had ordained for them.

As she walked, the idea grew and grew. Why (she wondered) hadn't it occurred to her before, as the one chance left? Naomi would hate it, and probably refuse at first, but she must be made to understand that it was her duty, not only as a wife (there were plenty of passages in the Bible to prove it), but as an agent of God. Why, it was almost another case of Esther and Ahasuerus, or even Judith and Holofernes. Look what they had done for God!

Yes, there was a chance of managing Philip, after all. If they fixed on him such new responsibilities, it might bring him to his senses.

Suddenly, in the midst of these torrential thoughts, she found herself at the very door of her own house, and, entering, she called out, "Naomi! Naomi!" in her loud, booming voice.

From her rocking-chair by the window, Naomi rose and answered her. She had been crying, perhaps all the afternoon, and her pale eyes were swollen and rimmed with red.

"Naomi," she said, flinging aside her hat and jacket, "I've had a new idea about Philip. I think we've been wrong in our way of managing him."

12

At the same moment, Philip was walking along the road that led out into the open country, talking, talking, talking to Mary Conyngham.

He had met her in a fashion the most natural, for he had gone to walk in the part of the town where Mary lived. There were odd, unsuspected ties between the people who lived on the Hill and those who lived in the Flats, and he had come to know of her return from Krylenko, his own foreman; for Krylenko had heard it from Irene Shane, who had seen Mary herself at the school that Irene kept alive in the midst of the Flats. Krylenko told him the news while they sat eating their breakfast out of tin pails and talking of Irene Shane. Once he heard it, there was no more peace for Philip: he thought about her while he worked, pulling and pushing great sheets of red-hot metal, while the thick smoke blew in at the windows of the cavernous shed. All through the morning he kept wondering what she was like, whether she had changed. He kept recalling her face, oval and dark, with good-humored blue eyes and dark hair pulled back in a knob at the back of her small head. That was the way he remembered her, and he tormented himself with doubts as to whether she had changed. She wasn't a girl any longer; she was the mother of two children, and a widow. She had been through troubles with her husband.

At lunch he scarcely spoke to Naomi and his mother, and he never uttered the name of Mary Conyngham, for something made him cautious: he could not say what it was, save that he felt he oughtn't to speak of her before the other two. He had to see Mary Conyngham; he had to talk with her, to talk about himself. He couldn't go on any longer, always shut in, always imprisoned in the impenetrable cell of his own loneliness. It was Mary Conyngham who could help him; he was certain of it.

He left Naomi at the door of the restaurant, telling her that he meant to go for a walk. He would return later to sleep. No, he didn't feel tired. He thought a walk would do him good.

And then, when he had left her, he walked toward the part of the town where Mary lived, and when he reached her street, he found that he hadn't the courage even to pass her house, for fear she might see him and wonder why he was walking about out there on the borders of the town. For an hour he walked, round and round the block encircling her house, but never passing it. It wasn't only that she might think him a fool, but she might be changed and hard. If she had changed as much as he himself had changed, it would only be silly and futile, the whole affair. But he couldn't go on forever thus walking round and round, because people would think him mad, as mad as his mother and Naomi believed him.

Crossing the street, he looked up, waiting for a wagon to pass, and there on the opposite side stood Mary Conyngham. She did not see him at once, perhaps (he thought) because she had not expected to see him, and so had not recognized him. She was wearing a short skirt, known as a "rainy daisy," though it was a bright, clear day. She looked pale, he thought, and much older—handsomer, too, than she had once been. All the tomboyish awkwardness had vanished. She was a woman now. For a moment he had a terrible desire to turn and run, to hide himself. It was a ridiculous thought, and it came to nothing, for as the wagon passed she saw him, and, smiling, she crossed the street to meet him. His heart was beating wildly, and the rare color came into his dark cheeks.

"Philip," she said, "I've been wondering where you were."

It gave him the oddest sensation of intimacy, as if the meeting had been planned, and he had been waiting all this time impatiently.

They shook hands, and Mary said, "I've just left your mother." And Philip blushed again, feeling awkward, and silly, like a boy in his best clothes, who didn't know what to do with his hands. He was dressed like a workman in an old suit and blue cotton shirt.

Suddenly he plunged. "I came out here on purpose. I wanted to see you."

"Have you been to the house?"

"No," he hesitated. "No . . . I've just been walking round, hoping to run into you."

It was five years since they had last seen each other, and longer than that since they had really been friends. Talk didn't come easily at first. Standing

there on the corner, they made conversation for a time
—silly, banal conversation—when each of them wanted
to talk in earnest to the other.

At last Philip said, "Are you in a hurry? Could I
come home with you?"

"No, I'm not in a hurry. I've left the children with
Rachel . . . Rachel is my sister-in-law. We share ex-
penses on the house. But I don't think we better go
home. Are you tired?" she asked abruptly.

"No."

"Because if you aren't, we might go for a walk. I
was afraid you might be, after working all night at
the Mills."

For a moment Philip looked at her sharply. "How
did you know I was in the Mills?"

She laughed. "Krylenko told me. I saw him yesterday. He was helping Irene teach English to a lot of
dirty and very stupid Poles."

"He's a nice fellow—Krylenko. I didn't know there
were such men down there."

"Nobody knows it without going down there. Shall
we walk a bit?"

They set out along Milburn Street, past the row of
houses surrounded by green leaves and bright trees.
It was the hill farthest from the Mills and the soot seldom drifted so far. As they drew nearer and nearer
to the open fields, the queer sense of restraint began a
little to melt away. They even laughed naturally as
they had done years before when they had played together.

"It was a funny thing," said Philip. "I've been
wanting to see you ever since I came back. That's why
I came out here this afternoon—on a chance of meet-

ing you. I came as soon as I heard you were home."

He was walking with his hands clasped behind him, his dark brows puckered into a fine line with the effort he was making. He didn't know how to talk to women, at least women like Mary, and, in spite of their old, old friendship, he felt shy with her. With her dead husband and her two children, she seemed so much older and wiser. Some odd, new complication had entered their relationship which made it all difficult and confused. Yet she seemed to take it calmly, almost sadly.

"Tell me," she said presently. "Philip, tell me about yourself. You don't mean to go back?" She halted and looked at him squarely.

"No, I don't mean to go back." And all at once he found himself pouring out to her the whole story. He told her how he hated it all from the beginning, how he had begun to doubt, how the doubts had tortured him; how he had prayed and prayed, only to find himself slipping deeper and deeper. He told her of the morning by the lake, of the terrible night of the drums, of the coming of the queer Englishwoman, and the fight that followed, in which his last grain of faith had gone. Suddenly, he realized that he was telling the whole story for the first time. He had never spoken of it before to any one. It was as if all the while, without knowing it, he had been saving it for Mary Conyngham.

"And so," she said, "you've come back to stay. Do you think you'll stay?"

He shrugged his shoulders. "I don't know. There's nothing else to do."

"And why did you go to work in the Mills?"

"I don't know. At least, I didn't know at the beginning."

"Was it because you wanted to work among the people in the Flats?"

"No . . . no . . . I'm through with meddling in other people's lives."

There was a bitterness in his tone which Mary must have guessed had some relation to the woman she had left a little while before; only Philip had always adored his mother. Emma Downes boasted of it.

"I think I went into the Mills," he was saying, "because I had to find something solid to get hold of . . . and that was the solidest thing I could find. It's awfully solid, Mary. And it's beginning to do the trick. At first I hadn't faith in anything, least of all myself, and now I've got something new to take its place. It's a kind of faith in man—a faith in yourself. I couldn't go on always putting everything into the hands of God. It's like cheating—and people don't do it really. They only pretend they do. If they left it all to God, I suppose things would work out somehow; but they don't. They insist on meddling, too, and when a thing succeeds then God is good and he's answered their prayers, and if it fails, then it is God's Will. But all the while they're meddling themselves and making a mess of things."

"And you don't mean ever to go back to the church?"

For a moment he didn't answer. Then he said in a low voice, "No . . . I don't believe any longer—at least, not in the way of the church. And the church—well, the church is dead so far as the world is concerned. It's full of meddling old women. It might disappear to-morrow and the world would go on just the same. That's one thing about the Flats. . . . Down there you get down to brass tacks. You know how little all the hubbub really means."

"Do people know how you feel?"

"No, they just think I'm a little mad. I've never told any one any of this, Mary, until now."

She looked at him shyly. "Your blue shirt suits you better than your black clothes, Philip. I always thought you weren't made for a preacher."

He blushed. "Perhaps . . . anyway, I feel natural in the blue shirt." He halted again. "You know, Mary, it's been the queerest thing—the whole business. It's as if I never really existed before. It's like being born again—it's painful and awful."

They were quite clear of the Town now. It had sunk down behind the rolling hills. They sat down side by side presently on the stone wall of the bridge that crossed the brook. The water here was clear and clean. It turned to oil further on, after it had passed through the Flats. For a time they sat in silence, watching the sun slipping down behind the distant woods that crowned Trimble's Hill. In the far distance the valley had turned misty and blue.

Presently Mary sighed suddenly, and asked, "And your wife? What's to be done about her? She's a missionary, too, and she still believes, doesn't she?"

A shadow crossed Philip's face. "Yes, that's the trouble. It's made such an awful mess. She's always lived out there. She's never known any other life, and she doesn't know how to get on here. That's the trouble. Sometimes I think she ought to go back . . . alone, without me. She'd be happier there."

For a moment there was a silence, and Philip fancied that she began to say something, and then halted abruptly; but he couldn't be certain. It may have only been the noise of the brook. He looked at her sharply, but she rose and turned her back.

"We'd better start back," she said. "It will be getting dark."

For a long time they walked side by side in silence—an odd silence in which they seemed to be talking to each other all the while. It was Mary who actually spoke.

"But you don't mean to go on forever in the Mills? Have you thought what you want to do?"

Again he waited for a long time before answering her. It must have seemed to Mary that he was being shy and cautious with her, that despite the pouring out of his story, there was still a great deal that he had kept hidden away. He had the air of a man who was afraid of confidences.

At last he said, "I don't know whether I ought to speak of it, but I do know what I want to do. It sounds ridiculous, but what I want to do is . . . is . . . paint." He blurted it out as if it required an immense effort, as if he were confessing a sin.

"Pictures?" asked Mary. "Do you know anything about it?"

"No . . . not very much. I've always wanted to, in a way. A long time ago, when I was a boy, I used to spend all my time drawing things." His voice fell a little. "But as I grew older, it seemed foolish . . . and the other thing came up . . . and I did that instead. You see, I've been drawing a bit lately. I've been drawing in the Flats—the engines and cranes and chimneys. They always . . . well, they fascinated me as far back as I can remember." When she did not answer, he said, "You remember . . . I used to draw when I was a kid . . ."

For a time she considered this sudden, fantastic outburst, and presently she said, "Yes, I remember. I still have the picture you made of Willie, the pony . . . and the tree-house. . . ." And then after another pause. "Have you thought about a teacher?"

"No . . . but . . . don't think I'm conceited, Mary . . . I don't want a teacher. I want to work it out for myself. I've got an idea."

She asked him if she might see some of the drawings.

"I haven't shown them to any one," he said. "I don't want to yet . . . because they aren't good enough. When I do a good one . . . the kind I know is right and what I meant it to be, I'll give it to you."

His secret, he realized suddenly, was out—the secret he had meant to tell no one, because he was in a strange way ashamed of it. It seemed so silly for any one in the Town to think of painting.

The odd, practical streak in Mary asserted itself. "Have you got paints? You can't get them here in the Town."

"No . . . I haven't needed them. But I'll want them soon. I want to begin soon."

"I'm going to Cleveland on Monday," she said. "I'll get them there . . . everything you need. You'd never find them here."

And then, since he had let escape his secret, he told her again of the morning by the lake at Megambo, and the sudden, fierce desire to put down what he saw in the procession of black women carrying water to the

young plantations. He tried to tell her how in a way
it had given him a queer sense of religious ecstasy.

It was almost dark now, and the fragrance of the
garden on the outskirts of the Town filled the air.

Mary smiled suddenly. "You know," she said, "I
don't think you really hated Africa at all. It wasn't
Africa you hated. You loved it. And I don't think
you mean to stay here all your life. Some day you'll
be going back."

He left her in the shadows as the older of her children, a tow-headed girl of three, came down the path
to meet her, calling out her name.

On returning to the slate-colored house, he opened
the door to find Naomi awaiting him.

"Supper is ready," she said. "I sent Essie to the
restaurant for it, so you wouldn't have to walk up
there."

He thanked her, and she answered, "I thought you'd
be tired after walking so long."

"Thank you. I did take a long walk. I wanted to
get into the open country."

While they ate, sitting opposite each other, beneath
the glow of the dome painted with wild-roses, he noticed that she was changed. She seemed nervous and
uneasy: she kept pressing him to eat more. She was
flushed and even smiled at him once or twice. He tried
to answer the smile, but his face seemed made of lead.
The effort gave him pain.

Suddenly he thought, "My God! She is trying to be
nice to me!" And he was frightened without knowing
why. It was almost as if, for a moment, the earth had
opened and he saw beneath his feet a chasm, vague and
horrible, and sinister.

He thought, "What can have changed her?" For lately there had grown up between them a slow and insinuating enmity that was altogether new. There were moments when he had wanted to turn away and not see her at all.

She poured more coffee for him, and he became aware suddenly that his nerves were on edge, that he was seeing everything with a terrible clarity—the little freckles on the back of her hand, the place where the cup was chipped, the very figures and tiny discolorations of the ornate wallpaper.

"Your mother won't be home till late," she said. "She's gone to report her talk with Mr. Slade to the ladies of the Union."

He wondered why she had told him something which he already knew. But he was kind to her, and tried not to seem different, in any way, from what he had always been. He was sorry for Naomi more than ever since her life had become such an empty, colorless thing.

At last he was finished, and thanking her again, he left her helping Essie to clear away the table, and went upstairs with a strange feeling that she had stayed behind to help only because she didn't want to be alone with him.

Undressing, he lay for a long time in the darkness, unable to sleep because of the acuteness which seemed to attack all his senses. He heard every small noise in the street—the cries of the children playing in the glare of the arc-lights, the barking of dogs, the distant tinkle of a piano. Slowly, because he was very tired, the sounds grew more and more distant, and he fell asleep.

He slept profoundly, as a man drowned in the long exhaustion of the Mills. He was awakened by something touching him gently at first, as if it were part of a dream. It touched him again and then again, and slowly he drifted back to consciousness. Being a man of nerves, he awakened quickly, all at once. There was no slow drowsiness and clinging mists of slumber.

He opened his eyes, but the room was in complete blackness, and he saw nothing. It must have been late, for even the sounds of the street had died away, to leave only the long pounding of the Mills that was like the silence. Somewhere, close at hand, there was a sound of breathing. For a second he thought, "I have died in my sleep."

Then the thing touched him again. It was a bit of metal, cold and rigid, not longer than a finger. And in a sudden flash he knew what it was—a metal hair-curler. The thing brushed his forehead. He knew then, quickly. It was Naomi come to him to be his wife. She was bending over him. The darkness hid her face. She made no sound. It was unreal, like something out of a dream.

13

In the Mills Philip had come to know the men who worked at his oven, one by one, slowly, for they were at first suspicious of him as a native from the Hills who came to work among them. It was Krylenko more than any of them who broke down the barrier which shut him away from all those others. Krylenko, he came presently to understand, was a remarkable fellow. He was young, not perhaps more than twenty-

five or six, a giant even among the big Poles, who
worked with the strength of three ordinary men. There
was a magnificence about his great body, with its supple muscles flowing beneath the blond, white skin.
Naked to the waist, and leaning on his great bar of
iron, there were times when he seemed a statue cut in
the finest Parian marble. It was this odd, physical
splendor that gave him a prestige and the power of
leadership, which would have come to nothing in a
stupid man; but Krylenko was intelligent, and hidden
within the intelligence there lay a hard kernel of peas-
ant shrewdness. He knew what it was he wanted and
he was not to be turned aside; he was, Philip had
come to understand, partly the creation of Irene Shane,
that pale, transparent wraith, who spent all her days
between the Flats and the great, gloomy house known
as Shane's Castle. She had found him in her night
class, a big Russian boy with a passion for learning
things, and she had taken him to help her. She had
perhaps discerned the odd thing about Krylenko, which
set him apart from the others, that he had a vision.
He had no ambition for himself, but his queer, mystical
mind was constantly illuminated by wonderful plans
of what he might do for his people. By this, he did not
mean his own country people, but all the hordes of
workers who dwelt in the rows of black houses and
spent half their lives in the Mills. To him they were,
quite simply, brothers—all the Poles, the Lithuanians,
the Italians, the Croats, even the negroes who came up
from the South to die slowly working over the acid
vats. In his own Slavic way he had caught a sense of
that splendor of the Mills which sometimes overwhelmed Philip. Only Krylenko saw, what was quite

true, that the people in the Flats belonged to another world from those on the Hill. They made up a nation within a nation, a hostile army surrounded and besieged.

He meant to help his people to freedom, even by doing battle, if circumstance demanded it. At times there was about him the splendor of the ancient prophets.

It was for this reason that he stayed in the pounding-sheds, as a simple foreman, refusing to go elsewhere, though he could have had after a time one of the easy places in the shipping-rooms. He might have been one of those men who, "working their way from the bottom of the ladder," turned to oppress his own people. There were plenty of shrewd, hard-headed, pitiless men like that—men such as Frick and Carnegie, who had interests in these very Mills. Only he wasn't concerned for himself. He had a queer, stupid, pig-headed idea of helping the men about him; and he was one of those fantastic men to whom Justice was also God.

He had his own way of going about it; and he was not a sentimentalist. He knew that to get things in this world, one had to fight; and so he had gone quietly about organizing men, one here, one there, into the dreaded unions. It had to be done secretly, because he would have been sent away, blacklisted and put outside the pale if the faintest suspicion of his activity reached the ears even of the terrified little clerks who talked so big. There were meetings sometimes in the room over Hennessey's saloon, with men who wandered into town on one train and out on the next. It was a slow business, for one had to go carefully. But even with all the care there were whispers of strange things going on beneath the rumbling surface of the Flats. There were rumors which disturbed the peace of the stock-brokers, and stirred with uneasiness the people on the Hill—the bankers, the lawyers, the little shopkeepers—all the parasite ants whose prosperity rested upon the sweat of the Flats. There were, too, spies among the workers.

They even said on the Hill that old Julia Shane and that queer daughter of hers had a finger in the pie, which was more than true, for they did know what was happening. In their mad, fantastic way they had even given money.

There was always a strange current of fear and sus-picion running beneath the surface, undermining here and there in places that lay below ground. In the first weeks Philip had become aware slowly of the sinister movement. He came to understand the suspicions against him. And then abruptly, bit by bit, perhaps because of his own taste for solitude and his way of go-ing off to sit alone in a corner eating his own lunch, Krylenko had showed signs of friendliness, stifled and hindered in the beginning by the strangeness which set apart a dweller in the Flats from one on the Hill. One by one, the other men came to drop their suspicions and presently Philip found himself joining in their coarse jokes, even picking up snatches of their outlandish tongues. He came, in a way, to be one of them, and the effect of the communion filled him with a sense of expan-sion, almost as if he could feel himself growing. In a life dedicated to loneliness, he felt for the first time that warm, almost sensual feeling of satisfaction in compan-ionship. He came to understand the men who worked at his own oven—Sokoleff, who drank whisky as if it were water, and sweated it all out as fast as he drank it, Krylenko himself, who was in love with an Italian girl who couldn't marry him until her orphaned brothers and sisters were grown, and Finke, the black little Croat who sometimes lost his head and talked wildly about revolution. And a dozen others—simple, coarse men, whose lives seemed plain and direct, filled too with suffering, though it was of a physical sort concerned with painful work, and childbirth, and empty stomachs, and so unlike that finer torture which Philip himself suffered.

And presently he found that the Mills were saving him—even his brain: the grimness, the bitter tang of the black life in the Flats, presented a savage reality which was to him like a spar in the open sea. There was no reality, he thought sometimes, even in his marriage to Naomi. It was all shadowy and unreal, filled with sound and fury which seemed baseless and even silly, when one thought of this other life of fire and steel. His own existence had been a futile, meaningless affair of vapors, swooning and ecstasies.

And then on the morning after Naomi had come to him, Krylenko fixed it for him to join the Union. To Philip it was a move that took on a significance out of proportion with the reality: it had an importance which for the others was lacking. He had entered the sinister conspiracy against his own people on the Hill; it marked the closing of a door behind him. He was certain now never to turn back.

All night and all morning he scarcely spoke to Krylenko and Finke and Sokoleff. He worked beside them, silent and sweating, his mind and soul in a confused state of alternate satisfaction and torment. Once or twice, he caught himself smiling into the depths of the burning ovens, like an idiot. He was smiling because of what had happened there in the dark in his room, with the pleasure of a boy come at last of age. It filled him with an odd, warm feeling of satisfaction and power. He was at last a man, like those others, Finke and Sokoleff and even Krylenko, who took such things as part of the day's routine, as they took eating and drinking. For them, a thing so commonplace couldn't mean what it meant to him. It couldn't give them that strange feeling of being suddenly set free after a long imprisonment. It couldn't mean a fever bred of long restraint that was vanished. And slowly through the long hours by the hot ovens his nerves grew relaxed and his mind cleared. The memory of the hot, tormenting nights at Megambo seemed distant and vague now. He was, as he had said to Mary Conyngham, being slowly born again. Something tremendous had happened to him. He was aware of a new strength and of a power over women, even women like his mother, and Naomi, terrified and hysterical in the darkness. He was free. A great light like a rocket had burst in the darkness.

At noon when the whistles blew, Krylenko, tucking in his shirt, said, "Come on and have a drink. . . . We gotta celebrate, all of us."

For a moment Philip hesitated. He had never drunk anything, even beer, but now there seemed a difference. What the hell difference did it make if you drank or not? These men about him all drank. It was the only pleasure they had, most of them, except what they found in the dismal, shuttered houses of Franklin Street. There was a reason now to drink. They would think he was celebrating his entrance into the Union, and all the time he'd be celebrating the other thing which they knew nothing about, which they wouldn't even understand.

"Yes," he said, "I'll go."

Hennessey's saloon stood at the corner of Halstead Street and the Erie tracks, just at the foot of the hill crowned by Shane's Castle. It was open night and day, and always filled with smoke and noise and drunken singing. Noise was its great characteristic— the grinding, squeaking sound of brakes on the endless freight-trains that passed the door, the violent, obscene voices of protesting drunks, the pounding of the Mills, and the ceaseless hammering of the tinny mechanical piano that swallowed nickels faster and faster as the patrons grew drunker and drunker. The only silence seemed to hang in a cloud about Mike Hennessey, the owner, a gigantic Irishman, with a beefy red face and carroty hair. He wasn't the original Hennessey. The founder, his father, was long since dead. In his day the famous Hennessey's had been only a crossroads saloon. There were no mills and furnaces. His customers were farmers. This silent Mike Hennessey knew his business: he watched men get drunker and drunker while the cash-register banged and jangled. He never spoke. He was afraid of no man, and he had a very special scorn for the Dagoes and their way of using knives to fight. He paid five hundred dollars a month to the mayor, which made the police both blind and deaf to the noise and lights of the saloon which had no closing hours, and a thousand more to veil in purity his row of shuttered houses in Franklin Street. There was a hard, flinty look in his cold blue eyes, that said:

"I know the price of everything in this bedlam of a Town. Every man and woman has a price."

But the hard blue eyes which never changed, widened ever so slightly for a brief second as the swinging doors opened and Philip came in with Finke and Krylenko and Sokoleff.

They sat at a table in the corner, where the mechanical piano growled and jangled. It was the full tide of drinking in the saloon, the hour when one shift of workers had left and another, dog-tired and black with soot, had only arrived. Most of them came unwashed from the Mills and their black faces together with the drifting smoke and clatter of sound gave the place the aspect of some chamber in Hell. The four companions began by drinking whisky, all of them but Philip perfectly straight. They would, Krylenko said, drink beer afterward to finish up.

The whisky, even diluted, burned and then warmed him. Finke and Sokoleff drank steadily, one glass after another, until the alcohol presently killed their weariness and Sokoleff began to grow hilarious and Finke to talk of revolution. For them the bad liquor took the place of rest, of sleep, of food, of cleanliness, even of decency. In the Flats it was useless to search for any decent thing, because comfort, food and warmth were not to be found there. Finke and Sokoleff had learned long ago that they lay only at the bottom of a glass filled many times with the rot-gut whisky that Hennessey sold.

Krylenko only drank a little and then said he must go, as he had to see Giulia before he went to bed. The great Ukrainian had washed himself carefully all over with cold water at the Mills, while the other three

waited, Finke and Sokoleff standing by and making
Rabelaisian jokes about his preparations for the
courtship. Krylenko took it with good-natured toler-
ance, but there was an odd, shining look in his small,
clear blue eyes.

Philip, sitting in a faint, warm haze, remembered the
scene with pleasure, conscious that he belonged to them
now. He was a member of the Union, one of them at
last, but more than that he had become like them a man.
He was drinking with them to celebrate.

Krylenko, taking leave of them, touched Philip on
the shoulder. "You better go home now and get some
sleep."

"No," said Philip; "I'm going to stay a while."

The big Russian's great hand closed on his shoulder
with a powerful but gentle pressure. "Look here,
Philip," he said, "you ain't like these two. You can't
stand it. You better go home now. They're just a
pair of hogs. Nothing hurts 'em."

But Philip felt hazy enough to be stubborn and a
little shrewd. He sided with Finke and Sokoleff, who
kept protesting noisily. He meant to have one more
drink—beer this time—and then he'd go.

Krylenko, shaking his big yellow head, went off to
see Giulia, and, as Philip watched his great shoulders
plowing their way through the mob, something odd
happened to him. It was as if a light had gone out;
instead of feeling jolly and a bit wild, he was seized
in the grip of melancholy. He wanted suddenly to weep.
He remembered what Krylenko had said about hogs,
and, staring in a queer daze at Finke and Sokoleff, he
saw them by some fantastic trick of the mind as two
pigs with smutty faces thrusting their noses into the

big drinking-glasses. He wanted suddenly to rise and wash himself all over with cold water as Krylenko had done—to wash away the smoke, the smell of sweat and the noise that filled the room. He didn't want to talk any more or listen to the lewd jokes which Finke and Sokoleff kept on making about Krylenko's courtship. He sat silently and stared into space.

And as the fumes of the alcohol filled his brain, the impulse to wash himself grew stronger and stronger. He came to feel vaguely that there were other things beside the soot and sweat that he wanted to wash away, and slowly he knew what it was. He wanted to wash away with cold water the memory of the night before, the fantastic memory of what had happened with Naomi.

Finke and Sokoleff had forgotten him. The one had gone off to stand by the bar talking red revolution, and the other was shouting wildly to stop "that Gott-damned piano." The room seemed to expand and then contract, growing vast and cavernous like the Mill shed and then pressing in upon him, squeezing the horrible noise tight against his ear-drums. He felt sick and filled with disgust. Suddenly he knew that he was drunk and he knew that he hadn't meant to be. It had happened without his knowing it. He was drunk, and last night he had slept with a harlot. Oh, he knew now. It sickened him. It might just as well have been a harlot, one of those women out of Hennessey's shuttered houses. It would have been better, because he wouldn't have to go back to a woman like that: he'd never see her again. And he wouldn't have that queer little knot, like a cramp in a weary muscle, that was almost hatred for Naomi.

The drunker he got, the clearer it all seemed. And then suddenly his tired brain gave way. He fell forward and buried his face in his hands. He knew now and he began to weep drunkenly. He knew now, because he had learned in a strange way during the darkness of the slate-colored house. He knew why it was that he had had to see Mary Conyngham; he knew why he had walked with her into the open country. He was in love with Mary Conyngham; he had been in love with her ever since he could remember. And it was Naomi who shared his bed.

Disgust enveloped him in physical sickness, and the old desire to wash himself in cold water returned passionately. What Krylenko had said was true. "You ain't like these two—just a couple of hogs." Krylenko knew with that shining look in his blue eyes. Krylenko had his Giulia, and he, Philip, had nothing . . . less than nothing, for he had bound himself in a terrible, sickening fashion to Naomi. It was all horrible. He was drunk and he wanted suddenly to die.

Some one touched his shoulder, and he raised his head. It was Hennessey, looking down at him out of the cold blue eyes.

"Look here," he said. "You're drunk enough. Get out of here and go home. Your Ma is Emma Downes, and I don't want to get mixed up with a hell-cat like her."

For a second Philip was blinded by rage. He wanted to kill Hennessey for the insult to his mother. He tried to get up, but he only knocked his glass on the floor, and then fell down beside it. He tried again to rise, and then Hennessey, cursing, bent over and picked him up as if he'd been a child, and carried him, plow-

ing through the heat and confusion, out the swinging
doors. In the open air, he placed him on his feet, holding him upright for a moment till he got a sense of his
balance. Then, giving him a little push, he said,
"There now. Run along home to your Ma like a good
little boy. Tell her not to let her little tin Jesus come
back again to Hennessey's place if she don't want him
messed up too much to be a good missionary."

14

In the slate-colored house, the Minerva Circle was
seated on the collapsible chairs from McTavish's, listening to a paper by Mrs. Wilbert Phipps on her visit to
the Mammoth Caves of Kentucky. To overcome the
boredom, some thought about their children and their
husbands, or even the hired girl, filling in the
time until the dreary reading was over, and they
might fall back again into gossip and recipes and
children's ailments. It was the price they paid for the
honor which came to each of them every eighteen
months of standing before the Minerva Circle and reading a paper to which no one listened.

The folding-doors between the parlor and the
sitting-room had been opened and those leading from
the parlor to the hall were closed. Upstairs Naomi lay
in bed with her hair still in steel curlers: she was too
ill to come down. She had wept hysterically all the
night and most of the morning. When Emma had tried
to comfort her with vague, soothing words about matrimony, nothing had made any difference. It was only
Aunt Mabelle's visit, colored by great chunks of wisdom and frankness drawn from her own experience and

conferences with many other married ladies upon a subject which she always found absorbing, that reduced Naomi at length to a calmer state of mind. And Mabelle was sitting by her now, nursing the baby, and pouring forth details of her own history, in an effort to forestall fresh outbursts.

Downstairs, in the dining-room and kitchen, Emma bustled about, scolding the slattern Essie, and thinking that it was just like Naomi to have chosen such a busy and awkward occasion for following her advice. So Emma had to look after all the refreshments herself. She was putting out the plates of fruit salad on the dining-room table, when she heard the knob of the front door turn. Pausing in her work, she saw the door open, gently and carefully, as Philip entered. His foot caught on the carpet, he tripped and fell.

In the next moment she knew. He was drunk. He couldn't get to his feet.

Behind the closed doors of the parlor the thin, refined voice of Mrs. Wilbert Phipps was saying, "And then the guide caught some fish in a net and showed them to us. They proved most interesting, as they were quite without eyes, and therefore blind. It seems that living so long in the darkness the eyes shriveled up in succeeding generations until they disappeared. I remember saying to Wilbert: 'Think of it! These fish are quite blind!' "

Philip, struggling to his feet, heard the word "blind." "Yes, I was blind too. But I'm not any longer. Naomi made a man of me. She made a man of me."

He laughed wildly, and Emma, clapping a hand over his mouth, put her arm about his shoulders and guided him up the stairs. She helped to undress him and put him to bed. She knew all the little knacks of doing it: she had learned long ago by caring for his father.

He didn't speak to her again, and buried his face in the pillow, biting into it with his strong, even teeth.

Belowstairs, Mrs. Wilbert Phipps was finishing her paper. "And so," she was saying in the flat voice she adopted for such occasions, "that was the visit that Mr. Phipps and I made to the Mammoth Cave. It was most interesting and not expensive. I advise you ladies all to make it at the earliest opportunity. We can never know enough of the geographical marvels of this, the greatest, freest and most noble nation under the protection of God."

Emma got down just in time. She congratulated Mrs. Phipps on the fascination of her paper, and regretted being able to hear only a little of it, but what she heard made her want to hear more: it was so fascinating. She did not say that the only part she heard was a sentence or two dealing with blind fishes.

It was Aunt Mabelle who "brought Naomi round." She had that quality of soft, insensitive people which, if allowed to expose itself long enough, becomes in the end irresistible. Aunt Mabelle was in her way a philosopher, possessing indeed even the physical laziness which gives birth to reflection. She was neither happy nor unhappy, but lived in a state of strange, cowlike contentment, which knew neither heights nor depressions. She was surprised at nothing, and through her long rocking-chair contemplation upon life and love, birth and death, she had shared the confidences of so many women that such behavior as Naomi's did not strike her as remarkable, but only to be listed in the vast category of human folly.

"Don't think you're remarkable or different," she told Naomi. "You're just like any other woman."

It was Aunt Mabelle who led Naomi into the routine of matrimony as a tried and experienced working elephant leads another, freshly captured, into the routine of piling teak logs and pushing carts. She made it all seem the most natural thing in the world.

But it was only after a week of hiding and of sudden outbursts of tears that Naomi returned to Philip—a new and uncomplaining Naomi curiously broken and acquiescent. Aunt Mabelle noticed the difference with the little round blue eyes that seemed too stupid and sleepy to notice anything; she saw that something very odd had happened to Naomi: nothing that was very odd in her (Mabelle's) experience in such cases, but odd only because it had happened to Naomi. It was as if she had found suddenly some reason for existence in a world where before she had no place, as if she enjoyed this newly discovered marital relationship.

Emma, too, noticed the difference—that Naomi began to take an interest in her appearance, and even went so far as to buy some ribbons and bits of lace which she sewed awkwardly on her somber woolen dresses. Her anemic cheeks at moments even showed the shadow of color. She went almost briskly to her choir rehearsals and made a feeble attempt at resuming her manufacture of calico mother-hubbards.

It was, thought Emma, working itself out. She was not one to discuss such things, and yet she knew that Naomi had followed her advice. Why, Naomi was almost like a bride. She was certain in the end to gain a hold over Philip, for he was not the sort whose eye wandered: he never looked at another woman. He wasn't

like his father. Emma told herself these things twenty
times a day. (And she knew things which she would
never admit knowing.) If things went well, he was
certain to come round in the end, for there was nothing
like a wife and family to bring a man to his senses.
When he was older and perhaps Bishop of East
Africa, and the youngest bishop of the church, he
would thank his mother for all her strength of
will. He would look back and understand then how
right she had been at the time when, for a moment, his
foot had strayed from the path. Then God would
bring her her just reward.

There was one thing she did not understand—the
intoxication of Philip. At first she succumbed to
righteous fury, filled with a wild desire to punish him
by shutting him in the storeroom as she had done when
he was a little boy. All the night after she had helped
him up the stairs, she lay awake, pondering what she
should do. The thing had frightened her in a fashion
she did not understand: it was an event which seemed
to thrust upward out of the shadowy depths of heritage, imperiling all her carefully made plans. It gave
her for the first time a sense of awe for her son, because it opened vistas of behavior of which she did not
believe him, a boy so carefully brought up, capable.
It was this fear which led her into paths of caution,
and prevented her from pouring out a torrent of reproach. When a week passed and then another without
any repetition of the disgraceful episode, she settled
back into her old sense of confident security. Philip
was her boy, after all. She could trust him. And fortunately no one had seen him drunk; no one knew.

But it troubled her that he never spoke of it. His

silence hurt her. Always he had told her everything, shared all his secrets and plans with her, and now he shut her out of everything. He was polite and kind to herself and to Naomi, but he never told them anything.

Still, he seemed to be less restless now, even if he was more silent. He was beginning, she thought, to soften a little. In the end, when it was all settled and he had returned to the arms of the Lord, she could perhaps sell her restaurant business and give herself over completely to missionary work and her clubs.

It wasn't that she had given up the idea of matrimony; it was only that she had laid it aside for the moment, since Moses Slade had said nothing in the least definite. He had been encouraging, and very friendly; he had taken her at her word and come to have his meals at the restaurant. On the occasion of his third visit, she said, "Perhaps you'd rather eat in my corner? A man like you, who is so prominent, is always stared at so."

So he had come to take his meals in the corner behind the screen, arriving after one, so that he never interfered with the family lunch of Philip, Naomi and herself. Sometimes she sat with him while he ate great plates of meat and potatoes and huge slices of pies. He was a vigorous man and an enormous eater. They talked usually of politics, and she thought more than once, "Of course, some people might think such a marriage undignified, but it wouldn't matter, because of all the influence I'd have. As the wife of a Congressman in Washington, I'd be a power for good."

They returned sometimes to the subject of their widowhood and loneliness, and once he seemed almost on the verge of speaking, when she was called to the telephone to speak to Mrs. Wilbert Phipps about her paper.

After a time she again urged him not to pay for his meals. It would be a pleasure, she said, to have such a distinguished man as her guest. One meal more or less meant nothing in the ocean of her prosperity. But he was wily and insisted that he could not impose upon her generosity. And then one morning she received from him a letter, saying that he had been called back to Washington suddenly, and would not be able to see her before leaving. He said nothing of marriage; it was a very polite, but a very cautious letter. And Emma resolved to put him out of her mind, and never again to ask him to have his meals at the Peerless Restaurant.

15

When Philip awoke to the sound of the alarm-clock on the night that followed the scene in the hall, he was quite sober again, though his head ached horribly. He was alone in the darkness and suffered from a wretched feeling of shame. It was as if he had plunged into some pit of filth which still clung to him, despite all the washing in the world. It was a conviction of shame, almost of sin, stronger than he had known since, as a little boy, he had listened to one of Emma's terrifying lectures upon purity and the future life. It concerned what had happened on the night before in this very room, it concerned Hennessey's saloon, and the memory of Hennessey's hard voice, "Go on home to your Ma!" and the vague memory of something which had happened in the hall while a voice said something about blindness. He wakened in the exact position in which he had fallen asleep, with his face half-buried in the pillows. He was dirty and unshaven. Slowly he remembered the events of the day before, one by one, but, fitting them together, he could not see how they had brought him here, soiled and filled with a sense of horror.

While he dressed, he tried to fathom what it was that had caused a collapse so sudden and complete, and it seemed to him that it all had very little to do with the chain of things that had happened yesterday; it lay deeper than that. It went back and back into the past. There were moments when it seemed to him that he had been moving towards this night ever since he had been born. It was as if he had no power because he did not even know what it was.

At the Mills, Sokoleff and Finke and Krylenko were already by the oven. They greeted him, as they always did, without comment. Of his drunkenness they said nothing, Sokoleff and Finke perhaps because they were themselves too drunk to have noticed it. He had arrived, sober and ashamed, with the fear that they would use it as an excuse of coarse jokes. And now they did not even remember. For them a thing like that was part of the day's business, just as rabbit-like love and its various counterfeits were things which one took for granted.

He didn't talk to them, even while they all sat eating their lunches. It was as if something had robbed him of the very power of speech. And he felt that they were more remote now and strange than they had ever been, even on the first night he had come there to work by the glowing ovens.

Only Krylenko seemed to understand anything at all. He laughed, and said, "You feel pretty bad after yesterday. Well . . . you'll sweat it out. You get over it quick like that. You can drink like a hog but you sweat it all out right away."

He grinned feebly and said nothing, but he remembered what Krylenko had said, "You ain't like those other fellows." It was true: he wasn't like them, and at the moment he wanted to be like them more than all else on earth. It seemed to him that salvation lay in drinking like a hog and living like a rabbit. He couldn't do it, because something walled him in and shut him away from that fierce turbulent current of life which he felt all about him and could never enter. It was the old hunger, more clear now and understandable, which had driven him to the Mills, seizing him on the night he stood on the Hill looking down upon the miraculous beauty of the Flats at night.

He knew now that he wasn't even free. Naomi hadn't freed him after all, and his celebration had been all for nothing, a bitter joke. He was still the same, only with a strange sense of having been soiled. Weary and sick and disgusted, he felt suddenly like a little child who wanted comforting, only it never occurred to him now to turn to his mother as he had once done. Something had happened, some mysterious snapping of the bonds which bound them together. He found himself wishing with a passionate feeling of self-reproach that he might not see her again. It was partly shame and partly because his love for her had vanished in some inexplicable fashion. It struck him with horror that he had no love any longer either for her or for Naomi. The one he respected because he owed her so much: she was so much stronger and more valiant than himself. The other he pitied because he understood through pitying himself that she, too, must be miserable.

He worked on in silence passionately, straining in every muscle, shoving and pushing the hot steel, until the patches of soot in the sides of the shed began to turn gray with the light of dawn. The sweat that streamed down his body seemed in some way to purify his soul, and at last he grew so weary that all his troubles seemed to lose themselves in the terrible heat and clamor of the pounding hammers.

Only one thing remained in his weary mind, and that was a fierce desire to see Mary Conyngham. If he saw her, he would have peace, because she would understand. She seemed to him like a cool lake into which he could plunge, bathing his whole soul, and his body too, for he understood now what love could be if the woman was Mary Conyngham. *Naomi had made a man of him.* . . .

But it was impossible ever to see her again, because he had nothing to offer her. He belonged now to Naomi, beyond all doubt. Naomi was his wife, she might even be the mother of his child. What could he offer to Mary Conyngham?

For Emma had done her work well. Her son *was* a decent sort, and not at all like his father.

In the weeks that followed he did not see Mary Conyngham. As if she had understood what happened during that walk into the open country, she sent him the paints she had bought, with a little note asking him to take them as a present from her on his return from Africa. She sent them to him at the Mills by the hand of Krylenko, and so put an end to the shameful hope that he would see her when she returned. It was marvelous how well she understood, and yet the very knowledge of her understanding made it all the more unbearable, for it was as if she said, "I know what has happened," and tragically, in the voice that seemed so much sadder than it had once been, "There's nothing to be done."

He kept the box of paints and brushes at Krylenko's boarding-house where he came to be regarded with a kind of awe by the Ukranians as an odd mixture of artist and lunatic. Without thinking why, he kept the whole affair a secret from Naomi and his mother. He told them that the afternoons when he worked, painting and rubbing out, painting and rubbing out, among the rows of dirty houses, were spent in walking or doing extra work at the Mills. It became slowly a sort of passion into which he poured his whole existence. It was only in those hours when he worked horribly to put on bits of canvas and wood that strange, smoky glamour which he found in the Flats, that he was able to forget Mary Conyngham and the dull sordid sense of uneasiness which enveloped all his existence in the slate-colored house. No one save Krylenko saw anything he painted, and Krylenko liked it all, good, bad and indifferent, with all the overwhelming vitality of his friendly nature. (He had come in a way to treat Philip as a child under his special protection.) Sometimes he puzzled his head over the great messes of black and gray and blue, but he saw, oddly enough, what Philip was driving at.

"Yes," he'd say, rubbing his nose with his huge hands. "It's like that . . . that's the way it *feels*. That's what you're after, ain't it?"

He never went again to Hennessey's saloon, although the memory of Hennessey's epithet clung and rankled in his brain. "I don't want to get mixed up with that hell-cat." He could, he thought, go and shoot Hennessey, but no good would come of it; nothing would be accomplished, and life would only become more horrible and complicated. He couldn't fight Hennessey, for the Irishman could break him across his knee. Once, a long while ago, when he was a boy, he would have flung himself at Hennessey, kicking and biting and punching, to avenge the insult to his mother, but all that seemed to belong vaguely to another life which no longer had anything to do with him. The epithet festered in his brain because there were times when it led to horrible doubts about his mother—that perhaps she wasn't, after all, so good and noble and self-sacrificing. It gave him a sudden, terrifying glimpse of what she must seem to others outside that circle in which she moved and had her whole existence. But that was only because they didn't know her as he knew her . . . for the good woman she was. At moments he even felt a fierce resentment toward her because she stood somehow between him and that rich savor of life which he felt all about him. If she had not existed he could have gone to Hennessey's place as much as he liked, drinking as much as he pleased. He could have come nearer to Sokoleff and Finke and even Krylenko.

She must be a powerful woman when a man like Hennessey feared her. . . . Hennessey, he thought sometimes, who was like some beast out of that other cruel jungle at Megambo.

As he lost himself more and more deeply in the effort to catch in color the weird fascination of the world about him, the anguish of the life at Megambo began to fade into the shadows of the existence which had belonged to that other Philip, who began to seem so

strange and distant. Sometimes, the sight of his
mother returning from church, or the sound of Naomi
pounding the tinny piano and singing revival hymns in
her loud voice (as if she were trying to recapture some
of her past glory), brought to his mind a sharp picture
of the other Philip, pale and shy and silent, dressed
always in dark clothes—a Philip who worshipped
a mother who was never wrong and respected a wife who
had no fear of the jungle; and the picture gave him an
odd flash of pity, as if the image had been that of some
stranger. His life now wasn't exactly happy, but it
was better than the life of that other Philip, for now
he stood with his feet fairly planted on the ground;
it was an existence that was real, in which he was aware
of a sinfulness that was really a temptation toward
sin. He wasn't tortured any longer by battling with
shadows. There were times when he was forced to laugh
(a trifle bitterly) at the memory of a Philip who had
suffered at his own doubts and agonies over the awful
prospect of turning his back upon the church. It was
finished, but no one would believe him, no one, except
Mary Conyngham.

He came to accept the attentions of Naomi, for he
could not see what else there was to do, and after
a time it became a relationship which he managed to
fit into the scheme of things as he went to work seven
days a week and ate three meals a day; but there was
no joy in it, save that obscure satisfaction which came
of knowing that like other men he had a woman who
belonged to him.

They never spoke of it to each other: it was a thing
which happened silently in the night, as if they both
were ashamed, and afterward Philip still had the

strange feeling that in some way he had been soiled.
It was, after all, exactly such a relationship as he
might have had with any of the women in Franklin
Street. If it was different, it was only because Naomi
was in love with him, and this love of hers sometimes
frightened him, because it made him more than ever her
prisoner. There sometimes came into her eyes that
same look of shining rapture that he had seen there in
the days when she was giving her life to God at Megambo. You could see it in the way she watched him.
Yet the word love had never been spoken between them,
and the possibility of children had never been uttered.

It was as if all her adoration of God had been turned
upon Philip.

Presently he began to drink, taking a glass on his
way to work, and another on his way home, but he did
not go to drink with any of the men from his own furnace. He did not go to Hennessey's; he went to a
saloon where the back room was filled with Polish girls
and no one had ever heard of Emma. The whisky made
him feel jolly and forget the slate-colored house. He
got there the feeling that he was himself, Philip
Downes, for the first time in his life, as if at last he
had been completely born. No one in the place had
ever heard of the other Philip. It was only an illusion
which came to him while the alcohol had possession of
his brain, and so he came to drink more and more regularly because it made him happy. With a glass or two
he was able to forget the life he shared with Naomi.

16

He was sitting one afternoon in Krylenko's room
working on a view of the Flats which included the oily

creek, a row of battered houses, and a glimpse of furnaces. For two days he had worked on it, and out of the lines and color there began to emerge something which he recognized with a faint sense of excitement as the thing he had been searching for. It grew slowly with each stroke of the brush, a quality which he could not have described, but something which he felt passionately. He was beginning a little to succeed, to do something which he would want to show, not to the world, but to . . . to . . . Mary Conyngham. He would send it to her as a gift, without a word. Certainly she wouldn't mind that. She would understand it as she understood all else. As he worked, his passion for painting and his love for Mary Conyngham became in a strange fashion blended and inextricable. It was as if he were talking to her with the line and color, telling her all the choked, overpowering, hot emotions that were kindled when he thought of her.

Presently, as the light began to fail, he put down his brushes, and, taking up his worn coat and hat, he closed the door to return to the slate-colored house. In that sudden exultation, even the prospect of encountering Naomi did not depress him. Feeling his way along the greasy hallway smelling of boiled cabbage and onions, he descended the stairs and stepped into the street. It was that hour between daylight and darkness, when sharp contours lose their hard angles, and ugliness fades mysteriously into beauty—the hour in the Flats when all the world changed magically from the squalor of daylight into the glowing splendor of the night.

Outside, the street was alive with dirty, underfed children. There seemed to be myriads of them, all drawn like moths out of the darkness towards the spots of light beneath each street-lamp. A great, ugly Ukranian sat on the steps rocking gently and playing a Little Russian song on a wheezy concertina.

For a moment, while Philip stood in the shadow of the doorway, looking down the long vista of the hot, overcrowded street, he felt again the old, poignant sense of the richness, the color that was born simply out of being allowed to live. And then suddenly he became aware of a familiar presence close at hand, of a voice heard in the twilight above the clamor of children, which made him feel suddenly ill.

Before the doorway of the next house he could see the dim figure of Irene Shane, a pale gray figure which seemed at times almost a ghost. The other woman he could not see in the hard reality, but he saw with all the painful clearness of an image called up by the sound of her soft voice. It was Mary Conyngham calling on some sick baby. He listened, hiding in the shadow, while a Polish woman talked to her in broken English. Then suddenly she turned away and with Irene Shane passed so near to the doorway that he could have touched her.

She was gone, quickly, lost in the crowd. He hadn't run after her and cried out what was in his heart, because he was afraid. His whole body was shaking; and he burned with a fire that was at once agony and delight, for the thing that had happened with Naomi made this other pain the more real and terrible.

For ten minutes he sat on the step of Krylenko's boarding-house, his head in his hands. When at last he rose to climb the hill, all the sense of exhilaration had flowed away, leaving him limp and exhausted. For weeks he had worked twelve hours a day in the Mills, painted while there was still daylight, and slept the little time that remained; and now he knew suddenly that he was horribly tired. His body that was so hard and supple seemed to have grown soft and heavy, his legs were like sacks of potatoes. Near the top of the hill, before the undertaking parlor of McTavish, he felt so ill that he had suddenly to sit down. And while he sat there he understood, with a cold horror, what had happened to him. It was the Megambo fever coming back. The street began to lose its colors, and fade into shadows of yellow before his eyes.

Behind him the door opened, and he heard a booming voice asking, "Anything the matter, Philip? You look sick."

Philip told McTavish what it was, and felt a feeble desire to laugh at the thought of being succored by the undertaker.

"I know," said McTavish. "It used to come back on me in the same way. I got a touch of it in Nicaragua, when I was a boy." Here he halted long enough to grunt, for he had bent down and was lifting Philip in his corpulent embrace bodily from the steps. He chuckled, "I was a wild 'un then. It's only since I got so damned fat that the fever left me."

He put Philip in one of the chairs before the stove. There was no fire in it now, but the door was left open for the old rips to spit into the ashes.

"You look sick—yellow as paint."

Philip tried to grin and began to shiver.

"It's nothing. I've often felt like this." The memory of the old fever took possession of him, setting his teeth on edge at the thought of the chill-hot horrors and all the phantasmagoria of jungle life which it invoked. Out of the terror of sickness, one thought remained clear—that perhaps this was the best way out of everything, to die here in the chair and let McTavish prepare what remained of him for the grave. He wouldn't then be a nuisance to any one, and Naomi, free, could go back to Megambo.

McTavish was pouring whisky down his throat, saying, "That'll make you stop shaking." And slowly warmth began to steal back. He felt dizzy, but a little stronger.

"I'll take you home," said McTavish, standing off and looking at him. "You know a fellow like you oughtn't to be working in the Mills. Why, man, you're thin as a fence-rail. I've been watching you when you went past—getting thinner and thinner every day. And you're beginning to look like an old man. A fellow of your age ought to be getting drunk and giving the girls a time. I wish to God I was twenty-six again."

He finished with a great booming laugh, which was meant to be reassuring, but which Philip, even through the haze of illness, knew was meant to hide his alarm. He gave Philip another drink, and asked suddenly, "What's the matter with you, anyway? There's something wrong. Why, any fool can see that." Philip didn't answer him, and he added, "You don't mean to go back to Africa. That's it, ain't it? I guessed that long ago, in spite of everything your Ma had to say. Well, if you was to go back like this, it'd be the end of you, and I propose telling your Ma so. I knew her well enough when she was a girl, though we don't hold much with one another now."

Philip suddenly felt too ill to speak to any one, to explain anything. McTavish had lifted him up and was carrying him toward the door, "Why you don't weigh no more than a woman—and a little woman at that."

He felt himself being lifted into McTavish's buggy. The fat man kept one arm about him, and with the other drove the horses, which on occasions pulled his hearse. At length, after what seemed to Philip hours, they drew up before the slate-colored house.

It was Emma herself who opened the door. McTavish, the debaucher of young men, she saw, had got Philip drunk, and was delivering him to her like a corpse.

"What does this mean?" she asked.

Philip managed to say feebly, "I haven't been drinking."

McTavish, still carrying him, forced his way past her into the hall. "Where do you want to put him? You've got a pretty sick boy here, and the sooner you know it the better."

They carried him upstairs and laid him on his and Naomi's bed. Naomi was in the room, and Mabelle was with her, and as they entered, she got up with a wild flutter of alarm, while McTavish explained. Philip asked for water, which Naomi went to fetch, and McTavish led Emma with him into the hall.

Downstairs, they faced each other—two middle-aged people, born to be enemies by every facet of their characters; yet, oddly enough, McTavish had once been a suitor for Emma's hand in those far-off days when Emma had chosen such a hopeless mate as Jason Downes. Sometimes, drawing deep out of his own experience, the philosophic McTavish had wondered how on earth he had ever fallen in love with Emma, or how she had come to be in turn the abject slave of such an amiable scamp as Downes. It made no sense, that thing which got hold of you, brain and body, in such a tyrannical fashion. (He was thinking all this again, as he stood facing the ruffled Emma beneath the cold glow of the green Moorish light.)

"Look here, Em," he was saying, "that boy has got to have a little peace. You let him alone for a time."

"What do you mean? What does a man like you, John McTavish, know about such things?"

The fat undertaker saw in a swift flash that the invincible Emma was not only ruffled, but frightened.

"Well, you know what I mean. The boy ain't like you. That's where you've always made a mistake, Em . . . in thinking everybody is like yourself. He's a bundle of nerves—that boy—and sensitive. Anybody with half an eye can see it."

"I ought to know my boy." She began to grow dramatic. "My own flesh . . . that I gave birth to . . . I ought to know what's good for him, without having to be told."

McTavish remained calm, save for an odd wave of hatred for this woman he had desired thirty years ago. "That's all right. You ought to know, Em, but you don't. You'd better let him alone . . . or you'll be losing him . . . too."

The last word he uttered after a little pause, as if intentionally he meant to imply things about the disappearance and death of Mr. Downes. She started to speak, and then, thinking better of it, checked herself, buttoned her lips tightly, and opened the front door with an ominous air.

"No, I ain't going till I've finished," he was saying. "I know you, Em. I've known you a long time, and I'm telling you that if you love that boy you'll stop tormenting him . . . you'll do it for your own good. If he gets well, I think I'll take a hand myself."

He went through the door, but Emma remained there, looking after the fat, solid form until it climbed into the buggy, and drove off, the vehicle swaying and rocking beneath the weight of his three hundred odd pounds. She was frightened, for she felt the earth slipping away from under her feet as it had done once before, a long time ago. The whole affair was slipping away, out of her control. It was like finding herself suddenly in quicksand.

Upstairs in the darkened room, Aunt Mabelle, left alone with Philip, pulled her rocking-chair to the side of the bed. She had news, she thought, which would cheer him, perhaps even make him feel better.

"Philip," she said softly. "Philip." He turned his head, and she continued, "Philip, I've got good news for you. Are you listening?"

Philip nodded weakly.

"Naomi is going to have a little baby . . . a little baby. Think of that!"

She waited, and Philip said nothing. He did not even move.

"Aren't you glad, Philip? Think of it . . . a little baby."

He whispered, "Yes . . . of course . . . I'm glad," and turned his face into the pillow once more.

Aunt Mabelle, excited by her news, went on, "You won't have to wait long, because she's already about four months along. She didn't want to talk about it.

She wasn't even sure what was the matter, but I dragged it out of her. I thought she was looking kind of peaked."

Then the door opened, and Emma and Naomi came in together. Naomi crossed to the bed, and, bending over Philip, said, "Here's the water, Philip." He stirred and she put her arm under his head while he drank. It seemed to him that all his body was alive with fire.

When he had finished, Naomi did an extraordinary thing. She flung herself down and burying her head against his thin chest, she began to sob wildly, crying out, shamelessly before Emma and Mabelle, "You mustn't be sick, Philip. You mustn't die . . . I couldn't live without you now. You're all I've got. . . . No . . . no . . . you mustn't die." She clung to him with terrifying and shameless passion. "I couldn't live without you . . . I couldn't . . . I couldn't . . . I'll never . . . leave you." Her long, pale hair came unfastened and fell about her shoulders, covering them both. "I'll never leave you. I'll do whatever you want."

It was Emma who seized her by force and dragged her off him; Emma who, shaking her, said in a voice that was horrible in its hatred, "You fool! Do you want to make him worse? Do you want to kill him?"

And Naomi cried out, "He's mine now. He's mine! You tried to poison him against me. You can't take him away from me any more. He belongs to me!"

It was horrible, but to Philip the scene had no reality; it came to him through the haze of his fever, as if it had been only an interlude of delirium.

When Naomi grew a little more calm, Aunt Mabelle said to her in a whisper, "I told him."

Naomi, still sobbing, asked, "Was he glad?"

"As pleased as Punch," said Aunt Mabelle. "It always pleases a man. It makes him feel big."

On the bed Philip lay shivering and burning. The room appeared to swell to an enormous size and then slowly to contract again till it was no bigger than a coffin. After a time, it seemed to him that he was already dead and that the three women who moved about the room, undressing him, fussing with the window-curtain, talking and sobbing, were simply three black figures preparing him for the grave. A faint haze of peace settled slowly over him. He would be able to rest now. He would never see them again. He was free.

17

It was not, after all, the old Megambo fever, but typhoid which had been lurking for months in the filth of the Flats. Irene Shane knew of it and Mary Conyngham and one or two doctors who were decent enough to take cases for which there was little chance either of pay or glory. It was typhoid that had brought Mary and Irene to talk to the Polish woman in the doorway next to Krylenko's boarding-house. Typhoid was a word that existed in an aura of terror; a disease which might strike any of the Hill people. So long as it happened in the Flats (and the fever lurked there winter and summer) it did not matter. But with Philip it struck at the people on the hills. The news spread quickly. There was another case and then another and another. The newspapers began to talk of it and suddenly the Town learned that there were sixty cases in the Flats and that eleven Hunkies and Dagoes were already dead.

When Emma first heard that the illness was typhoid, she snorted and said, "Of course! What could you expect? He got it working in the Flats among those Hunkies and Dagoes. They throw all their slops right into the streets. They ought to be shut off and a wall placed around them. They always have typhoid down there. Some day they'll have a real epidemic and then people will wake up to what it means—bringing such animals into a good clean country!"

The doctors, summoned by Emma in her terror, told her that Philip's case was doubly serious because he had already had fever twice in Megambo and because his whole body was thin and sick. He fell into a state of stupor and remained thus. He seemed to have no resistance.

For days terror racked Emma and Naomi. Each of them prayed, secretly and passionately, begging God to spare the life of the man who became suddenly the only possession in the world which they cherished. And out of their fight there was born a kind of hostility which made their earlier distrust of each other fade into oblivion. There were hours and days when they scarcely addressed each other, when it seemed that the slightest disagreement might hurl them into open warfare. Mabelle was always in the house, moving about, comforting Naomi and exasperating Emma by her sloppy ways.

Indeed, the perpetual sight of Mabelle and her squalid overfed brat in her neat house filled Emma with a distaste to be equaled only by such a calamity as the discovery of vermin in one of her beds. But she found herself suddenly delivered into Mabelle's hands; for Mabelle was the only person who could "do anything with" Naomi. If Emma approached her, she grew tense and hysterical. And it was, of course, impossible to think of ridding herself of both: you couldn't turn from your home the woman who was to be the mother of your grandchild.

Mabelle she hated, too, for her passionate and morbid absorption in the subjects of love and childbirth; she seemed to Emma to stand as a symbol of obscenity, who must as such have tortured her brother Elmer. She was a symbol of all that side of life which Emma had succeeded in putting out of her mind for so many years.

But there was one other person who had the power of calming Naomi. This was the Reverend Castor, who, since Naomi's condition prevented her from appearing in the choir, came himself two or three times a week to comfort her and inquire after her husband. Except for Mabelle, he seemed to be Naomi's only friend.

"He is," she told Emma, " a very sympathetic man, and he reminds me of my father. He is just the same build and bald in the same way."

The Reverend Castor had a beautiful voice, low and mellow and filled with rich inflections which Mrs. Wilbert Phipps had once spoken of as an "Æolian harp." He could have had, people said, a great success as an Evangelist, but he was so devoted to his bedridden wife that he would not leave her, even for such a career. The church, they said, was indeed fortunate to keep him, even though it was at the price of his own misfortune. Words of condolence and courage spoken in the rich voice had a strange power of rousing the emotions. Once or twice Emma had come upon him sitting in the twilight of the parlor talking to Naomi of illness and faith, of death and fortitude, in so moving a fashion that the tears came into her eyes and a lump into her throat. And he was a good man—a saint. One felt it while talking to him. He was a man who believed, and had devoted his whole life to the care of a sick wife.

Sometimes Mabelle lingered long after the hour when she should have been in her kitchen preparing supper for Elmer. There were in the Reverend Castor's voice intimations of things which she had never found in her own chilly husband.

As Naomi's time drew nearer, the conversation of Mabelle grew proportionately more and more obstetrical.

They compared symptoms and Mabelle's talk was constantly sprinkled with such remarks as, "When I was carrying Jimmy," or, "When Ethel was under way." She even gave it as her opinion that Naomi, from the symptoms, might be having twins.

She appeared to have a strange, demoralizing effect upon Naomi, for the girl came presently to spend all the day in a wrapper, never bothering to dress when she rose. And Emma discovered that for days at a time she did not even trouble to take off the metal bands which she used for curling her long, straight hair. The two of them sat all day long in rocking-chairs while little Jimmy, who was beginning to walk a little, crept from one piece of furniture to another. He had already ruined one corner of the Brussels carpet in the parlor.

Meanwhile, in the great walnut bed Philip lay more

dead than alive. There were long periods when he recognized no one and simply lay as if made of stone, white, transparent, with a thin, pinched look about the temples. The lines seemed to have faded from his face, giving him a pathetic, boyish look. The only life lingered in the great dark eyes which in his fever were larger and more burning than ever. The doctors who came and went sometimes shook their heads and expressed belief that if the patient could be got to show any interest in the life about him there was hope. But he appeared to have no desire to recover. Even in those moments when his wife gave way and, weeping, had to be taken from the room, he only stared at her without speaking.

Failing to take into account the terrible vitality which came to him from Emma and the toughness of that father whom none of them had ever seen, they marveled that he could go on living at all. Yet week after week passed when he grew no better or worse. None of them knew, of course, about Mary Conyngham and how the thought of her sometimes came to him and filled him with a fierce desire to live. When his sick brain cleared for a little while, he knew with a strange certainty that he could not die leaving her behind, because in some way life would be left incomplete. It was a thought which troubled him, as he was troubled when he could not get a picture to come right because he was not yet a good painter.

And then one day Emma's own doctor took her aside in the hall and said, "There's one thing you must understand, Mrs. Downes. No matter how much your son wants to return to Africa, you mustn't let him go. If he gets well and tries to go back, it will be the end of him. I know he'll want to go back, but it'll be suicide to send him where there's fever."

When the doctor had gone, Emma put on her hat and jacket and went for a walk. It was a thing she never did, for there were no moments in her busy life to be wasted simply in walking; but there seemed no other way to find solitude in a world filled with Naomi and Mabelle, little Jimmy and the trained nurse. She had to be alone, to think things out.

She saw clearly enough that, whatever happened, there was now no chance of Philip's going back to Africa and the knowledge filled her with a blank, inexplicable feeling of frustration. But after she had grown more calm, she began to feel more like herself and thus more able to cope with her troubles.

. Philip could not go back, and he was to have a child. But if he could not go back to duty, neither, she saw, must he be allowed to return to the Flats. The one, surely, was just as dangerous as the other, and the Mills carried with them a sense of failure and disgrace. No, up to now she had been patient in the belief that he would return to his senses; but the time for patience had passed.

The old feeling of her own strength and righteousness began to return to her in great surging waves of confidence.

John McTavish! What did he know of her husband's weakness? Or Philip's weakness? How could he know that both of them were the sort who had to be guided? John McTavish! (She snorted at the thought.) A waster, a vulgar man, about whom gathered the riffraff of the Town. What had he ever done for the good of any one?

She had a sudden desire to see Moses Slade. Somehow she felt he'd understand her problem and approve her strong attitude. There was a man who did things. A distinguished man! A man who'd made his mark! Not a good-for-nothing like John McTavish.

The old possibility of marrying Moses Slade kept stealing back over her. Through pride and a faint sense of being a woman rejected, she tried not to think of it, but it was no good trying to put it out of her mind because it was always stealing back upon her unawares. Perhaps if she sent him a postcard, a pretty view of the new park, it would serve to remind him of her without being, properly speaking, a piece of forwardness. The temptation kept pricking her. It would be splendid to be the wife of a Congressman, and it would solve the difficulty of Philip. She could turn over the restaurant to him and Naomi.

Nearly two hours passed before she returned to the house, but in that time all life seemed to have become subdued and conquered once more. It had all been worked out. She sat down at once and wrote a perfectly impersonal message to Congressman Slade on the back of a picture postcard of the new monument to General Tecumseh Sherman that adorned dubiously the new park. On the way to the restaurant she posted it. As she left the house she heard Naomi sobbing alone in the corner of the darkened parlor, and a great wave of contempt swept over her for people who were not strong enough to manage their own lives.

On the same night the Reverend Castor led his congregation, or a fraction of it, in addressing to the Lord words of supplication and entreaty on behalf of "their brother Philip Downes, who lay at the point of death." He begged that Philip, who had sacrificed his health, might be spared "to carry on the noble work among the black and sinful children of the great African continent."

As he prayed, with arms extended and face upturned to heaven, the fine nose, the shapely dome of his head and imposing expanse of his chest, took on a classic, moving dignity. As the sonorous voice, trembling with emotion, rolled over the heads of his flock more than one woman felt herself slipping dimly into the grip of strange disturbing emotions.

He prayed longer than usual, painting for the Lord a moving and luxurious picture of the trials suffered by His servant; in Old Testament phrases he finished by calling the attention of God to the suffering of Naomi, who sat at home, ill herself, praying for the life of the husband she loved with such noble and selfless devotion.

When he had finished, there were tears in all eyes, and Emma, seated near the back, was sobbing in a warm mist of suffering and glory. In some way his eloquence had purified them all. It was as if each one of them had passed with Philip through the flame of suffering. They felt purged and clean and full of noble thoughts, almost ready at last to enter the Kingdom of Heaven.

The sound of "Amens!" trembled in the air and before it had died away completely, Miss Swarmish, an old maid with a mustache, struck out several loud chords on the tinny piano and in her booming voice led them in singing, *Throw out the Life Line!* They sang with militant enthusiasm, their voices echoing in the vast, damp basement of the church. It was an oblique glorification of Philip, the renegade, who lay unconscious in the slate-colored house. It was as if they, too, were forcing him back.

When they had finished the orgy of music and the Benediction was spoken, the usual stir was silenced suddenly by Emma's rich voice. She had risen to her feet at the back of the room and was standing with her hands clasped on the back of the chair before her.

"Brothers and sisters," she was saying, in a voice rich with emotion, "I know that all of you feel for me in the illness of my son. I have felt for some time that I should speak to you about him" (here, overcome by feeling, she coughed and hesitated) "to make an answer to the talk that has come to my ear from time to time. I feel that to-night—to-night is the time—the occasion ordained by God. I have very little to say. You know that his health has been wrecked forever by his work among our ignorant, sinful brothers in Africa. He is lying at the point of death. Your prayers have touched me to the depths of my heart, and if it is God's will, surely they will help towards his recovery." (Here she hesitated once more.) "People wondered why he came back. It was because his health was ruined. People wondered why he went into the Flats to work. It was because he wanted to know the life there. He has been through a great spiritual struggle. He fell ill because he was tormented by the wish to go back to his post, to those ignorant black men who live in darkness. If he recovers . . ." (her voice broke suddenly) "if he recovers . . . he can never go back. The doctors have told me that it would be nothing short of suicide. He has given his health, perhaps his life, in carrying forward our great purpose of sending the light to heathen."

She hesitated for a moment as if she meant to say more, and then sat down abruptly, too overcome for speech. For a moment there was silence, and then one by one women began to gather about her, sobbing, to offer comfort. It was a touching scene, in which Emma managed to control herself after a time. Surrounding her, they moved out of the church in a sort of phalanx. Two or three of them even followed her a little way down the street. But it was her brother, Elmer, who accompanied her home. In his stiff, cold way he proposed to let bygones be bygones.

"At a time like this," he said, "it's not right for a brother and sister to quarrel." And then, after an awkward silence, "I've no doubt that when Philip is well again, he'll come to his senses and behave himself."

He stopped at the slate-colored house for Aunt Mabelle, who had come over to sit with Naomi, and before they left, all of them, even Naomi, seemed to have changed in some way, to have grown more cheerful, as if the Heavenly joy of the prayer-meeting still clung like perfume to their very garments. Things, they all felt, were beginning to work themselves out.

18

When he had closed the roll-top desk in his study and locked the door after him, the Reverend Castor turned his steps toward the parsonage, still lost in the exalted mood which, descending miraculously upon the congregation, had risen to a climax in the noble words of Mrs. Downes. There was a lump in his throat when he thought of the goodness of women like her. She'd had a hard life, bringing up her boy, feeding and cloth-

ing him, and finding time, nevertheless, to care for his
soul and give herself to church work. It was women
like her who helped you to keep your faith, no matter
what discouragements arose.

For a moment, a suspicion of disloyalty colored his
meditations and he thought, "If I had only been blessed
with a wife like Emma Downes!"

But quickly he stifled the thought, for such wickedness came to him far too often, especially in the moments when he relaxed and allowed his mind to go its
own way. The thing seemed always to be lying in wait,
like a crouching animal stealing upon him unawares.
"If only I'd had some other woman for a wife!" The
thing had grown bolder and more frequent as the years
piled up. He would be fifty years old in another
month. It kept pressing in upon him like the pain of
an aching tooth. Soon he'd be too old to care. And
he would die, having missed something which other men
knew. He was growing older every day, every minute,
every second . . . older, older, older.

In a sudden terror, he began to repeat one of the
Psalms in order to clear his mind and put to rout the
grinning, malicious thought. He said the Psalm over
three times, and then found that God had sent him
strength. Walking the dark, silent street, he told
himself that there were others far worse off than he.
There was poor Naomi Downes with the husband she
worshipped dying hourly, day and night, in the very
house with her. She, too, had courage, though she
wasn't as strong as her mother-in-law. She wasn't
perhaps as fine a character as Emma, but there was
something more appealing about her, a weakness and
a youth that touched your pity. It was terrible to see

a young girl like that with her husband dying and a baby coming on. He remembered that he must go again to-morrow and pray with her. It was odd (he thought) how little prayer seemed to comfort her—a girl like that who was a missionary and the daughter of missionaries. He must have a talk with her and try to help her. . . . She seemed to be losing her great faith. . . .

He was on the front porch of the parsonage now, turning his key in the lock, and something of the wild emotion of the prayer-meeting still clung to him. It had been a glorious success. He was still thinking of Naomi as he closed the door, and heard a whining voice from the top of the stairs.

"Is that you, Samuel?"

He waited for a moment and then answered, "Yes, my dear."

"What kept you so late? I've been frightened to death. The house was full of noises and I heard some one walking about in the parlor."

"We prayed for Philip Downes," he said, turning out the light.

The whining voice from above-stairs took on an acid edge. "And you never thought about your poor suffering wife at home all alone. I suppose it never occurs to you to pray for *me!*"

He stood in the darkness, waiting, unwilling to climb the stairs until her complaints had worn themselves out. The voice again: "Samuel, are you there?"

"Yes, Annie."

"Why don't you answer me? Isn't it enough to have to lie here helpless and miserable?"

"I was turning out the light."

"Well, I want the hot-water bottle. You'll have to heat water. And make it hot, not just lukewarm. It's worse again. It's never been so bad."

As he went off to the kitchen, fragments of her plaints followed him: "I should think you'd have remembered about the hot-water bottle!" And, "If you'd had such pain as mine for fifteen years. . . ."

Yes, fifteen years!

For fifteen years it had been like this. The old wicked thought came stealing back into his mind. If only he had a wife like Emma Downes or her daughter-in-law, Naomi . . . some one young like Naomi. He was growing older, older, older. . . .

He began again to repeat the Psalm, saying it aloud while he waited by the stove for the kettle to boil.

19

In the Flats the number of deaths began to mount one by one with the passing of each day. When disease appeared in any of the black, decaying houses, it had its way, taking now a child, now a wife, now a husband, for bodies that were overworked and undernourished had small chance of life in a region where the very air stank and the only stream was simply an open sewer. Doctors came and went, sometimes too carelessly, for there was small chance of pay, and to the people on the Hill the life of a worker was worth little. The creatures of the Flats were somehow only a sort of mechanical animal which produced and produced and went on producing.

The churches went on sending missionaries and money to the most remote corners of the earth; the clergymen prayed for the safety of their own flocks, while their congregations sat frightened and resentful, believing that somehow the people in the Flats had caused the catastrophe. It could not be (they reasoned) that God would send such a calamity upon a Town so Godfearing.

Irene Shane and Mary Conyngham closed their school because there was no longer any time to teach when people were ill and dying to right and left. Mary sat night after night at the beds of the dying. She saw one of Finke's thirteen children die and then another and another. She listened to his cursing and drunken talk of revolution, and all the while she knew bitterly enough that those of the family who remained would be happier because they would have more to eat.

The Mills went on pounding and pounding; they were building new furnaces and new sheds. There seemed no end to it. It did not matter if people in the Flats died like flies, because there were always more where they came from—hordes of men and women and children who came filled with glorified hopes to this new country.

One day Mary read in the papers that the man who owned the Mills, himself a German immigrant, had built himself a marble palace on Fifth Avenue and would now divide his time between Pittsburgh and New York. He was becoming a gentleman: he had engaged an expert, a cultivated man of taste, to fill his New York house with pictures brought from Europe. The Town *Gazette* printed an editorial drawing a moral from the career of the great magnate. See what could be done in this great land of God-given opportunity! A man who had begun as an immigrant. But it said nothing

of the foundations on which the marble palace rested.
It appeared to have arisen miraculously with the aid
and sanction of God, innocent of all connection with
the stinking Flats.

Mary, watching the spectacle about her, felt her
heart turning to stone. If she was to be saved from
bitterness, it would only be, she believed, through the
touching faith of the ignorant wretches about her.
She came to feel a sympathy for the cursing of a man
like Finke: she herself even wanted at times to curse.
She understood the sullen drunkenness of men like
Sokoleff. What else was there for them to do? Something—perhaps a sense of dull misery, perhaps a terror
of death—had slowly softened their resentment toward
herself and Irene Shane. Once they had been looked
upon as intruders come down from the Hills to poke
about in filthy hallways and backyards filled with piles
of rubbish and rows of privies. But it was no longer
possible to doubt them. The two women, gently bred
and fastidious, slept night after night at the school in
the midst of the Flats. They sat up night after night
by the beds of the dying.

There were times when Mary wondered why Irene
Shane poured out all her strength in succoring these
wretched people. She sensed deep in Irene a strange
kind of unearthly mysticism which made her seem at
times stubborn and irritable. It was a mysticism
strangely akin to that groping hunger which had always tormented Philip. The likeness came to her suddenly one night as she sat by the bed of one of Finke's
dying children. It seemed to her a strange and inexplicable likeness in people so different. Yet it was true
—they were both concerned with shadowy problems of

faith and service to God which never troubled the more practical Mary. And Irene, she fancied, was prey to a sense of atonement, as if she must in some way answer to God for the wickedness of a father long dead and a sister who was, as the Town phrased it, "not all she should have been." There was, too, that hard, bitter old woman who lay dying and never left Shane's Castle —old Julia Shane, the queen ant of all the swarming hive.

As for herself, Mary knew well enough why she had come to work in the Flats: she had come in order to bury herself in some task so mountainous and hopeless that it would help her to forget the aching hurt made by John Conyngham's behavior with Mamie Rhodes. It required a cure far more vigorous even than a house and two children to make her forget a thing like that.

She had been, people said, a fool to put up with such behavior. But what was she to do? There were the children and there was her own devotion to John Conyngham, a thing which he had thrown carelessly aside. It wasn't even as if you suffered in secret: in the Town a thing like that couldn't be kept a secret. The very newsboys knew of it. She had found a sort of salvation in working with Irene Shane. People said she was crazy, a woman with two small children, to go about working among Hunkies and Dagoes; but she took good care of her children, too, and she supplied the people in the Flats with what no amount of such mystical devotion as Irene Shane could supply: she had a sound practical head.

She was an odd girl (she thought) when you came to consider it, with a kind of curse on her. She had to have some one to whom she could give herself up completely, pouring out all the soul in a fantastic devotion. John Conyngham had tired of it, perhaps (she sometimes thought) because he was a cold, hard, sensual man who had no need for such a thing. A woman like Mamie Rhodes (she thought bitterly) suited him better. If she had been married to Philip, who needed it so pathetically. . . .

In the long nights of vigil, she thought round and round in circles, over the same paths again and again. . . . And before many nights had passed she found herself coming back always to the thing she knew and tried constantly to forget . . . that it had been Philip whom she loved always, since those very first days in the tree-house. It seemed to her that at twenty-eight her life, save for her children, was already at an end. She was a widow with only memories of an unhappy married life behind her and nothing to hope for in the future. Philip was married and, so Krylenko told her, about to have a child of his own. She didn't even know whether he even thought of her. And yet, she told herself, fiercely, *she did know*. He had belonged to her always, and she knew it more than ever while they had sat on the bridge, during that solitary walk into the open country.

Philip was *hers*, and he was such a fool that he would never know it. He was always lost in mooning about things that didn't matter. *She* could save him: she could set straight his muddles and moonings. He needed some one who thought less of God and more of making a good pie and keeping his socks darned.

She herself had never thought much about God save when her children were born and her husband died, and even then she had been only brushed by a consciousness of some vast and overwhelming personal force. Life, even with its pain, seemed a satisfactory affair: there was always so much to be done, and it wasn't God that Philip needed but pies and socks and a woman who believed in him.

She knew every day whether he was better or worse and she found herself, for the first time in all her life, praying to God to spare his life. She didn't know whether there was a God or whether He would listen to one who only petitioned when she was in need, but she prayed none the less, believing that if there *was* any God, He would understand why it was she turned to Him. If He did not understand, she told herself rebelliously, then He was not worthy of existing as God.

She did not go to the slate-colored house, though she did ask for news on one occasion when she met Emma in the street. She understood that Emma had resented her friendship for Philip, even when they were children, and so avoided seeming to show any great interest. But she heard, nevertheless, sometimes from Krylenko who had even gone to the door to inquire, and sometimes from the doctor, but most of the time it was McTavish who kept her informed.

McTavish was the only person whom she suspected of guessing her secret.

After she had stopped day after day at his undertaking-parlors, he looked at her sharply one day out of his humorous little blue eyes, and said, "If Philip gets better, we've got to help him." Then he hesitated for a moment and added, "Those two women are very bad for him."

He was, she understood, feeling his way. When she

agreed, by not protesting, he went on, "You ought to have married him, Mary, when you had a chance."

"I never had a chance."

"I thought perhaps you had. . . . I understand. She began her dirty work too soon."

Mary knew well enough whom he meant by "she." It struck her that he seemed to hate Emma Downes with an extraordinary intensity.

"Still it may work out yet," he said. "Sometimes things like that are a little better for waiting."

She did not answer him, but spoke about the weather, and thanked him and said good-by, but she felt a sudden warmth take possession of all her body. *"Still it may work out yet."* He never spoke of it again, but when she came in on her way up the hill, he always looked at her in the same eloquent fashion. It was odd, too, that the look seemed to comfort her: it made her feel less alone.

It was from Krylenko that she first heard news of the catastrophe that was coming: he told her and Irene Shane, perhaps because he had confidence in them, but more, perhaps, because he knew that in the end they were the only ones beyond the borders of the Flats to whom he might look for sympathy. The news frightened her at first because there had never been any strike in the Town and because she knew that there was certain to be violence and suffering and perhaps even death. She understood that the spirit which moved the big Ukranian was an eternal force of the temper which had made bloodshed and revolution since the beginning of time. It shone in his blue eyes—the light of fanaticism for a cause. The thing, he said, had been brewing for a long time: any one with half an intelligence could have seen it coming. And Mary knew more than most, for she knew of the hasty, secret meetings in the room over Hennessey's saloon with men who came into the Town and out again like shadows. She watched the curious light in Krylenko's eyes in turn kindle a light in the pale eyes of an unecstatic old maid like Irene Shane. She felt the thing spreading all about her like a fire in the thick underbrush of a forest. It seemed to increase as the plague of typhoid began to abate. In some mysterious way it even penetrated the secure world settled upon the Seven Hills.

She had, too, a trembling sense of treason toward those whom the Town would have called her own people —but her heart leaped on the day when Krylenko told her that Philip, too, was on their side. He was, the Ukranian said, a member of the new Union: they had celebrated his joining months ago at Hennessey's saloon. It made Philip seem nearer to her, as if he belonged not at all to the two women who guarded him. Krylenko told her on the day when every one was certain that Philip was dying, and it served to soften the numb pain which seemed to blind her to all else in the world.

In the afternoon of the same day, Irene Shane said to her, "My mother is dying, and I've cabled to my sister, Lily, to come home."

20

When Moses Slade was not in Washington, he always went on Sundays to the Baptist Church which stood just across the street from Emma's house of worship. It was not that he was a religious man, for he had enough to do without thinking about God. The service bored him and during the sermon he passed the time by turning his active mind toward subjects more earthly and practical, such as the speech he was to make next week at Caledonia, or what answer he would have for the Democratic attack upon his vote against the Farmers' Relief Bill. (How could they understand that what was good for farmers was bad for industry?) In the beginning, he had fallen into the habit of going to church because most of his votes came from church-going people: he went in the same spirit which led him to join sixteen fraternal organizations. But he had gone for so long now that he no longer had any doubts that he was a religious, God-fearing man. (In Washington it did not matter: he could sit at home on Sunday mornings in old clothes drinking his whisky with his feet up on a chair while he read farm papers and racing news.)

Of all the citizens of the Seven Hills, he alone appeared in the streets on Sunday mornings clad in a Prince Albert and a top-hat. Any other citizen in such a fancy-dress costume would have been an object of ridicule, but it was quite proper that he—the Honorable Moses Slade, Congressman—should be thus garbed. He carried it off beautifully; indeed, there was something grand and awe-inspiring in the spectacle of the big man with thick, flowing hair and an enormous front, standing on the steps of the First Baptist Church, speaking to fathers and mothers and patting miserable children imprisoned in stiff Sunday clothes.

On one hot September Sunday he was standing thus (having just patted the last wretched child) when the doors of the church opposite began to yield up its

dead. Among the first to descend the Indiana limestone steps appeared the large, handsome figure of
Emma, dressed entirely in dark clothing. Moses Slade
noticed her at once, for it was impossible not to notice
such a magnetic personage, and he fancied that she
might go away without even knowing he was there.
(He would never learn, of course, that she had hurried
out almost before the last echo of Reverend Castor's
Benediction had died away, because she knew that the
Baptist Church was always over a little before her
own.)

In that first glance, something happened to him
which afterward made him feel silly, but at the moment had no such effect. A voice appeared to say, "I
can't wait any longer," and excusing himself, he hurried, but with an air of dignity, down the steps of his
church, and, crossing the street in full view of the now
mingling congregations, raised his glistening top-hat,
and said, "Good-morning, Mrs. Downes."

Emma turned with a faint air of surprise, but with
only the weakest of smiles (for was she not in sorrow?)
"Why, Mr. Slade, I didn't know you were back."

"May I walk a way with you?"

"Of course, it would be a pleasure."

Together they went off beneath the yellowing maples,
the eyes of two congregations (to Emma's delight)
fastened on them. One voice at least, that of the
soured Miss Abercrombie, was raised in criticism.
"There's no fool," she observed acidly, "like an old
one."

When they had gone a little way beyond the reach
of prying eyes and ears, Moses Slade became faintly
personal in his conversation.

"I appreciated your sending me that postcard," he said.

"Well, I thought you'd like to see the new monument to General Sherman. I knew it was unveiled while you were away, and seeing that you took so much interest in it. . . ." Her voice died away with a note of sadness. The personal touch had filled them both with a sense of constraint, and in silence he helped her across the street, seizing her elbow as if it were a pump-handle.

Safely on the opposite side, he said, "I was sorry to hear of the illness of your son. I hope he's better by now."

Emma sighed. "No . . . he's not much better. You see, he gave up his health in Africa working among the natives." She sighed again. "I doubt if he'll ever be well again. He's such a good boy, too."

"Yes, I always heard that."

"Of course, he may not live. We have to face things, Mr. Slade. If God sees fit to take him, who am I to be bitter and complain? But it isn't easy . . . to have your only son. . . ." She began to cry, and it occurred to Moses Slade that she seemed to crumple and grow softly feminine in a way he had not thought possible in a woman of such character. He had never had any children of his own. He felt that she needed comforting, but for once words seemed of no use to him—the words which always flowed from him in an easy torrent.

"You'll forgive me, Mr. Slade, if I give way . . . but it's gone on for weeks now. Sometimes I wonder that the poor boy has any strength left."

"I understand, Mrs. Downes," he said, in a strange, soft voice.

"I always believe in facing things," she repeated. "There's no good in pretending." She was a little better now and dabbing her eyes with her handkerchief. Fortunately, no one had passed them: no one had witnessed the spectacle of Emma Downes in tears, walking with Congressman Slade.

Before the slate-colored house, they halted, and Mr. Slade asked, "Would you mind if I came in? I'd like to hear how the boy is."

She left him in the parlor, sitting beneath the enlarged portrait of the late Mr. Downes, while she went off up the stairs to ask after Philip. Naomi and Mabelle were there talking, because Naomi no longer went out on account of her appearance, and Mabelle, who always went to sleep in church, avoided it whenever possible. Emma did not speak to them, but hurried past their door to the room where Philip lay white and still, looking thin and transparent, like a sick little boy.

Downstairs, in the darkened parlor, Moses Slade disposed his weight on the green plush, and, leaning on his stick, waited. His mind seemed to be in utter confusion, his brain all befogged. Nothing was very clear to him. He regarded the portrait of Emma's husband, remembering slowly that he had seen Downes years ago, and held a very poor opinion of him. He had been a clever enough fellow, but he never seemed to know where he was going. Emma (he had begun already with a satisfactory feeling of warmth to think of her thus) was probably well rid of him. She had made a brave struggle of it. A fine woman! Look how she behaved about this boy! She believed in facing things. Well, that was a fine, brave quality. He, too, believed in facing things. He couldn't let her go on alone like this. And he began to think of reason after reason why he should marry Emma Downes.

She was gone a long while, and presently he found his gaze wandering back to the portrait. The dead husband seemed to gaze at him with an air of mockery, as if he thought the whole affair was funny. Moses Slade turned in his chair a little, so that he did not look directly at the wooden portrait.

And then he fell to thinking of Philip. What was the boy like? Did he resemble his father or his mother? Had he any character? Certainly his behavior, as far as you could learn, had been queer and mysterious. He might be a liability, yes, a distinct liability, one which was always making trouble. Perhaps he (Moses Slade) ought to go a little more slowly. Of course the boy might die, and that would leave everything clear, with Emma to console. (He yearned impatiently to console her.) It was a wicked thought; but, of course, he wasn't actually *hoping* that the boy would die. He was only facing things squarely, considering the problem from every point of view as a statesman should.

Again he caught the portrait smirking at him, and then the door opened, and Emma came in. She had been crying again. He stood up quickly and the old voice said, "I can't wait any longer." He took her hand gently with a touch which he meant to be interpreted as a sympathetic prelude to something more profound. She didn't resist.

"Well?" he asked.

Emma sank down on the sofa. "I don't know. They thought he'd be better to-day, and . . . and, he isn't."

"You mustn't cry—you mustn't," he said in a husky voice.

"I don't know," she kept repeating. "I don't know what I'm to do. I'm so tired."

He sat down beside her, thankful suddenly that the room was dark, for in the darkness courtship was always easier, especially after middle-age. He now took her hand in both his. There was a long silence in which she gained control of herself, and she did not withdraw her hand nor resist in any way.

"Mrs. Downes," he said presently in a husky voice. "Emma. . . . Mrs. Downes. . . . I have something to ask you. I'm a sober, middle-aged man, and I've thought it over for a long time." He cleared his throat and gave her hand a gentle pressure. "I want you to marry me."

She had known all along that it was coming. Indeed, it was almost like being a girl once more to see Moses Slade, man-like, working his way with the grace of an elephant toward the point; but now it came with the shock of surprise. She couldn't answer him at once for the choke in her throat. For weeks she had borne so much, known such waves of sorrow, that something of her unflagging spirit was broken. She thought, "At last, I am to have my reward for years of hard work. God is rewarding me for all my suffering."

She began to cry again, and Moses Slade asked quickly, "You aren't going to refuse—with all I can give you. . . ."

"No," she sobbed, and, leaning forward a little, as if for support, placed her free hand upon his fat knee. "No . . . I'm not going to refuse . . . only I can't quite believe it. . . . I've had such a hard time. I'd begun to think that I should never have a reward."

Suddenly he leaned over and took her awkwardly in his arms. She felt the heavy metal of his gold watch-chain pressing into her bare arm, and then she heard footsteps descending the stairs in the hallway. It was Mabelle going home at last. She was certain to open the door, because Mabelle couldn't pass a closed door without finding out what was going on behind it.

"Wait!" said Emma, sitting up very straight. "You'd better sit on the other chair."

Understanding what it was she meant, he rose and went back to the green plush. The steps continued, and then, miraculously, instead of halting, they went past the door and out into the street.

The spell was broken, and Moses Slade suddenly felt that he had made a fool of himself, as if he had been duped by an adventuress.

"It's Mabelle," said Emma, who had ceased weeping. "My brother Elmer's wife. She has such a snoopy disposition, I thought we'd better not be found . . . found . . . well, you understand." She blew her nose. "You've made me happy . . . you don't know what it's like to think that I won't have to go on any more . . . alone . . . old age is all right, if you're not alone. . . ."

"Yes, I understand that!" He was a little upset that she treated the affair as if they were an elderly pair marrying for the sake of company in adjoining rocking-chairs. That wasn't at all the way he had looked upon it. In fact, he had been rather proud at the thought of the youthful fervor which had driven him to cross the street a little while before. By some malicious ill-fortune. Mabelle's footsteps had cut short

the declaration at the very moment when he had been
ready to act in such a way as to establish the whole
tone of their future relationship.

"Yes, I understand that," he repeated, "but there's
no use talking about old age. Why, we're young—
Emma—I suppose I can call you Emma?"

She blushed. "Why, yes, of course."

"You wouldn't mind if I called you just Em? That
was my mother's name, and I always liked it."

"No, don't call me Em. It's a name I hate—not on
account of your mother, of course . . . Moses."

She couldn't think why she objected to the name: she
had been called Em all her life, but somehow it was
connected with the vague far-off memory of the romantic Jason Downes. He had called her Em, and it
seemed wrong to let this elderly, fleshy man use the
same name. It seemed vaguely sacrilegious to put this
second marriage on the same basis as the first. She
had *loved* Jason Downes. She knew it just now more
passionately than she had ever known it.

"You understand," she said, laying one hand gently
on his.

"Yes, of course, Emma."

They were standing now, awkwardly waiting for
something, and Moses Slade again suddenly took her
in his arms. He pinched her arm, ever so gently—just
a little pinch; and then he began at once to make a
fool of himself again.

"When shall it be?" he asked. "We must fix a date."

She hesitated for a moment. "Don't ask me now.
I'm all confused and I've had so much to worry me.
We mustn't be hasty and undignified—a man in your
position can't afford to be."

"We can be married quietly . . . any time. No one would know how long I'd been courting you." Then he suddenly became romantic. "The truth is that I've wanted to marry you ever since that day you came to see me. So it's been a long time, you see."

For a moment she was silent and thoughtful. At last she said, "There's one thing we ought to consider, Moses. I don't know about such things, but you'll know, being a lawyer. It's about my first husband. You see they never found his body out there in China. They only know he disappeared and must have been killed by bandits. Now what I mean is this . . . he mightn't be dead at all. He might have lost his mind or his memory. And if he turned up . . ."

Moses Slade looked at her sharply. "You *do* want to marry me, don't you, Em . . . I mean Emma. . . . You're not trying to get out of it?"

"Of course I want to marry you. I only mentioned this because I believe in facing things."

"How long has he been gone?"

"It's twenty-four years this January. I remember it well. It was snowing that night, just after the January thaw. . . ."

He checked what would have been a long story by saying, "Twenty-four years . . . all alone without a husband. You're a brave little woman, Emma." He made a clicking sound with his tongue, and looked at her fondly. "Well, that's a long time . . . long enough for him to be considered dead under law. But we'll have him declared dead by law and then we won't have to worry."

Emma was staring at the floor with a curious fixed

look in her eyes. At last she said, "Do you think that would be right? He might still be alive. He might come back."

Moses Slade grew blustering, as if he were actually jealous of that shadow of the man who kept looking down at him with an air of sardonic amusement.

"It won't make any difference if we declare him dead. Besides, he hasn't got any right to you if he *is* alive."

It wasn't that she was simply afraid he might return; the source of her alarm went much deeper than that. She felt that she couldn't trust herself if he did return; but of course she couldn't explain that to Moses.

"It wasn't quite that," she murmured, and, conscious that the remark didn't make sense, she asked quickly, "How long ought it to take?"

"A couple of months."

"We could be married after that?"

"Yes, as soon as possible."

Moses Slade took her hand again. "You've made me a happy man, Emma. You won't regret it." He picked up his hat. "I'd like to call to-night. Maybe you'd go to evening service with me?"

"No, I think we'd better not let any one know about it till it's settled."

"Maybe you're right. Well, I'll come to the restaurant to-morrow for lunch."

He kissed her again, a bit too ardently, she felt, to be quite pleasant, and they went into the hall. At the same moment the figure of Naomi appeared, descending the stairs heavily. She was clad only in a nightgown and a loose kimono of flowered stuff. Her hair, still in curl-papers, lay concealed beneath a kind of mob-cap of bright green satin, trimmed with soiled lace. It was impossible to avoid her.

"Naomi," said Emma, in a voice of acid, "this is Mr. Slade—Moses, my daughter-in-law, Naomi."

Naomi said, "Pleased to meet you." Moses Slade bowed, went through the door, and the meeting was over.

When the door closed, Emma stood for a moment with the knob in her hand. Naomi was watching her with a look of immense interest and curiosity strangely like the look that came so often into the eyes of Mabelle when curiosity about the subjects of love and childbirth became too strong for her feeble control.

"Is that Mr. Slade . . . the Congressman?" asked Naomi.

"Yes, it is." There was something in Naomi's look that maddened her, something that was questioning, shameless, offensive, and even accusing.

"What made him come to see us?"

Emma controlled herself. She felt lately that it was all she could bear always to have Naomi in the house.

"He came to ask about Philip."

"I didn't know that he knew Philip."

"He didn't, but he's an old friend of mine." The lie slipped easily from her tongue.

"Philip's better," Naomi answered. "He opened his eyes and looked at me. I think he knew me."

"Did he speak?"

"No, he just closed them again without saying any-thing."

Emma moved away from the door as Naomi turned

into the dining-room. "Naomi," she called suddenly, "is the Reverend Castor coming this afternoon?"

"Yes . . . he said he was."

"Surely you're going to put on some clothes before he comes?"

"I was going to fix my hair."

"You must put on some clothes. I won't have you going about the house all day looking like this—half dressed and untidy. You're a sight! What will a man like Mr. Slade think—a man who is used to Washington where there's good society."

Naomi stared at her for a moment with an unaccustomed look of defiance in her pale eyes. (Emma thought, "Mabelle has been making her into a slattern like herself.")

"Well, in my condition, clothes aren't very comfortable. I think in my condition I might have some consideration."

Emma began to breathe heavily. "That has nothing to do with it. When I was in your condition I dressed and went about my work every day. I wore corsets right up to the end."

"Well, I'm not strong like you. . . . The doctor told me . . ."

Emma broke in upon her. "The doctor didn't tell you to go about looking like a slattern all day! I wish you'd tell Mabelle for me that I'd like to come home just once without finding her here."

The fierce tension could not endure. When it broke sharply, Naomi sat down and began to cry. "Now you want to take her away from me," she sobbed. "I've given up everything to please you and Philip . . . everything. I even gave up going back to Megambo, where the Lord meant me to be. And now I haven't got anything left . . . and you all hate me. Yes, you do. And Philip does too sometimes. . . . He hates me. . . . You wanted me to marry him, and now see what's come of it. I'm even in this condition because you wanted me to be." She began to cry more and more wildly. "I'll run out into the street. I'll kill myself. I'll run away, and then maybe you'll be happy. I won't burden you any longer."

Emma was shaking her now, violently, with all the shame and fury she felt at Moses' encounter with this slatternly daughter-in-law, and all the contempt she felt for a creature so poor spirited.

"You'll do no such thing, you little fool! You'll brace up and behave like a woman with some sense!"

But it was no good. Naomi was simply having one of her seizures. She grew more hysterical, crying out, "You'd like to be rid of me . . . both of you. You both hate me. . . . Oh, I know . . . I know . . . I'm nothing now . . . nothing to anybody in the world! I'm just in your way."

Emma, biting her lip, left her abruptly, closing the door behind with ferocious violence. If she had not gone at once, she felt that she would have laid hands on Naomi.

Moses Slade, bound toward his own house, walked slowly, lost once more in a disturbing cloud of doubts. With Emma out of sight, the ardent lover yielded place to the calculating politician. He suffered, he did not know why, from a feeling of having been duped. The sight of Naomi so untidy and ill-kempt troubled him. He hadn't known about the child. The girl must

be at least seven months gone, and he hadn't known it.
Of course (he thought) you couldn't have expected
Emma voluntarily to mention a subject so indelicate.
Nevertheless, he felt that she should have conveyed
the knowledge to him in some discreet fashion. Even
if the boy did die, the situation would be just as bad,
or worse. If he left a widow and a child. . . . He felt
suddenly as if in some way Emma herself had tricked
him, as if she herself were having a child, and had
tricked him into marrying her to protect herself. . . .

In a kind of anguish he regretted again that he had
been so impetuous in his proposal to the widow Barnes
that he had shocked her into refusal. *She* wasn't so
fine-looking a woman as Emma, but she was free, without encumbrances or responsibilities, without a child.
Of course, Emma would never know that in the midst
of his courtship he had been diverted by the prospect
of Mrs. Barnes. She would never know what had been
the reason for the months of silence. . . .

21

Since the reconciliation, the Sunday dinner at Elmer
Niman's had again been resumed, and Emma, on her
way there, suffered as keenly from doubts as her suitor
had done on his homeward journey. Now that the
thing was accomplished, or practically so, she was
uneasy. It was not, she reflected, a simple thing to
alter the whole course of one's life at her age. There
would be troubles, difficulties, for Moses Slade was not,
she could see, an easy man to manage. To be sure, he
was less slippery than Jason had been: a Congressman could never run off and disappear. But, on the

other hand, he was as rocklike and solid as his own portly figure.

She faced the thing all the way to Elmer's house, examining it from every possible angle, except the most important of all—the angle of ambition. In the bottom of her heart, hidden and veiled by all the doubts and probings, there lay a solid determination to marry Moses Slade. The restaurant was a complete success, enlarged to a size commensurate with the possibilities of the Town. Nothing more remained to be done, and she was still a healthy, vigorous woman in the prime of life. As the wife of Moses Slade, new vistas opened before her. . . . There had never been any doubt about her course of action, but she succeeded in convincing herself that she was going slowly and examining every possibility of disaster.

What she found most difficult to bear was the lack of a confidante. Even though, as she admitted to herself, it was silly to think of such a thing as love between herself and Moses, she had nevertheless an overwhelming desire to share the news with some one. It was almost as strong as the feeling she had experienced twenty-seven years earlier after accepting Jason's declaration. She could not, she felt, go in safety beyond the borders of a discreet hinting to any of her woman friends: a mere rumor soon spread among them with the ferocity of a fire in a parched forest. Naomi was the last person to tell, especially since that queer Mabelle look had come into her eyes. And her brother? No, she couldn't tell him, though she supposed he would be pleased at her marrying so solid a man. It wasn't clear to her why she couldn't bring herself to tell him, save that it was connected vaguely with the memory of his behavior on the occasion of announcing her engagement to Jason. He might behave in the same fashion again; and on the first occasion he had only forgiven her when Jason had vindicated his opinion by disappearing. Elmer, she knew, loved to say, "I told you it would end like this."

There remained only Philip, and he was too ill to be told; but when she thought of it, she began to doubt whether she would have told him if he had been well.

It was the first time since his return that she had had need to confide in him, and now she found herself troubled by the feeling that it wouldn't be easy. Until now she had gone bravely on, ignoring the changes in their relations as mother and son, but now that a test had arisen, she saw that there had been a change. She saw, despite herself, that he had become in a way a stranger—her boy, who had always loved her, whom she worshipped with a maternal passion too intense to be put into words. Her boy, whose very character she had created as she had created his flesh, had become a stranger with whom she couldn't even discuss her own plans. Once he would have believed that whatever she did was right.

As she thought of it, she walked more rapidly. Why, she asked herself, had this happened to her? Hadn't she given all her life to him? Hadn't she worked her fingers to the bone? Hadn't she watched and guarded him from evil and sin, kept him pure? Had she ever thought of anything but his welfare and saving him from the pitfall of his father's weaknesses? A lump came into her throat, and a moisture into her eyes. What had she done to deserve this?

She felt no resentment against him. It was impossible to blame him in any way. He was a good boy, who had never caused her any trouble—not trouble in the real sense, for his doubts about his calling were temporary, and perhaps natural. Since he could never go back to Africa, he would in the end settle down with some church of his own. He might even perhaps become a bishop, for certainly he was more clever than most preachers, a thousand times more clever than the Reverend Castor, and more of a gentleman, more of what a bishop ought to be. And after this illness perhaps he would see the light once more. Perhaps the Lord had sent this illness for just that reason.

No, Philip was a perfect son. She was sure that he still loved her.

She tried to hate the Mills, but that was impossible, and in the end the suspicion came to her that the change was due in some way to Naomi. It must be Naomi. She had always thought that Naomi disliked her. Why, she didn't know. Hadn't she done everything for Naomi? Hadn't she treated her as if she were her own daughter?

And her only reward was spite and jealousy.

While she thought of it, it occurred to her that the change in Philip—the *real* change—his slipping away from her—had begun at the time that Naomi became his wife in more than name: until that time he had always been her boy who adored her. Suddenly, she saw it all clearly; it was Naomi for whom she had done everything, who had stolen Philip from her.

Her tears were dried by the time she reached her brother's front step, but the lump in her throat was still there, and it remained all through the lunch, so that at times she felt that she might suddenly weep, despite herself. In her sorrow, she paid little heed to her brother's usual long speeches, or to Mabelle's idiotic interruptions. But she was able to despise Mabelle with a contempt which made any previous emotion pale by comparison. Because Mabelle was Naomi's friend, she, too, seemed responsible for what had happened.

After lunch, when Mabelle had gone out to the kitchen for a time, Emma took her brother aside in the grim parlor, and said, "Elmer, I have something to ask of you."

He looked at her sharply, in a way in which he had looked at her for years on occasions when he thought she might be asking for money. It had never yet happened, but the unguarded look of alarm had never wholly died since the moment that Jason Downes left his wife penniless.

"It's not what you think," said Emma coldly. "It's only about Mabelle. I want you to keep her from coming to the house so often."

"But why, Emma?"

"You don't know that she spends all her days there. I never go home without finding her . . . and I think she's bad for Naomi . . . just now."

"How bad for her?"

He was standing with his hands clasped behind him, watching her. For a moment she looked squarely into his eyes, hesitating, wondering whether she dared speak the truth. Then she took the plunge, for she felt suddenly that Elmer would understand. There was a bond between them not of fraternal affection (for there were times when they actually disliked each other), but a tie far stronger. He would understand what she meant to say, because he was, in spite of everything, very like her. They were two people who had to rule those about them, two people who were always right. She knew that he understood her contempt for Mabelle as a woman and as a housekeeper; the fact that Mabelle was his wife made little difference.

"You'll understand what I mean, Elmer. You know that Mabelle doesn't keep house well. You know she's . . . well, lazy and untidy. And that is why she's bad for Naomi. Naomi wasn't meant for a wife and mother, I'm afraid. She's a miserable failure at it. I'm trying to put character into her, to make something of her . . . but I can't, if Mabelle's always there. She undoes all I can do."

He unclasped his hands, and, after a moment, said, "Yes, I think I know what you mean. Besides, Mabelle ought to be at home looking after her own house a little. You'd think that she couldn't bear the sight of it. She's always gadding." He turned away. "She's coming now. I'll speak to her, and if she still bothers you let me know."

Mabelle came through the swinging beaded portières. "It's too bad Naomi couldn't come, too, for lunch. It's a pity she feels like she does about being seen in the street. I have tried to make her sensible about it. Why, when I was carrying Ethel . . ."

Both of them gave her black looks, but Mabelle, seating herself at once in the rocking-chair, rattled on without noticing.

22

The inspiration came to Emma at the evening service, when she was struck again by the quality of sym-

pathy in the voice and countenance of the Reverend
Castor. He, of course, was the one with whom to discuss the problem of her marriage. He would understand, and he would be able, as well, to give her advice.
Nor did he ever betray all the ladies of his congregation who came to him with their troubles. And he
had been so sympathetic over Philip's long illness, showing so deep a solicitude, calling at the house three or
four times a week.

Almost at once she felt happier.

At the end of the service, she waited until he had
shaken hands with all the congregation, smiling and
making little jests with them, as if he had not done so
twice a day for fifty-two Sundays a year, ever since
he had felt the call. When they had all gone, she
said, "Could I take a moment of your time, Reverend
Castor? I want advice over something that worries
me."

It was a request he heard often enough, from one
woman after another—women who asked advice upon
every subject from thieving hired girls to erring husbands. There were times when he felt he could not
endure listening to one more woman talk endlessly
about herself. It wearied him so that he wanted to
flee suddenly, leaving them all, together with the hand-
shaking and the very church itself, behind him forever.
Sometimes he had strange dreams, while he was awake,
and with his eyes wide open, of fleeing to some outlandish place like those marvelous islands in the South
Seas where there were none of these things. And then
to calm his soul, he would tell himself cynically that
even in those islands there were women.

He led her to his study, which he had been driven

to establish at the back of the church, since there was no peace in the parsonage from the complaining voice above-stairs. There the two of them sat down. It occurred to Emma that he looked very white and tired, that there were new lines on his face. He couldn't be an old man. He wasn't much older than herself, yet he was beginning to look old. It was, she supposed, the life he led at home. A clergyman, of all people, needed an understanding, unselfish wife.

"And now," he was saying, "I'm always pleased to help, however I can in my humble way."

He was a good man, who never sought to evade his duty, however tired he was. He wanted, honestly, to help her.

She began to tell him, constructing an approach to the fact itself by explaining what a lonely, hard life she had had since the death of her husband in China. She touched upon the Christian way in which she had brought up her boy, and now (she said) that he was a grown man and married and would soon have a parish of his own (since he could not return to Africa) she would be left quite alone. She wanted the rest which she had earned, and the companionship for which she would no doubt hunger in her old age. These were the reasons why she had accepted the offer of Moses Slade. Yet she was troubled.

She leaned back in her chair and sighed. What did he think? Could he help her to decide?

The study was a gloomy room, lighted in the day-time by a single sooty Gothic window and at night by a single jet of gas. There was a roll-top desk, a long heavy table, a cabinet where the choir music was kept, and two or three sagging, weary leather chairs. Before he answered her, the tired eyes of the Reverend Castor rested for a time on the meager furniture as if he had lost himself in deep thought. She waited. This attitude was, however, merely professional, and wholly misleading. He was not in deep thought. He was merely thinking, "She doesn't want advice. She only wants to talk about herself. Whatever I say will make no difference. She means to marry him, no matter what happens."

But because this was his work he spoke at last, setting forth one by one all the arguments she had repeated to herself earlier in the day, concluding with the remark, "The reasons on the other side you have put very well yourself."

Emma stirred in the springless leather chair. "Then what do you advise?"

"Mrs. Downes, it is a matter that no one can decide but yourself. Pray God to help you, and do what you think is right."

He was troubled, and, in a vague way, disturbed and unhappy, because in the back of his mind the worm of envy was at work, gnawing, gnawing, gnawing—a sinful worm that gave him no peace. Moses Slade was free to marry again, and he had chosen Emma Downes. He had thought of Emma Downes for himself, in case . . . (the wicked thought returned to him again like a shadow crossing his path) . . . in case Annie's illness carried her off at last. It seemed to him that all the world was going past him, while he remained behind, chained to a complaining invalid.

Emma rose, and, after he had turned the gas out and locked the door, they went out together. It was a clear, quiet night, when for once there seemed to be no soot in the air, and the stars seemed very close. For a moment they both stood listening, and at last Emma said, "Am I right, or am I growing deaf? Do the Mills sound very far away to-night . . . sort of weak?"

He listened, and then said, "Yes, it's queer. They sound almost faint."

There was another silence. And Emma gave a low, groaning sound. "Maybe that's it . . . maybe they've gone out on strike."

"There'll be trouble," said the Reverend Castor. "It makes me kind of sick to think of it."

They bade each other good-night, and went their ways, the Reverend Castor hurrying along, because he was more than an hour late. He knew that when he arrived she would be out of her bed, standing at the upper window looking for him, her mind charged with the bitter reproaches she had thought out to fling at him, torturing sarcasms dealing with what had kept him so long in the study. She had an obsession that he meant to be unfaithful to her; she never ceased to hint and imply the most odious things. She was always accusing him of disgraceful things about women. . . .

As he came nearer and nearer to the parsonage, he was seized by a terrible temptation to turn away, to disappear, never to enter the doors of his home again. But a man of God, he knew, couldn't do a thing like that. And now God—even God—seemed to be deserting him. He couldn't drive these awful thoughts from his mind. He began desperately to repeat his Psalm.

Turning past the hedge, he saw that there was a light in the upper window, and against the lace cur-

tains the silhouette of a waiting figure, peering out
eagerly.

When Emma entered the house, she discovered that
all the lights were on, that Philip had been forgotten,
and that his nurse and Mabelle were with Naomi, who
was being forced to walk up and down. Mabelle sat
giving advice and saying repeatedly that she never
had such trouble even with her first baby. In a little
while, the doctor came, and seven hours later Mabelle's
predictions were vindicated, for Naomi gave birth at
last to twins, a boy and a girl. At about the same
hour the last echo of the pounding at the Mills died
away into silence, and the last fire in the blast-furnace
died into ashes. In the room next to Naomi's, Philip
opened his eyes, called for a drink of water, and for
the first time in four months knew that his head was
clear and that his body was not burning or shaking.
It was an extraordinary thing, the nurse observed, as
if his children coming into the world had called him
back to life.

He came back to consciousness out of a strange
country peopled with creatures that might have haunted
a Gothic nightmare, creatures who seemed as confused
and unreal as the fantastic world on which they moved.
Sometimes his mother was present, moving about, oddly
enough, against the background of the jungle at
Megambo, moving about among the niggers, converting
them in wholesale lots. At times she would disappear
suddenly, to return almost at once, driving before her
with Lady Millicent Wimbrooke's rawhide whip whole
troops of natives, dressed completely, even to bonnets
and shoes, like the people one saw in Main Street.
And then she would feed them at the Peerless

Restaurant, which seemed to have been set up intact on the borders of the gloomy forest. Once Lady Wimbrooke appeared herself with her portable-bath and rifle, and shooting about her carelessly, she drove all of them, including Emma, out of the restaurant into Main Street, which appeared miraculously to have sprung up just outside the door. Once outside, he discovered that all of them—Emma herself and the niggers, were walking stark naked in the car-tracks in the middle of the street. He, himself, seemed to be carrying a banner at the head of the parade on which was written in fiery letters, "Let God look out for himself. We will do the same." And at the corner he found Mary Conyngham waiting to keep a tryst, and neither he nor she seemed to take any notice of the fact that he was as naked as the day he was born.

And Naomi was there, too, always in the background, only she was not the Naomi he knew, but a large woman with a soft, powerful body, like Swanson's, above which her pale face peered out comically from beneath a sunbonnet woven of reeds. Once or twice he had mistaken her for Swanson playing a joke on him.

At other times he seemed to be back in the Mills, or in Hennessey's saloon, where Emma entered presently and broke all the mirrors; and then all of them were suddenly squeezed out of the doors to find themselves in the jungle, which appeared to have sprung up all about them, impenetrable save for a single path in which was stuck a cast-iron guide-post, reading, "To the Mills." The air was filled with the sound of distant thunder, but he could not make out whether it was the distant sound of tom-toms, or the pounding of monstrous steel hammers. Oddly enough, it seemed quite natural, as if the trees, the jungle and the Mills belonged thus together.

And Mary Conyngham was always there. It seemed that she was married to him, and that they had somewhere a family of children which he had never seen and could not find.

Once he witnessed a horrible sight. He saw Emma pursuing the black virgin who had long ago been eaten by the leopards. The virgin, naked, save for her ornaments of copper wire, ran to the lake, and across the water, skimming the surface like a kingfisher of ebony, and, as Emma gave chase, she sank like a stone, disappearing beneath the brassy surface without a sound.

For a long time after he returned to life, memories of the dead, nightmarish world clung to him like wisps of the haze that sometimes veiled the lake at Megambo in the wet season. He did not know how long he had been ill, and at times it seemed to him that he had died and was not living at all. His body felt light as air, but when he tried to raise it, it failed him, slipping back in a miserable weakness. And then, bit by bit, as the memories of the delirium faded into space, the hard, barren world about him began to take shape . . . the starched lace curtains at the windows, which Emma kept clean despite all the soot, the worn rocking-chair, the table at the side of the bed crowded with medicines, and, finally, the strange figure of the nurse. And then he understood that Naomi must be somewhere near at hand, and his mother. He had a vague feeling that they must have become old now, and gray, after all the years he had been ill.

It was Emma whom he saw first, and recognized. She came into the darkened room, and stood silently by the side of the bed until he, conscious that there was some one near him, opened his eyes, and said in a weak voice, "Is that you, Ma?"

Without answering him, she fell on her knees beside the bed and took his head in her hands, kissing him passionately again and again on his forehead. She wept and said over and over again, "Philip, my boy! The Lord has given me back my boy!"

There was something frightening in the wildness of her emotion. The nurse, hearing her weeping, came in to warn her that she must be calm, and Philip said weakly, "It's all right. I understand. She's always been like that."

Once it would never have occurred to him to speak thus, as if he were detached from her and stood quite apart, protecting her. Protecting Emma! Something had happened to him during that long night of four months' delirium.

When his mother had gained control of herself once more, she sat down by the side of the bed, and, taking his hand, she held it clasped passionately in hers, while she sat looking at him, without once speaking. For some reason, he could not look at her, perhaps because in the intensity of her emotion she was asking from him a response which he could not give. He was ashamed, but it was impossible to pretend. Instead of any longer seeming almost a part of her, he was detached now in a strange, definite fashion. In his weakness, it seemed to him that he was seeing her for the first time and he was ashamed and sorry for her. He knew that before long she, too, would understand that there was a difference, that in some way their relationship had been broken forever. The old Philip was dead, and the new one suddenly pitied her from a great distance, as he pitied Naomi. It was as if the weakness gave him a clairvoyance, a second sight, which illuminated all the confusion of mind that had preceded the long night.

Lying there, with his eyes closed, her passionate cry, "Philip, my boy!" burned itself into his brain. He was, he knew, unworthy of that consuming love she had for him.

After a long time he heard her asking, "Philip, are you awake?"

"Yes, Ma." But he did not open his eyes.

"I have some good news that will delight you."

What could it be? Perhaps she had arranged his return to Megambo. She would think that was good news.

"It's about Naomi. You're a father now, Philip . . . twice a father, Philip. You've two children. They were twins."

The knot of perplexity which had been tormenting his brain suddenly cleared away. Of course! That was what he couldn't remember about Naomi. She had been going to have a baby, and now she had had two. Still he did not open his eyes. It was more impossible now than ever. He did not answer her, and presently Emma asked, "You heard what I said, Philip?"

"Yes, Ma."

"You're glad, aren't you?"

He answered her weakly, "Of course . . . why, of course, I'm glad."

Again there was a long silence. He was ashamed again, because he had been forced to lie, ashamed because he wasn't proud, and happy. His mother sat there trying to raise his spirits, and each thing she said only drove them lower. In that curious clarity of mind which seemed to possess his soul, he knew with a kind of horror that he had wanted to waken alone, free, in a new country, where he would never again see Naomi, or his mother, or the lace curtains, or the familiar, worn rocking-chair. That, he saw now, was why he had wanted to die. And now he was back again, tied to them more closely than ever.

At last he said in a low voice, "It was like Naomi, wasn't it . . . to have twins?"

"What do you mean?"

He hesitated a moment, and then said, "I don't know . . . I'm tired . . . I don't know."

Again a silence. Deep inside him something kept urging him to break through all this web which seemed to be closing tighter and tighter around him. The last thought he could remember before slipping into the nightmare returned to him now, and, without knowing why, he uttered it, "There won't be any more children."

"Why?" asked Emma. "What are you trying to say?"

"Because I don't mean to live with Naomi ever again. It's a wicked thing that I've done."

She began to stroke his forehead, continuing for a long time before she spoke. She was having suddenly to face things—things which she had always known, and pretended not to know. At last she said, "Why is it a wicked thing to live with your lawful wife?"

The world began to whiz dizzily about his head. Odd flashes of light passed before his closed eyes. It seemed to him that he must speak the truth, if he were ever to open them again without shame.

"Because she's not really my wife . . . she's just like any woman, any stranger . . . I never loved her at all. I can't go on . . . living like that. Can't you see how wicked it is?"

Emma was caught in her own web, by the very holy principles she upheld—that it was wrong to marry some one you did not love. It was this same thing which disturbed her peace of mind about Moses Slade.

"You loved her once, Philip, or you wouldn't have married her."

"No, I didn't know anything then, Ma." The color of pain entered his voice. "Can't you see, Ma? I wasn't alive then. I never loved her, and now it's worse than that."

The stroking of his forehead suddenly ceased. "I don't know what you're talking about, Philip. . . . We'd better not go on now. You're tired and ill. Everything will be different when you are well again."

For a second time there came to him a blinding flash of revelation. He saw that she had always been like that: she had always pushed things aside to let them work themselves out. An awful doubt dawned upon him that she was not always right, that sometimes she had made a muddle of everything. A feeling of dizziness swept over him.

"But it will break her heart, Philip," she was saying. "She worships you. . . . It will break her heart."

Through a giddy haze he managed to say, "No . . . I'm so tired. . . . Let's not talk any more." He felt the nightmare stealing back again, and presently he was for some strange reason back at Megambo, sitting under the acacia-tree, and through the hot air came the sound of voices singing, in a minor key:

"Go down to the water, little monkey,
To the life of lives, the beginning of all things."

He thought wildly, "I've got to get free. I must run . . . I must run."

Emma, holding his hand, felt the fever slipping back. She heard him saying, "Go down to the water, little monkey," which clearly made no sense, and suddenly she sprang up and called Miss Bull, the nurse.

"It's odd," said Miss Bull, white and frightened, "when he was so much better. Did anything happen to upset him?"

"No," said Emma. "Nothing. We barely talked at all."

The nurse sent Essie for the doctor, reproaching herself all the while for having allowed Emma to stay so long a time by the bed. But it was almost impossible to refuse when a woman like Mrs. Downes said, "Surely seeing his mother won't upset him. Why, Miss Bull, we've always been wonderful companions— my boy and I. He never had a father, you see. I was both mother and father to him." Miss Bull knew what a gallant fight she'd made, for every one in the Town knew it. A widow, left alone, to bring up her boy. You couldn't be cruel enough to stop her from seeing her own son.

When the doctor came and left again, shaking his head, Emma was frightened, but her fright disappeared once more as the fever receded again toward morning, and when at last she fell asleep, she was thinking, "He doesn't belong to her, after all. He's never belonged to her. He's still my Philip." There was in the knowledge a sense of passionate triumph and joy, which wiped out all else—her doubts about Moses Slade, her worry over Philip's future, even the sudden, cold terror that gripped her as she felt the fever stealing back into his thin, transparent hand. He didn't belong to Naomi. Why, he almost hated her. He was still her boy. . . . And she had defeated Naomi.

In the darkness the tears dampened the pillow. God had not, after all, forsaken her.

PART THREE

THE STABLE

AT the back of the great Shane house there clustered a little group of buildings arranged in plantation style. There were a laundry, a kennel, an office and a stable with a double row of box-stalls. The whole was overgrown with dying vines and was connected with the big white-trimmed brick house by a sort of gallery, roofed but open on the sides. The buildings were empty now, since the old woman had taken to her canopied bed, save for the pair of fat old horses who never went out any more and now stood fat and sleek, groomed carefully each day by the old negro who acted as groom and general factotum. One daughter had given up her life to the poor and the other to the great world and no one cared any longer if the hinges rusted on the stable doors and the great wrought-iron gates sagged at the entrance to the park. Ghosts haunted the place—the ghost of the wicked old John Shane who had built the Castle, the ghosts of all the great who had stayed at the Castle in the glamorous days before the coming of the black Mills. Old Julia Shane lay dying, aloof, proud, rich and scornful. Nobody cared. . . .

When the strike came the whole park fell into a state of siege, walled in on the one side by the Mills and on the other by the filthy houses of the steelworkers. The warfare raged just outside its borders. Sometimes in the night a shot sounded in the darkness.

But neither side invaded the territory: it remained in some mysterious way neutral and sacred, as if the lingering spirit of the old woman who lay dying in the smoke-blackened house held the world at bay. The doctor came twice daily, making his way bravely through the black district of the strike; once each day, the old nigger Hennery went timorously across the Halstead Street bridge to fetch food. Irene Shane and sometimes Hattie Tolliver, a cousin who came to "take hold," went in and out. Otherwise the place lay deserted and in solitude, waiting.

Early in December, when the first blackened snow lay among the dead trees of the park, Irene Shane and Mary Conyngham visited the stables. It was the first time Irene had gone there since she was a young girl and kept a pony called Istar. To Mary Conyngham it was a strange place never before visited. They were accompanied by the old nigger Hennery.

Above the stalls of the fat horses there was a room once occupied by a coachman, which now lay empty save for a table, two or three chairs, an iron stove and a bed. At each end of the room there was a big window partly covered by the vines that overran the whole building. It was here that the two women and the old negro came.

Irene, dressed in her shabby gray clothes, opened the door of the harness-closet, looked inside, and then regarded the room with a sweeping glance. "This ought to serve, very well," she said.

Mary was pleased. "It's perfect, I should think."

"Put those newspapers in the stove, Hennery, and light them," said Irene. "He can't work here unless there's some means of heat."

The papers went up in a burst of flame. The stove worked perfectly.

The two women looked at each other. "Will you tell him, then?" asked Mary.

"Yes . . . Krylenko will tell him. I don't know him at all."

Suddenly Mary kissed the older woman on the cheek. It was an odd, grotesque gesture, which failed of all response. It was like kissing a piece of marble to kiss a woman like Irene Shane.

"Thank you, Irene," she said.

Irene ignored the speech, and turned to the old negro. "Clean the room out, Hennery. There's a Mr. Downes coming here to paint now and then."

"What? Pitchers?" asked Hennery.

"Yes, pictures. He's to come and go as he likes. You needn't worry about him."

They left him raising clouds of dust with a worn stable-broom. It did not strike him that there was anything extraordinary in the arrangement. He had come to Shane's Castle a buck nigger of eighteen, when John Shane was a bachelor. He was sixty-five now. Anything, he knew, might happen at Shane's Castle. Life there possessed a sort of subterranean excitement.

As he swept he kept thinking that Miss Lily was already on her way home from Paris, coming to see her Mammy die. She hadn't been home in seven years. When Miss Lily came home, everything was changed. All the excitement seemed to rise above the surface, and all life changed and became a tingling, splendiferous affair. Even the presence of death in the Castle couldn't dampen the effect of Miss Lily.

2

With that first fall of snow the fever began to lose a little its hold upon the twice-stricken community. As it waned the new terror came to take its place—a terror that, like the fever, rose out of the black of the Flats.

Bristling barriers of ugly barbed-wire sprang up overnight and for days each train brought in criminals shipped from the slums of a dozen cities to protect the sheds and furnaces. In the beginning it was neither the strikers, nor the men who owned the Mills, but the Town itself which suffered. Business in the shops bordering the diseased area fell off; but, far worse than that, there began to occur one after another, with terrifying regularity, a whole series of crimes. Houses were broken into, a woman was attacked at twilight in the raw, new park, two fat business men were held up and beaten, and the Farmers' and Industrial Bank, the institution of the corrupt Judge Weissman, was robbed and then quickly failed under mysterious circumstance. It was the gunmen brought in to make war on the strikers who committed the crimes, but it was the strikers who were accused. Save for Philip and Mary Conyngham, and perhaps McTavish, they had no friends on the Hills. The Shanes could not be counted, since they stood apart in an isolation of their own. A panic-stricken community began to imagine innumerable horrors. The newspapers wrote editorials predicting anarchy and dissolution. They talked of the "sacred rights of property" and used clouds of similar high-sounding phrases. Moses Slade, seeing perhaps a chance to harvest new crops of votes by "standing by his community in such a crisis," returned to head a sort of vigilance committee whose purpose was to fasten all crime upon the strikers.

By this heroic act he soon rose high in the esteem of Emma, so high indeed that it seemed to wipe out all her doubts concerning her marriage. It was an action of which she approved with all her spirit. She herself went about talking of "dirty foreigners" and the need of making laws to exclude them from a nation favored by God, until Moses took her aside and advised her not to talk in such a vein, because the very strength of the Mills depended on new hordes of cheap labor. If they throttled immigration, labor would rule. Didn't she understand a simple thing like that?

She understood. Moses Slade seemed to her a paragon. "Why," she told Philip, "he understands all the laws of economics."

Philip, restless and convalescent, listened to her in silence. He even met the Honorable Moses Slade, who eyed him suspiciously as a cat and asked about his future plans.

"I haven't any," said Philip. "I don't know what I mean to do," and so put Moses Slade once more upon a bed of pins and needles concerning Emma's qualifications as a bride.

The omnipresence of the Congressman's name in Emma's conversation had begun to alarm Philip. He saw presently that she meant to tell him something, and after a time he came to guess what it was. He saw that she was breaking a way through his prejudices and her own; and in that odd sense of detachment born

of the fever he faced the idea with disgust. It was
not only that he disliked Mr. Slade; it seemed to him
that there was something disgraceful in the idea of his
mother marrying again after so many years. It was
in a strange way a disloyalty to himself. Moses Slade
was a new ally in the forces against him. The idea came
to torment him for hours at a time, when he was not
pondering what was to be done about Naomi, how he
could escape from her without hurting her too deeply.

The two women, Naomi and his mother, hovered
over him with the solicitude of two women for a man
whom they had snatched from death. In these first
days when he came downstairs to sit in the parlor
there was always one of them with him. Naomi left
him only long enough to nurse the twins. She was, as
Mabelle observed, very fortunate, as she was able to
feed them both, and there were not many women,
Mabelle remarked with a personal pride, who could say
the same. And under Mabelle's guidance Naomi
adopted the same methods: the moment the twins set
up a wail they were fed into a state of coma. Mabelle
had great pride in them, as if she had played in some
way a part in their very creation. She was always in
the house now, for Emma's request and Elmer's com-
mands were of no avail against her instinct for human
companionship. With the twins crying and little Jimmy
running about, the house seemed overrun with children.
And little Jimmy had turned into what Mabelle described as "a whiner."

"I don't know what to do about him," she said.
Her method was to cuff him over the head, thus changing the whine instantly into a deafening squall.

Naomi used her own convalescence as an excuse for

clinging to the soiled flowered kimono and the green
mob-cap.

It was a state of affairs which could not long endure
and the climax arose on the afternoon when Emma, returning unexpectedly, found a scene which filled her
with horror. In his chair by the window sat Philip,
looking white and sick. Behind him on the sofa Naomi
in wrapper and mob-cap fed the twins. Little Jimmy
sat on the floor pulling photographs out of the album
at the back of the family Bible. Draping the backs of
the mahogany chairs hung white objects that were unmistakably diapers. Two of the objects were even
hung to dry upon the very frame of Jason Downes'
enlarged photograph!

For a moment Emma simply stood in the doorway in
a state of paralysis. At the sight of her Naomi sat up
defiantly and Mabelle smiled blandly. Philip, wearily,
did not even turn to witness the picture. And then,
quickly, like a bird of prey, Emma swooped upon the
diapers, gathering them up in a neat roll. Then she
turned on Naomi.

"It's the last time I want this to happen in my
house." She seized the family Bible from Jimmy, who
began to squall, setting off the twins like matches
brought too close to a fire. "I won't have it looking
like a bawdy-house," she cried. "With you sitting here
all day in a wrapper, like a chippy waiting for trade."
Words that she would have denied knowing came to her
lips in a stream.

This time Naomi did not weep. She sprang up from
the sofa as if to attack Emma. "Take care what you
say! Take care what you say! You old hypocrite!"

Emma turned suddenly to Philip. "You hear what she called me!"

And Naomi, like an echo, cried, "You heard what filthy names she called me."

Mabelle, terrified, rolled her cowlike eyes, and tried to stifle Jimmy's screams. Philip did not even turn. He felt suddenly sick.

Naomi was saying, "If I hadn't all the work to do. . . . If I had the right kind of husband—"

Emma interrupted. "I took care of my child and did all the work as well. I never complained or made excuses."

"You didn't have twins. . . . Sometimes my back fairly breaks. Oh, if I had the right kind of husband, I wouldn't be in your dreary old house!"

Emma turned again, "Philip . . . Philip. . . ."

But Philip was gone. She saw him, hatless and without an overcoat, running through the snow that had begun to come down slowly and softly as a white eiderdown.

3

He only stopped running when he grew so weak that he could no longer make an effort. He had gone, without knowing why, in the direction of the Mills, and presently he found himself, with a savage pain just beneath his heart, sitting on the steps of McTavish's undertaking parlors. It was almost dark, and the air was cold and still; he felt it creeping about him as the heat went out of his body. He knew that if he caught cold he would die and suddenly he wanted to live, horribly. It was as if that sickening scene had

in some way released him from the bondage of the
two women. They seemed all at once to belong to
another world in which he played no rôle, a world
strange and horrible and fantastic. Even the twins
did not seem to be his children, but creatures born
somehow of the two women and all they stood for in
his tired mind. They were two squalling tomato-
colored infants in whom he could take no interest—a
judgment sent by fate as a punishment for his own
weakness and indecision. He grew bitter for the first
time and out of the bitterness there was born a new
strength.

Sitting there in the softly falling snow, he resolved
to go his own way. He couldn't desert Naomi and
his children, but he could tell her that he was through
with her once and for all. And he saw suddenly the
whole sickening depth of the tangle—that it was her
fault no more than his, that she had suffered as much
as himself, that perhaps in the end she would suffer
more, because (he knew it with a kind of disgust) she
loved him with all her soul and body.

Beating his arms against his body, he rose and
turned the handle of the door. McTavish was inside,
alone, sitting by the stove. At the sound of the handle
turning, he looked up and grinned.

"Hello, Philip," he said, and then quickly, "What
the hell are you doing out without a coat or hat?"

Philip grinned, and the very grin hurt his face, as
if it had been frozen by the cold. "I came out in a
hurry . . . I wanted to borrow a coat and hat off
you."

McTavish rose and stretched his great arms, yawning, watching Philip all the while. "Driven out?" he asked at last, with a sharp look.

"Yes," said Philip quietly. "Driven out." He knew suddenly that McTavish understood. He remembered all at once what he had said, "I knew your Ma before you were born. You can't tell me anything about her."

"Here," suddenly the undertaker was pouring whisky. "Here, drink this. I'll get you a coat."

He disappeared into that portion of the establishment where the dead were kept, and returned in a moment bearing a coat and hat. The curious, pungent odor of the place clung to him.

"Here," he said. "It's all I've got. You couldn't wear my clothes. You'd be drowned in them." He laid the coat and hat on a chair by the stove. "These ought to about fit you. They belonged to Jim Baxter, who got bumped off at the grade-crossing while comin' home drunk last week. His wife has never come for 'em. I guess he won't need a coat where he is now." He sat down and took Philip's wrist, feeling the flow of blood. "Feel better now? Your heart seems all right."

"I've always been strong as an ox."

"It ain't the same after you've had a fever."

They sat in silence for a moment and then McTavish asked, "You don't mind wearin' a dead man's clothes?"

"No," said Philip. "No." Anything was better than going back to the slate-colored house.

"When you're in my business, you get over squeamish feelings like that. Dead men and live ones are all the same, except you know the dead ones are mebbe missing a lot of fun."

"No . . . I don't mind, Mr. McTavish." Philip

looked up suddenly. "There's one thing you could do for me. You could send word around to the house that I'm not coming home to-night."

A grin lighted up the big face. "Sure I will. . . . I'll take the word myself." After a pause, "Where will you go?"

"I don't know . . . somewhere." He rose and put on Jim Baxter's coat and hat. "I'm going down to the Flats now."

"Your friends have been raising hell down there."

"Yes . . . that's why I want to go down there now. . . . They'll think I'm dead."

"No . . . they won't think that. That Dago friend . . . Krylenko . . . is that his name? He's been asking for you, and Mary Watts . . . Mary Conyngham she is now, she's been asking, too . . . almost every day."

He must have seen the sudden light come into Philip's eye, for he said suddenly, turning to the window, "There's a good girl . . . a brave one, too."

"Yes," said Philip.

"She's the kind of a wife a man ought to have. There aren't many like her."

"No."

There was a long silence and McTavish said, "They can't win down there . . . everything's against 'em. It'll be over in two months and a lot of 'em never be able to get work within ten miles of a mill ever again."

Philip said nothing. He thrust his hands deep into the pockets of Jim Baxter's coat.

"They tried it too soon. They weren't strong enough. They'll win some day, but the time isn't yet."

Philip looked at him sharply. "I'm on their side.

I know what it's like down there. Nobody else knows, except Irene Shane and Mary Conyngham."

"Does your Ma know it?" asked McTavish, with a grin.

"She must know it. She pretends not to."

"And the Reverend Castor?"

"No . . . I suppose he doesn't."

Philip thanked him abruptly, and went out of the door. When he had gone, McTavish poked up the fire, and sat staring into it. "I'm a regular old woman in some ways," he thought, "trying to meddle in people's affairs. But it needs a whole army to cope with Em."

4

Outside, the world of the Flats lay spread out before him no longer alive with flame and clamor, but still now and cold and dead beneath the softly falling snow. There was no glow of fire; no wheel turned. Only the locomotives shrieked and puffed backward and forward over the shining rails. The streets were alive with people: they stood in little groups in the snow. On the bridge a little knot of them surrounded a speaker unknown to him, who harangued them in three tongues, urging them not to lose faith. At Hennessey's corner the lights cast a glow over the fallen snow—it was really white now that there was no longer any soot—and the tinny piano sent forth its showers of brassy notes into air that was no longer filled with the pounding of gigantic hammers. And the saloon was filled to the doors. Now and then a drunken Pole or Croat fell through the doors into the street. He saw what McTavish meant. They weren't strong enough yet.

They were so weak that Hennessey alone could defeat them: his banging cash register could swallow up their strength. He was a better friend of the Mill owners than all the men brought in to break the strike.

As he followed the path that lay among the garbage heaps by the side of the oily brook, it occurred to him that it was odd how strong he felt on this first sally from the house. He was strong, and suddenly so content that he forgot even the scene from which he had fled, running like a madman. It was as if he gained strength from treading the very soil of the Flats, as if it came to him from the contact of all these human creatures battling for existence. And among them he was lost, alone as he had been on those rare happy hours at Megambo when he had gone off into the jungle at the peril of his life. The snow fell all about him, silently, into the oil-muffled brook.

Crossing a vacant lot where the rubbish lay hidden beneath a carpet of snow, he came at last to the familiar doorway which he had not seen since the night six months before when he stood hidden in its shadow listening to the voice of Mary Conyngham. Feeling his way along the dark passageway, smelling of coal-gas and cabbage, he came at last to Krylenko's door. He knocked and the familiar voice called out something in Russian.

Pushing open the door, he saw Krylenko sitting on the edge of his iron bed with his head in his hands. There was no light in the room, but only the reflection of a rubbish fire some one had built in the yard outside the house. For a moment Philip stood leaning against the door, and when Krylenko did not raise his head, he said, "It's me . . . Philip Downes."

When he saw Krylenko's face, he knew that the strike was lost. Even in the reflected firelight, he seemed years older. He was thin, with deep lines on either side of his mouth.

"Oh, it's you, Feeleep. . . . I thought it was the old woman."

He rose and put a match to the gas and then peered closely into Philip's face, with the look of a man waking from a deep sleep.

"It's you. . . . Sit down."

Philip knew the room well. It was small and square, with no furniture save a bed, two pine chairs and a washstand. Above the bed there was a shelf made by Krylenko himself to hold the dangerous books that Irene Shane and her mother had given him . . . John Stuart Mill and Karl Marx and a single volume of Nietzsche.

"And how do you feel . . . huh?" asked Krylenko, seating himself once more on the bed.

"All right. Look at me."

"Kind-a skinny."

"You, too."

"Yeah! Look at me!" Krylenko said bitterly. "Look at me. . . . A bum! A failure! No job! Nothing."

"It's not as bad as that."

"It will be." He looked up. "Did yuh pass Hennessey's place?"

"Yes."

"Well, you see what it is . . . trying to make a lot of pigs fight. All they want is to quit work and get drunk. That's all it means to them."

"It's not over yet."

"It will be . . . I'm gonna fight it to the end. They're startin' to operate the B chain to-night . . . a lot of niggers from the South that ain't organized." He got up and went over to the window, standing with his back to Philip. "We can make trouble for another month or two and then I'm finished, and me . . . I'm out of a job for good . . . down . . . on the blacklist. You know what that means."

It was an eloquent back, big, brawny and squared with defiance, despite all the tone of despair in his voice. The rumpled, yellow hair fairly bristled with vitality and battle. Philip thought, "He's not done yet. He's going on. He's got something to believe in . . . to fight for. For him it's only begun. He's got a giant to fight . . . and I'm fighting only two women."

Suddenly Krylenko turned. "Look," he said. "Look," pointing out of the window. "That's what they're up to now. They've bought up all the loose houses and they're turning the strikers out in the snow . . . on a night like this, God damn 'em. Look!"

Philip looked. Across the street in the falling snow lay a pitiful heap of odds and ends of some Slovak household . . . pots, kettles, battered chairs, blankets, a mattress or two. A woman and four small children, none of them more than six, stood drearily watching.

"And it's a hell of a thing to do. . . . A free country, hell! It belongs to a lot of crooked rich men." Suddenly, he thrust his big fist through the pane of glass and the tinkling fragments fell into the snow in the yard. "We're finished this time . . . but we've only begun!" He laughed. "The windows don't matter. They bought this house, too. A lot of niggers are movin' in to-morrow."

The blood was running from his cut knuckles and he bound them round silently with a red cotton handkerchief. Presently, he said, "You're looking for your paints and pictures. . . . They ain't here. . . . Mrs. Conyngham took 'em away."

"Mrs. Conyngham!"

"Yeah. . . . She came and got 'em herself. She's fixed up a place for you up at Shane's Castle . . . in the stable. I was to tell you and I forgot. She did it when she heard about the Mills buyin' up this row of houses. It's in the stable and you're to go up there whenever you want. There's a stove and everything."

He spoke in agitation, as though the paints, the pictures, were nothing compared to his own troubles. A little thing, of no use! Suddenly he turned, "And you, what are you goin' to do?"

"When?"

"Now you're finished, too. They've done with you, too. You're one of 'em. Don't forget that."

Yes, that was a thing he hadn't thought of. There must be people in the Town who hated him the way they hated the Shanes, and perhaps Mary Conyngham . . . as renegades, traitors. And while he waited there in the squalid room, watching Krylenko sitting with his head buried in his hands, there came to him for the first time a curious, intoxicating sense of satisfaction in being one of that odd little band—Krylenko, the saintly Irene, the dying old woman in Shane's Castle, and Mary Conyngham. The wind had begun to rise, and with it little gusts of snow swirled in through the broken window. He thought suddenly,

"We are the leaven in the lump." He was not quite certain what he meant by that; he only knew that the lump was concerned vaguely with that mass of materialism and religion which made the character of the Town . . . a religion tamed and shopworn and subdued to commercial needs, a faith worn down to the level of convenience. Groping, it seemed to him that he was beginning to emerge at last, to be born as a soul, an individual.

"I mean to paint," he said suddenly.

"That won't feed you . . . and your children."

"No . . . I'll manage somehow." Nothing seemed impossible . . . nothing in the world . . . if he could only shake himself free. He thought, without any reason, "Krylenko is no more one of the mill workers than I am. If he were really one of them, he would be drunk now in Hennessey's place. There is something which sets him apart. . . . He isn't one of them either. He's as unhappy as I am."

Looking up, he asked suddenly, "And what about Giulia? Are you going to marry her?"

Without raising his hand, Krylenko answered, "No . . . that's finished now. If we'd won, it would have been all right. But now . . . it's no good . . . I'll be nothing but a tramp and bum."

He spoke in a strange, dead voice, as if he were saying, "It's a snowy night," as if something had died in him.

"No . . ." he repeated. "That's all finished. But you . . . you've got everything before you . . . and that girl . . . Mrs. Conyngham. . . ." He looked up suddenly, "She has faith in you . . . that's something." He looked at the great, nickeled watch he carried. "I've gotta go now. I've got to see about putting up tents for all of 'em who've been thrown out of their houses. It's a hell of a night to live in a tent." Rising, he took up his black felt hat. "What are you going to do?"

Philip wakened suddenly out of a haze of thought. "Me! I want to stay here to-night."

"Here in this room?"

"Yes."

"All right. . . Turn in there." He pointed to the rickety iron bed. "I'll be out most of the night, gettin' coal and blankets. See you later."

When he had gone, Philip felt suddenly ill again, and hopelessly weary. He lay down on the bed wrapped in Jim Baxter's overcoat, and in a moment fell asleep.

At two, when Krylenko finally returned, there was a little drift of snow by the broken window. Going over to the bed, he stood for a time looking down at Philip, and then, with a great gentleness, he lifted him, and, drawing out the blanket, laid it over him, carefully tucking in the edge to keep out the cold. When he had finished, he lay down, keeping well over to the edge in order not to disturb Philip. It was all done with the tenderness of a strong man fostering the weak, of a great, clumsy father protecting a little boy.

5

In the morning Philip awakened to find Krylenko already gone. It was still snowing as he went out into the empty street and made his way toward the shed where there was always hot coffee for the strikers and their families. He stood there among them, drinking his coffee and feeling the old sense of satisfaction of being in a world stripped bare to those things which lay at the foundations of life. This was solid, with a rawness that bit into the soul. He took out a pencil and on a bit of newspaper began to sketch fragments of the scene about him—a Croat woman who was feeding coffee to her three small children out of a clumsy teacup, a gigantic, bearded Slovak and his wizened, tubercular wife, a baby wrapped in the ragged remains of a pair of overalls, a thin, white, shivering girl, with the face of a Madonna. They were simply sketches, reduced to the very skeletons of drawing, yet they were in a way eloquent and moving. He felt intoxicatingly sure of his hand, and he saw all at once that they were the best things he had ever done. Set down on the face of columns of printing, they caught the cold misery and the dumb bravery of these puzzled, wretched people, suffering silently in the midst of a hostile, foreign country. Looking at the sketches, he saw that by some ironic chance he had chosen to draw directly upon an editorial condemning them. He began to read. The fragment was torn, and so had no beginning. ". . . sacred rights of property must be protected against the attacks of men little better than brutes who have come, infected with poison of socialism and anarchy, to undermine the institutions of a great, free and glorious nation favored by God. These wretches must be treated as they deserve, without consideration, as beasts bent upon tearing down our most sacred institutions and destroying our God-given prosperity."

It was signed in bold black type with the name

MOSES SLADE. He was quite safe in his attack, thought Philip: foreign-born mill workers had no votes.

A hand touched Philip's shoulder and a voice said, "Give me that." It was Krylenko. "I can use it," he said. "I know just where it belongs."

He gave it to Krylenko without a word.

From the steaming coffee-shed he made his way through a street filled with people and bordered with pitiful little heaps of shabby household goods like that which he had seen from Krylenko's window the night before. He passed Hennessey's place and, crossing the railroad tracks, came within the area of the Mills. It was silent here. Even the trolleys had ceased to run since one car had had its windows shattered. Beyond this he came to the great iron fence that shut in the park of Shane's Castle. At the gates he turned in, following the drive that ran between rows of dead and dying Norway spruce up to the house that crowned the hill. It was silent in the park and the falling snow half veiled the distant gables and odd Gothic windows of the big house. Among the dead trees it occurred to him that there was a peace here which did not exist elsewhere in the whole Town. It was an enchanted place where a battered old woman, whom he had seen but once or twice, lay dying.

Following the drive, he passed the wrought-iron portico and the little cast-iron Eros who held a ring in his outstretched hand and served as a hitching-post. The towering cedars that gave the place a name— Cypress Hill—which all the world had long ago forgotten, loomed black and melancholy against the sky. And, turning the corner, he came suddenly within sight of the stables.

Before the door an old negro swept away the falling snow with a worn and stubby broom. He did not hear the approach of Philip, for he was deaf and the snow muffled the sound of footsteps. It was only when Philip said "Good-morning" that he turned his head and, grinning, said, "You must be Mr. Downes."

"Yes."

"The room's all ready for you."

The old man, muttering to himself, led the way. At the top of the stairs, he said, "If I'd knowed you was a-comin' I'd a-had a fire."

The place was all swept and in order and in one corner stood all the things which Mary Conyngham had carried there from Krylenko's room. The sight of them touched him with emotion, as if something of Mary herself clung to them. He wanted to see her more than he wanted anything in the world. He stood looking out of the window while the old nigger waited, watching him. He was sure that in some way she could wipe out the sickening memory of that awful scene. The window gave out over the Mills, which lay spread out, cold and desolate and silent, save for the distant K section, where smoke had begun to drift from the chimneys. He would paint the scene from this window, in all its dreary bleakness—in grays and whites and cold blues, with the faintest tinge of pink. It was like a hell in which the fires had suddenly burned to cold ashes. No, he must see Mary. He had to see her. He couldn't go on like this. It wasn't possible for any human creature to be thirsty for so long— thirsty for peace and honesty and understanding.

He began to see himself in the mawkish light of one who suffered and was put upon, and what had been impossible before began in the light of self-pity to seem possible.

He had (he knew) to go back to the slate-colored house. Turning, he said to the old nigger, "I'm coming back," and then halting, he asked, "How's Mrs. Shane?"

"She ain't no better, sir. She's dying, and nothin' kin save her." Suddenly the black face lighted up. "But Miss Lily's come back. She came back last night."

"Yes?"

"You don't know Miss Lily, mebbe."

"No. . . . I've seen her years ago riding through the Town."

"Then you don't know what she's like. . . . The old Missie can die now that Miss Lily's come home. She jus' couldn't die without seein' Miss Lily."

Philip scarcely heard him. He was thinking about his own troubles, and Lily Shane was a creature who belonged to another world whose borders would never touch his own. Even as a boy, looking after her as she rode in the mulberry victoria up Park Avenue, it never occurred to him that he would ever come nearer to her. There was something magnificent about her that set her apart from all the others in the Town. And there was always the wicked glamour that enveloped one who, it was whispered, had had a child out of wedlock and then declined to marry its father.

How could Lily Shane ever touch the world of Uncle Elmer and Naomi and Emma and Mabelle? No, she did not exist for him. She was like one of the actresses he had followed furtively along Main Street as a boy, because a mysterious, worldly glamour clung to those ladies who appeared in town one night and disappeared the next into the great world. No creature could have been more remote than these coryphées from the slate-colored house and the prayer-meetings of the Reverend Castor.

6

It was the Reverend Castor himself who greeted Philip on the doorstep when he reached home at last. Philip would have avoided him, but the clergyman was coming down the path as he turned into it and so there was no escape.

He greeted Philip with a smile, saying, "Well, it's good to see you about again, my boy. We had a bad time over you . . . thought you weren't going to make the grade."

Philip grinned. "I'm not so easy to be rid of." He felt a sudden refreshing sense of superiority over the preacher, strange in all his experience. It was simply that he had no longer any awe of him as a man of God.

The Reverend Castor coughed and answered, "Oh! My dear boy. We didn't want to be rid of you. That's the last thing. . . ." He protested nervously and added, "I just dropped in for a moment to see how your wife was doing . . . and the twins. You ought to be proud, my boy, of two such fine babies . . . two. Most people are thankful for one."

"I would have been, too."

"You don't mean you aren't delighted with what God has sent you?"

"No . . . of course not . . . I was only making a

joke." It hardly seemed honest, Philip thought, to give God the credit for the twins.

"I suppose we'll be having Mrs. Downes back with us in the choir soon. . . . Since Mrs. Timpkins has moved to Indianapolis I've asked your wife to be the leader and the librarian of the music."

"Yes . . . she ought to be back soon. She seems strong again."

There was an awkward silence, and the Reverend Castor's kindly blue eyes turned suddenly aside. He started to speak and then halted abruptly and seized Philip's hand a second time. "Well, good-by. I must be off."

He was gone quickly, and for a moment Philip stood looking after him, puzzled by his strange, nervous manner. He was sorry for this poor man, whom he had always disliked. It was a sorrow he could not explain, save that his life must be a hell with a wife like his, and all the women of the parish on his neck. He did his duty, the Reverend Castor. He never shirked. It was good of him to call on Naomi. She would like such attention from the head of her church. It would bring back to her, Philip thought, some of the old glory and importance that had waned steadily since the night they had got down from the train, shivering, and fearful of what lay before them.

And she would be pleased at being asked to lead the choir and take care of the music. It was odd what little things brought happiness to her. She had need of the little things, for he meant to hurt her. He was certain now that it was the only way out. It would be easier for her to face the truth.

He found her sitting in the parlor where the

Reverend Castor had left her. She was dressed for the first time since the twins were born, and she had been crying. As he entered, she came over to him and, putting her arms about his neck, pressed her head against Jim Baxter's overcoat, and said, "I'm ashamed, Philip . . . I want to die. I couldn't help it yesterday. It's the way I feel! I feel so tired."

The whole action disturbed him horribly. She had never done such a thing before; she had never done more than kiss him chastely. He freed himself and, still holding her hands, said, "I understand. It's all over now and I understand."

She began to cry again helplessly, pitifully. "You'll forgive me? You'll forgive me?"

"There's nothing to forgive. I understand it." He pushed her gently into a chair, and sat down beside her, silently, wondering how he could bring himself to say what he *had* to say.

"It's because I'm so unhappy, Philip. . . . I've been unhappy ever since we left Megambo . . . ever since that Englishwoman stopped there. I wish to God we'd never seen her."

"Let's not think about her. She had nothing to do with it."

"And it's so awful in this dreary house. I'm nothing here, Philip. . . . I'm less than a hired girl. Your Ma hates me. . . ." He tried to speak, but she cried out passionately, "I can't go on living here . . . I can't . . . I can't."

As he sat there, all his horror of scenes, of that wretched scene in the same room the evening before, swept over him. It was like a physical sickness rising into his throat and choking him. He was confused, too, with a sense of impotent rage.

"And after you ran away she told Mabelle she was never to enter the house again. . . . Now I haven't any one."

No, she hadn't any one, but she didn't know yet how alone she really was.

"Naomi," he said quietly. "Naomi . . . listen to me . . . try to control yourself."

"Yes. . . . Yes. . . . I'm trying to." Her pale, homely face was even paler with weeping. Her eyes were swollen beneath the transparent lashes and her nose was red.

"Naomi . . . would you like to have a house of your own?"

"Oh, Philip . . . yes."

"I don't mean a whole house, but a place to live . . . two or three rooms where you'd be away from my mother."

"Yes . . . yes. I'd do better. I'd take care of things . . . if I had a chance in my own place. Oh, Philip—if you'd only be kind to me."

He stroked her hand suddenly, but it was only because he pitied her. "I try to be kind, Naomi."

"You've been so hard to me . . . just like a stone— ever since we left Megambo. Oh, I knew it . . . I knew even when. . . ." She broke off suddenly, without finishing. Philip looked away, sick with misery. He pitied her, but he could not love her. She went on and on. "Out there I had something to live for . . . I had my work. I loved it. It was the only life I'd ever known. It was everything. And here . . . there's nothing. I don't know how to live here."

"There are the children," he said in a quiet voice.

"Yes . . . but that's not what I mean. It's my soul I'm thinking of. It's rotting away here. . . ."

"Mine was rotting at Megambo." She did not answer him, and he said, "There's church work to do, and now Reverend Castor wants you to lead the choir."

"But it's not the same, and they're all jealous of me . . . all those women . . . jealous because I'm more important because I've been a missionary, and jealous because Reverend Castor shows me favors. Oh, I know. I don't belong here, and they don't want me here. Oh, I don't know what's to become of me!"

There was a long silence, in which they sat there, dumbly trying to find some way out of the hopeless muddle, trying to patch together something which was now in tatters, if it had ever existed at all. Philip's thin jaw was set in that hard, stubborn line that made even his mother afraid.

"Naomi," he said presently, "I'll get you a place to live. It won't be much, for I haven't much money, but you'll be free . . . to do what you please. Only . . . only, Naomi . . . I . . . I . . ." Suddenly, his head fell forward, and he buried his face in his hands. In a voice that was hardly audible he said, "I don't want to live with you any longer. It's . . . it's all over."

For a long time there was no sound in the room, save the ticking of the great onyx clock beneath the picture of Jason Downes. Naomi didn't even sob; but presently she said, in a voice like the voice of a deaf person, "Philip, you mean you're going to leave me?"

"No," he said slowly. "No . . . it's not that exactly. I shan't leave you. I'll come and see you every day and the children—only I won't sleep in the house. I'm going to sleep where I work."

In the same dead voice she asked, "You're not going back to the Mills?"

"No, I'm not going back to the Mills . . . they wouldn't have me now. I'm going to paint. . . ."

"Pictures?"

"Yes . . . pictures. That's what I've always wanted to do and now . . . now, nothing can stop me." There was in his voice a sudden cold rasp, as of steel, which must have terrified her. He thought, "I've got to do it, if I'm to live. I've got to do it."

She said, "But you could have a good congregation. You could preach."

"No, that's the last thing I could do. I'm through with all that."

"Oh, my God! Oh, my God!"

He raised his head, and saw that she was biting her handkerchief. "Naomi," he said. "Naomi," and the sound of her name seemed to precipitate a sudden climax. She fell on her knees and beat them with her fists.

"You won't do that, Philip. You can't . . . you can't leave me for everybody to mock at. Say that you won't . . . I was wrong in the beginning, but now I'll do anything. I'll lie down and let you walk over my body!"

"Naomi," he said. "Please! For God's sake!"

"Oh, don't you see! It's different now . . . I love you. Don't you see that makes it different?"

"It can't make it different, Naomi. I can't pretend what isn't true . . . it's a thing a man can't do."

Suddenly she stopped sobbing and looked up at him,

her face all white and contorted. "You can't say that! You can't mean it! It isn't true!"

"It's true, Naomi. I can't help myself. I wish to God I could!"

"And you didn't love me . . . even . . . even then?"

He made a heroic effort. "No . . . not even then."

She flung herself on the floor, pressing her face against the carpet, moaning and moaning. Kneeling down, he picked her up bodily and laid her on the sofa. Bending over her—

"Naomi . . . listen to me. It's not my fault. It's not yours. It's all a muddle. Nobody's to blame."

Then she sat up suddenly. "Yes, there is. It's your mother who's to blame. She made me marry you. It all began with that. I didn't want to . . . I didn't want to marry any one, but I wanted to have a mission of my own. She did it. She's to blame, and now she hates me. She thinks I've stolen you from her."

She buried her face in the cushions and lay sobbing. After a time, Philip said, "Naomi . . . listen to me. You didn't steal me from her."

"Who did then?" said Naomi's muffled voice.

"I don't know. It just happened. I suppose it's one of the things that happen in life. I've grown up now. I've grown up since we went to Megambo. That's all. I know my own mind now."

"Oh, you're hard, Philip . . . harder than flint." She sat up slowly. "I'll do anything for you. You can wipe your feet on me. I can't let you go now . . . I can't . . . I can't!" She began suddenly to laugh. "I'll do anything! I'll prove to you I can keep house as well as your mother. I'll show you how I can care for the children. They're your children, too. I'll learn to cook . . . I'll do anything!"

He did not answer her. He simply sat staring out of the window like an image carven of stone. And he was saying to himself all the while, "I can't yield. I daren't do it. I can't—not now." And all the while he felt a kind of disgust for the nakedness of this love of Naomi's. It was a shameful thing. And during all their life together he had thought her incapable of such love.

She kept moaning and saying, over and over again, "I've got nothing now. I'm all alone . . . I've got nothing now."

He rose, and laid a hand on her shoulder. "I'm going now, Naomi. I'm not going to the restaurant. I'll come back this afternoon. It'll be all right. We'll work it out somehow."

She looked up at him. "You've changed your mind?"

"No, I don't mean that. No, it's better this way."

"I'll show you, Philip, what a good wife I can be."

He picked up his hat, Jim Baxter's hat, and suddenly he thought, "The old Philip is dead—as dead as Jim Baxter. I've dared to do it."

Aloud he said, "Let's not talk any more now. I'll be back in an hour or two when you feel better."

Then he went away, and outside the house, among the lilacs, he was suddenly sick.

7

He found a tiny flat of three rooms over a drugstore halfway up the hill from the railway station. It had been occupied by the family of a salesman who traveled for a house which manufactured false teeth. He had been promoted to a western territory where, with the great boom in the silver mines, the market for gold teeth had risen enormously.

He was a little fat man, with enormous black mustaches, all aglow with his promotion. "It's the best gold tooth territory in America," he told Philip.

The apartment rented for thirty dollars a month. The bubbling salesman would leave the furniture behind for two hundred and fifty dollars. Philip could move in the day after to-morrow.

He left the place, his whole body warmed by the satisfaction of having acted, of having done something definite. But the thing was not settled yet, because his mother still remained to be told.

He found her in the kitchen of the restaurant, superintending the preparation of mince-meat according to a recipe of her own which eliminated all intoxicating liquors. Standing over the negress who did the work, she was the essence of vigor and authority, her face crimsoned by the heat of the place, her hair all in disorder.

"Ma," he said to her. "I have something I want to discuss with you."

After bidding the negress wait until she returned, she followed him quickly, surprised and troubled by the look in his eye and the set of his jaw. The talk took place at the table behind the screen where Moses Slade came every day to eat.

"It's about Naomi, Ma . . . I've taken some rooms for her to live in. She won't trouble you any longer. We'll move out on Tuesday."

She looked at him for a moment in astonishment.

"But, Philip," she said, "you ought to have consulted me. You mustn't do that. We can't even think of it."

"The rent is paid. I've bought furniture."

"Where did you get the money?"

"I used what Grandpa left me."

"I thought you'd pledged the interest on that to the mission."

"I've taken it back. I took it back before I was sick."

She didn't say anything for a long while. She saw suddenly that he was changed, more hardened even than she had feared. He didn't even come to her any longer for advice. He had shut her out altogether. At last she said, "But, Philip, what will people think—when I've a house big enough for you all?"

"I don't care any longer what people think. I can't go through any more scenes like yesterday. Besides, a man has a right to his own house."

"But, Philip . . . my house is your house. I've worked all these years and sacrificed. . . . Oh, you don't know what it's meant sometimes. I wouldn't even let Uncle Elmer help me—so that you'd have the house for your own. It wasn't for myself. . . . I could have got along somehow."

He looked away from her at the mustard-pot in the center of the table. "You know that you can't get on with Naomi—and she hates living in your house."

"I can try . . . we can both try. If only she'd take a little interest and not make the place into a pig-stye."

"You know she won't change."

"Philip, I'll do anything . . . I'll put up with

Naomi . . . I won't say a word, only don't leave me now after all the years when I'm an old woman."

She saw the stubborn jaw set in a hard line. The sight of it stirred a sudden, turbulent emotion: it was his father's jaw over again, terrifying in its identity. What had she done to deserve such treatment from these two men to whom she had given up all her life without once a thought of herself? She had worked for them, sacrificed. . . .

Philip was saying, "It won't make any difference. Even if you and Naomi never spoke to each other. You'd be hating each other all the time. Don't you see? That's what I can't stand."

She reached over and touched his hand. "Philip . . . once you used to come to me with everything, and now . . . now you treat me like a stranger . . . me, your own mother. Why don't you come to me? I want to share your life, to be a part of it. It's all I live for. You're all I've got."

He felt her trying to capture him once more. What she said was true . . . you couldn't deny it. She had given her whole life to him. Every word she spoke hurt him.

"I don't know, Ma. Nothing has happened except maybe that I'm grown up now. I'm a man. I've got to decide things for myself."

It was that hard, brutal jaw which she couldn't overcome. It had thwarted her always. With Jason, when his jaw was set thus, it was as if his heart had turned to stone.

"Where did you go last night?"

He told her, and the answer frightened her. In the

Flats, in a Dago's boarding-house, her son had passed a night.

"Where did that coat come from?"

"It belonged to Jim Baxter, who was killed at the grade-crossing last week. I borrowed it from McTavish."

"So you've been seeing him."

"Yes, he told you I wouldn't come home, didn't he?"

"Yes," she said, with a sudden flash of anger. "Yes . . . he told me. I wish you wouldn't see so much of him, Philip. He's a wicked man."

He made no response to this sudden, feeble sally of the old authority. He had, she discovered with awe, that old trick of his father's—of not answering in an argument unless he had something to say. It was an unfair method, because it always kept the argument upon the level of reason, excluding all the force of the emotions.

"And I'm not coming home any more to sleep, Ma. That's all finished."

He must have seen the look of fear in her eyes. It was that look he had seen there whenever, for a moment, she seemed to lose control of that solid world she had built up.

"But, Philip . . . it's your house . . . your own home. You've never had any other." He said nothing, and she asked, "Where are you going to sleep?"

Slowly, and then carefully, so that it would hurt her as little as possible, he told her about the stable at Shane's Castle, and his plan of painting. She listened, half believing that she could not be in her right mind, that what she heard was only part of a nightmare. She kept interrupting him, saying, "But, Philip, you never told me . . . I didn't know," and when he had finished, she said abruptly, "That wasn't the plan I had for you, Philip; I've been talking with Reverend Castor and he thinks we could arrange to get you a good congregation."

"No . . . that's all finished. It's no use even talking of it."

She went on, ignoring him. "And if that didn't please you, I thought . . . well, you could take the restaurant because, well . . ." she looked away from him, "you see, I'm thinking of getting married."

She saw his face grow red with anger. "Not to that humbug, Moses Slade!"

"Yes, Philip. But it's wrong of you to call him a humbug. He's a distinguished man, a good man, who stands for the best in the community."

"He's a hypocrite and a humbug!"

An uncontrollable rage took possession of him. It was impossible that he was to have Moses Slade, the humbug who had written that editorial about the strike, for a stepfather. No, it was outlandish, too impossible, that a good woman like his mother should be taken in by that lecherous old rip.

"Philip," she was saying. "You don't understand. I've been alone always . . . except for you—ever since your father died. It would be a good marriage, a distinguished marriage, and I wouldn't be alone in my old age."

"You couldn't marry him. You couldn't marry a fat old man like that."

He fancied that he saw her wince. "It isn't a question of love, Philip, at our age. It's companionship.

I'm very fond of him, and he's been thoughtful—so thoughtful all the time you were sick."

"It's disgusting!"

It was odd, what had happened—that he found himself for the first time in his life taking a high hand with his mother. It was an intoxicating sensation.

"If I give him up, I'll be giving up a great opportunity for good. As a Congressman's wife, there's no end to the things I could accomplish. . . ." She began to cry. "But I'll give him up . . . I'll give him up if you won't turn your back on your poor mother. I'd do anything for you, Philip. You're all I've got, and I hoped for so much—to see you one of the great men of the church, a Christian leader, fighting on the side of God."

"It's no good, Ma. I won't go back to that."

One of the waitresses appeared suddenly from behind the screen. "Mrs. Downes . . ." she began.

"Go away! Go away! I'll talk to you later."

The girl disappeared.

"And that isn't all, Ma. I'm not going to live with Naomi any more. I'm through with that. I meant what I said when I was sick."

"Philip—listen to me, Philip!"

"No . . . I'll come to see her and the children. But I'm through."

"What will people think? What will they say?"

"You can tell them I've got a night job. . . . Nobody'll know, except Aunt Mabelle, where Naomi is going to live. Nobody will see me come or go. It's in Front Street."

"Front Street! Why, that's on the edge of the Flats! You can't do that!"

He looked at her for a long time in despairing silence. "My God, Ma! Can't you see? Can't you understand? From now on, I'm going to stand on my own. I'm going to work things out. I've got to get out of this mess. . . . I've *got* to."

He rose abruptly, and put on his hat.

"Philip," she asked, drying her eyes, "where are you going now?"

"I'm going to buy blankets for myself."

"Philip, listen to me. For God's sake, listen! Don't ruin everything. I've a right to something. I'm your mother. Doesn't that mean anything?"

He turned for a moment hesitating, and then quickly said, "Ma, don't talk like that, it isn't fair."

Without another word, he put on his hat and hurried out of the restaurant.

Once outside, the cold air cleared his head, and he was thankful that he had been hard as a stone. Again he was sorry for Emma in a vague, inexplicable fashion; she could never understand what it was that made him hard. She couldn't see why he had to behave thus.

"I wish to God," he thought bitterly, "that I'd had a mother who wasn't a fine woman. Life would have been so much easier. And I can't hurt her . . . I can't. I love her."

And suddenly he saw that in all their talk together nothing had really been settled. Nothing had been changed or decided.

8

He went that night to sleep in the room above the stable, and on the following Tuesday Naomi and the twins moved into the three rooms above the drugstore in Front Street. Emma stayed home from the restaurant all day, going and coming to and from the newly established household. She did and thought of everything, so that Naomi in the end gave up, and, sitting on the imitation-tapestry davenport, simply watched her mother-in-law arrange the new household. Mabelle was there, too, with little Jimmy, in the way most of the time, or making suggestions which Emma ignored. She was a creature whose feelings were not easily hurt and all Emma's bitter remarks seemed to have left no trace. When they had left Naomi with the three rooms in order, she even walked home with Emma, dragging the tired and whining Jimmy behind her.

As she hurried through the darkness after Emma's tall, robust form, she panted, "Well, things might go better now. I always think young people ought to start out in a house of their own."

"Yes," said Emma, certain from the remark that Naomi hadn't told Mabelle the whole truth.

"It's funny what a change has come over Philip. He's much nicer than he used to be."

"What on earth do you mean by that, Mabelle?"

Here Jimmy set up a yell—"I don't wanna walk! I wanna be carried!"

"All right, dear, only you mustn't cry. Little men don't cry."

"Well, I do. I'm tired. I don't wanna walk!"

"All right, dear." She bent down and picked up the child. He continued to whine, but at least their progress was not retarded.

"If he were my child, Mabelle," said Emma, "I'd

just leave him sitting on the curb till he got good and ready to walk. I never had any trouble with Philip. He's always been *obedient* and respectful."

"But Jimmy's delicate, and I'd rather carry him than have him whine."

"He's whining in any case," said Emma, acidly.

Mabelle was puffing now beneath her burden and the long steps of Emma. But she managed to say, "What I mean about Philip is . . . that he's more masterful now. He's a man. He's the kind of a man that women have a right to be afraid of."

Emma snorted. "Don't talk such rot, Mabelle. If you'd read less trash."

"It's funny about him taking up with the Shanes."

Naomi *had* told her, then, about the stable. And Mabelle was a sieve: whatever you told her poured right on through. "He hasn't taken up with the Shanes. He's simply using their stable to work in. That's not the same thing. Why, he barely knows them—except that half-crazy old maid, Irene. And he doesn't know the others at all."

"Then it must be that Mary Conyngham. She's friends with them."

"Mary Conyngham!" repeated Emma. "Mary Conyngham! Why, he hasn't seen her in years!" But the shock of the name turned her suddenly thoughtful, so that she walked at a slower pace, mercifully for Mabelle.

"Well, he *might* have seen her," persisted Mabelle. "She's mixed up with Irene Shane's school for the Dagoes and Hunkies. They all belong to the same crowd . . . all thinking they can make something out of a lot of bums." For a moment she was so completely winded that she could not speak. When she recovered her breath, she said, "I remembered the other night that they'd been sweet on each other once."

Still Emma walked furiously in silence, and presently Mabelle said, "Of course, I didn't say anything about her to Naomi. She might be upset just now."

"No," said Emma, "and don't say anything to her about it or to any one else. It's nonsense."

"Well, I didn't know. I was just interested in Philip, and Naomi, and in his queer behavior, and I always find that when a man goes off his head like that, there's a woman about somewhere."

"I forbid you, Mabelle, to speak of it to any one." She halted and took Mabelle by the shoulder. "You understand? That's the way silly talk gets started."

Mabelle was silent as they resumed their way, but presently she said, "That Lily Shane . . . she's come home to see the old woman die."

"They're a bad lot, all of 'em," said Emma, "and I guess she's the Jezebel of the lot."

"I hate to see a good boy like Philip getting mixed up with people like that."

"He's not getting mixed up, I tell you."

"What am I to tell people about him, Em, if they ask me?"

"Tell them that he's going to be an artist. You might say, too, that he has a fine talent, and later he's going to New York to study."

She had thought it all out. There was only one method—"to take the bull by the horns." If Philip wasn't one day to be a bishop, he might be a great artist and paint great religious pictures like the man who did the Sistine Madonna or the Flight into Egypt.

The voice of Jimmy interrupted her thoughts. "Aren't we nearly home? I'm hungry!"

"Yes, dearie. That's your house right there. . . . See the one with the red light in the window?"

"I don't like Aunt Em. I wish she'd go away."

"Shh! Jimmy! Shh! He's tired, Em, that's all— the poor little thing."

They reached the house with the red light in the window, and bade each other good-night.

"Remember what I said," was Emma's final word.

After she left the gate, only one thought occupied the mind of Emma, the thought that it was Mary Conyngham who had stolen Philip from them both— from herself and Naomi. "Mary Conyngham, of course," she told herself. "What a fool I've been not to think of her before! It *would* be like her and her superior ways. The Watts always thought nobody good enough for 'em but the Shanes—that bawdy old woman and her two daughters—one a lunatic and the other a harlot. Yes, Mary Conyngham could carry on to her heart's content there in the Flats, and no one would know of it. The Shanes would only help her. Shane's Castle had been like a bawdy-house in the days when old John Shane was still living."

She was in a savage humor, born partly of her irritation at Naomi's helplessness, and partly of disgust at Mabelle's feeble-minded chatter; and now she had found an object on which to pin it. It was Mary Conyngham who lay at the root of everything: it explained why Mary had stopped her that day to ask about Philip.

"Mabelle," she thought, "is a dangerous woman, going about and saying things like that when she *knows* nothing."

Mabelle was a constructive gossip. Having nothing to keep her occupied, she sat about all day thinking up things, putting two and two together, pinning odd pieces of stories together to construct a whole, but she *did* have (thought Emma) an uncanny way of scenting out scandal; her only fault was that she sometimes told the story before in fact it had happened. She came upon a scrap, the merest suspicion of some dubious story, and presently after days of morbid brooding it reappeared, trimmed and garnished to perfection, with such an air of reality about it that if it wasn't true, it might easily have been.

It was the uncanny faculty of Mabelle's that really troubled Emma. Her suspicion of Mary Conyngham frightened her even while it gave her satisfaction. It occurred to her that Philip was now quite beyond control, as his father had sometimes been. Anything might happen. She dared not think of it. For a moment she felt the quick shadow of foreboding, of some tragedy that lay ahead, beyond the power of anything to prevent.

She shook it off quickly, thinking, "That is nonsense. I can still bring Philip to his senses."

Inside the house, she prepared her own supper, and spent an hour in clearing up her own house, putting from sight every trace of Naomi.

At nine o'clock Moses Slade came to call. He was in a furious temper. He brought with him a labor periodical, called *The Beacon*.

"It was marked," he said, "and sent to me through the mail."

Opening it, he showed her the desecration of his most admired editorial. It was a fragment of the local newspaper, stained and torn, which read, ". . . sacred rights of property must be protected against the attacks of men little better than brutes, etc., etc.," and signed in large black letters MOSES SLADE. On the face of the printing some irreverent hand had made a series of drawings in pencil—a Croat woman feeding her three small children with coffee out of a clumsy tin cup, a gigantic, bearded Slovak and his wizened, tubercular wife, a baby wrapped in the remains of a ragged pair of overalls, a thin, shivering girl with the face of a Madonna. The whole had been photographed and reproduced.

Underneath them was a line which read, "These are the brutes of the Honorable Moses Slade who have endangered our most sacred institutions and destroyed our God-given prosperity." And beside it was a caricature of Slade himself, gross, overdressed, with flowing locks and a leering expression, beneath which was written: "Puzzle—find the beast on these two pages."

He banged the table with his hamlike fist. "By God, I'll find out who did it, and make him pay for his impudence! I'm not a force in this Town for nothing!"

Emma turned faintly pale, but she only said, "It's shameful, I think, Moses, but what can you expect from such people? They have no respect for our institutions . . . our excellent Congressmen."

But she knew well enough who had made the drawing.

9

In the flat in Front Street, Philip put the last chair in place, washed his face and hands at the sink in the kitchen, and went in to look at the sleeping twins. They lay side by side, fat, rosy, healthy children, such as women like Naomi or Mabelle were certain to bear. He was alone in the room, and, after a time, he bent down and touched the fine, soft dark hair that covered their small, round heads. They were like him, and so, he supposed, like his father, with eyes that one day would be the same clear blue. It struck him suddenly that there was something ruthless in the operation of Nature which took no account of all the structure of habits and laws of man. It took no account of the fact that he had never loved Naomi, or that neither of them had really wanted these children. Nature had wanted children, and it did not matter how they were created, so long as the act of creation occurred. All man's ideas of love, of lawful wedlock, of sentimentality, had nothing to do with it. And it was impossible to imagine stronger, healthier children.

He fell to stroking the soft head of the little girl, and, slowly, in her sleep, she stirred and, groping with a fat, pink hand, found one of his fingers, and clutched it tightly. Something in the touch of the soft, plump hand melted him suddenly. She was so soft, so helpless, reaching out trustfully. And for the first time he felt a sudden quick pride and delight. These were *his* children; he knew that he loved them, despite everything, Naomi and his mother and all the trouble he had been through. They were *his* to care for and

protect and set on their way in life. That was a
wonderful thing. When he thought of it, he was frightened; and yet (he reflected) he would perhaps understand far better than most fathers how to help them.
He had learned, he thought, bitterly, by his own blunder-
ing.

The little girl still clung tightly to his finger, and
presently he found himself smiling, without knowing
it. He was, oddly enough, suddenly happy, and conscious that no matter what fate befell him, it was good
to be alive. He wasn't sorry any longer that he had
helped to bring into existence these two fat, funny
little morsels of life. He almost laughed, and then,
bending down, he kissed first one and then the other
on the tops of their round, dark little heads. They
were his: he was a father. And it had happened without his wanting it, almost without his understanding
how it had happened.

He was still bending over them when the door opened
and, with a sense of falling spirits, he heard Naomi
come in. Ever since that horrible day in his mother's
parlor, she had made an effort to dress completely and
neatly, but somehow it was impossible for her to accomplish it entirely. Little wisps of sandy hair fell
down over the back of her high tight collar. Her
white petticoat, showing itself an inch or two below
her skirts, dragged on the floor. There was a smudge
of the dust left behind by the dental salesman's wife
on one side of her face. She might set herself in order
a dozen times a day, but always, in some mysterious
way, she was in disarray. At Megambo, it hadn't
made any difference: in a place like that such things
were lost in the whole cataclysm of disorder. But here

in a civilized place, it was different. It was as if Naomi could not cope with the problems of decent living.

At the sound of the opening door, Philip straightened up quickly, as if ashamed to be found thus, caressing his children. But Naomi had seen him, and smiled—an odd, twisted, pitiful smile, which was like a knife turned in his flesh, for behind it lay a whole regiment of ghosts, of implications. It was as if he saw suddenly what happiness there might be in life, if he himself had been different, if Naomi had been a different woman, if he had only been able to love her. He couldn't change: he saw again how ruthless a thing Nature could be. Some one had meddled with her plans, and so the misery resulted. It was not that he thought these things: the whole impression happened far more quickly than any process of thought. It was a sudden, pitiful flash of illumination. What hurt him most was the faint hint of bitterness in her smile, a hint almost of mockery, a shadow which had crossed her pale, freckled face without her knowing it. But until now, he hadn't thought her capable of suffering in that way.

It frightened him by making him feel weak and yielding.

Perhaps if she had been a more clever woman, she could in that moment have changed the whole course of his life. Long afterward when he thought of the scene (and it always remained one of his clearest memories of her) he saw that it *could* have been done. But then he saw that if she had been a more clever woman he might have loved her in the beginning.

She came over and stood by his side. "What are we

to call them, Philip? We've never even spoken of it."
She said it in a flat voice, as if they had been puppies or
kittens, and not children—*his* children—at all.

"I don't know."

"I've been thinking about the girl. Your mother
would like to call her Emma, but I'd like it if you'd
call her Naomi."

He knew before she had finished what she had meant
to say, and he knew, too, that he hated both names.
To go on for the rest of his life, even as an old man,
calling his child "Emma" or "Naomi". . . .

"She's your child, too, Naomi. You have a choice
in the matter."

"I wanted you to be pleased." There was a humbleness in her voice which made him feel ill.

"And the boy—have you thought of him?"

"I want to call him Philip, of course."

(No, he couldn't do that: it was like wishing them
bad luck.)

"No, I hate the name of Philip. You can call the
girl Naomi. You bore her, and you've more of a right
to name her than Ma has. But—no, we won't call the
boy Philip. We'll think of something else."

"I'd like to have her called Naomi . . . and then
you'd think of me sometimes, Philip."

He looked at her sharply. "But I do think of you.
Why should you say that?"

"Oh, I don't know . . . just in case anything happened to me. That's why I'd like to call him Philip."

"No . . . no . . . any other name."

He took up his hat. "What are you going to do
with the twins on Sundays and choir practice nights?"

"I don't know. I'd thought of asking Mabelle to

stay with them . . . but she lives such a long way off. Maybe I'd just better give it up."

"No, you mustn't do that. I'll come and stay with them. I'd like to."

"You don't mind my leading the choir, Philip?"

"No, of course not."

"Because I want you to be pleased. I want it to be a new start now, here in this new house."

He didn't answer, and after an awkward pause, she said, "I wouldn't go at all, but I think Reverend Castor needs me. He's got so many worries. Yesterday when I was talking to him, he began all at once to cry . . . not out loud, but the tears just came into his eyes. His wife's an awful woman. He's been telling me about her. And now that Mrs. Timpkins has moved away, there's no one to take the choir who knows anything about music."

"Of course, go by all means."

He was glad for two reasons, because he knew she liked the importance of leading the choir, and because he would have these evenings alone with the children— *his* children—who had been born in reality as he stood looking down at them a moment before.

"Good-night, Naomi," he said abruptly.

"Philip. . . ."

"Yes."

"Philip, you won't stay?"

"No, Naomi. . . . It wouldn't look right."

There was a pause.

"Sometimes you're like your mother, Philip."

He went out and in his agitation found himself half-way down the flimsy pine stairway before he remembered his overcoat. When he returned and opened the door of the little flat, he heard the sound of sobbing, a horrible choked sound, coming from the bedroom. She had not made a scene. She had not wept until he was gone, for she was trying to please him.

10

It was a clear night, and very cold, when the moonlight painted the snow and the black houses of the Flats with a luminous blue light. As he walked, the hard-packed snow creaked and whined beneath his heels. The stars, for all their brilliance, seemed infinitely remote. As he walked, a little cloud of frozen breath trailed behind him.

By the railroad-tracks and in the narrow streets that bordered them, the Flats were empty. The houses stood silent and black. The fires, the little piles of household goods, were gone now, and with them the miserable, shivering women and children. At Hennessey's corner there was the usual blaze of light, the jagged clamor of the mechanical piano, and the sound of drunken voices behind the swinging-doors. The lights, the sounds, hurt him in an inexplicable fashion, filling him with an acute and painful sense of loneliness.

It was an emotion which changed, as he entered the park, to one of vague fear. Inside the rusted gates the park lay frozen and solitary in the brilliant moonlight. The deep shadows were blue along the drive, black where the outline of a dead tree fell across the snow. The bits of statuary—the Venus of Cnidos, the Apollo Belvedere, the cast-iron Cupid—all had little caps and collars of frozen snow. The windows of the big house lay shuttered and dark, save for a room in

the corner where little bars of yellow light filtered out.
It was perhaps the room where Lily Shane sat waiting
for her mother to die.

As he turned the corner on the stable side, there
came to him all at once a feeling that he was not alone
in the park. There were other creatures there, too, not
human perhaps, but the ghosts of all the men and
women who had been there in the gaudy days of the
Castle when the trees were still alive, and the garden
neatly kept, and the stable filled with horses. There
had always been a mystery about the place, and for
him, who had never seen the place while it was alive,
it was a mystery enveloped in a romantic glamour.
He understood suddenly how people are able to invest
a place with the character of their own existence. It
was the wicked old John Shane, dead so long that he
had become a legend, and his dying widow, who owned
this silent frozen park filled with dead trees. . . . It
would still be theirs and theirs alone long after they had
turned to dust, until at last the house was pulled down
and the park buried beneath clamorous steel sheds and
roaring furnaces. And even then . . . as long as
there remained alive one person who remembered them,
the place would be known as Shane's Hill, where once
the Castle stood. It was an odd sort of immortal-
ity. . . .

He saw, too, that the slate-colored house was like
his mother: she had stamped it forever as her own,
and that the huts at Megambo were oddly like Naomi,
who had been so happy in them. And he saw suddenly why he had hated both places and how in a way
they explained both his mother and Naomi, and the
power they both possessed of making him wretched.

This cold park and the silent house, peopled by creatures that were dead, seemed a dark and sinister place, yet it had, too, a sense of splendor, of barren grandeur, that for more than half a century had dominated the Town. It existed still in the very midst of the clamorous Mills.

The stable was silent, save for the sound of the fat horses tramping in their stalls, and in his room overhead the stove still burned, filling the room with warmth. It was a plain enough room, empty save for the iron cot where he slept, a table, two chairs and his painting materials. Yet for him a pleasant place. He had for the first time in all his life a sense of coming home. It was his; and it suited him with its barren emptiness. It was like the cell of a monk, bare and cold, and free of everything which might distract from a contemplation of the great mystery.

He did not trouble to light the kerosene lamp. The cold moonlight flooded in through the window, casting in black filigrees on the bare floor the shadow of the drooping vines that fell across the panes. Against the walls and ceiling the flames in the belly of the stove cast another pattern, different, outlined of warm and glowing light.

For a long time he stood there, his hands clasped behind him, looking out of the window, seized once more by the enchantment of the beauty with which the night invested all the expanse of the Flats. Far off, under the shadow of one of the seven hills, the flames of the furnaces in the Jupiter plant raised an arc of glowing light. He saw in his imagination all the spectacle that existed there—the bodies of the black men, the dancing shadows cast by the glaring lights, the angry hiss and bubble of boiling white-hot metal. He could smell the curious, pungent odor of burning coke. He saw the movement, the unearthly splendor, the immense energy that filled the whole scene.

Just beneath the hill, the sheds and furnaces lay in black shadows. There were fires there, built by the Mill guards, that burned like the red eyes of giants asleep in the velvety darkness. There was the sudden wild screech of an express locomotive, and a long serpent-like monster, lighted from within like a firefly, rushed through the darkness.

He was glad suddenly to be alone, for the solitude brought him a strange peace like the peace that had come to him at times when he went alone at dawn along the borders of the lake at Megambo. It was the peace of complete aloofness, of detachment from all that troubled him—a mysterious exaltation like death perhaps, in which no one could share. No, not even Mary Conyngham. . . . Mary Conyngham. . . . He found himself repeating the name idly in his brain. Now, in this moment of solitude, even Mary Conyngham did not trouble him. It was as if he were free suddenly of his body and existed only as a spirit.

Presently, he put his hand across his eyes, pressing them with a kind of anguish. He knew that he believed again; he knew that he had always believed. He had never lost his faith. It was only that until now he had followed a bogus God. It was only that he didn't believe in that harsh, commonplace, ugly God of Naomi and Emma and the Reverend Castor. It was a different sort of God—One who was concerned with a kind of beauty and splendor which they did not know . . . the beauty of all that scene outspread below him, of that savage energy which cast a distant glow against the sky; it was the beauty of those two children, his children, called into existence because He willed it, the sinister beauty of the park and of people like old John Shane and his widow who lived on even after they were dead and dying, the beauty even of that coffee-shed filled with shivering women and children, and the fires in the street. He was the God, too, of those black women pouring the water of the burning lake over the belly of an obscene idol—a God concerned with the whole glowing tragic spectacle of living.

Presently his hands dropped to his side once more, and, looking out of the window, he saw that the park was no longer empty. There was some one there—a woman—walking up and down in the moonlight. She was wrapped in furs and she was no ghost, for in the cold air, the moonlight and the frost of her breath made a little halo about her uncovered head. She was walking round and round the ruined dead English garden, which must have had its own ghosts of lark-spurs and foxgloves and lavender and mint and primulas—all the ghosts of flowers long dead, killed by the soot of the Mills.

And then all at once, he divined who the woman must be. She was Lily Shane, walking in the moonlight.

She turned at last, and, going carelessly through the deep snow, returned to the big, darkened house.

Philip lay down on the iron cot, and toward morning he fell asleep. But in the long hours while he lay there, watching the pattern of warm light on the ceiling, he became aware slowly of a whole new world born of a strange, mystical understanding, that had come to him as he stood by the window in the brilliant moonlight . . . a world which belonged to him alone, which none could intrude upon or destroy. He fell asleep in peace, aware vaguely that for a time he had escaped from Naomi and Uncle Elmer, from Mabelle—even from his own mother.

It was at noon on the following day that old Julia Shane fell into a sleep from which she did not awaken. The old nigger, standing in the snow by the stable door, told him the news. The old man wept like a little child. "It's the end of something, Mr. Downes," he said. "It's all over now, and I expect I ain't got much longer on this earth, myself. It ain't the same no longer."

All that day Philip stayed in the room above the stable, struggling passionately, with his stubborn jaw set like a steel trap, over paints and canvas, trying to capture, while the mood was still on him, the strange things he had seen in the dead park and the desert of silent Mills beyond. But in the end, when it grew too dark to work any longer, there was only a mass of blacks and grays, blues and whites, upon the canvas.

At eight o'clock, he went to the Flats to sit with the twins while Naomi went to choir practice.

11

The choir met in the room of the church which was given over on the Sabbath to "the infant class" of the Sunday School for children under six. It was a large, barren room, with large chromos of Biblical scenes decorating the walls—the soldiers of Moses returning from the Promised Land, Moses smiting the Rock, the same as an Infant being discovered in the Bulrushes by a Princess dressed in garments as gaudy and inaccurate as those of a music-hall Cleopatra, Noah and his family receiving the Dove and Olive Branch. In the center of the room two dozen lilliputian chairs sat ranged in a circle, save on the occasions of choir practice, when a dozen adult chairs were brought in from the main Sunday School room to accommodate members of the choir.

Naomi arrived early, and, admitting herself with the private key that was her badge of office, turned on the gas and seated herself at the upright piano. There was no piano in the flat by the railroads, and she fell at once to playing, in order to recover her old careless facility. She had no sense of music; yet music was to her only what wine is to some temperaments: it served to unlock the doors of the restraining prison which forever shut her in. She played relentlessly in showers of loud, banging notes, heedless of discord and strange harmonies; and the longer she played, the more shameless and abandoned became the character of her playing. To-night she played from a none too sure memory *The Ninety and Nine* and *Throw Out the Life Line* (her favorites) and then *I'm a Pilgrim, I'm a Stranger*, which always made her want to cry, and then with a strong arm and a loud pedal she swept into *Ancient of Days*, which filled her with the strangest, emotional grandeur. There was a splendor in it which made her feel noble and heroic: it filled her with a sense of beauty and power. She saw herself vaguely as a barbarian queen, like Sheba, riding on an elephant, surrounded by guards and servitors. The image in her mind bore a strange resemblance to her memory of a highly painted artificial blonde, clad principally in sequins and crimson satin, whom she had once seen riding an elephant in the circus parade—a lady advertised as "the ten-thousand-dollar beauty." But always when she had finished *Ancient of Days*, and the last note had died away, she was left with a melancholy feeling of depression and a sense of wickedness. The world about her became after one of these musical debauches a sad and unbearable place.

To-night, alone in the bare, unattractive room, she poured into the music all the pent-up emotions of days . . . all her hatred of Emma, her fear of the new life on which she had embarked, but, most of all, that curious passionate half-wicked feeling she had for Philip. Beneath the spell of *Ancient of Days* this emotion for him seemed to become purified and free of all restraint. She poured into the banging, careless chords all the things which she could never bring herself to tell him—how the sight of him standing by the crib had made her feel suddenly ill with warm voluptuous feeling, how there were times when she wanted to lie down before him and beat her head on the floor to show him how she felt, how she wakened out of a sound sleep in the midst of the night with her hands aching to touch his face and his dark hair. In the splendor of the hymn it was as if all those things were realized. For a time she *was* that fantastic, barbaric queen of her imagination and Philip was her lover, dressed like one of the soldiers in the chromo of the return from the Promised Land, and sometimes in an overwhelming wave of wickedness she saw him as she had seen him on the night of the drums, standing half naked by the light of the dying fire.

It was thus that she saw him to-night, and, as if she meant to preserve the wild romantic feeling, she played and sang the whole hymn over again in her loud, flat voice. She was wildly happy, for in the end it seemed that Philip really belonged to her, and that they were alone once more by the lake at Megambo. They weren't even missionaries and Swanson wasn't there. And he loved her.

When she had finished, the spell clung to her until the last chord, held deliberately by the use of the loud pedal, died away, leaving her weak and exhausted, and prey suddenly to the horrible, sickening depression. She let her head fall forward on the piano. She wanted to cry, but she couldn't cry, because people would be coming in at any moment. And suddenly she felt the touch of a hand on her shoulder and a voice saying, "That was splendid, Mrs. Downes! That's the sort of music that will bring them to the Lord!"

It was the Reverend Castor. He had come in quietly, without a sound, and had been sitting there all the while listening to her while she desecrated the sanctity of a hymn with all her fleshly emotions. She tried to gain control of herself, and, without looking up, mopped her eyes and nose with her handkerchief. But it was no good: when she looked up he saw that she had been crying. She was blushing with shame, and the color made her seem almost pretty.

"Why, you've been crying!" he said.

She choked, recovered herself, and answered, "Yes . . . I . . . I can't help it. . . . It always makes me cry—that hymn."

He laid a big, bony, masculine hand on her shoulder. "But you mustn't cry . . . Mrs. Downes. You mustn't cry. . . . It's something to be joyful over."

She looked (he thought) so young and pitiful and unhappy. If it were only possible to comfort her, to take her on his knee as if she were a little child. It was no more than that, this feeling toward her. He wanted to comfort her. But you couldn't do that, of course, especially if you were a preacher.

"I watched your face while you were singing," he said. "It was a beautiful sight . . . so filled with joy and hope and exaltation . . . like the face of one who has seen a vision. It was an inspiration—even to me, a man of God."

She thought, "Oh, I *am* wicked. I *am* wicked!" And aloud, suddenly, without knowing why, she said, "Oh, I'm so unhappy!"

"But why, Naomi?"

He had called her by her name, without thinking, and suddenly he was frightened. He always thought of her thus, as if she had been his own child, and now the thought had slipped into words. He saw that she had noticed it, for she was blushing and avoided his eyes. She did not answer his question, and suddenly he said, "You mustn't mind that . . . that . . . Mrs. Downes. . . . It only means . . . that . . . well, I always think of you as Naomi because I think of your mother-in-law as *the* Mrs. Downes."

Still looking away, she answered, "I know . . . I know. . . . It's all right. You may call me that if you want, only . . . only not in front of the others. I didn't. . . . I think it would make me feel less alone."

And then the door creaked, and Mrs. Wilbert Phipps came in. The Reverend Castor began fingering the piles of music, and Naomi began again to pound the piano with an hysterical violence.

"Good-evening, Mrs. Phipps."

"Good-evening, Reverend Castor."

"I've been looking over the anthems for next Sunday."

"We haven't sung *O the Golden, Glowing Morning* for a long while."

"No . . . but that's an Easter hymn!"

"But we *have* sung it before on other occasions . . . it's so moving."

"What do you think, Mrs. Downes?"

Naomi stopped in the midst of her playing. "I think it would be fine. It's so full of joy."

One by one the others arrived. Each had his favorite, some song which he or she found moving. Naomi, troubled and unhappy, yielded to their choice. She was not, it was plain to be seen, to be a leader save in name alone. The eleven singers took their seats. There was a rustling of music and Naomi plunged noisily into:

> "O the Golden, Glowing Morning!
> Stars above and Stars adorning!"

The voices rang out loud and clear, filling the infants' classroom with a wild joy that seemed almost improper in so bare and chaste a place. They went on through a whole program of anthems and hymns, singing more and more loudly. At last, as the clock banged out eleven, the orgy of music came to an end, leaving them tired but happy, and filled with a strange excitement. At the piano, Naomi turned away to collect the sheets of music. There was a bustle of farewells and small talk and, one by one, or in pairs, the singers drifted out. It had been a happy evening: the happiness of these evenings in the infants' classroom held the choir together. In all the dreary Town of slate-colored houses, the weekly orgy of singing provided a half-mystical joy that elsewhere did not exist. It was, for all the pious words that were chanted, a sort of pagan festival in which men and women found a wild, emotional abandon. It was from choir practice that Mrs. Swithers had run off with the county auditor, leaving behind a husband, an aged mother and three small children.

The music was kept in a cabinet in the Reverend Castor's study, and before the others had all gone, Naomi hurried off to place it there. The depression had begun to settle over her once more, leaving her a prey to uneasiness. The drawer of the cabinet was jammed, and while she pulled and tugged at it, she heard the singers in little groups passing the door. She heard the dry Mrs. Wilbert Phipps say in a curious, excited voice, "No, Hanna, you mustn't say that here. Wait until we get out," and then the banging of the door. She pulled and tugged desperately at the drawer. The door banged again, and again. Without thinking, she counted the number of times it had closed . . . ten times! They must all have gone, and she was left alone. She knew suddenly that she must escape before the Reverend Castor appeared. She could not stay alone with him there in the study. She could not. She could not. . . . Suddenly, in a wave of terror, she let the music slip to the floor, and turned to escape, but at the same moment the Reverend

Castor came in. He stood for a second, looking at her with a queer, fixed expression in his kindly gray eyes, and then he said, gently, "What is it, Naomi? Did I frighten you?"

In her struggle with the drawer, her hat had slipped to the back of her head and her hair had fallen into disarray. Her pale face was flushed once more.

"No," she said. "I just couldn't get that awful drawer open."

"I'll do it for you."

She couldn't escape now. She couldn't run past him out of the door. It would be too ridiculous. Besides, she had a strange, wicked desire not to escape. She sat down on one of the shabby leather chairs and put her hat straight. The Reverend Castor stooped without a word and gathered up the music, and then, with one hand, he opened the drawer easily. She saw it happen with a chill of horror. It was as if the drawer had betrayed her.

She rose quickly and said, "It *really* wouldn't open for me. It *really* wouldn't. . . . I tried and tried." (He would think she had planned it all.)

But when he turned toward her, he said gently, "Yes, I know. It's a funny drawer. It sticks sometimes like that." He was so calm and so . . . usual, she had suddenly, without knowing why, a queer certainty that he understood what was happening there deep inside her, and was trying to still her uneasiness. The knowledge made her want to cry. If only for a second Philip would treat her thus. . . .

He was rubbing his hands together. "Well, that *was* what I call a real choir practice. We've always needed some one like you, Naomi, to put spirit into them. It's the way you make the piano talk. Why, it was like a new choir to-night."

She looked away from him. "I tried my best. I hope they liked it."

"It was wonderful, my child."

There was a sudden, awkward silence, and Naomi said nervously, "Well, I ought to be going."

She moved toward the door, and the Reverend Castor took up his hat and coat. "I'll walk with you, Naomi. I want some air."

Despite herself, she cried out in a sudden hysteria, "No, no. You mustn't do that."

"But it isn't safe down there by the railroads."

"Oh, I'm not afraid." She kept moving slowly toward the door.

"But I don't mind the walk, Naomi. It's no walk for a strong man like me."

"Oh, it isn't that. . . ." She hesitated for a moment. "I don't mean that. . . . I don't know how to explain, only . . . only you never walked home with Mrs. Timpkins when she was leading the choir . . . and . . . you see, if any one saw us. . . ."

He looked suddenly at the floor, and a great sigh escaped him—a heart-breaking sigh, filled with the ghosts of disillusionment, of misery and disappointment.

"Yes . . . I know," he said gently. "I understand."

The door closed behind her, and she was outside in the snow. She kept hearing the sigh. It haunted her as she hurried, confused and out of breath, down the long hill. She felt so sorry for him . . . a kind, good man like that. And all at once she began to cry silently.

There was no sound, but only tears and a lump in her throat.

12

The suspicion of Mary Conyngham, planted by Mabelle in the mind of Emma, lay there for days, flourishing upon fertile soil until at last it took on the sturdy form of reality and truth. In her pain at Philip's coldness toward her and in her anger at the spectacle of an existence which had become as disorderly and unmanageable as her own house during Naomi's presence in it, the thought of Mary Conyngham seldom left her. It burned her mind as she sat behind the cash-register, while she lay in bed at night alone in the house she had meant always to be Philip's house. It gave her no peace. What right, she asked herself, had Mary Conyngham to steal her boy? Bit by bit, she built up the story from that one shred of gossip dropped by Mabelle.

She saw now that the name of Mary Conyngham explained everything. Mary had never gone to church, and perhaps hadn't any faith in God, and so she had aggravated Philip's strange behavior. It was probably Mary or the thought of her, that put into Philip's head that fantastic idea of going to work in the Mills, in a place which had nearly cost him his life. She must have seen him almost every day. Why, she was even friendly with the Polacks and Dagoes. Who could say what things she hadn't been guilty of down there in the Flats, where no decent person ever went? There was probably truth in the story that Irene Shane slept with that big Russian—what was his name—who had had the boldness to come to the very door when Philip was ill. No, all sorts of orgies might go on in the Flats and no one would ever know. It was awful, degrading of Philip, to have mixed himself up with such people.

And presently she began to suspect that Mary lay at the source of Philip's behavior toward Naomi. A man didn't give up living with his wife so easily unless there was another woman. A man didn't do such things. Men were different from women. "Why," she thought, "I've lived all these years without a man, and never once dreamed of re-marrying. I gave up my life to my son."

It was Jason's fault too (she thought). It was Jason's bad blood in Philip. The boy wouldn't have behaved like that if it hadn't been for his father before him. That was where the weakness lay.

And now Mary probably came to see him at that room over the stables at night, and even in the daytime, because there was nothing to stop her coming and going. No one in the Flats would care, especially now, in the midst of the strike, and the Shanes wouldn't even take notice of such a thing. Shane's Castle had always been a sort of bawdy-house, and with the old woman dead the last trace of respectability had vanished. . . .

She remembered, too, that Mary hadn't been happy with her husband. Being married to a man like that who ran after women like Mamie Rhodes did something to a woman. Why, she herself could remember times when Jason's behavior made her, out of revenge, want to be unfaithful to him; and if it could happen to her (Emma) why, what would be the effect on a godless woman like Mary Conyngham?

For a time she considered boldly the plan of going to Philip himself and forcing him to give up Mary Conyngham. Surely she could discuss a thing like that with her own son, to whom she had been both father and mother. There must be, no matter how deeply it lay buried, still a foundation of that sound and moral character which she had labored so long to create. "If only," she thought, "I could make him feel again as he once felt. If only I could get through to the *real* Philip, my Philip, my little boy." But he was hard, as hard as flint.

Twice she planned to go alone to the stable of Shane's Castle, and once she got as far as the bridge before she lost courage and turned back. Always a shadow rose up between her and her resolution—the shadow of that day when, hidden by a screen in the corner of the restaurant, she had pled with him passionately, only to find herself beating her head against a wall of flint, to hear him saying, "You mustn't talk like that. It's not fair"; to see the thin jaw set in a hard line. No, she saw that it was impossible to talk to him. He was so strange and unruly that he might turn his back on her forever. The thought of it filled her with terror, and for two nights she lay awake, weeping in a debauch of self-pity.

But one thing was changed. In all the trouble with Philip, her doubts over marrying Moses Slade seemed to have faded away. At times when she felt tired and worn she knelt in her cold bedroom and thanked God for sending him to her. They could be married in two more months, and then . . . then she would have some one to comfort her. She couldn't go to him with her troubles now, lest the weight of them should frighten him. No, she saw that she must bear all her suffering

alone until God saw fit to lift the cross from her
shoulders.

One afternoon when Moses Slade had left, still
breathing fire and thunder against Krylenko, she sat
for a long time alone behind the screen, in the restaurant, looking out of the window. Her eyes saw nothing
that passed, for she was seeing far beyond such things
as shop-fronts and trolley-cars. She was thinking,
"What has come over me lately? I haven't any character any more. I'm not like Moses, who goes on fighting
like an old war horse. I've let things slide. I haven't
faced things as I should. I've humored Philip, and
see what's come of it. When I kept hold on the reins
everything went well, and now Philip's ruining himself
and going straight to the Devil. I should never have
allowed Naomi to leave the house. She's wax in his
hands, with all her softness—she can never manage him
and he needs to be managed just as his father did. If
I'd treated his father the way Naomi treats Philip
. . . God knows what would have happened."

She began automatically to stack the dishes on the
table before her, as if she had gone back to the days
when the restaurant had been only a lunch-room and
she had herself waited on her customers.

"I must take hold," she told herself. "There's only
one thing to do . . . only one thing. . . . I must go
and see Mary Conyngham. I must talk to her face to
face and have it out. He's my son. I bore him. I gave
him life, and I have a right to save him."

A kind of feverish energy took possession of her. It
seemed that she could no longer sit there seeing the
whole structure of her life going to ruin. She would

save Philip. She would die knowing that he was a bishop. She would marry Moses Slade and go to Washington and work there to save the country from chaos, from drink, from strikes. She would rise in the end, triumphant as she had always been. She had been weak: she had rested at the time when she should have worked. She needed to act. She *would* act, no matter what it cost her. She *would* save Philip and herself.

In a kind of frenzy she seized her hat and coat and left the restaurant.

It was a warm day when the snow had begun to melt and the pavement was deep with slush. She hurried, wet to the knees, fairly running all the way, so that by the time she reached Mary Conyngham's house her face was scarlet and wet with sweat.

Mary was in, but she was upstairs with the children, and the hired girl bade her wait in the parlor. There she seated herself on a rosewood chair, upholstered in horsehair, to mop her face and set her hat straight. And slowly the room began to have a strange effect upon her. Though the room itself was warm, it was as if she had come into a cool place. The rosewood furniture was dark and cool, and the great marble slab of the heavy mahogany commode. The wax flowers and the glass dome that protected them were cool, and the crystal chandelier and the great silver-bordered mirror. The whole room (queer and old-fashioned, Emma thought indignantly) was a pool of quiet . . . a genteel room, a little thread-bare, but nevertheless possessed of an elegance all its own.

It exerted the queerest effect on Emma, dampening her spirits and extinguishing the indignation that a little while before had roared in her bosom like the flames in the belly of one of the furnaces. She began suddenly to feel tired again and filled with despair.

"It's like her to keep an older woman waiting," she thought. "Probably she knows well enough why I've come."

She began to tap the carpet with the toe of her shoe and at last she rose and began to walk about, as if she felt that only by activity could she throw off from her the softening effect of that quiet room. She halted presently before the oval portrait, framed in gilt, of Mary's mother, a very pretty woman, with dark hair and a spirited eye . . . a woman such as Mary might have been if she hadn't married that John Conyngham and had her spirit subdued. Well (thought Emma) she seemed nevertheless to have too much spirit for her own good or the good of any one else.

She was standing thus when Mary came in, dressed in a mauve frock, and looking pale and a little nervous. Emma thought, "She knows why I've come. It's on her conscience. She's afraid of me already."

"I'm sorry, Mrs. Downes," said Mary, "but my sister-in-law has gone out, and I couldn't come down until both children were asleep."

It was odd, but her voice had upon Emma the same effect as the room. It seemed to sap the foundations of her assurance and strength by its very gentleness. It was strange how subdued and quiet Mary seemed, almost as if (Emma thought suspiciously) she had forgotten her early troubles and was now shamelessly and completely happy. Feeling that if she did not begin at once, she would not accomplish her plan, Emma plunged.

"It's about Philip I've come to see you," she said. "I knew that you were interested in him."

Mary admitted the interest shamelessly.

"I don't know what's happened to him. He's so changed . . . not at all the boy he used to be."

"Yes, he's very different. . . . I think maybe he's happier now."

"Oh, he's not happy. No one could be happy in his state of mind. Why, he's even abandoned God. . . . Something, some one has gotten hold of him."

The shadow of a frown crossed Mary's smooth brow. She had the air of waiting . . . waiting. . . . She said, "Perhaps I've chosen the wrong word. I mean that he seems on a more solid foundation."

"Do you call what he's doing solid?"

"If it's what he wants to do."

"He doesn't know his own mind."

"I mean he's more like the real Philip. I think he *is* the real Philip now."

Emma's fingers began to strum the arm of her chair nervously. "I don't know what you're talking about, but if you mean that the old Philip wasn't real, why, I think you're saying a crazy thing. It's this new one who's queer. Do you mean to insinuate that I, his own mother . . . the one who bore him . . . who gave him life, doesn't know who the real Philip is?"

It was clear that she was "working herself up." Mary did not answer her at once, but when she raised her head, it was to say, with a curious, tense quietness, "No . . . if you want the truth, Mrs. Downes, I don't think you know Philip at all. I think that's really what's the matter. You've never known him."

Emma found herself suddenly choked and speechless. "Do you know what you're saying? I've never had any one say such a thing to me before . . . *me*, his own mother! Why, do you know what we've been to each other . . . Philip and me?" She plunged into a long recital of their intimacy, of the beautiful relationship that had always existed between them, of the sacrifices she had made. It went on and on, and Mary, listening, thought, "That's how she talks to him. That's why he can't get free of her." Suddenly she hated Emma. And then she heard Emma saying, in a cold voice, "Of course, I suppose in one way you do know him better than I do—in one way."

"What are you trying to say?"

"You know what I mean. You ought to know . . . you . . . you . . . who have stolen him away from me and from his own wife."

Mary's fingers dug suddenly into the horsehair of her chair. She felt a sudden primitive desire to fling herself upon Emma, to pull her hair, to choke her. The old tomboyish spirit, dead for so long, seemed suddenly to breathe and stir with life. She thought quickly, "I mustn't. I mustn't. It's what she'd like me to do—to put myself on a level with herself. And I mustn't, for Philip's sake. It's all bad enough as it is." She grew suddenly rigid with the effort of controlling herself. She managed to say in a quiet voice, "I think you're talking nonsense. I think you're a little crazy."

"Crazy, am I? That's a nice thing to say!"

"I have talked to Philip just once since he came home, and that was on the day I met you in the street. I didn't try to find him. He came to me."

"Do you expect me to believe that?"

"It's the truth. Beyond that I don't care what you believe."

"I want you to leave him alone."

Suddenly Mary stood up. "I *was* leaving him alone. I meant never to see him, but I won't leave him alone any longer. He would have been mine except for you. He's belonged to me always and he needs me to protect him. No, I won't leave him alone any longer."

All at once she began to cry, and turning, she ran from the room and up the stairs. Emma, left behind on the horsehair sofa, felt suddenly foolish and outwitted. She was certain that Mary meant not to come back, but she remained in the cool, quiet room for a long time, as if her dignity demanded such an action. And at last, baffled and filled with a sense of flatness, she rose and walked out of the house.

The whole visit had been a failure, for it hadn't come properly to a climax. It was ended before it began. But she had (she felt) done her best, all that a mother could do to save her only son. She had laid herself open to insult. . . . A block from Mary's house she discovered that in her agitation she had forgotten her gloves. She halted abruptly, and then resumed her way. They didn't matter. They were old gloves, anyway.

She couldn't bring herself to go back and enter that depressing house again.

Upstairs in the room where the two children were asleep in their cribs, Mary lay on the bed and wept. Until this moment her love had seemed a far-off, distant thing, to be cherished sadly and romantically as hopeless, but now, all at once, it had become unbearably real. She saw Philip in a new way, as some one whom she might touch and care for with all the tenderness that had been wasted upon John Conyngham. She saw him as a lonely man who wanted one thing above all else from a woman, and that was understanding; and it was tenderness that she wanted to give him more than all else on earth. In the midst of her grief and fury, she meant to have him for her own. It seemed to her suddenly that it was only possible to free him from that terrible woman by sacrificing herself. If she gave herself—soul and body and heart—to Philip, she could save him. "He is mine," she kept sobbing, half-aloud. "He is mine . . . my own dear Philip." Why (she asked herself) should she care at all for gossip, for the sacrifice of her own pride, for all the tangle that was certain to follow? He needed her, though she doubted whether the fact had ever occurred to him, and she needed him, and it had been so ever since they were children, and would be so when they were old. All at once she felt a sudden terror of growing old. She seemed to feel the years rushing by her. She knew that she could not go on thus until she died.

And after a little while, when her sobbing had quieted a little, she began to see the thing more coldly. She saw even that Philip was fantastic and hopeless, trying to escape as much from himself as from his mother and from Naomi. She saw even that he was impossible. She doubted whether there was in him the chance of happiness. Yet none of it made any difference, for those were the very reasons perhaps why she loved him. They were the reasons too, perhaps, why at least three women—his mother, his wife and herself—had found themselves in a hopeless tangle over him. It was simply that without knowing it he made demands upon them from which they could not escape. He had even touched Irene Shane in whose cold life men played no part. Mary loved him, she saw now, without reason, without restraint, and she knew that because she loved him she must save him from his own weakness and lead him out of his hopeless muddle into the light.

Because she was a sensible woman, the sudden resolution brought her a certain peace. She coldly took account of all the things that might follow her decision, and knew that she was decided to face them. She *had* to help him. It was the only thing that mattered.

As she stirred and sat up on the edge of the bed, the youngest child moved and opened its eyes, and Mary, in a sudden burst of joy, went over and kissed it. Bending down, she said, "Your mother, Connie, is a wicked woman." The child laughed, and she laughed too, for there was a sudden peace and delight in her heart.

13

Philip had spent the morning of that same day among the tents where the strikers lived in the melting snow. He had made sketches, a fragment here, a fragment there—tiny glimpses that were in their own way more eloquent than the lifting of the whole curtain. They were a weekly affair now, done regularly on a fragment of some denunciating speech or editorial. They appeared weekly in the *Labor Journal*. Now he chose an editorial in which the Chairman of the Board of Mill Directors made a speech filled with references to Christ and appeals to end the strike and return to an era of Peace on Earth; now it was an address from the

Governor of the State—a timid man, a bit of a fool, and destined one day to be President of the Nation. Moses Slade suffered twice more, for his pompous bombastic speeches made irresistible subjects for burlesque. But, as the weeks passed, Philip found himself less and less interested in making propaganda for the workers, and more and more concerned with the purity of his line. The room above the stable came to be papered in sketches made on bits of newsprint or fragments of butchers' brown paper. A frenzy of work took possession of him, and for whole days at a time he never left the place, even to see his children. There were even times when he forgot the very existence of Mary Conyngham. But he did go faithfully twice a week to stay with the twins so that Naomi might go to choir practice. It was, he knew, the only pleasure which lay in his power to give her.

The importance of the thing appeared to make her happy, and to diminish the aching sense of strain that was never absent when they were together. She began, little by little, to grow used to a husband whose only activities were those of a nursemaid, but she still tried pathetically to please him. She made a heroic effort to dress neatly and keep the house in order (although there were times when he spent his whole visit to the twins in putting closets in order and gathering the soiled clothing into piles), and she never spoke any more of his coming back to her. The only fault seemed to be a jealousy which she could not conquer.

She kept asking him questions, disguised in a pitiful air of casualness, about what the Shanes' house was like, and whether he thought Lily Shane as beautiful a woman as she was supposed to be. Once she even

asked about Mary Conyngham. He always answered
her in the same fashion—that he had never been inside
the Shanes' house, and did not know Lily Shane, and
had spoken to Mary Conyngham but once since he had
come home. Sometimes he fancied that it was more
than mere jealousy that prompted her questions: he
thought, too, there was something in them of wistful
curiosity about a world filled with people she would
never know. She still had the power of rousing a pity
which weakened him like an illness.

He did tell her at last that he *had* seen Lily Shane
three or four times walking in the park, once in the
moonlight, and that he thought she was a beautiful
woman; but he never told her how the figure of Lily
Shane was inextricably a part of that strange illuminating vision that came to him as he stood by the vine-
clad window. It was, he believed, the sort of thing no
one would understand, not even Mary. Naomi would
only think him crazy and go at once to tell his mother.
They would begin all over again humoring him as a
madman or a child. No, he did not know Lily Shane,
and yet he did know her, in a strange, unearthly, mystical fashion, as if she stood as a symbol of all that
strange, sensuous world of which he had had a single
illuminating intuition as he stood by the window. It
was a world in which all life was lived on a different
plane, in which tragedies occurred and people were
happy and unhappy, but it was a world in which success
and happiness and tragedy and sorrow were touched
by grandeur. There was in it nothing sordid or petty,
for there were in it no people like Uncle Elmer and
Naomi and Mabelle. One could enter it if one knew
how to live. That, he saw, was a thing he must learn—

how to live, to free himself of all that nastiness and intolerance and pettiness of which he had suddenly become aware. He had to escape from all those things which the old Philip, the one who was dead, had accepted, in the blindness of a faith in a nasty God, as the ultimate in living.

This new Philip, prey to a sickening awareness, had been working all the morning in the Flats and ate with Krylenko at the tent where the homeless strikers were fed soup and coffee and bread, and, on returning to the stable, he lay down on the iron bed and fell asleep. He did not know how long he lay there, but he was awakened presently by a curious feeling, half a dream, that some one had come into the room with him. Lying quietly, still half-lost in a mist of sleep, he became slowly aware that some one was walking softly about beyond the screen. Rising, he pushed it aside and, stepping out, saw who it was. Standing in the shadow near the window, peering at the drawings, was Lily Shane, hatless, with her honey-colored hair done in a knot at the back of her neck, her furs thrown back over her shoulders. At the sound of his step, she turned slowly and said, "Oh! I thought there was no one here. I thought I was alone."

It was a soft voice, gentle and musical, exactly the right voice for such a figure and face. At the sound of it, he was aware suddenly that he must appear ridiculous—coatless, with his hair all rumpled. It was the first time he had ever spoken to such a woman, and something in her manner—the complete calm and assurance, the quiet, almost insolent lack of any apology, made him feel a gawky little boy.

"I . . . I was asleep," he said, desperately patting down his hair.

She smiled. "I didn't look behind the screen. Hennery told me you hadn't come in." But there was a contradiction behind the smile, a ghost of a voice which said, "I *did* look behind the screen. I knew you were there."

And suddenly, for the first time, Philip was stricken by an awful speculation as to how he looked when asleep. He knew that he was blushing. He said, "It doesn't matter. It's your stable, after all."

"I didn't mean to disturb you. I've stayed longer than I meant to . . . but—you see . . . "—she made a gesture toward the drawings—"I found all these more fascinating than I expected. I knew about you. My sister told me . . . but I didn't find what I expected. They're so much better. . . . You see, it's always the same. I couldn't believe it of the Town. Can any good thing come out of Nazareth?"

He began to tremble a little. He'd never shown them to any one save Krylenko, who only wanted pictures for propaganda and liked everything, good and bad. And now some one who lived in a great world such as he could scarcely imagine, thought they were good. Suddenly all the worries, the troubles, slipping from him, left him shy and childlike.

"I don't know whether they're good or bad," he said, "only . . . only I've *got* to do them."

She was standing before the painting of the Flats seen from the window, over which he had struggled for days. She smiled again, looking at him. "It's a bit messy . . . but it's got something in it of truth. I've seen it like that. It was like that one moonlight night

not so long ago. I was walking in the garden . . .
late . . . after midnight. I noticed it."

She sat down in one of the chairs by the stove. "May
I stay and talk a moment?"

"Of course."

"Sit down too," she said.

Then he remembered that he was still without a coat,
and, seizing it quickly, he put it on and sat down. His
mind was all on fire, like a pile of tinder caught by a
spark. He had never seen anything like this woman before. She wasn't what a woman who had led such a
life should have been. She wasn't hard, or vulgar, or
coarse, as he had been taught to believe. She must
have been nearly forty years old, and yet she was
fresh as the morning. And in her beauty, her voice,
her manner, there was an odd quality of excitement
which changed the very surface of everything about her.
Her very presence seemed to make possible anything
in the world.

She was saying, "What do you mean to do about it?"

"About what?"

She made a gesture to include the drawings. "All
this."

It seemed to him for the first time that he had
never thought of what he meant to do about it. He
had just worked, passionately, because he had to work.
He hadn't thought of the future at all.

"I don't know . . . I want to work until I can find
what I know is here . . . I mean in the Mills and in the
Flats. And then . . . some day . . . I . . . I want
to go back to Africa. . . . I've been to Africa, you
know. I was a missionary once." He thought that from
the summit of her worldliness she might laugh at him

for being a missionary; but she didn't laugh. She clasped her hands about her knee, and he saw suddenly that they were very beautiful hands, white and ringless, against the soft, golden sables. He wanted to seize a pencil and draw them.

She didn't laugh at him. She only said, "Tell me about that . . . about Africa . . . I mean."

And slowly he found himself telling the whole story, passionately, as he had never told it before, even to Mary Conyngham. He seemed to find in it things which he hadn't seen before, strange lights and shadows. He told it from beginning to end, and when he had finished, she said, looking into the fire, without smiling, "Yes, I understand all that. I've never been religious or mystical, but I've always had my sister Irene. I've seen it with her. You see I'm what they call a bad lot. You've probably heard of me. I'm only thankful I'm alive and I try to enjoy myself in the only world I'm sure of."

He went on, "You see, when I've learned more, I want to go back and paint that country. It had a fascination for me. I guess I'm like that Englishwoman . . . Lady Millicent . . . the one I told you about. She said there were some people who couldn't resist it."

When he finished, he saw that all his awe of her had vanished. He knew her better than any one in the world, for she had a miraculous way of understanding him, even those things which he did not say. The desire for the jungle and the hot lake swept over him in a turbulent wave. He wanted to go at once, without waiting. He was thirsty for a sight of the reedy marshes. The procession of black women moved somehow across the back of the room beyond Lily Shane.

He was hot all at once, and thirsty for the water they carried up the slope to the parched ground.

She understood what he was trying to tell her . . . she had caught a magnificence, a splendor, that was not to be put into words. He wasn't afraid any more, or shy. It was as if she existed in an aura of contagious lawlessness.

She took out a cigarette from a lacquered box. "Do you mind if I smoke?"

"No."

"I didn't know. . . . "

He watched her curiously. There lay in the soft curve of her body, in the long slim leg crossed over the other, in the curve of the fur thrown back across her shoulders, in the poise of her arm, all the perfection of some composition designed and executed by a great artist. It was a kind of perfection he had never dreamed of, something which had arisen mysteriously during years out of the curious charm of her own personality. It was, too, a completeness born of the fearlessness which he had sensed for a moment by the window. Suddenly he thought, "Some day I shall be of that world. I shall succeed and become great. And Mary, too, will share it."

He had almost forgotten Mary, but it was only, he told himself shamefully, because she had been there with him all the while. It was almost as if she were a part of himself: whatever happened to him must happen also to her. It was not that he had fallen in love with this stranger, or even that he desired her: the emotion was something far beyond all that, a sort of dazzled bewilderment shot through with streaks of hope and glamour which brought near to him that world in which people were really alive.

Suddenly he summoned all his courage. He said, blushing under his dark skin, "I want to draw you. I want to make a picture of you."

She moved a little and smiled.

"No," he said, quickly. "Like that. Don't move."

He wanted to capture the grace and elegance of the pose, so that he might have it always, as a little fragment, caught and held, of this thing which he knew to exist, beyond his reach. She sat quietly. "Yes, of course . . . only it's almost dark now . . . "

He seized a pencil and a bit of paper, working swiftly, as he had done at the soup-kitchen. He must hurry (he thought) or she would be gone again back to Paris. She appeared presently to have forgotten him, and sat, with the remnant of the cigarette hanging from her long white fingers, while she stared into the fire. There was a curious sense of repose in the whole body, and a queer sadness too. She might have been quite alone. He had the feeling that she had forgotten his existence.

He worked nervously, with long, sure strokes, and with each one he knew that he was succeeding. In the end he would fix her thus forever on a fragment of paper. And then suddenly he heard some one enter the stable below, and, fumbling with the door, open it and hurry up the steps. He went on, pressed by the fear that if he were disturbed now the thing would never be finished. He *had* to have it. It would be a kind of fetish to keep off despair.

It was Lily Shane who moved first, stirred perhaps by a sense of being watched. As she moved, Philip turned too, and there, half-way up the stairs where she had halted at sight of them, stood Naomi, staring.

She was breathless, and beneath a carelessly pinned hat, from which wisps of hair escaped, her face showed red and shining as a midsummer day. For one dreadful moment the three remained silent, staring at each other. Lily Shane stared with a kind of bored indifference, but there was in Naomi's eyes a hurt look of bewilderment. Suddenly she turned back, as if she meant to go away again without speaking to either of them. Philip knew the expression at once. She had looked thus on the day that Lady Millicent appeared out of the forest with the Arab marching before her. It was the look of one who was shut out from something she could not understand, which frightened her by its strangeness.

It was Lily Shane who moved first. The burnt cigarette dropped from her fingers and she stamped on it. The action appeared to stir Naomi into life.

"Philip," she said. "I came to tell you that your Pa has come home."

14

It was Emma herself who saw him first. Returning flustered and upset from the call upon Mary Conyngham, she entered the slate-colored house closing the door stormily behind her. She would have passed the darkened parlor (where since Naomi's departure the shades were always kept drawn to protect the carpet), but, as she explained it afterward, she "felt" that there was some one in the room. Peering into the darkness, she heard a faint sound of snoring, and, as her eyes grew accustomed to the darkness, she discerned the figure of a man lying on her best sofa, with his feet resting on the arm. He was sleeping with his mouth open a little way beneath a black mustache, waxed and curled with the care of a dandy.

As she stood there in the midst of the room, the figure in the shadows took form slowly, and suddenly she knew it . . . the dapper, small body, dressed so dudishly, the yellow waistcoat with its enormous gold watch-chain, and cluster of seals. She knew, with a sudden pang, even the small, well-shaped hand, uncalloused by any toil, that lay peacefully at rest on the Brussels carpet. For a second she thought, "I've gone suddenly crazy from all the trouble I've had. What I'm seeing can't be true."

It took a great deal of courage for her to move toward the sofa, for it meant moving in an instant, not simply across the Brussels carpet, but across the desert of twenty-six years. It meant giving up Moses Slade and all that resplendent future which had been taking form in her mind only a moment before. It was like waking the dead from the shadows of the tomblike parlor.

She did not lack courage, Emma; or perhaps it was not courage, but the headlong thrust of an immense vitality which now possessed her. She went over to the sofa and said, "Jason! Jason Downes!" He did not stir, and suddenly the strange thought came to her that he might be dead. The wicked idea threw her into an immense confusion, for she did not know whether she preferred the unstable companionship of the fascinating Jason to the bright future that would be hers as the wife of Moses. Then, all at once, she saw that the gaudy watch-chain was moving up and down slowly as he breathed, and she was smitten abruptly by memories twenty-six years old of morning after morning when she had wakened, full of energy, to find Jason lying beside her sleeping in the same profound, conscienceless slumber.

"Jason!" she said again. "Jason Downes!" And this time there was a curious tenderness in her voice that was almost a sob.

He did not stir, and she touched his shoulder. He moved slowly, and then, opening his eyes, sat up and put his feet on the floor. He awakened lazily, and for a moment he simply sat staring at her, looking as neat and dapper as if he had just finished an elaborate toilet. Again memory smote Emma. He had always been like this: he had always wakened in the mornings, looking fresh and neat, with every hair in place. It was that hair-oil he persisted in using. Now that he'd come home, she would have to get antimacassars to protect the furniture against Jason's oily head.

Suddenly he grinned and said, "Why! Hello! It's you, Em." It wasn't a sheepish grin, but a smile of cocky assurance, such as was frozen forever upon the face of the enlarged portrait.

"Jason . . . Jason! Oh, my God! Jason!" She collapsed suddenly and fell into the mahogany-veneer rocker. It was a strange Emma, less strange perhaps to Jason Downes than she would have been to the world outside, for suddenly she had become all soft and collapsed and feminine. All those twenty-six years had rolled away, leaving her helpless.

As if he had left the house only that morning, he sat on the arm of the chair and kissed her. He patted her hands and said, "You mustn't cry like that, Em. I can't bear to hear you. It breaks me all up."

"If you knew how long I'd waited!" she sobbed.

"Why didn't you even write? Why didn't you tell me you were coming?"

He seemed a little proud of himself. "I wanted it to be a surprise."

He led her to the sofa and sat there, patting her hand and smiling, and comforting her while she wept and wept. "A surprise," she echoed. "A surprise . . . after twenty-six years. . . ." After a time she grew more calm, and suddenly she began to laugh. She kept saying at little intervals, "If you knew how I've waited!"

"I'm rich now, Emma," he said with the shadow of a swagger. "I've done well out there."

"Out where . . . Jason?"

"Out in Australia . . . where I went."

"You were in Australia?" He wasn't in China at all, then. The story was so old that she had come to believe it, and with a sudden shock of horror she saw that they would now have to face the ancient lie. He hadn't been in China, and he hadn't been killed by bandits. Here he was back again, and you couldn't keep a man like Jason shut up forever in the house. The Town would see him. She began once more to cry.

"There, there, Em!" he said, patting her hand again, almost amorously. "Don't take it so hard. You're glad I did come back, ain't you?"

"I don't know . . . I don't know. You don't deserve anything . . . even tears . . . after treating a wife the way you've treated me. Don't think I'm crying because I'm glad you're back. It's not that. I ought to turn you out. I'd do it, too, if I was an ordinary woman."

She saw then that she still had to manage everything, including Jason. She saw that he was as useless as he had always been. She would have to "take hold." The feminine softness melted away, and, sitting up, she blew her nose and said, "It's like this, Jason. When you went away, I said you'd gone to China on business. And when you didn't come back, I said I hadn't had any letters from you and something must be wrong. You see I pretended I heard from you regularly because . . . I wanted to protect you and because I was ashamed. I didn't want people to think you'd deserted me after everybody had warned me against you. And so Elmer. . . ."

"And how's he?" said Jason. "Cold boiled mutton, I call 'im."

"Wait till I finish my story, Jason. Try to keep your mind on what I'm saying. And so Elmer set the Government to investigating. . . ."

"They were looking for me? The *United States Government* itself?" There was in his voice and manner a sudden note of gratification at his importance.

"Yes . . . they hunted all over China."

Jason was grinning now. "It's lucky they was looking in China, because I was in Australia all the time."

"And they said you must have been killed by bandits . . . so I put on black and set out to support myself and Philip."

"Why didn't old pious Elmer help you out? I wouldn't have gone away, except that I knew 'e was rich enough to look out for you."

"Elmer's tight, and besides I didn't want him to be pitying me and saying, 'I told you so' every time I asked him for a cent."

"And Philip? You haven't told me about him yet."

"We'll come to him. We've got to settle this other thing first. You see, Jason, we've got to do something about that lie I told . . . it wasn't really a lie because I told it for your sake and Philip's—to protect you both."

"Yes, it is kind-a awkward." He sat for a moment, trying to bring his volatile mind into profitable operation. At last he said, "You oughtn't to have told that lie, Em."

"I told you why I told it. God will understand me if no one else will."

"Now, Em, don't begin on that line. . . . It was always the line I couldn't stand. . . . You ain't no bleedin' martyr."

She looked at him with a sudden suspicion. "Jason, where did you pick up this queer talk . . . all the queer words you've been using?"

"Australia, I guess . . . living out among the cockneys out there." He rose suddenly. "Em, I can't sit any more in this dark. I can't think in a tomb." He went over and drew up the window-shades. As the fading winter light filled the room, he looked around him. "Why, it ain't changed at all! Just the same . . . wedding parlor suite and everything." His glance fell on the wall above the fireplace. "And you still got my picture, Em. That was good of you."

She showed signs of sobbing again. "It's all I had. . . ."

He was looking at the picture with a hypnotic fascination. "It's funny, I ain't changed much. You'd never think that picture was taken twenty-six years ago." He took out a pocket mirror and began comparing his features with those in the enlarged photograph. What he said was true enough. Time had left no marks on the smooth, good-looking face, nor even on a mind that was like a shining, darting minnow. He was as slim and dapper as ever. The hair was much thinner, but it was still dark, and with the aid of grease and shrewd manipulation you couldn't tell that he was really bald. Emma, watching him, had an awful suspicion that it was dyed as well; and the elegant mustaches too. She would be certain to discover, now that he had come back to share the same room and bed. She had a sudden, awful fear that she must look much older than he.

"I'm a little bald," he said ruefully, "but nothing very much."

"Jason," she said sternly. "Jason . . . we've got to settle this thing . . . now . . . before we do anything else. Did any one see you?"

"No, I don't think so." He replaced the pocket mirror with a mild, comic air of alarm at the old note of authority in her voice.

"You must think of something . . . you're better at such things than I am." He had, she remembered, the proper kind of an imagination. She knew from experience how it had worked long ago when he had given her excuses for his behavior.

He looked at her with an absurd air of helplessness. "What can we say? I suppose you could say I lost my memory . . . that I got hit on the head." Suddenly a great light burst upon the empty face. "I *did* get a fall on the steamer going out. I fell down a stairway and for three days I didn't know a thing. A fall like that might easily make you lose your memory. . . . A thing like that *might* happen." As if the possibilities of such a tale had suddenly dawned upon him, his face became illumined with that look which must come at times into the faces of great creative artists. He said, "Yes, I *might* have lost my memory, not knowing who I was, or where I came from, and then, after twenty-six years, I got another fall . . . how? . . . well out of the mow on my ranch in Australia, and when I came to, I remembered everything—that I had a wife in America. It's true—it might happen. I've read of such things."

Listening to him, Emma felt the story seemed too preposterous, and yet she knew that only heroic measures could save the situation. The bolder the tale, the better. It was, as he said, a story that *might* be true. Such things *had* happened. She could trust him, too, to make the tale a convincing one: the only danger lay in the possibility of his doing it *too* well. It occurred to her in the midst of her desperate planning that it was strange what wild, incredible things had happened in her life . . . a life devoted always to hard work and Christian living.

Jason's glittering mind had been working rapidly. He was saying, "You see, there's the scar and everything." He bent down, exposing the bald spot that was the only sign of his decay. "You see, there it is— the scar."

She looked at him scornfully, for the crisis of her emotion had passed now, and she was beginning to feel herself once more. "Now, Jason," she said, "I haven't forgotten where that scar came from. You've always had it. You got it in Hennessey's saloon."

For a second the dash went out of him. "Now, Em, you're not going to begin on that, the minute I get home." And then quickly his imagination set to work again, and with an air of brightness, as if the solution he had thought of vindicated him completely, he said, "Besides I wasn't bald in those days and nobody ever saw the scar. And the funny thing is that it was on that exact spot that I fell on the boat. It enlarged the scar." He looked at her in the way he had always done when he meant to turn her mind into more amiable channels. "Now, isn't that queer? It enlarged the scar."

It was clear that she meant not to be diverted from the business at hand. "I suppose that's as good a story as any. We've got to have a story of some kind. But you must stick to it, Jason, and don't make it too good. That's what you always do . . . make it too good." (Hadn't she, years ago, trapped him time after time in a lie, because he could not resist a too elaborate pattern of embroidery?)

She said, "But there's one thing I've got to do right away, and that is send word to Naomi to tell Philip."

"Who's Naomi?"

"She's Philip's wife."

"He's married?"

"He's been married for five years."

He made a clucking sound. "We're getting on, Em."

"And there's more than that. You're a grandfather."

The smooth face wrinkled into a rueful expression. "It's hard to think of myself as a grandfather. How old is the child, or the children?"

"They're twins."

He chuckled. "He did a good job, Philip."

"Now, Jason. . . ."

"All right, but how old are they?"

"Four months . . . nearly five."

"I must say that Philip took 'is time about it. Married five years. . . . Well, we didn't waste any time, did we, Em."

"Jason!"

She hated him when he was vulgar. She decided not to go into the reasons why Philip and Naomi had been married four years without children, because it was a thing which Jason wouldn't understand—sacrificing the chance of children to devote yourself to God. There was nothing spiritual about Jason. It was one of his countless faults.

"But who did 'e marry, Em? You haven't told me."

"Her name was Naomi Potts. You wouldn't know who she was. Her people were missionaries, and she was a missionary too."

"Oh, my God!"

"I won't have you blaspheming."

"And what's Philip like?"

"He was a missionary too. . . . He was three years in Africa . . . until his health broke."

"Oh, my God!" He grew suddenly thoughtful, moved perhaps by the suspicion that she had succeeded in doing to his son what she had failed to do to him.

She was at the door now. "I won't listen to you talking like that any longer." She turned in the doorway. "Don't go out till I come back. You mustn't be seen till we've worked this thing out. I've got to send word to them all."

When she had gone, he picked up his hat, took a cigar from his vest pocket and lighted it. In the hallway, he shouted at her, "Are we still using the same room, Em? I'll just move in my things and wash up a bit."

In the sitting-room Emma sat down and wrote three notes—one to Naomi, one to Mabelle, and the third to Moses Slade. With a trembling hand she wrote to him, "God has sent Jason, my husband, back to me. He came to-day. It is His will that we are not to marry. Your heartbroken Emma."

She summoned the slattern Essie, and, giving her instructions of a violence calculated to impress Essie's feeble mind, she bade her deliver the three notes, Mr. Slade's first of all. But once outside the sight of Emma, the hired girl had her own ideas of the order in which she meant to deliver them, and so the note to Moses Slade arrived last. But it made no difference, as the Honorable Mr. Slade, bearing a copy of the *Labor Journal*, was at the same moment on his way to Emma's to break off the engagement, for he had discovered the author of the libelous drawings. The latest one was signed boldly with the name, "Philip Downes." He never arrived at Emma's house, for on his way he heard in Smollett's Cigar Store that Jason Downes had returned, and so he saved himself the trouble of an unpleasant interview. For Essie, in the moment after the returned prodigal had made known to her his identity, had put on a cast-off hat of Emma's and set out at once to spread the exciting news through the Town.

When she returned at last from delivering the three notes, Emma was "getting Jason settled" in the bedroom he had left twenty-six years before. Essie, tempted, fell, and, listening outside the door, heard him recounting to his wife a wonderful story of having lost his memory for a quarter of a century. But one thing tormented the brain of the slattern Essie. She could not understand how Emma seemed to know the whole story and to put in a word now and then correcting him.

At the sound of Emma's footsteps approaching the door, Essie turned and, fleeing, hid in the hall closet, from which she risked her whole future by opening the door a little way to have a look at the fascinating Mr. Downes. Her heart thumped wildly under her cotton blouse at the proximity of so romantic a figure.

15

It seemed that something in the spirit of the irrepressible Jason Downes took possession of the house, for Emma turned almost gay, and at times betrayed signs of an ancient coquetry (almost buried beneath so many hardening years) in an actual tendency to bridle. For the first time since Jason had slipped quietly out of the back door, the sallow dining-room was enlivened by the odors, the sounds, the air of banqueting: a dinner was held that very night to celebrate the prodigal's return. Elmer came, goaded by an overpowering curiosity, and Mabelle, separated for once from Jimmy, her round, blue eyes dilated with excitement and colored by that faintly bawdy look which so disturbed Emma. And Philip was there, of course, and Naomi, paler than usual, dressed in a badly fitting new foulard dress, which she and Mabelle had "run up at home" in the hope of pleasing Philip. The dress had been saved for an "occasion." They had worked over it for ten days in profound secrecy, keeping it to dazzle Philip. It was thick about the waist, and did not hang properly in the back, and it made her look all lumpy in the wrong places. In case Philip did not notice it, Mabelle was to say to him, "You haven't spoken about Naomi's pretty new dress. She made it all herself—with her own hands." They had carefully rehearsed the little plot born of Mabelle's romantic brain.

But when Naomi arrived at the slate-colored house, she took Mabelle quickly into a corner and said, "Don't speak of the dress to him." And when Mabelle asked, "Why not?" she only answered, "You can do it later, but not to-night. I can't explain why just now."

She couldn't explain to Mabelle that she was ashamed of the dress, nor why she was ashamed of it. She couldn't say that as she stood on the stairs of the stable and saw a handsome woman, in a plain black dress, with her knees crossed, and furs thrown back over her fine shoulders, that the pride of the poor little foulard dress had turned to ashes. She couldn't explain how she had become suddenly sick at the understanding that she must seem dowdy and ridiculous, standing there, all red and hot and disheveled, staring at them, and wanting all the time to turn and run, anywhere, on and on, without stopping. She couldn't explain how the sight of the other woman had made the foulard dress seem poor and frowzy, even when she put on the coral beads left her by her mother, and pinned on the little gold fleur-de-lys watch her father had given her.

When she first arrived, she kept on her coat, pretending that the house was cold, but Emma said, "It's nonsense, Naomi. The house is warm enough," and the irrepressible Mabelle echoed, "That's what I say,

Emma. She ought to take it off and show her pretty new dress."

Naomi had looked quickly about her, but Philip hadn't been listening. He was standing with Uncle Elmer beside his father, who was in high spirits, talking and talking. He wouldn't notice the dress if only she could keep people from speaking of it.

She hadn't spoken of Lily Shane to Philip. All the way back to the flat by the railroad they had talked of nothing but his father and the poor bits of information she had been able to wring from the excited Essie; and when they arrived it was to find Mabelle waiting breathlessly to discuss it with them. She had been already to the slate-colored house and seen him with her own eyes. She didn't stay long (she said) because she felt as if she were intruding on honeymooners. Did they know that he had lost his memory by a fall on the boat going out to China, and that it had only come back to him when he had a fall six months ago out of the mow on his ranch in Australia? Yes, it was Australia he had been to all this time. . . .

She went on and on. "Think of it," she said. "The excitement of welcoming home a husband you hadn't seen in twenty-six years . . . like a return from the dead. I don't wonder your Ma is beside herself."

Naomi heard it all, dimly, as if all Mabelle's chatter came to her from a great distance. She should have been excited, but she couldn't be, with something that was like a dull pain in her body. She could only keep seeing Lily Shane, who made her feel tiny and miserable and ridiculous—Lily Shane, whom Philip said he didn't even know, and had never spoken to. Yet he knew her well enough to be making a picture of her.

He never thought of making a picture of his own wife.

She felt sick, for it was the first time she had ever seen herself. She seemed to see at a great distance a pale, thin, freckled woman, with sandy hair, dressed in funny clothes.

And then she would hear Mabelle saying through a fog, "Your Ma wants you to come right up to supper. You can get Mrs. Stimson—the druggist's wife—to sit with the twins."

Mabelle hurried off presently, and Mrs. Stimson came in duly to sit with the twins. She gave up the evening at her euchre club because the excitement of sitting up with the grandchildren of a man who had returned after being thought dead for twenty-six years was not to be overlooked. She would hear all the story at first hand when Philip and Naomi returned, before any one else in the Town had heard it. She could say, "I sat with the twins so that Philip and Naomi could go to supper with Mr. Downes himself. I heard the whole thing from them."

As they went up the hill to the slate-colored house, Naomi said nothing, and so they walked in silence. She had begun to understand a little Philip's queer moods, and she knew now that he was nervous and irritable. She had watched him so closely of late that she had become aware of a queer sense of strain which once she had passed over unnoticed. She had learned not to speak when Philip was like that. And as they climbed the hill, the silence, the strain, seemed to become unbearable. It was Philip who broke it by crying out suddenly, "I know what you're thinking. You're thinking I lied to you about Lily Shane. Well, I didn't. Before God, I never spoke to her until to-day, and I wouldn't have, even then, but she came to my room without my asking her."

For a moment, she wanted to lie down in the snow and, burying her face in it, cry and cry. She managed to say, "I wasn't even thinking of her. Honestly I wasn't, Philip. And I believe you."

"If that's so, why do you sulk and not say anything?"

"I wasn't sulking. I only thought you didn't want to talk just now."

"I hate it when you act like a martyr." This time she was silent, and he added, "I suppose all women do it . . . or most women . . . it's what Ma does when she wants to get her way. I hate it."

She thought, "He said 'most women' because he meant all women but Lily Shane." But she was silent. They did not speak again until they reached the slate-colored house.

It wasn't really Naomi who lay at the bottom of his irritation, but the thought of his father. The return troubled him. Why should he have come now after twenty-six years? It was, he thought, almost indecent and unfair, in a way, to his mother. He tried, when he was not talking to Naomi, to imagine what he must be like—a man who Emma said had gone out to China to make money for his wife and child, a man who adored her and worshipped his son. He was troubled, because the moral image created by his mother seemed not to fit the enlarged, physical portrait in the parlor. In these last years he had come to learn a lot about the world and about people, and one of the things he had learned was that people *are* like their faces. His mother was like her large, rather coarse and energetic face;

Naomi was like her pale, weak one; and Lily Shane and Mary and Uncle Elmer and even Krylenko and McTavish were like theirs. It was impossible to escape your own face. His father, he thought, couldn't escape that face that hung in the parlor.

When the door opened and he stepped into the parlor, he saw that his father hadn't escaped his face. He felt, with a sudden sensation of sickness, that his father was even worse than his face. It was the same, only a little older, and the outlines had grown somehow dim and vague from weakness and self-indulgence. Why, he thought again, did he ever come back?

But his mother was happy again. Any one could see that.

And then his father turned and looked at him. For a moment he stared, astonished by something in the face of his son, something which he himself could not perhaps define, but something which, with all the sharp instincts of a sensual nature he recognized as strange, which had little to do with either himself or Emma. And then, perhaps because the astonishment had upset him, the meeting fell flat. The exuberance flowed out of Jason Downes. It was almost as if he were afraid of his son—this son who, unlike either himself or Emma, was capable of tragedy and suffering. His eyes turned aside from the burning eyes of his son.

"Well, Philip," he said, with a wild effort at hilarity, "here's your Pa . . . back again."

Philip shook hands with him, and then a silence fell between them.

But it was Jason Downes who dominated the family gathering. Philip, silent, watched his father's spirits mounting. It seemed to him that Jason had set himself deliberately to triumph over his dour, forbidding brother-in-law, and to impress his own son. It was as if he felt that his son had a poor opinion of him, and meant to prove that he was wrong in his judgment.

He told the whole story of the voyage out, of his fall down a companionway, and the strange darkness that followed. Once more he bowed his head and exhibited the scar.

"But," said the skeptical Elmer sourly, "you always had that scar, Jason. You got it falling on the ice at the front gate."

"Oh, no. The one before was only a small one. The funny thing was that I struck my head in exactly the same place. Wasn't that queer? And then when I fell out of the mow I hit it a third time. That's what the doctors in Sydney said made it so serious." For a moment, conscious that the embroidering had begun, Emma looked troubled and uneasy.

And Mabelle, with a look of profound speculation, asked, "And what if you hit it a fourth time? Would that make you lose your memory about Australia?"

Jason coughed and looked at her sharply, and then said, "Well, no one could say about that. If it happened again, it would probably kill me."

"Well," said Mabelle, "I must say I never heard a more interesting story . . . I never read as interesting a one in any of the magazines . . . not even in the *Ladies' Home Journal*."

For a moment Philip wanted to laugh at Mabelle's question, but it wasn't a natural desire to laugh: it sprang from a blend of anger and hysterics. He loathed the whole party, with Mabelle and her half-witted questions, his mother with all her character gone in the silly blind admiration for her husband, Uncle Elmer and his nasty, mean questions, and Naomi, silent, and looking as if she were going to cry. (If only she wouldn't sulk and play the martyr!) And Mabelle's half-witted questions were worse than Uncle Elmer's cynical remarks, for they made him see suddenly that his father *was* lying. He was creating a whole story that wasn't true, and he was enjoying himself immensely. If it *was* a lie, if he had deliberately deserted his wife and child, why had he come back now?

Jason went on and on, talking, talking, talking. He told of his ranch of eighteen hundred acres and of the thousands of sheep he owned and of the sixty herders employed to take care of them. He described the long drouths that sometimes afflicted them, and told a great deal about Melbourne and Sydney.

"Your Pa," he said, addressing Philip, "is an important man out there." And the implication was, "You don't think much of him, but you ought to see him in Australia."

But Philip was silent, and thought, "He's probably lying about that, too," and, as the conversation went on, he thought, "He's never said anything about women out there. He's never spoken about that side of his life, and he's not the kind to leave women alone."

"And I suppose you'll be wanting to take Emma back to Australia," said Uncle Elmer, regarding Jason over his steel-rimmed spectacles.

"No . . . I won't be doing that. After all, her life is here, ain't it? I shall have to go back from time to time to look after my affairs, but . . ."

"Don't speak of that now," Emma interrupted, "when you've only just arrived."

"But we have to face these things," said Jason.

Suddenly Emma turned away from the table to the doorway where Essie, in terror of interrupting the party, yet fascinated still by the spell of Jason's narrative, stood waiting. She was standing, as she always stood, on the sides of her shoes.

"What is it, Essie? What are you standing there for?"

"There's a man come to see Mr. Downes."

"What does he want?"

"He's from the newspaper."

"Tell him to come back to-morrow."

But Jason had overheard. He rose with the napkin still tucked into the fawn-colored vest. "No, Essie. . . . Tell him I'll speak to him now."

"But, Jason. . . ."

"Yes, Em. . . . I might as well get it over."

There was no holding him now; but Emma succeeded in thrusting forward a word of advice.

"Remember, Jason, what the newspapers are like. Don't tell them too much."

A shadow crossed her face, and Philip thought suddenly, "Ma knows he's lying too, and she's afraid he'll overdo it." And then a more fantastic thought occurred to him—that she knew for a good reason that he was lying, that perhaps she had planned the lie to cover up an earlier one.

"I must say it's all very remarkable . . . how Jason's affairs have turned out," said Elmer. "I never would have thought it."

"You never believed in him," said Emma, with an air of triumph, "and now you see."

To Philip the whole room, the table, the people about

it, the figure of the slattern Essie standing in the doorway, all their petty boasting and piety and lying, became suddenly vulgar and loathsome. And then, almost at once, he became ashamed of himself for being ashamed, for they were *his* people. He had no others. It was a subtle, sickening sort of torture.

16

Emma was herself forced to go in at last and send away the newspaper man, for Jason would have kept him there the rest of the night, telling a story which became more and more embroidered with each rash recounting. And when, at last, the reporter had gone, the others came in and sat about while Jason continued his talk. But the evening died slowly, perhaps because of Elmer's suspicions, or Naomi's curious depression, or Philip's own disgust and low spirits. Jason found himself talking presently against a curious, foreboding silence, of which he took no notice. Only Emma and Mabelle were still listening.

It was Elmer who at last broke up the party, pushing the rotund and breathless Mabelle before him. In the door Mabelle turned, and, shaking her head a little coquettishly, said, "Well, good-night, Jason. Goodnight, Emma. I feel like I was saying 'good-night' to a honeymoon couple." And the bawdy look came into her eyes. "There'll never be any second honeymoon for Elmer and me. We've got our family now and that's all done."

Still tittering, she was dragged off by her husband. When she had gone, Jason said, "Mabelle is a cute one, ain't she, and a funny one too, to be married to a mausoleum like Elmer."

"Now, Jason, it's all patched up between you and Elmer. There's no use beginning all over again."

Naomi and Philip had put on their wraps, and were standing by the door, when Jason suddenly slapped his son on the back. "We've got to get better acquainted, son. You'll like your Pa when you know him better. Nobody can resist him." He winked at Emma, who turned crimson. "Ain't it so, Em. Least of all, the ladies." And then to Philip again, "I'll come and see you in the morning."

Philip turned quickly. "No, I'll come and fetch you myself. You wouldn't find the way."

"I want to see the twins the first thing."

"I'll come for you."

He had resolved that his father was not to come to the stable. He saw that Emma hadn't even told his father that he wasn't living with his wife. The stable had suddenly become to him a kind of temple, a place dedicated to that part of him which had escaped. There were things there which his father wouldn't understand, and could only defile. The stable belonged to him alone. It was apart from all the others—his father, his mother, Naomi, Uncle Elmer and Aunt Mabelle.

Emma was standing before Naomi, holding her coat open, so that she might examine the dress underneath. She was saying, "You must come up some afternoon, Naomi, and I'll help you make the dress right. It hangs all wrong at the back, and it's all bunchy around the armholes. You could make it all right, but, as it is, it's . . . it's sort of funny-looking."

All the way back to the Flats neither of them spoke at all: Philip, because there was a black anger and rebellion burning in him, and Naomi, because if she had tried to speak, she would have wept. She felt as though she were dead, as if in a world made up of Philip and his father and Emma she no longer had any existence. She was only a burden who annoyed them all. And the dress . . . it was only sort of "funny-looking."

He left Naomi at the door of the flat with an abrupt "good-night." It was after midnight, and the moon was rising behind the hill crowned by Shane's Castle, throwing a blue light on the mist that hung above the Flats. In the far distance the mist was all rosy with the light from four new furnaces that had begun once more to work. The strike was slipping slowly into defeat, and he understood that it meant nothing to him any longer. He had almost forgotten Krylenko.

As he passed through the rusted gates of the park, there drifted toward him from among the trunks of the dead trees, a faint, pungent odor that was hauntingly familiar and, as he climbed the drive between the dead trees, it grew stronger and stronger, until at last he recognized, in a sudden flash of memory which brought back all the hot panorama of the lake and the forest at Megambo, that it was the smell of gunpowder, the smell that clung to his rifle when he had stood there by the barricade beside Lady Millicent killing those poor niggers. It was a faint, ghostly smell that sometimes died away altogether and sometimes came in strong waves on a warm breeze filled with the dampness of the melting snow.

At the top of the hill, the big house lay dead and blind, without a sign of life, and, as he turned the corner, he saw that near the stable lay the remnants of a fire which had burnt to a heap of embers. His foot touched something that was wet and slippery. He looked down to discover a great stain of black on the snow. For a moment he stared at the stain, fascinated, and suddenly he knew what it was. It was a great stain of blood.

In the distance, among the trees, he discerned a light, and after a moment he discovered a little group of men . . . three or four . . . carrying a lantern, which they held high from time to time, as if searching for something. And then, all at once, as he moved forward again, he almost stepped upon a woman who lay in the snow at the entrance to the rotting arbor covered with the vines of the dying wistaria. She lay face down with one arm above her head in a posture that filled him for a moment with a sense of having lived through this same experience before, of having seen this same woman lying face down . . . dead . . . for she was unmistakably dead. He knelt beside her, and, turning the body on its side, he remembered suddenly. She lay like the black virgin they had found dead across the path in the tall grass at Megambo . . . the one they had left to the leopards.

Trembling, he peered at the white face in the moonlight. The woman was young, and across one side of the face there was a little trickle of blood that came from a hole in the temple. She was dressed in rags, and her feet were wrapped in rolls of sacking. She was the wife or daughter of some striker. It occurred to him suddenly that there was something pitifully lonely in the sight of the body left there, forgotten, by the embers in the dead park; it had the strangest effect upon him. He rose and tried to call to the little group of searchers, but no sound came from his throat, and he began suddenly to cry. Leaning against one of the pillars of the arbor, he waited until his body had ceased to tremble. It was a strange, confused feeling, as if the whole spectacle of humanity were suddenly revealed in all its pathos, its meanness, its grandeur, and its cruelty. It was a brilliant flash of understanding, but it passed almost at once, leaving him weak and sick. And then, after a moment, he found his voice again, and shouted. The little party halted, and looked about, and he shouted a second time. Then they came toward him, and he saw that two of them carried shotguns and that one of them was McTavish.

The woman was dead. They picked her up and laid her carefully on one of the blackened marble benches of the garden, and McTavish told him what had happened. In the Town they had forbidden the strikers to hold meetings, hoping thus to break the strike, but the Shanes, Irene and Lily (for the old woman was dead), had sent word to Krylenko that they might meet in the dead park. And so the remnant of those who had held out in the face of cold and starvation had come here to listen to Krylenko harangue them from a barrel by the light of a great fire before the stables. There had been shouting and disorder, and then some one inside the Mill barrier—one of the hooligans (they hadn't yet discovered who did it) turned a machine-gun on the mob around the fire. It had only lasted an instant—the sharp, vicious, staccato sound, but it had taken its toll.

"It's a dirty business," concluded McTavish in disgust. He wasn't jolly to-night. All the old, cynical good-humor had gone out of him, as if he, too, had seen what Philip saw in that sudden flash as he leaned against the decaying arbor.

They took a shutter from the windows of the stable and, placing the body of the girl upon it, set off down the hill between the dead walls of the pine-trees. For a long time Philip stood in the soiled, trampled snow, looking after them, until a turn in the drive hid the lantern from view behind the pine-trees.

17

The room above the stable was in darkness, but as he came up out of the staircase he saw that there was a woman sitting by the window, silhouetted against the moonlight beyond. He thought, "It must be Lily Shane, but why is she here at this hour of the night?" And then a low, familiar voice came out of the darkness, "It's only me, Philip . . . Mary." She spoke as if he must have known she was there, waiting for him.

He struck a match quickly and lighted the kerosene lamp, at which she rose and came over to him. By the flickering, yellow light he saw that she had been crying.

"It's been horrible, Philip. I saw it all from the window while I was waiting for you."

"I know . . . we just found a dead woman in the snow."

He was possessed by a curious feeling of numbness, in which Mary seemed to share, as if the horror of what had taken place outside wiped out all the strangeness of their meeting thus. Death, it seemed, had brushed by them so closely that it had swept away all but those things which lay at the foundation of existence—the fact that they loved each other, that they were together now, and that nothing else was of any importance. They were, too, like people stunned by horror. They sat by the stove, Philip in silence, while Mary told him what she had seen. For a long time it did not even appear strange to him that she should be there in his room at two o'clock in the morning.

He heard her saying, "Who was the woman they killed?"

"I don't know. She looked Italian."

There was a long silence and at last it was Mary, the practical Mary, who spoke. "You must wonder why I came here, Philip . . . after . . . after not seeing you at all for all this time."

He looked at her slowly, as if half-asleep. "I don't know. I hadn't even thought of it, Mary . . . anything seems possible to-night, anything seems possible in this queer park." And then, stirring himself, he reached across the table and touched her hand. She did not draw it away, and the touch gave him the strangest sense of a fathomless intimacy which went back and back into their childhood, into the days when they had played together in the tree-house. She had belonged to him always, only he had been stupid never to have understood it. He could have spoken out once long ago. If only he, the *real* Philip, had been born a little sooner, they would both have been saved.

And then, suddenly, he knew why she had come, and he was frightened.

He said, "You heard about my father?"

She started a little, and said, "No."

"He came back to-night. It was awful, Mary. If

he'd only stayed away! If he'd never have come
back. . . . "

So he told her the whole story, even to his suspicion
that his father was a liar, and had deserted him and
his mother twenty-six years before. He told her of the
long agony of the reunion, describing his father in
detail. And at the end, he said, "You see why I wish
he'd never come back. You *do* see, don't you, Mary
. . . if he'd stayed away, I'd never have thought of him
at all, or at least only as my mother thought of him.
But he isn't like that at all. I don't see how she can
take him back . . . how she can bear to have him
about."

She wanted to cry out, "Don't you see, Philip?
Don't you see the kind of woman she is? If you don't
see, nothing can save you. She's worse than he is, because he's harmless." But she only said quietly, "Perhaps she's in love with him. If that's true, it explains
anything."

"Maybe it's that. She must be in love with him."

Mary thought, "Oh, Philip! If you'd only forget
all the things that don't matter and just live, you'd
be so much happier!" She wanted him to be happy
more than anything in the world. She would, she knew,
do anything at all to make him happy.

Presently she said, "She came to see me this afternoon, Philip . . . your mother. That's why I'm here
now. She said horrible things . . . that weren't true
at all. She said . . . she said . . . that I'd been living
with you all along, and she'd just found out about it.
She said that I came here to meet you in the stable.
She's hated me always . . . just because I've always

been fond of you. She said I'd tried to steal you from her."

For a moment he simply sat very still, staring at her. She felt his hand grow cold and relax its grasp. At last he whispered, "She said that? She said such things to you?"

"Yes . . . I ran away from her in the end. It was the only thing I could do."

Then all at once he fell on his knees and laid his head in her lap. She heard him saying, "There's nothing I can say, Mary. I didn't think she'd do a thing like that . . . and now I know, I know what kind of a woman she is. Oh, I'm so tired, Mary . . . you don't know how tired I am!"

She began to stroke his dark hair, and the sudden thought came to her with horror that in her desire for vengeance upon Emma Downes, it was not Emma she had hurt, but Philip.

He said, "You don't know what it is, Mary,—for months now . . . for years even, I've been finding out bit by bit . . . to have something gone that you've always believed in, to have some one you loved destroyed bit by bit, in spite of anything you can do. I tried and tried, but it was no good. And now . . . I can't hold out any more. I can't do it . . . I hate her . . . but I can never let her know it. I can never hurt her . . . because she really loves me, and it's true what she says . . . that she did everything for me. She fed and clothed me herself with her own hands."

Again Mary wanted to cry out, "She doesn't love you. She doesn't love any one but herself!" and again she kept silent.

"And now it's true . . . what she said . . . you've stolen me away from her, Mary. She's made it so. I'm through now . . . I can't go on trying any more."

Still stroking his head, she thought, "He's like a little boy. He's never grown up at all." And she said, "I was so angry, Philip, that I came here. I didn't care what happened; I only thought, 'If she thinks that's the truth, it might as well be, because she'll tell about it as the truth.' I didn't care any longer for anything but myself and you."

His head stirred, and he looked up at her, seizing her hands. "Is that true, Mary?" He kissed her hand suddenly.

"It's true . . . or why else should I be here, at this hour?" He was hopeless, she thought: he didn't live for a moment in reality.

He hadn't even thought it queer of her to be sitting there in his room long after midnight with his head on her knees. And suddenly she thought again, "If I'm his mistress, I can save him from her altogether. Nothing else can break it off forever."

He was kissing her hands, and the kisses seemed to burn her. He was saying, "Mary, I've loved you always, always . . . since the first time I saw you, but I only knew it when it was too late."

"It isn't too late, Philip. It isn't too late."

He was silent for a time, but she knew what he was thinking. He wasn't strong enough to take life into his own hands and bend it to his own will, or perhaps it wasn't a lack of strength, but only a colossal confusion that kept him caught and lost in an immense and hopeless tangle. Until to-night she hadn't herself been strong enough to act, but now a kind of intoxicating recklessness had seized her—the sober, sensible Mary Conyngham. She meant to-night to take him and comfort him, to make them both, for a little time, happy. To-morrow didn't matter. It would have been better if there were no to-morrow, if they could never wake at all.

It was Philip who spoke first. After a long silence, he said in a whisper, "I can't do it, Mary . . . I can't. It isn't only myself that matters. It's you and Naomi too. It isn't her fault any more than mine."

For a moment she wished wickedly that he had been a little more like John Conyngham, and then almost at once she saw that it was his decency, the very agony of his struggle, that made her love him so profoundly. And she was afraid that he would think her wicked and brazen and fleshly. It was a thing she couldn't explain to him.

There were no words rich enough, strong enough, to make him understand what it was that had brought her here. She had thought it all out, sitting for hours there by the window, in the light of the rising moon. She had felt life rushing past her. She was growing old with the passing of each second. She had seen a man killed, and afterwards Philip had himself come upon the body of a dead woman lying in the snow. Nothing mattered, save that they come together. What happened to her was of no consequence. Some terrible force, stronger than either of them, had meant them for each other since the beginning, and to resist it, to fight against it unnaturally as Philip was doing, seemed to her all at once a black and wicked sin.

He freed himself suddenly and stood up. "I can't

do it, Mary. I'll go away. . . . You can spend the night here and leave in the morning. No one in the Town will know you haven't spent the night at Shane's Castle."

"Where will you go?"

"I'll go to the tents. I'll be all right."

She suddenly put her hand over her eyes, and, in a low voice, asked, "And . . . what's to come after, Philip?"

"I don't know . . . I don't know. I don't know what I'm doing."

"We can't go on . . . I can't . . . "

"No . . . I'd rather be dead."

Suddenly, with a sob, she fell forward on the table, burying her face in her hands. "You belong to your mother still, Philip . . . you can't shake off the hard, wicked things she's taught you. Oh, God! If she'd only died . . . we'd have been married to each other!"

She began to cry softly, and, at the sound, he stopped the mechanical business of buttoning his coat, and then, almost as if he were speaking to himself, he said, "Damn them all! We've a right to our happiness. They can't take it from us. They can't . . . "

He raised her face from the table and kissed it again and again with a kind of wild, rude passion that astonished her, until she lost herself completely in its power. Suddenly he ceased, and, looking at her, said, "It doesn't matter if to-morrow never comes. I love you, Mary . . . I love you. That's all that matters."

They were happy then, for in love and in death all things are wiped out. There, in the midst of the dead and frozen park, she set him free for a little time.

18

The morning came quickly in a cold gray haze, for the furnaces, starting to work one by one as the strike collapsed, had begun again to cover the Flats with a canopy of smoke. It was Mary who went first, going by the back drive, which led past the railway-station. And with her departure the whole world turned dark. While she had been there with him, he was happy with the sense of security that is born of companionship in adventure, but as her figure faded presently into the smoke and mist that veiled the deserted houses of the Flats, the enchantment of the night gave way to a cold, painful sense of actuality. The whole night had been, as some nights are in the course of lives that move passionately, unreal and charged with strange, intangible currents of fire and ice. During that brief hour or two when he had slept, years seemed to have passed. The figure of his father had become so remote that he no longer seemed cheap and revolting, but only shallow and pitiful. Even the memory of McTavish and the two men with the lantern standing over the dead woman in the snow was dim now and unreal.

It was only the sight of the trampled, dirty snow, the black spot where the fire had been and the pool of blood at the turn of the drive that made him know how near had been all these things which had happened during the night. And the park was no longer beautiful and haunted in the moonlight, but only a dreary expanse of land filled with dead trees and decaying arbors. The old doubts began slowly to torment him once more— the feeling of terror lest Naomi should ever discover what had happened, and the knowledge that he had betrayed her. There was, too, an odd new fear that he might become such a man as his father. It was born in that cold, gray light, of a sudden knowledge that deep inside him lay sleeping all the weaknesses, all the sensuality, of such a man. After what had happened in the night, he saw suddenly that he might come like his father to live in a shallow world that shut out all else. He was afraid suddenly, and ashamed, for he had been guilty of a sin which his father must have committed a hundred times.

Yet he had, too, an odd new sense of peace, a soothing, physical, animal sort of peace, that seemed to have had its beginnings months ago, in the moments of delirium when he had wanted to live only because he could not die without knowing such an experience as had come to him in the night. It was, he supposed, Nature herself who had demanded this of him. And now she had rewarded him with this sense of completeness. Nature, he thought, had meant his children to be Mary's children, too; and now that couldn't be . . . unless . . . unless Naomi died.

It was a wicked thought that kept stealing back upon him. It lay in hiding at the back of his mind, even in the last precious moments before Mary had left, when she stood beside the stove making the coffee. He had thought again and again, "If only Naomi died . . . we could be like this forever." Watching her, he had thought, despite all his will to the contrary, of what love had been with Naomi and what with Mary. And he had told himself that it wasn't fair to think such things, because he had never loved Naomi: at such moments he had almost hated her. Yet she had loved him, and was ashamed of her love, so that she made all their life together a sordid misery. And Mary, who had been without shame, had surrounded her love with a proud and reckless glory. Yet, in the end, it was Mary who hid, who stole away through the black houses of the Flats as if she had done a shameful thing, and it was Naomi who bore his children. For a moment he almost hated the two helpless little creatures he had come so lately to love, because a part of them was also a part of Naomi.

As he stood by the window, all wretched and tormented, he saw coming across the trampled snow the battered figure of Hennery. He was coming from the house, and his bent old figure seemed more feeble and ancient than it had ever been before. He entered the stable, and Philip heard him coming painfully up the stairs. At the sight of Philip, he started suddenly, and said, "You scared me, Mr. Downes . . . my nerves is all gone. I ain't the same since last night." He took off his hat and began fumbling in his pockets. "I got a letter for you . . . that strike feller left it for you . . . that . . . I doan' know his name, but the feller that made all the trouble."

He brought forth a piece of pale mauve paper that must have belonged to Lily Shane, but was soiled now from contact with Hennery's pocket.

"He was in the house all night," said Hennery, "a-hiding there, I guess, from the police, and he's gone now."

Then he was silent while Philip opened the note and read in the powerful, sprawling hand of Krylenko:

"I've had to clear out. If they caught me now, they'd frame something and send me up. And I'm not through fighting yet. The strike's bust, and there's no good in staying. But I'm coming back. I'll write you from where I go.

"Krylenko."

He read it again and then he heard Hennery saying, "It was a turrible night, Mr. Downes . . . I guess it was one of those nights when all kinds of slimy things are out walkin'. They're up and gone too . . . both of them . . . the girls, Miss Lily and Miss Irene. And they ain't comin' back, so Miss Lily says. She went away, before it was light, on the New York flier. Oh, it was a turrible night, Mr. Downes . . . I've seen things happenin' here for forty years, but nothin' like last night . . . nothin' ever."

He began to moan and call on the Lord, and Philip remembered suddenly that the half-finished drawing of Lily Shane had disappeared. She had carried it off then, without a word. And slowly she again began to take possession of his imagination. For a moment he tried to picture her house in Paris where his drawing of her would be hung. She had gone away without giving him another thought.

Hennery was saying over and over again, "It was a turrible night . . . something must-a happened in the house too. The Devil sure was on the rampage."

He stood there, staring out of the window, suffering from a curious, sick feeling of having been deserted. "By what? By whom?" he asked himself. "Not by Lily Shane, surely, on whom I had no claims . . .

whom I barely knew." Yet it was Lily Shane who had
deserted him. It was as if she had closed a door behind
her, shutting him back into the world of Elmer and his
mother and Jason Downes. The thing he had glimpsed
for a moment was only an illusion. . . .

19

When Hennery had gone off muttering to himself,
Philip put on his coat and went out, for the room had
become suddenly unendurable to him. He did not know
why, but all at once he hated it, this room where he had
been happy for the first time since he was a child. It
turned suddenly cold and desolate and hauntingly
empty. Running down the stairs, he hurried across the
soiled snow, avoiding the dark stain by the decaying
arbor. He went by that same instinct which always
drove him when he was unhappy towards the furnaces
and the engines, and at Hennessey's corner he turned
toward the district where the tents stood. They presented an odd, bedraggled appearance now, still hous-
ing the remnant of workers who had fought to the end,
all that little army which had met the night before in
the park of Shane's Castle. Here and there a deserted
tent had collapsed in the dirty snow. Piles of rubbish
and filth cluttered the muddy field on every side. Men,
women and children stood in little groups, frightened
and helpless and bedraggled, all the spirit gone out of
them. There was no more work for them now.
Wherever they went, no mill would take them in. They
had no homes, no money, no food. . . .

Lost among them, he came presently to feel less
lonely, for it was here that he belonged—in this army

of outcasts—a sort of pariah in the world that should have been his own.

At the door of one of the tents, he recognized Sokoleff. The Ukranian had let his beard grow and he held a child of two in his arms—a child with great hollow eyes and blue lips. Sokoleff, who was always drunk and laughing, was sober now, with a look of misery in his eyes. Philip shook his free hand in silence, and then said, "You heard about Krylenko?"

"No, I ain't heard nothin'. I've been waitin' for him. I gotta tell him a piece of bad news."

"He's gone away."

"Where's he gone?"

Philip told him, and, after a silence, Sokoleff said, "I suppose he had to beat it. I suppose he had to . . . but what are we gonna do . . . the ones that's left. He's the only one with a brain. The rest of us ain't good for nothin'. We ain't even got money to get drunk on."

"He won't forget you."

"Oh, it's all right for him. He ain't got nobody . . . no children or a wife. He ain't even got a girl . . . now."

For a moment the single word "now," added carelessly after a pause, meant nothing to Philip, and then suddenly a terrible suspicion took possession of him. He looked at Sokoleff. "What d'you mean . . . now?"

"Ain't you heard it?"

"What?"

"It was his girl, Giulia . . . that was killed last night."

Philip felt sick. In a low voice he asked, "And he didn't know it?"

"I was to tell him, but nobody's seen him. I'm damned glad he's went away now. I won't have the goddamned dirty job. He'll be crazy . . . crazy as hell."

And then Philip saw her again as he had seen her the night before, lying face down in the snow . . . Krylenko's Giulia.

"She oughtn't to have went up there," Sokoleff was saying. "But she was nuts on him . . . she thought that he was the best guy on earth, and she wanted to hear his speech. . . ." The bearded Slovak spat into the snow. "I guess that was the last thing she ever heard. She musta died happy. . . . That's better than livin' like this."

And Krylenko had been hiding in Shane's Castle all night while Giulia lay dead in the snow outside.

The sick baby began to cry, and Sokoleff stroked its bare head with a calloused paw covered by black hair.

All at once Philip was happy again; even in the midst of all the misery about him, he was gloriously, selfishly happy, because he knew that, whatever happened, he had known what Krylenko had lost now forever. He thought suddenly, "The jungle at Megambo was less cruel and savage than this world about me."

20

To Jason Downes the tragedy in the park of Shane's Castle had only one significance—that it tarnished all the glory of his astonishing return. When the papers appeared in the morning, the first pages were filled with the news of "the riot precipitated by strikers last night." It recounted the death of a Pole and of Giulia Rizzo, and announced triumphantly that the strike was broken at last. And far back, among the advertisements of Peruna and Lydia Pinkham's Compound, there appeared a brief paragraph or two announcing the return of Jason Downes, and touching upon the remarkable story of his accident and consequent loss of memory. There were, doubtless, people who never saw it at all.

But he made the most of his return, walking the round of all the cigar-stores and poker-rooms which he had haunted in his youth. He even went to Hennessey's saloon, beginning to thrive again on the money of the strike-breakers. But he found no great triumph, for he discovered only one or two men who had ever known him and to the others he was only Emma Downes' husband, whom they barely noticed in the excitement of discussing the riots of the night before. Even his dudishness had dated during those long twenty-six years: he must have heard the titters that went up from poolroom loafers at the sight of the fauncolored vest, the waxed mustaches and the tan derby. He was pushed aside at bars and thrust into the corner in the poolrooms.

Half in desperation, he went at last to find an audience in the group of old men who sat all day about the stove of McTavish's undertaking-parlors. They were old: they would remember who he was. But even there the clamor of the tragedy drowned his tale. He found the place filled with Italians—the father and the seven orphaned brothers and sisters of Giulia Rizzo. The father wept and wrung his hands. The older children joined him, and the four youngest huddled dumbly in a corner. It was Jason's own son, Philip, who was trying to quiet them. He nodded to his father, gave him a sudden glance of contempt, and then disappeared with McTavish into the back room where the undertaker had prepared Giulia for her last rest. For a moment Jason hung about hopefully, and then, confused and depressed by the ungoverned emotions of the Italians, he slipped out of the door, and up the street toward the Peerless Restaurant. He was like a bedraggled bantam rooster which had lost its proud tail-feathers, but as he approached the restaurant he grew a bit more jaunty: there was always Em who thought him wonderful. . . .

Behind the partition of the undertaking-rooms, Philip and McTavish stood looking down at Giulia. The blood had been washed away and her face was white like marble against the dark coil of her hair. She was clothed in a dress of black silk.

"It was her best dress," said McTavish. "The old man brought it up here this morning."

Philip asked, "Are they going to bury her in the Potters Field? Old Rizzo hasn't got a cent, with all these children to feed."

"No, I've arranged that. I fixed it up with the priest. She had to be buried in consecrated ground . . . and . . . and I bought enough for her. I ain't got any family, so I might as well spend my money on something."

21

Philip saw his father at the restaurant, but there was little conversation between them, and Emma kept talking about the riot of the night before, observing that, "now that the police had tried something besides coddling a lot of dirty foreigners, the strike was over in a hurry."

At this remark, Philip rose quietly and went out without another word to either of them. At home he found the druggist's wife sitting with the twins. Naomi, she said, was out. She had gone to see Mabelle. Mrs. Stimson wanted more details of his father's return, and also news of what had happened at Shane's Castle. After answering a dozen questions, he went away quickly.

At four o'clock his father came and saw the twins, diddling them both on his feet until they cried and Mrs. Stimson said, with the air of a snapping-turtle, "I'm going to leave them with you. Naomi ought to have been home two hours ago, and I've got a household of my own to look after." (Even for her poor Jason appeared to have lost his fascination.)

At seven when Philip came in to sit with the twins while Naomi went to choir practice, he found little Naomi crying and his father asleep in the Morris-chair by the gas stove. Jason had removed his collar and wrapped himself in a blanket. With him, sleeping was simply a way of filling in time between the high spots in existence: he slept when he was bored, and he slept when he was forced to wait.

Holding the baby against him, and patting its back softly, Philip approached his father and touched him with the toe of his shoe. "Pa!" he said. "Pa! Wake up!"

Jason awakened with all the catlike reluctance of a sensual nature, stretching himself and yawning and closing his eyes. He would have fallen asleep a second time but for the insistence of Philip's toe, the desperate crying of the child, and Philip's voice saying, "Wake up! Wake up!" There was something in the very prodding of the toe which indicated a contempt or at least a lack of respect. Jason noticed it and scowled.

"I just fell asleep for a minute," he said. "It couldn't have been long." But all the cocksureness had turned into an air of groveling apology.

"Where's Naomi?"

"She went off to Mabelle's." He took a pair of cigars from the yellow waistcoat and asked, "Have a cigar?"

"No. Not now." Philip continued to pat the baby's fat back. Suddenly he felt desperate, suffocated and helpless. The cry of the child hurt him.

He said, "She's been at Mabelle's all day."

"I do believe she said she'd be back after choir practice." He lighted the cigar and regarded the end of it thoughtfully. Philip began to walk up and down, and presently his father said, without looking at him, "You ain't living with Naomi, are you? I mean here in this house? You ain't sleeping with her?"

"No . . . I'm not."

"I thought so. Your Ma was trying to make me believe you was." He cocked his head on one side. "But I smelled a rat . . . I smelled a rat. I knew something was wrong."

Philip continued his promenade in silence.

"How'd you ever come to hook up with Naomi?"

"Because I wanted to . . . I suppose."

Jason considered the answer thoughtfully. "No, I don't believe you did. I ain't very bright, but I know some things. No man in his right mind would hook up to anything as pious as Naomi. . . ." He saw that Philip's head tossed back and his jaw hardened, as if he were going to speak. "Now, don't get mad at your Pa . . . your poor old Pa . . . I know you don't think much of 'im, but he's kind-a proud of you, just the same. And he don't blame you for not living with Naomi. Why, the thought of it makes me kind-a seasick."

Again a silence filled by little Naomi's heartbroken crying.

"Why, she ought to be home now looking after her children instead of gadding about with preachers and such. Your Ma was always pious, too, but she was a good housekeeper. She never allowed religion to interfere with her bein' practical."

Philip, distracted, unhappy, conscience-stricken, and a little frightened at Naomi's queer avoidance of him, was aware, too, that his father was saying one by one things he'd thought himself a hundred times. It occurred to him that Jason wasn't perhaps as empty and cheap as he seemed. It was almost as if an affection were being born out of Jason's hopeless efforts toward an understanding. If only little Naomi would stop squalling. . . .

His father was saying, "No, I'm proud of you, my boy. D'you know why?"

"No."

"Because of the way you stand up to your Ma. It takes a strong man to do that, unless you learn the trick. I've learned the trick. I just let her slide off now like water off a duck's back. I just say, 'Yes, yes,' to her and then do as I damned please. Oh, I learned a lot since I last saw her . . . a hell of a lot. There's a lotta women like her . . . especially American women—that don't know their place."

The baby stopped screaming, sobbed for a moment, and then began again.

"It wasn't her piousness that drove me away. I could have managed that. It was her way of meddlin'."

Philip stopped short and turned, looking at his father. "Then you *were* running away from us when you fell and hit your head?"

"I wasn't runnin' away from *you*."

Philip stood in front of the chair. "And you didn't lose your memory at all, did you?"

Jason looked up at him with an expression of astonishment. "No . . . of course not. D'you mean to say she never told you the truth . . . even you . . . my own son?"

"No . . . I guess she was trying to protect you . . . and made me believe my father wasn't the kind to run away." (The cries of the baby had begun to beat upon his brain like the steel hammers of the Mill.)

"Protect me, hell! It was to protect herself. She didn't want the Town to think that any man would desert her. Oh, I know your Ma, my boy. And it would have took a hero or a nincompoop to have stuck with her in those days." He knocked the ash from his cigar, and shook his head sadly. "But I oughtn't to have run away on your account. If I'd 'a' stuck it out, you wouldn't have got mixed up in the missionary business or with Naomi either. You wouldn't be walkin' up and down with that squallin' brat—at any rate, it wouldn't be Naomi's brat. I guess the missionary business was her way of gettin' even with me through you." He shook his head again. "Your Ma's a queer woman. She's got as much energy as a steam engine, but she never knows where she's goin', and she always thinks she's the only one with any sense. And my, ain't she hard . . . and unforgivin' . . . hard as a cocoanut!"

"She forgave you and took you back."

"But she's been aching to do that for years. That's the kind of thing she likes." His chest swelled under the yellow vest. "Besides, I always had a kind of an idea that she preferred me to any other man she's ever seen. Your Ma's a passionate woman, Philip. She's kind of ashamed of it, but deep down she's a passionate woman. If she'd had me about all these years she wouldn't have been so obnoxious, I guess."

The baby had ceased crying now, and, thrusting its soft head against the curve of Philip's throat, was lying very still. The touch of the downy little ball against his skin filled him with pity and a sudden, warm happiness. The poor little thing was trusting him, reaching out in its helpless way. He didn't even mind the things that his father was saying of his mother. He scarcely heard them. . . .

"I thought," said Jason, "that we'd cooked up that story about my memory for the Town and for old pie-faced Elmer. I thought she'd tell you the truth, but I guess she don't care much for the truth if it ain't pleasant."

Philip continued to pat little Naomi, more and more gently, as she began to fall asleep. In a low voice he asked, "You're going to stay now that you've come back, aren't you?"

"No, I gotta go back to Australia."

Philip looked at his father sharply. "You aren't going back to stay, are you?"

"I gotta look after my property, haven't I?"

"Why did you ever come back at all?"

Jason considered the question. "I suppose it was curiosity . . . I wanted to see my own son, and well . . . I wanted to see what had happened to your Ma after all these years, and then it is sort of fun to be a returned prodigal. Nothing has happened to your Ma. She's just the same. She accused me of bein' drunk this morning when I'd only had a glass. She carried on something awful."

"Have you told her you're going back to stay?"

"No . . . I've just told her I'm going back." He looked at Philip suddenly. "I suppose you think I'm lyin' about all that property in Australia. Well, I ain't. I'll send you pictures of it when I get back . . . I ought to have brought them. I can't guess why I didn't."

He rose and put on his coat. "I'd better be movin' on now, or she'll be sayin' I've been hangin' around bars. Have you eaten yet?"

"Yes . . . at the railroad lunch counter."

"That's a hell of a life for a married man."

He stood for a moment looking at little Naomi, who lay asleep on Philip's shoulder. Then, shyly, he put out his finger and touched the downy head gently. "They're fine babies," he said. "I wouldn't have thought a poor creature like Naomi could have had 'em."

Philip laid the child gently beside her brother and stood looking down at them.

"Philip," his father began. Philip turned, and, as if the burning gaze of his son's eyes extinguished his desire to speak, Jason looked away quickly, and said, "Well, good-night." He turned shyly, and Philip, aware that he was trying to pierce through the wall that separated them, felt suddenly sorry for him, and said, "Yes, Pa. What was it you meant to say?"

Jason coughed and then with an effort said, "Don't be too unhappy . . . and if there's somebody else . . . I mean another girl . . . why, don't torture yourself too much about it. Your Ma has made you like that. . . . But she's got queer ideas. We ain't alive very long, you know, and there ain't any reason why we should make our brief spell miserable."

Philip didn't answer him. He was looking down again at the children, silent, with the old, queer, pinched look about the eyes, as if he were ill again. He saw suddenly that his father wasn't such a fool, after all, and he *was* human. He was standing there with his hat in his two hands, looking childish and subdued and very shy.

Philip heard him saying, with another nervous cough, "Well, good-night, Philip."

"Good-night."

The door closed and Philip sank down wearily into a chair, resting his head on the edge of the crib. Presently he fell asleep thus.

22

On that night the singing at choir practice reached a peak of frenzy. While Philip sat sleeping beside the crib, Naomi was pounding her heart out on the stained celluloid keys of the tinny piano in the Infants' Class-room. She played wildly, with a kind of shameless abandon, as if she wanted to pour out her whole story of justification; and the others, taking fire from her spirit, sang as they had never sung before.

During the afternoon, the old Naomi—the stubborn, sure Naomi of Megambo—had come to life again in some mysterious fashion. She even put on the new foulard dress in a gesture of defiance to show them—Philip and his mother—that, however "funny-looking" it might be, she was proud of it. And then neither of them had seen her wearing it, Philip because she was avoiding him, and Emma because chance had not brought them together. She had gone up to Mabelle's bent upon telling her that she had come to the end of her endurance. She had meant to ask Mabelle's advice, because Mabelle was very shrewd about such matters.

And then when she found herself seated opposite Mabelle she discovered that she couldn't bring herself to say what she meant to say. She couldn't humble her pride sufficiently to tell even Mabelle how Philip treated her. She had finally gone home and then returned a second time, but it was no use. She couldn't speak of it: she was too proud. And she knew, too, that whatever happened she must protect Philip. It wasn't, she told herself, as if he were himself, as he had been at Megambo. He was sick. He really wasn't responsible. She cried when she thought how she loved him now; if he would only notice her, she would let him trample her body in the dust. Mabelle's near-sighted blue eyes noted nothing. She went on rocking and rocking, talking incessantly of clothes and food and a soothing syrup that would make little Naomi sleep better at night.

During the day she had formed a dozen wild projects. She would go back to Megambo. She would return to her father, who was seventy now, and would welcome her help. She would run off to a cousin who lived in Tennessee. She would join another cousin who was an Evangelist in Texas: she could play the piano and lead the singing for him. In any of these places she would find again the glory she had known as Naomi Potts, "youngest missionary of God"; she wouldn't any longer be a nobody, unwanted, always pushed aside and treated as of no consequence.

But always there were the twins to be considered. How could she run off and forget them? And if she did run away, Emma and perhaps even Philip would use it as a chance to rid themselves of her forever. She fancied that she saw now how Emma had used her, willing all the while to cast her off when she was no longer of any service. She told herself again and again, as if she could not bring herself to believe it, that she loved the twins—that she loved them despite her aching back and the hours she was kept awake by their crying. But she remembered that she had never been tired at Megambo: no amount of work had tired her. She hadn't wanted the twins: she'd only gone to Philip because Mabelle and Emma told her that she must and because Mabelle said that men liked children, and that going to Philip would give her a hold over him. And now . . . see what had come of it! Philip scarcely noticed her. Before she lived with him, it hadn't mattered to her, but now—now she always carried a weight about inside her. Her heart leaped if he took the least notice of her.

No, she saw it all clearly. She must run away. She couldn't go on, chained down like a slave. But if she ran away, she'd lose Philip for ever, and if she stayed, he might come back to her. The children belonged to both of them. They were a bond you could never break, the proof that once, for a little time, he belonged to her. She saw that he, too, was chained after a fashion. He belonged to her in a way he belonged to no other woman. In the sight of the Lord any other woman would always be a strumpet and a whore.

At last, as it was growing dark, she found herself sitting on a bench in the park before the new monument to General Sherman. It was raining and her coat was soaked and her shoes wet through. The rain ran in little trickles from her worn black hat. It was as if she had wakened suddenly from a dream. She wasn't certain how she came to be sitting on the wet bench with the heavy rain melting the snow all about her. She thought, "I must have been crazy for a time. I can't go on like this. I've got to talk to some one. I've got to . . . I've got to!" She began to cry, and then she thought, "I'll speak to the Reverend Castor to-night after choir practice. He'll help me and he's a good man. He'll never tell any one. He's always been so kind. It was silly of me to think things about him. I was silly to be afraid of him. I'll talk to him. I've got to talk to some one. He'll understand."

When the practice was finished, the Reverend Castor came out of the study to bid the members good-night. In the dim light of the hallway, as Naomi passed him, he looked at her and smiled. She saw that his hands were trembling in a way that had come over him lately, and the smile warmed her, but at the same time weakened her. There was a comfort and a kindliness in it that made her want to cry.

Once inside the study, she found that the drawer of the cabinet was jammed again, as it had been on that first night. While she tugged at it, she heard him outside the door saying good-night one by one to the choir. Putting down the music, she began again to struggle with the drawer, and then suddenly, as if the effort was the last she could make, she collapsed on the floor and began to weep.

She heard the door open and she heard the Reverend Castor's deep, warm voice saying, "Why, Naomi, what's the matter?"

She answered him, without looking up. "It's the drawer," she said. "It's stuck again . . . and I'm . . . I'm so tired."

He went over to the cabinet and this time he was forced to struggle with it.

"It's really too heavy for you, my dear girl . . . I'll fix it myself in the morning." He replaced the music and when he attempted to close the drawer again it stuck fast. "Now it won't close at all. But I can fix it. I'm handy about such things."

His hands were trembling, and he looked white and tired. He talked with the air of a man desperately hiding pits of silence. When he turned, Naomi still sat on the floor, her body bent forward. Her worn, rain-soaked hat had fallen forward a little, and she was sobbing. He sat down in the great stuffed leather chair. It was very low, so that he was almost on a level with her.

"My poor child," he asked, "what is it? Is it something I can help?"

"I don't know. I wanted to talk to some one. I can't go on. I can't . . . I can't."

He laid his big hand on her shoulder with a gentleness that seemed scarcely real, and, at the touch, she looked up at him, dabbing her eyes with a handkerchief that had been soaked with tears hours earlier. As she looked at him, some old instinct, born of long experience with unhappy women, took possession of him. He said, "Why, you've got a new dress on, Naomi. It's very pretty. Did you make it yourself?"

For a second a look almost of happiness came into her face. "Why, yes," she said. "Mabelle helped me . . . but I made most of it myself."

His other hand touched her shoulder. "Here," he said, "lean back against my knee and tell me everything that's making you unhappy. . . ." When she hesitated, he said, "Try to think of me as your father, my child. I'm old enough to be your father . . . and I don't want to see you unhappy."

She leaned against his knee with a sudden feeling of weak collapse. It was the first time any one had been kind to her for so long, and, strangely enough, she wasn't afraid of him any longer. The old uneasiness seemed to have died away.

"Tell me, my child."

The damp handkerchief lay crushed into a tiny ball in her red, chapped hand. For a long time she didn't speak, and he waited patiently until she found words. At last she said, "I don't know how to begin. I don't know myself what's happened to me . . . I don't know. Sometimes I think I must be black with sin or going crazy . . . sometimes I can't think any more, and I don't know what I'm doing. . . . It was like that to-day . . . all day. . . . I've been going about like a crazy woman."

And then, slowly, she began, in a confused, incoherent fashion, to tell him the whole story of her misery from the very beginning at Megambo when the Englishwoman had suddenly appeared out of the forest. It all seemed to begin then, she said, and it had gone on and on ever since, growing worse and worse. She hadn't any friends—at least none save Mabelle; and the others didn't want her to see Mabelle. Besides, Mabelle didn't seem to help: whatever she advised only made matters worse.

The Reverend Castor interrupted her. "But I'm your friend, Naomi . . . I've always been your friend. You could have come to me long ago."

"But you're a preacher," she said. "And that's not the same thing."

"But I'm a man, too, Naomi . . . a human being."

And then she even told him about Emma while he interrupted her from time to time by saying, "Can it be?" and, "It hardly seems possible—a woman like Emma Downes, who has always been one of the pillars, the foundation-stones, of our church! How much goes on of which we poor blind creatures know nothing."

And Naomi said, "I know. No one will ever believe me. They'll all believe that I'm nothing and that she's a good, brave woman. I can't fight her, Reverend Castor. I can't . . . and sometimes I think she tries to poison him against me."

The trembling hand came to rest once more on her shoulder. There was a long silence, and presently he said, in a low voice, "I know, my child . . . I know. I've suffered, too . . . for fifteen years."

She had begun to sob again. "And now there are other women . . . more than one, I'm sure. I pray to God for his soul. I pray and pray to God to return him to me . . . my Philip, who was a good man and believed in God. He's changed now. I don't know him any more. To-night I don't think I love him. I've come to the end of everything."

He began to pat her shoulder, gently, as if he were comforting a child, and for a long time, they stayed thus in silence. At last he said, "I've suffered, too, Naomi . . . for years and years. . . . It began almost as soon as I was married, and it's never stopped for an hour, for a moment since. It gets worse and worse with each year." Suddenly he covered his face with his hands and groaned. "I pray to God for strength to go on living. I have need of God's help to go on at all. I, too, need some one to talk to." His hands dropped from his face, and he placed one arm about her thin, narrow shoulders. She did not draw away. Still sobbing, she let her whole weight rest against him. She was so tired, and she felt so ill. A strange, gusty and terrifying happiness took possession of the tired, nerve-racked man. Just to touch a woman thus, to have a woman kind to him, to have a woman who would trust him, was a pleasure almost too keen to be borne. For fifteen acid years he had hungered for a moment, a single moment, like this. He did not speak, conscious, it seemed, that to breathe might suddenly shatter this fragile, pathetic sense of peace.

Naomi had closed her eyes, as if she had fallen

asleep from her long exhaustion; but she wasn't sleeping, for presently her pale lips moved a little, and she said in a whisper, "There's nothing for me to do but run away or kill myself . . . and then I'll be out of the way."

He did not tell her at once, without hesitation, that she was contemplating a great sin. He merely kept silent, and, after a time, he murmured, "My poor, poor child . . . my tired child," and then fell once more into silence. They must have remained thus for nearly an hour. Naomi even appeared to fall asleep, and then, starting suddenly, she cried out. His arm ached, but he did not move. He was, it seemed, past such a small discomfort as an aching arm. And he was struggling, struggling passionately, with a terrible temptation, conscious all the while that each minute added to the bitterness of the reproaches that awaited him on opening the parsonage door. It was long after eleven o'clock, and he should have returned ages ago. He thought, "I can't go home now. I can never go home again. I can never open that door again. I would rather die here now. One more time might drive me mad . . . I mightn't know what I was doing . . . I might. . . ."

The free hand again closed over his eyes, as if to shut out the horrible thing that had occurred to him. Naomi had opened her eyes and was looking up at him. For a second he thought, "Has she seen what was in them?"

Her lips moved again. "I don't care what happens to me any longer."

Suddenly, without knowing what he was doing, he bent down and took her in his arms, "Naomi . . .

Naomi . . . do you mean that? Answer me, do you mean that?"

She closed her eyes wearily. "I don't care what happens to me."

He held her more tightly, the odd, gusty pleasure sweeping over him in terrifying waves. "Naomi . . . will you . . . will you go away . . . now . . . at once, and with me?"

"You can do with me what you want, if you'll only be kind to me."

"We've a right to be happy. We've suffered enough." She did not answer him, and he said, "God will understand. He's merciful. We've had our hell here on earth, Naomi . . . Naomi . . . listen to me! Will you go now . . . at once?" A curious, half-mad excitement colored his voice. "I've got money. I've been putting it aside for a long time, because I've thought for a long time I might want to go away . . . I've been saving it, a dime and a quarter here and there where I could squeeze it. I've got more than two hundred dollars. I thought that sometime I'd have to run away. But I meant to go away alone . . . I never knew . . . I never knew." He began abruptly to cry, the tears pouring down the lined, tired face. "We'll go somewhere far away . . . to South America, or the South Sea Islands, where nobody will know us. And we'll be free there, and happy. We've a right to a little happiness. Oh, Naomi, we'll be happy."

She appeared not to have heard him. She lay in a kind of stupor, until, raising her body gently, he stood up and lifted her easily into the big leather chair, where she lay watching him, her eyes half-closed, her mouth set in a straight, hard line, touched with bitterness.

The Reverend Castor moved quickly, with a strange vigor and decision. The trembling had gone suddenly from his hands. His whole body grew taut and less weary, as if he had become suddenly young. He had the air of a man possessed, as if every fiber, every muscle, every cell, were crying out, "It's not too late! It's not too late! There is still time to live!" He approached the desk, and, unlocking the drawer, began taking out money—a thin roll of bills, and then an endless number of coins that tinkled and clattered as they slid into his pockets. There must have been pounds of metal in dimes and nickels and quarters. He filled his vest pocket with cheap cigars from a box on the desk, and then, turning, went over to Naomi, and, raising her from the chair, smoothed her hair and put her hat straight, with his own hands. Then he kissed her chastely on the brow, and she, leaning against him, murmured, "Take me wherever you like. I'm so tired."

For a moment they stood thus, and presently he began to repeat in his low, rich, moving voice, *The Song of Songs.*

"For, lo, the winter is past, the rain is over and gone. The flowers appear on the earth; the time of the singing of birds is come, and the voice of the turtle is heard in our land. . . ."

The words had upon her a strange effect of exaltation, the same that had come over her when she sat by the piano, carried away by her emotions. She wasn't Naomi any longer. Naomi seemed to have died. She was a gaudy Queen, and Solomon in all his glory was her lover. She seemed enveloped by light out of which the rich, vibrant voice was saying, *"Until the day break, and the shadows flee away, turn, my beloved, and be thou like a roe or a young hart upon the mountains of Bether.*"

A little while after, as the clock on the firehouse struck midnight, the door of the study closed, and two figures hurried away into the pouring rain. They were a tired, middle-aged preacher and a bedraggled woman, in a queer, homemade dress of figured foulard, and a soaked coat and hat; but there was a light in their eyes which seemed to illumine the darkness and turn aside the rain.

23

Philip wakened slowly, conscious of being stiff and sore from having slept in a cramped position, and thinking, "It must be late. Naomi will be home soon." And then, looking up at the clock, he saw that it was after one. He rose and went over to it, listening for the tick to make certain that it was working properly. He looked at his own watch. It, too, showed five minutes past one. He listened for a moment to the sound of the rain beating upon the tin roof and then he went into the other two rooms. They were empty, and, suddenly, he was frightened.

Giving a final look at the twins, he seized his hat, and, hurrying down the steps, roused the long-suffering Mrs. Stimson and told her that Naomi hadn't yet come home. He begged her to leave her door open, so that she might hear the twins if they began to scream, and without waiting to hear her complaints he rushed out into the rain.

It fell in ropes, melting the snow and running off down the hill in torrents. To-morrow, he knew dimly, there would be a flood in the Flats. The water would rise and fill the stinking cellars of the houses. Those few families who lived in tents must already be soaked with the cold downpour. The streets were deserted, and the shops and houses black and dark. Once he caught the distant glint of light on the wet black slicker of a policeman. Save for this, he seemed to be alone in a town of the dead.

From a long way off he saw the light in the church study, and the sight of it warmed him with quick certainty that Naomi must still be there. Some urgent thing, he told himself, had arisen at choir practice. He ran down the street and through the churchyard, and at the door of the study he knocked violently. No one answered. The place was empty. He opened the door. A drawer of the cabinet stood half-open with a pile of music thrust into it carelessly. A drawer of the desk was open and empty. The gas still flickered in the corner. Passing through the study, he went into the church itself. It was dark, save for a dim flare that made the outlines of the windows silhouettes of gray set in black. The empty church frightened him. He shouted, "Naomi! Naomi!" and, waiting, heard only an echo that grew fainter and fainter . . . "Naomi! . . . Naomi! . . . Naomi! . . ." until it died away into cold stillness. Again he shouted, and again the mocking, receding echo answered him. . . . "Naomi! . . . Naomi! . . . Naomi! . . ." His own voice, trembling with terror, came back to him out of the darkness: "Naomi! . . . Naomi! . . . Naomi!"

He thought, "She's not here, but she might be at the parsonage. In any case, Reverend Castor will know something." And then, "But why did he go away leaving the gas lighted and the study unlocked?" He turned back and, running, went through the dark church and the lighted study out into the rain.

There was a light still burning in the parsonage, and as he turned into the path he saw that a figure, framed against the light, stood in the upper window. At first he thought, "It's Reverend Castor," and then almost at once, "No . . . it's his wife. She's waiting for him to come home."

He knocked loudly at the door with a kind of desperate haste, for a terrible suspicion had begun to take form. Whatever had happened to Naomi, every moment was precious: it might save her from some terrible act that would wreck all her life and the Reverend Castor's as well. He knocked again, and then tried the door. It was locked, and he heard an acid voice calling out, "I'm coming. I'm coming. For Heaven's sake, don't break down the door!"

The key turned, and he found himself facing a figure in a gray flannel dressing-gown, dimly outlined by the slight flicker of gas. He could barely distinguish the features—thin, white and pinched . . . the features of a woman, the Reverend Castor's wife.

"Who are you . . . coming at this hour of the night to bang on people's doors?" It was a thin, grating voice. As his eyes grew accustomed to the light, he saw a face of incredible repulsion. It was a mean face, like that of a malicious witch.

"I'm Philip Downes. I'm trying to find my wife. She didn't come home from choir practice."

A look of evil satisfaction suddenly shadowed the woman's face. "She wasn't the only one that didn't come back. Like as not they're still there, carrying on in the church. I guess it wouldn't be the first time."

He didn't care what she was saying, though the sound of her voice and the look in her cold blue eyes made him want to strangle her.

"They aren't there. I've just come from the church."

He fancied that he heard her chuckle wickedly, but he couldn't be certain. He heard her saying, "Then he's done it. I always knew it would happen."

He seized her by the shoulders. "Done what? What do you mean?"

"Let go of me, young man! Why, he's run off with your wife, you fool! I always knew he'd do it some day. Oh, I knew him . . . Samuel Castor . . . I haven't been married to him for fifteen years for nothing!"

He wanted to shake her again, to make her talk. "If you knew, why didn't you tell me?"

"Because it might have been any woman. It wasn't just your wife. I wasn't sure who it would be." She began to laugh again, a high, cackling laugh. "I told him he'd do it. I told him so every night. I knew it was going to happen." She seemed to find delight in her horrible triumph.

"Where have they gone?"

"How do I know where they've gone? He's gone to hell for sure now, where he can't torment me any more. He's left me—a poor invalid . . . without a cent or any one to look after me. God knows what'll become of me now. But he's done it. I always told him he would. He's a fine man of God! He's left a poor invalid wife . . . penniless and sick."

There was a kind of wild delight in her voice and manner, as if she had been trying all these years to destroy him and had at last succeeded. She seemed to receive this last calamity as the final crown of her martyrdom. She was happy. To Philip it seemed suddenly that by wishing it, by thinking of nothing else for fifteen years, she had made the thing happen—just as it was Emma who had made happen the thing she wanted to believe—that Mary had stolen him from her.

He waited no longer. He ran past the malicious figure in the greasy dressing-gown, out again into the rain. He heard her saying, "He didn't even think of my hot-water bottle . . . the scoundrel . . ." and then the horrible voice was drowned by the sound of the downpour.

Without quite knowing how he got there, he found himself, soaked and shivering, inside the baggage-room at the railway station. Everything else was closed, but in the shadows among the gaudy, battered trunks of some theatrical company, the baggageman dozed quietly. He was shaken into consciousness to find a madman standing before him, white and trembling, and dripping with water.

"Tell me," Philip asked, "did any one leave the Town on the one o'clock?"

The man looked at him sleepily, and growled something about being wakened so roughly.

"Tell me. I've got to know!"

He scratched his head. "Why, yes. I do mind somebody gettin' on the one o'clock. Come to think of it, it was what's-his-name, the preacher."

"Reverend Castor?"

"Yes . . . that's the one . . . the big fellow."

"Was he alone?"

"I dunno. . . . He was alone for all I know. I didn't see no one else."

Philip left him, and, outside, stood for a moment in the shelter of the platform shed, peering into the distance where the gleaming wet rails disappeared into the dimness of fog and jewel-like signal lights. And all at once he hated the Flats, the Mills, the whole Town, and then he laughed savagely: even his beloved locomotives had betrayed him by carrying Naomi off into the darkness.

There was nothing to do now. What was done was done. He was glad he hadn't gone to the police to find her. If they didn't know, it would keep the thing out of the papers for a little time, and the two of them might come back. There was only that crazy old woman in the parsonage who need be feared; it was impossible to imagine what she might do. He hadn't really thought of her until now, and, as he walked through the rain, up the hill again, to his mother's house, her horrid image kept returning to him as she stood in her greasy dressing-gown screaming at him in triumph, "I knew it would happen some day. I always told him he'd do it!"

He thought, "I never knew it was as bad as that. No one knew." It seemed to him that God would forgive a man any sin who must have suffered as the Reverend Castor.

He was no longer conscious of the downpour, for he was already as wet as if he had jumped into the brook, and as he walked, all the deadly sickness of reaction began to sweep over him. He was tired suddenly, so

tired that he could have lain down in the streaming
gutter in peace; the whole thing seemed suddenly to
lose all its quality of the extraordinary. In his weariness it seemed quite a usual experience that a man
should be searching the Town for a wife who had run
away with the preacher. It was as if the thing hadn't
happened to himself, but as if he saw it from a great
distance, or had heard it told him as a story. To-
morrow (he thought), or the next day, they would be
telling it everywhere in the Town, in every cigar-store
and poolroom, about the stove at McTavish's undertaking parlors. They would hear of it even in
Hennessey's saloon. All at once a sudden flash of
memory returned to him—of Hennessey standing above
him, saying, "Run along home to your Ma like a good
little boy. Tell her not to let her little tin Jesus
come back to Hennessey's place, if she don't want him
messed up too much to be a good missionary . . . I
don't want to be mixed up with that hell-cat."

In that queer mood of slackness, he was certain now
of only one thing—that he could stay no longer in the
same Town where Naomi and the Reverend Castor had
lived, where Giulia Rizzo had been killed, where that
pathetic uprising of workmen asking justice had been
beaten down. He couldn't stay any longer in the same
place with his own father. He wanted to go away, to
the other side of the earth. Any place, even the savage,
naked jungle at Megambo was less cruel than this black
and monstrous Town.

At the slate-colored house he hammered on the door
for twenty minutes without getting any answer, and
at last he went to the side of the house and tossed
stones against the window behind which his mother

and father were passing what Mabelle called "a second honeymoon." After a moment a head appeared at the window, and his mother's voice asked, "Who's there? For God's sake, what's the matter?"

"It's Philip . . . let me in!"

She opened the door to him in her outing-flannel gown and a flowered wrapper which he had never seen her wear before. It was, he supposed, a best wrapper which she had kept against the homecoming she had awaited for years. Her head was covered coquettishly by a pink boudoir cap trimmed with lace. As he closed the door behind him, she said, "For God's sake, Philip. What's the matter? Have you gone crazy?"

He smiled at her, but it was a horrible smile, twisted and bitter, and born of old memories come alive, and of a disgust at the sight of the flowered wrapper and the coquettish lace cap. "No, I'm not crazy this time —though I've a right to be. It's about Naomi . . . she's run away. . . ."

"What do you mean?"

"And she hasn't gone alone. She's run away with the Reverend Castor."

"Philip! You *are* crazy. It's not true!"

"I'm telling you the truth. *I know.*"

She sat down suddenly on the stairs, holding to the rail for support. "Oh, my God! Oh, my God! What have I done to deserve such a thing? When will God bring me to the end of my trials?"

He made no move to comfort her. He simply stood watching, until presently she asked, "How do you know? There must be a mistake . . . it's not true."

Then he told her bit by bit the whole story, coldly and with an odd, cruel satisfaction, so that no doubt remained; and for the first time in his memory he saw her wilt and collapse.

"You see, Ma, there can't be any doubt. They've gone off together."

Suddenly she seemed to make a great effort. She sat up again and said bitterly, "I always thought something like this would happen. She was always flighty . . . I discovered that when she lived here. She wasn't any good as a wife or as a mother. She wouldn't nurse her own children. No . . . I think, maybe, you're well rid of her . . . the brazen little slut."

"Don't say that, Ma. Whatever has happened is our fault. We drove her to it." His words were gentle enough; it was his voice that was hard as flint.

"What do you mean? How can you accuse me?"

"We treated her like dirt . . . and it wasn't her fault. In some ways she's better than either of us."

She looked at him suddenly. "You're not planning to take her back if she comes running home with her tail between her legs?"

"I don't know . . . I have a feeling that she'll never come back."

"Leaving her children without a thought!"

"I don't suppose she left them without a thought . . . but sometimes a person can be so unhappy that he only wants to die. I know . . . I've been like that. Besides, she never wanted the children any more than I wanted them."

"How can you say such a wicked thing!"

His face looked thin and pinched and white. The water, all unnoticed, had formed a pool about his feet on the immaculate carpet of Emma's hall. He was shaking with chill. He was like a dead man come up out of the sea. And deep inside him a small voice was born, which kept saying to him, "It's that ridiculous woman in a flowered wrapper and pink cap who lies at the bottom of all this misery." It was a tiny voice, but, like the voice that the Reverend Castor had tried to still by repeating Psalms, it would not die. It kept returning.

"It's not wicked. It's only the truth . . . and it's only the truth I care about to-night. I don't give a damn for anything else in the world . . . not for what people think, or about what they say. They can all go to hell for all I care." His face was white and expressionless, like the face of a man already dead. It was the voice that was terrible.

"You needn't swear, Philip." She showed signs of weeping. "And I never thought my boy would turn against his own mother——not for any woman in the world."

"Now don't begin that. I'm not your boy any longer. I've got to grow up sometime. I'm not turning against you. I'm just sick to death of the whole mess. I'm through with the whole thing."

She wiped her eyes with a corner of the ridiculous flowered wrapper, and the sight made him want to laugh. The tiny voice grew more clamorous.

She was saying, "I won't wake your Pa and tell him. He's no good at a time like this." (Philip thought, "I don't know. He might do better than any of us.") "And I'll dress and come down to the twins. And you ought to get on some dry clothes." She rose, turned all at once into a woman of action. "I'll take care of the twins."

"No," he said abruptly. "I can do that."

"You don't know about their bottles."

"I *do* know . . . I've done them on the nights Naomi went to choir practice. I don't want you to come . . . I want to be alone with them."

"Philip . . . I'm your mother. . . . It's my place. . . ."

"I want to be alone with them. . . ."

He looked so wild that she seized his shoulders and said, "You're not thinking anything foolish, are you?"

"I don't know what I'm thinking. I can't bear to think of her running off like that. I can't bear to think of how we treated her. . . . If you mean that I'm thinking of killing myself, I'm not . . . I can't do that. I've got to think of little Philip and Naomi. If it wasn't for them . . . I might do anything."

Suddenly in a wild hysteria, she put her arms about him, crying out, "Philip! Philip! My boy! Don't say such things—it's not you who's talking. It's some one else . . . it's a stranger . . . somebody I never knew . . . somebody I didn't bear out of my own body." She shook him passionately. "Philip! Philip! Wake up! Be your old self . . . my son. Do you hear me, darling? You *do* love me still. Tell me what's in your heart . . . what the voice of your real self is saying."

In the violence of her action, the pink lace cap slipped back on her head, exposing a neat row of curl-papers, festoons and garlands (thought Philip in disgust) of their second honeymoon. He didn't resist her. He simply remained cold and frozen, one cold, thin hand thrust into his pocket for warmth. Then suddenly the hand touched something which roused a

sudden train of memory, and when at last she freed
him, he drew out a pair of worn gloves.

"I think I'll go home now," he said in the same
frozen voice. "Before I go, I must give you these.
Mary Conyngham sent them to you. I think you left
them at her house when you went to call." It was as
if he said to her, "It's true . . . what you thought
about Mary and me. It's true . . . now."

She took the gloves with a queer, mechanical gesture, and without another word he turned and went
out, closing the door. When he had gone, she sat
down on the steps again and began to weep, crying
out, "Oh, God! Oh, God! What have I done to deserve such trouble! Oh, God! Have pity on me!
Bring my son back to me!"

Suddenly, in a kind of frenzy, she began to tear the
gloves to bits, as if they were the very body of Mary Conyngham. In the midst of her wild sobbing, a voice came
out of the dark at the top of the stairs, "For Heaven's
sake, Em, what are you carrying on about now?"

It was Jason standing in his nightshirt, his bare legs
exposed to the knees. "Come on back to bed. It's cold
as Jehu up here."

By the time Philip reached the Flats, the rain had
begun to abate a little, and the sky beyond the Mills
and Shane's Castle to turn a pale, cold gray with the
beginning of dawn. The twins were awake and crying
loudly. Poking up the fire in the kitchen range, he
prepared the bottles and so quieted them before taking
off his soaked clothing. The old feeling of being soiled
had come over him again, more strongly even than on
the day in Hennessey's saloon, and when he had un-

dressed and rubbed warmth back into his body, he drew hot water from the kitchen range, and, standing in a washtub by the side of the cribs where he could restore the bottles when they fell from the feeble grasp of the twins, he scrubbed himself vigorously from head to foot, as if thus he might drive away that sordid feeling of uncleanness.

At last he got into the bed beside the cribs—the bed which he had never shared with Naomi, and to which it was not likely that she would ever return. He had barely slept at all in more than two days, but it was impossible to sleep now. His mind was alive, seething, burning with activity like those cauldrons of white-hot metal in the Mills; yet he experienced a kind of troubled peace, for he had come to the end of one trouble. He knew that with his mother it was all finished. In the moment he had given her the gloves, he knew that he didn't love her any more, that he no longer felt grateful to her for all that she had done for him. There was only a deadness where these emotions should have been. It was all over and finished: it would be better now if he never saw her again.

And the twins . . . they must never go to her; whatever happened, she must never do to them what she had done to him. He would protect them from her, somehow, even if he died.

The day that followed was one of waiting for some sign, some hint, some bit of knowledge as to the whereabouts of Naomi and the Reverend Castor. Like the day after a sudden death in a household, it had no relation to ordinary days. It was rather like a day suspended without reality in time and space. Philip went about like a dead man. His father came and sat with him for a time, silent and subdued, and strangely unlike his old exuberant self.

It was Emma alone who seemed to rise above the calamity. "It is," she said, "a time for activity. We must face things. We mustn't give in."

She went herself to call upon the editors of the two newspapers and by some force of threats and tears she induced them to keep silence regarding the affair until some fact was definitely known. It was a triumph for her, since neither editor had any affection for her, and one at least hated her. From the newspaper offices she went at once to call upon the invalid in the parsonage. She found the miserable woman "prostrated," and in the care of Miss Simpkins, head of the Missionary Society. Before five minutes had passed, she understood that she had arrived too late. Miss Simpkins had been told the whole story, and in turn had communicated it, beyond all doubt, to a whole circle of hungry women. The invalid was still in the same state of triumph. It seemed to Emma that she saw no disgrace in the affair, but only a sort of glory and justification. It was as if she said, "People will notice my misery at last. They'll pay some attention to me. They'll give up pitying him and pity me for a time." It was impossible to argue with her. When Emma left, she said to herself savagely, "The old devil has got what was coming to her. She deserved it."

Once a trickle of the scandal had leaked out, there was no stopping it: the news swept the Town as the swollen waters of the brook flooded the pestilential Flats. It reached Mary Conyngham late in the afternoon. For a time she was both stunned and frightened, as if the thing were a retribution visited with horrible speed upon herself and Philip. And then, quickly, she thought, "I must not lose my head. I've got to think of Philip. I've got to help him." She fancied him haunted by remorse and self-reproaches, creating in his fantastic way all manner of self-tortures. One of them at least must keep his head, and she was certain that the one wouldn't be Philip. And she was seized with a sudden terror that the calamity might shut him off from her forever: it was not impossible with a man like Philip who was always tormenting himself about troubles which did not exist. She found to her astonishment that she herself felt neither any pangs of conscience nor any remorse. What she had done, she had done willingly, and with a clear head: if there had ever been any doubts they were over and done with before she had gone to the stable.

She dared not, she knew, go and see him, and thus deliver herself into the hands of his mother; for she knew well enough that Emma would be waiting, watching for just such a chance. She would want to say to Philip, "You see, it's the judgment of God upon you for your behavior with Mary Conyngham." For a second there came to Mary a faint wish that she had never turned Emma's accusation into truth, but it died quickly. She knew that nothing could ever destroy the memory of what had happened on the night of the slaughter in the dead park.

She decided at last to write to him, and late that night, after she had torn up a dozen attempts (because writing to a man like Philip under such circumstances was a dangerous business) she finished a note and sent it off to him. She wrote: "My Darling . . . I can't come to you now. You know why it is impossible.

And I want to be with you. It is killing me to sit here alone. If you want to meet me anywhere, send word. I'd go to hell itself to help you. You mustn't torment yourself. You mustn't imagine things. At a time like this, you must keep your head. For God's sake, remember what we are to each other, and that nothing else in the world makes any difference. I love you, my boy. I love you . . . Mary."

Then she addressed the note, and, as a safeguard against Emma, printed *"Personal"* in large letters on the outside of the envelope. It was too late to find any one to deliver the note and the post-office was closed. At last she put on a hat and coat and went herself to leave it under the door of the drugstore, where the druggist would be certain to deliver it in the morning. When she came home again, she lay down in the solitude of the old Victorian parlor, and before long fell asleep. It was two o'clock when she wakened, frightened, and shivering with cold.

Mr. Stimson, the druggist, found the letter in the morning, and laid it aside until he had swept out the store. Then he had breakfast and when a Pole with a cut on the side of his head came in to have it bandaged, he quite forgot the letter. It was only after ten o'clock when a boy came bringing a telegram for Philip that he remembered it suddenly. The note and the telegram were delivered together.

The telegram was brief. A man and woman believed to be Samuel Castor and Mrs. Philip Downes were found dead by suicide in a Pittsburgh boarding-house. Would Mr. Downes wire instructions, or come himself. It was signed, "H. G. Miller, Coroner."

24

The rooming-house stood in one of the side streets in the dubious quarter that lay between the river wharfs and the business district—a region of Pittsburgh once inhabited by middle-class families, and now fallen a little over the edge of respectability. It was one of a row of houses all exactly alike, built of brick, with limestone stoops, and all blackened long ago by the soot of mills and furnaces. Number Twenty-nine was distinguished from the others only by the fact that the stoop seemed to have been scrubbed not too long ago, and that beside the sign "Rooms to Let to Respectable Parties," there was another card emblazoned with a gilt cross and bearing an inscription that was not legible from the sidewalk. Philip and McTavish, peering at the house, noticed it, and, turning in at the little path, were able to make out the words. The card was stained and yellow with age, and beneath the cross they read, "JESUS SAID, 'COME UNTO ME.'"

For a moment, McTavish gave Philip an oblique, searching look, and then pressed the bell. There was a long wait, followed by the sound of closing doors, and then a tired little woman, with her hair in a screw at the back of her head, stood before them, drying her hands on a soiled apron.

Philip only stared at her, lost in the odd, dazed silence that had settled over him from the moment the telegram had come. He seemed incapable of speech, like a little child in the care of McTavish. It was the fat undertaker who lifted his hat and said, "This is Mr. Downes, and I'm the undertaker." He coughed suddenly, "The Coroner told us that . . . they had left some things in the room."

The little woman asked them in, and then began suddenly to cry. "I've never had such a thing happen to me before . . . and now I'm ruined!"

McTavish bade her be quiet, but she went on and on hysterically. In all the tragedy, she could, it seemed, see only her own misfortune.

"You can tell me about it when we're upstairs," said McTavish, patting her arm with the air of a bachelor unused to the sight of a woman's tears, and upset by them. "Mr. Downes will wait down here."

Then Philip spoke suddenly for the first time. "No . . . I'm going with you. I want to hear the whole thing. I've . . . I've *got* to know."

There was a smell of cabbage and onions in the hallway. As McTavish closed the door, the whole place was lost in gloomy shadows. The tired woman, still sobbing, and blowing her nose on the soiled apron, said, "It's upstairs."

They followed her up two flights of stairs to a room at the back. It was in complete darkness, as if the two bodies were still there, and as she raised the window-shade there came into view a whole vista of dreary backyards littered with rubbish and filled with lines of newly washed clothing. The gray light revealed a small room, scarcely a dozen feet square, with a cheap pine table, a wash-bowl, pitcher and slop-jar, two chairs and a narrow iron bed. On the walls hung a bad print of the Sermon on the Mount and a cheaply illuminated text, "Come unto Me, all ye that labor and are heavy laden." The bed was untouched, save for two small depressions at the side away from the wall.

Near the door there were little rolls of torn newspaper—the paper (Philip thought, with a sudden feeling of sickness) with which they had stuffed the cracks
of the door to imprison the smell of gas. A newspaper
and a Bible lay on the table beside the wash-bowl.

"I left everything just as it was," said the woman;
"just as the Coroner ordered."

Those two depressions on the side of the bed suddenly took on a terrible fascination for Philip. It
was as if they were filled by the forms of two kneeling
figures who were praying.

"Here's the bag they brought," said the woman. She
bent down and opened it. "You see it was empty. If
I'd known that . . . but how was I to know?" It was
a cheap bag made of paper and painted to imitate
leather. It stood in a corner, mute, reproachful, empty.

Philip was staring at it in silence, and McTavish
said again, "Maybe you'd better go downstairs and
wait."

For a moment there was no answer, and then Philip
replied, "No, I mean to stay. I've got to hear it."

The woman began to tell her story. They had come
to the rooming-house about nine o'clock in the evening.
"I remember the hour because Hazel—that's the girl
that helps me with the house—had finished the dishes
and was going to meet a friend." She had one room
empty, and she was only too glad to rent it, especially
to a clergyman. Oh, he had told her who he was. He
told her he was the Reverend Castor and that the woman
with him was his wife. They were, he said, on their
way east, and came to the rooming-house because he

had heard Mr. Elmer Niman speak of it once as a cheap, clean, respectable place to stay at when you came to Pittsburgh. "You see," she explained, "I'm very careful who I take in. Usually Methodists and Baptists. They recommend each other, and that way I do a pretty good business, and it's always sure to be respectable." She sighed and said, "It wasn't my fault this time. I never thought a preacher would do such a thing, and being recommended, too, by Mr. Elmer Niman."

They went, she said, right up to their room, and, about half-past ten, when Hazel came back, she heard voices singing hymns. "They weren't singing very loud . . . sort of low and soft, so as not to disturb the other roomers. So I thought it was a kind of evening worship they went through every night, and I didn't say anything. But one of my other roomers came to me and complained. I was pretty near undressed, but I put on a wrapper and went up to tell them they'd have to be quiet, as other people wanted to sleep. They were singing, *Ancient of Days*, and they stopped right away. They didn't even say anything."

The woman blew her nose again on her apron, sighed, and went on. "So I went to sleep, and about one o'clock my husband came in. He's so crippled with rheumatism he can't work much and he'd been to a meeting of the Odd Fellows. It must have been about one o'clock when he waked me up, and after he'd gotten into bed and turned out the light, I told him that I'd rented the empty room. And he said, 'Who to?' and I told him a Reverend Castor and his wife. He

sat up in bed, and said, 'His wife!' as if he didn't believe me, and I said, 'Yes, his wife!' And then Henry
got out of bed and lit the gas, and went over to his
coat and took out a newspaper. I thought it was
kind-a funny. He opened it, and looked at it, and
said, 'That ain't his wife at all. It's a woman who sings
in his choir. The scoundrel, to come to a respectable
house like this!' And then he showed me the newspaper, and there it all was about a preacher in Mil-
ford who'd run away with a choir singer. And there
was his name and everything. You'd have thought
he'd have had the sense to take some other name if
he was going to do a thing like that."

McTavish looked at her quietly. "I don't think he'd
ever think of a thing like that. He was a good man.
He was innocent."

The woman sniffed. "I don't know about that. But
it seems to me a good man wouldn't be trapsin' around
with another man's wife."

The look in McTavish's eyes turned a little harder.
When he spoke, his voice was stern. "I know what I
mean. *He was a good man.* He had a hellion for a
wife. She deserved what she got and worse."

Something in the quality of his voice seemed to irri-
tate the woman, for she began to whine. "Well, you
needn't insult me. I was brought up a good Christian
Methodist, and I'm a regular churchgoer, and I know
good from bad."

McTavish turned away in disgust. "All right! All
right! Go on with your story."

"Well," said the woman, "Henry—that's my husband—said, 'You must turn them out right away. We
can't have the house defiled by adulterers!'" Her

small green eyes turned a glare of defiance at McTavish. "That's what they were—adulterers."

"Yes," said McTavish wearily. "There's no denying that. But go on."

"So I got up, and went to their room and knocked. I smelled gas in the hall and thought it was funny. And then I knocked again and nobody answered. And then I got scared and called Henry. He was for sending for somebody to help break down the door, and then I turned the knob and it was open. They hadn't even locked it. It just pushed open, easy-like. The room was full of gas, and you couldn't go in or strike a match and you couldn't see anything. But we left the door open, and Henry went to get the police. And after a time I went to open the window, and when I pulled up the window-shade and the light from the furnaces came in, I saw 'em both a-lyin' there. He was sort of slumped down beside the bed and she was half on the bed a-lyin' on her face. They'd both died a-prayin'."

The thin, dreary voice died away into silence. McTavish looked at Philip. He was sitting on one of the stiff pine chairs, his head sunk on his chest, his fingers unrolling mechanically bit by bit the pieces of newspaper with which the door had been stuffed. Automatically he unrolled them, examined them and smoothed them out, putting them in neat piles at his feet. They were stained with tears that had fallen silently while he listened. And then, suddenly, he found what he had been looking for. He handed it to McTavish without a word, without even raising his head.

It was a scrap torn hastily to stuff the door, but in the midst of it appeared in glaring headlines:

"PREACHER ELOPES
WITH MISSIONARY

*Romance begins at choir
practice. Woman a
former Evangelist"*

The editors had kept their word to Emma, but the
story had leaked out into the cities nearby.

McTavish read it in silence, and turned to the woman.
Philip did not even hear what they were saying. He
was thinking of poor Naomi lying dead, fallen forward
on the bed where she had been praying. It was poor
Naomi who had made that ghastly depression in the
gray-white counterpane. He saw what had happened.
He saw them coming in, tired and frightened, to this
sordid room, terrified by what they had done in a
moment of insanity. He saw them sitting there in
silence, Naomi crying because she always cried when
she was frightened. And perhaps he had taken the
newspaper out of his pocket and laid it on the table
and as it fell open, there was the headline staring at
them. They must have seen, then, that they were
trapped, that they could neither go on nor turn back.
In their world of preachers and Evangelists and prayer
there was no place for them. And presently they must
have noticed the print of the Sermon on the Mount, and
at last the framed text—"Come unto Me, all ye that
labor and are heavy laden. . . ." They must have
seen the text written in letters of fire, inviting them,
commanding them— "Come unto Me, all ye that labor
and are heavy laden. . . ." It must have seemed the
only way out. And then they had sung hymns until

the harpy had knocked at the door and bade them be silent.

The depression in the bed kept tormenting him. The two figures kneeling there, praying, praying for forgiveness, until one of them slumped down, unconscious, and the other was left alone, still praying. . . . Which one of them had gone first? He hoped it was Naomi, for she would be so frightened at being left alone. For the one who was left alone, those last moments must have seemed hours. And Naomi must have been frightened. She was destroying herself—a sin which once she had told him was the unforgivable.

He saw then that the faith which had given her strength in that far-off unreal world at Megambo must have been failing her for a long time. It must have died before ever she set out on the mad journey that ended in this wretched room. Or she must have been mad. And then, all at once, the memory of her figure kneeling in the dust of the Mission enclosure rose up and smote him. He saw her again, her face all illumined with a queer, unearthly light. She had been ready then to die by the bullets of the painted niggers. She should have died then, happy in the knowledge of her sacrifice. He had saved her life—he and that queer Englishwoman—only that she might die thus, praying alone, lost, forgotten. . . .

She should have died at Megambo—a martyr.

Suddenly he heard the voice of the tired little woman, "And here is her hand-bag." She held it out to McTavish, a poor morsel of leather, all hardened and discolored by the rain. "That's how we found her address. It was written on a card."

McTavish opened it mechanically, and turned it up-side-down. A few coins rattled out. He counted them . . . eighty-five cents. The woman opened a drawer of the table. "And here is his." The worn wallet contained a great amount of silver and ninety odd dollars in bills. They had meant to start life again with ninety odd dollars.

"They must have been mad," said McTavish. He touched Philip's shoulder. "Come . . . we'd better go."

Philip rose in silence, and McTavish turned toward the Bible that lay open on the table. "Was that theirs?" he asked.

"No, that's mine. I keep Bibles in all my rooms."

McTavish turned toward the door, and she said, "The bag . . . ain't you going to take the bag?"

McTavish turned toward Philip.

"No," said Philip. "You may keep it."

The woman frowned. "I don't want it. I don't want any of their things left in my house. I've suffered enough. They ruined me. I don't want my house polluted."

McTavish started to speak, and then thought better of it. He simply took up the bag and followed Philip. They went down the two flights of odorous stairs and out of the door. The policeman who had accompanied them was waiting on the sidewalk. As the door closed, they heard the woman sobbing and calling after them that she, an honest, God-fearing woman, had been ruined.

In silence they turned their backs on the dingy house, with the sign, "Rooms to Let to Respectable Parties," and the emblazoned text, "JESUS SAID, 'COME UNTO ME. . . .'"

Half-way down the block, McTavish said, "You mustn't think about it, Philip. You mustn't brood. You had nothing to do with it."

"How can I help thinking about it?" He could only see them kneeling there by the bed praying until the end, innocent save that they had tried to escape from a life which circumstance or fate had made too cruel for them to bear. They had died without ever knowing the happiness which had come to him and Mary. He saw bitterly that there was not even any great dignity in their death, but only a pathos. They had not even known a poor tattered remnant of human happiness. They had simply run away, fleeing from something they could not understand toward something that was unknown.

"How can I ever think of anything else?"

25

The Reverend Castor was buried from his own house, and Naomi from the flat over the drugstore. Emma had proposed that the services should be held in the slate-colored house, but Philip refused. It seemed wrong that Naomi should enter it again, even in death. He would not even allow any mourners save the family. His mother and father were there, Jason in a curious state of depression, more than ever like a bedraggled bantam rooster, and Mabelle bringing both Ethel and little Jimmy, who kept asking in loud whispers where Cousin Naomi had gone, and why he wasn't supposed to speak of her. Mabelle herself repeated over and over again, "I can't believe it. She was so cheerful, though she did seem a bit nervous and fidgety that last day. She came twice to see me. I suppose she wanted to tell me something," and, "What strikes me as funny is that nobody ever suspected it. There wasn't any talk about them at all. It was like a flash out of the blue." It was impossible to silence her tongue. Even during the service she whispered to Jason, "Don't she look pure and sweet? You just can't believe that things like this happen. Life is a funny thing, I always say. It was just like a flash out of the blue."

And "pie-faced" Elmer was there too, all in dingy black. He read the service, looking like the Jewish god of vengeance. He only spoke once or twice in a ghoulish whisper, but his eyes were eloquent. They said, "You see the wages of sin . . ." and, "This is what comes of Philip abandoning God."

Once the service was interrupted when little Philip, wakened by the singing of *Crossing the Bar* by the hired quartet, stirred in his crib and began to cry.

Naomi was buried in the dress of figured foulard. Mabelle observed that in the coffin it looked all right. Naomi, she said, looked so young and so natural.

26

The Mills began once more to pound and roar. The flames of the furnaces again filled all the night sky with a rosy glow. The last miserable remnants of the strikers drifted away and the tent village disappeared, leaving only a vacant lot, grassless and muddy with the turn of winter. The strike and the slaughter in the park of Shane's Castle, even the tragedy of Naomi and the Reverend Castor, were at last worn to shreds as subjects of conversation. Life moved on, as if all these things counted for nothing, as if the Shanes, and Krylenko, poor Giulia Rizzo, Naomi and the Reverend Castor, had never existed. In the church, Elmer Niman read the services until a suitable preacher was found. The bereft and invalid Mrs. Castor disappeared in the obscurity of some Indiana village, where she went to live with a poverty-stricken cousin.

As for Philip, he stayed on in the flat, hiring an old negress, whom McTavish knew, to care for the twins. A sort of enchantment seemed to have taken possession of him, which robbed him even of his desire to go away. Emma came nearly every day to question old Molly about the children, to make suggestions and to run her finger across tables in search of dust. She did not propose that he return to the slate-colored house, for she seemed now to be afraid of him, with the fear one has of drunkards or maniacs—a fear which had its origin in the moment he had taken the worn gloves from his pocket and given them to her. There was, too, a wisdom in the fear, a wisdom which had come to her from Jason on that same night, after she had returned to the marital bed.

For Jason had said to her, when she had grown calm, "Em, you never learn anything. If you lived to be a hundred, you'd still be making a mess of things."

And she had cried out, "How can you say such a thing to me . . . after all I've suffered . . . after all I've done? It's you who've made a mess of your life."

"My life ain't such a mess as you might think," he had replied darkly. "But let me tell you, if you don't want to lose that boy altogether, you'll let him alone.

He ain't no ordinary town boy, Em. He's different.
I've found that out. I don't know how we produced
'im. But if you don't want to lose him, you'll let him
alone."

She didn't want to lose him. There were times when
she hardened her heart toward him, thinking he was
ungrateful and hard to allow a hussy like Mary Conyngham to stand between him and his mother; and again
she would think of him as her little boy, her Philip,
for whom she would work her fingers to the bone. But
she was hurt by the way he looked at her, coldly, out
of hard blue eyes, as if she were only a stranger to him.
She felt him slipping, slipping from her, and at times
she grew cold with fear. She "let him alone," but she
could not overlook her duty toward him and his children. They were, after all, her grandchildren, and a
man like Philip wasn't capable of bringing them up
properly, especially since he had lost his faith. And
with a mother like theirs, who had such bad blood,
they would need special care and training . . . she
resolved not to speak of it for the moment, but, later
on, when they were a little older. . . .

But it was Mabelle who was the most regular visitor
at the flat. She came with a passion for always being
in the center of things; she clung to the tragedy, and
came every day to break in upon Philip's brooding
solitude, to chatter on and on, whether he listened
or not. She brought little Jimmy's old toys for the
twins, and she dandled them on her knee as if they
were her own. There were times when Philip suspected
her of being driven by a relentless curiosity to discover
more of what had happened on the terrible day, but he
endured her; he even began to have an affection for

her, because she was so stupid and good-natured.

She was sitting there one morning, playing with little Philip and little Naomi, when she said suddenly, "You know I often think that all that trouble in the park at Shane's Castle . . . killing all those people . . . had something to do with Naomi's being so upset. You see, when she heard that morning about the people being killed there, she got worried about you. She was nearly crazy for fear that something had happened to you, and she went herself to the stable to find you, and when she didn't find you there she was sort of crazy afterward. She came up and talked to me in a crazy way until she heard from your Pa that he'd seen you at McTavish's. When I think of it now, I see that she was sort of unbalanced and queer, though I didn't notice it at the time."

Philip, barely listening to her, took little notice of what she was saying, for he had come long ago to allow her to rattle on and on without heeding her; it was only a little while afterward that it had any significance for him. It was as if what she had said touched some hidden part of his brain. When she had gone, and he began indifferently to think of it, it seemed to him that he remembered every word exactly as she had spoken it. The words were burned into his mind. *"She was nearly crazy for fear something had happened to you, and she went herself to the stable to find you."*

When Mabelle had gone, he could think of nothing else.

Since the morning after the slaughter in the park, he had never returned to the stable. The place which he had once thought of as belonging to himself alone was spoiled now: it had been invaded by Lily Shane

and poor Naomi, and even by Mary . . . even by
Mary. There were times when he resented her having
come there, and times, too, when his remorse over
Naomi made him feel that Mary had come deliberately,
to tempt him, that what they had done was not a beautiful, but a wicked thing, which would torment him until
he died. The place was spoiled for him, since it had
come in a ghastly way to stand as a symbol of all
those things which he believed had driven Naomi into
madness.

But he knew, too, that he must return one day to
the stable. It was filled with his belongings, the sketches
pinned to the walls, the unfinished canvas of the Flats
at night on which the paint must long since have caked
and turned hard. (He knew now that it would never
be finished, for he could never bring himself to sit there
again by the window, alone, watching the mists stealing over the Mills.) After Mabelle had gone, he kept
thinking that Naomi was the last one to enter the
place. It was as if her spirit would be there awaiting
him.

And then all at once there came to him a sudden
terrifying memory: he had gone away that morning
leaving behind unwashed the dishes he and Mary had
used at breakfast. He had sent Mary away, promis-
ing to wash them himself, and then, troubled by the
remorse of the gray dawn, had gone off, meaning to do
it when he returned. They were still lying there—the
two plates, the two coffee-cups, the very loaf of bread,
turned hard and dry, and nibbled by the mice. And
Naomi had gone there, "crazy for fear something had
happened" to him. She had seen the remnants of that
breakfast. In all the uproar and confusion he had for-

gotten. . . . She had known then; she must have known before she ran away. . . .

For a moment he thought, "I must be careful, or I shall go crazy. It must feel like this to lose one's mind." He thought, "It was I who did it. I drove her away. I killed her myself. She thought that I was lying to her all along. I wasn't lying. I wasn't lying. I was telling her the truth. . . . It would have been the truth, even now, to the end, if Mary hadn't come then. She must have been crazy. Both of us must have been crazy."

And then, after a time, he thought, "I've got to be calm. I've got to think this thing out." There wasn't, after all, any reason why there shouldn't have been two plates and two cups. Any one might have been having breakfast with him . . . any man, Krylenko, or even McTavish. Oh, it was all right. There couldn't have been anything wrong in that.

And then he thought bitterly, "But if it had been Krylenko, Naomi wouldn't have believed it. She'd be sure it was a woman. She'd think it was Lily Shane . . . Lily Shane, who wouldn't have looked at me. She was jealous of Lily Shane."

None of it was any good—none of this self-deception. It wasn't a man who had had breakfast with him. It was a woman—Mary Conyngham, only Naomi had believed it was Lily Shane. Thank God! It wasn't the same as if he and Mary together had driven her away to death in that horrible rooming-house. He'd never have to think of that after he and Mary were married. Naomi had believed the woman was Lily Shane.

Suddenly he pressed his hands to his eyes, so savagely that for a moment he was blinded. "I'm a fool. It's just the same, even if she did think that it was some other woman."

The stable began to acquire for him a horrid fascination, so powerful that he could no longer stay away from it. He *had* to return, to see the place with his eyes, to see the tell-tale cups and plates. Perhaps (he thought) some miracle had happened. Old Hennery might have removed them after he left, or perhaps he had himself washed them and put them away in the harness-closet without remembering it. Such a thing could happen. . . . In all the tragedy, all the confusion, the ecstasy of those few hours, he might have done it, without knowing what he did. Or afterwards, in all the stress of what had happened, he might have forgotten. Such things had been known to occur, he told himself, such lapses in the working of a brain. There were, after all, moments of late when he was not certain of what was happening—whether he was alive or dead, or whether Naomi had really killed herself, praying by the side of that wretched bed. . . .

But immediately he said, "I'm a fool. I'm like my father. I'm not thinking of what *did* happen, but what I wish had happened. It's like his story of losing his memory."

When the old negress Molly returned from marketing, he gave her the twins and went off like a madman to the stable. He traversed the area of the Mills, passed Hennessey's place, and entered the dead park, but when he came to the stable, it took all his courage to enter.

He climbed the creaking stairs with his eyes closed, groping his way until he stood at the top. Then he opened them and looked about.

The place had a wrecked and desolate look. The dust and the soot of the Mills, filtering in through the decaying windows, covered everything. At some time during the storm the roof had begun to leak, and the water, running down the walls, had ruined a dozen sketches and soaked the blankets on the bed, and in the middle of the room on the table stood the coffee-pot, the dried loaf of bread gnawed by the mice, the soiled cups and plates, and a saucer with rancid butter on it.

There wasn't any doubt of it—the things were there, just as they had been left by him and Mary.

He sat down weakly in one of the chairs by the table, and lighted a cigarette. Suddenly he leaned back with his eyes closed. He didn't care any longer. He was tired. He had come (he thought) to the end of things, and nothing any longer made any difference—neither his mother, nor his father, nor Naomi, nor even Mary. He wanted only to be alone forever, to go off into some wilderness where there was no human creature to cause him pain. He wanted to be a coward and run away. In solitude he might regain once more that stupid faith which had once given him security. It wasn't that he'd ever again be glad to be alive: it was only when you believed you could make God responsible in a way for everything. Whatever happened, it was the Will of God. He hadn't been alive: it was only when he had turned his back on God that he had begun to understand what it meant to be alive. And now that, too, was past: he saw now that he wasn't strong enough to live by himself. He was, after all, a coward, without the courage of a person like Mary. She had, he saw, no need of a God to lean upon. No, he wasn't even like his father, whom no tragedy had the power to touch. He was like her—like his mother. He needed God as an excuse. She was safe: nothing could touch her, nothing could ever change her. She always had God to hold responsible. . . .

The forgotten cigarette, burning low, scorched his fingers, and, dropping it, he stepped on it mechanically, and, rising from the chair, saw suddenly a woman's handkerchief lying on the table among the dishes. It lay there, folded neatly, beneath a covering of dust and soot. He thought, "It must have been Naomi's. She must have dropped it here." The thing exerted an evil fascination over him. He wanted to go away, but he couldn't go, until he knew whose handkerchief it was. It couldn't have been Lily Shane's, for he or Mary would have noticed it. It couldn't have been Mary's: for she wouldn't have gone away from the table with it lying there, neat and unused, in full sight on the table. It must have belonged to Naomi. He wanted to go away without even looking, but he had not the strength. It lay there tormenting him. He would never have any peace if he went away in ignorance.

At last his hand, as if it moved of its own will, reached out and picked it up. It left behind a small square free of dust on the surface of the table. It was a tiny handkerchief, frail and feminine, and in the corner it was marked with initials. They were . . . M.C. There wasn't the slightest doubt. . . . M.C. . . . M.C. . . . Mary Conyngham.

He saw then what must have happened—that Mary had dropped it somewhere in the room, and Naomi, searching for some clue, had found it and left it lying behind on the table. It was Naomi's hand that had placed it there on the table, Naomi's hand that had last touched it.

Naomi had known who the woman was. In the next moment he had, in some unaccountable way, a curiously clear vision of an iron bed with a small depression where some one had knelt to pray.

After a long time, he rose, and, leaving the handkerchief on the table, went down the stairs once more. He never returned again to the room above the stable.

27

While Philip sat in the dust and soot of the dead stable, his father waited for him at the flat. He danced the twins for a time on his knee, and set them crowing by giving a variety of imitations of birds and animals which he had learned in Australia, but, after a time, the old spirit flagged. He wasn't the same gay, blithe creature that Emma found awaiting her in the darkened drawing-room. Even the waxed mustaches seemed to droop a little with weariness. For Jason was growing old in body, and he knew it. "My sciatica," he said, "will not let me alone."

"For an active, nervous man like me," he had told Emma only that morning, "there ain't much left when his body begins to get old."

Even his return home had been in a way a failure. He began now to think he ought never to have come back. Emma was the only one pleased by his return. "You'd have thought," he told himself, "that she'd have forgotten me long ago and taken to thinking about other things." It was pretty fine to have a big, handsome woman like Emma give you all her devotion.

Yes, she was glad enough to see him, but there was his boy, Philip, whom he hardly knew. He'd never get to know Philip: he couldn't understand a boy like that. And this Naomi business. It was too bad, and of course it was a scandal, but still that didn't make any difference in the way you enjoyed living. The truth was that Philip ought to be kind-a glad to be rid of her. It wasn't a thing he could help, and he'd behaved all right. If there *was* another woman, Philip had kept it all quiet. There wasn't any scandal. And now, if he wanted to marry her, he could—if she wasn't married too. No, he couldn't understand Philip. Emma had done something to him.

The return was a failure. He hadn't even had any glory out of it, except on that first night when he'd had his triumph over pie-faced Elmer; but who wanted a triumph over a thing like Elmer? No, he'd been forgotten, first in the excitement of the riot when they'd killed a couple of dirty foreigners, and then by Naomi running off and killing herself with a preacher. Em wouldn't let him say that preachers were a bad lot but he had his ideas, all the same. The Town had forgotten all about him—him, a man who lost his memory, and who had been thought dead for twenty-six years. Of course he hadn't *quite* lost his memory, but he might have lost it. . . .

And then he was homesick. The Town wasn't home to him any more. It was no more his *real* home than Philip was his *real* son, or Emma his *real* wife.

He was thinking all these things, mechanically rolling a ball back and forth to the twins, when Philip came in. At first Jason didn't notice him, and when he did look up, the drawn, white look on the face of his strange son frightened him. He tried to jest, in a wild effort to drive away that sense of depression.

"Well, here I am," he said brightly. "Back again like a bad penny." Philip didn't answer him, and he said, "I just ran in to say I'm going home day after to-morrow."

"Home?" asked Philip, with a look of bewilderment.

"Yes . . . home to Australy."

"Oh." Then the boy pulled himself together with an effort. "But I thought this was your home."

"No . . . not really. You see, I've lived out there most of my life. And this darned Town has changed so, it don't seem the same any longer. It's all full of new people . . . and foreigners. Most of 'em have never heard of me."

"What'll Ma think?"

"I don't know. I haven't told her, but she knows I had to go back some day. She'll think I'm comin' back. She'll have that to look forward to."

"You're not coming back . . . ever?"

"It ain't likely. They say an animal wants to go home when he's dying. Well, that's me. I want to go home."

"But you're not dying."

"No, but I ain't as young as I once was. I don't want there to be no mistake." He appeared to grow even more dejected. "If I'm out there, I'll know where I am. It's no place for a man like me here in this Town. Why, there ain't room to breathe any more." He took a cigar out of his yellow waistcoat pocket and offered it to Philip, who refused it instinctively, and then accepted it, moved by the pathetic effort at friendliness. The little man wanted to tell him something;

he wanted to treat him as a son, to create suddenly a bond that had never existed. He held a match for the cigar and then lighted his own. "It's like this, Philip," he said. "I've been thinking it over. You don't want to stay in this Town any more?"

"No."

"It's no place for a fella like you any more than it is for one like me. We've got to have room to breathe and think. I often think that. It's a nasty place, this Town—no room for a fella to do as he wants . . . always somebody a-watchin' of 'im."

Philip scarcely heard what he was saying, but he did notice the return of the haunting, half-comic accent. It was the first time that he had ever seen his father grave, the first time a serious thought had ever pierced the gay, shiny surface. And suddenly he felt a queer affection for the little man. Jason was making so great an effort that his face had turned red as a turkey-cock's.

"It's like this, Philip. . . . Why don't you come away with me to Australia? It's a fine life, and I'm rich out there." He waited for a moment, and when Philip didn't answer, he said, "You could begin all over again—like a new person. I know you could, because I did it myself . . . I started all over." Again he waited. "There's nothing to keep you, is there? No woman?"

He always thought of women first—his father. Philip turned slowly. "Yes . . . there is."

"Does she count as much as that?"

"Yes."

"You could marry her and take her along, couldn't you? She ain't a married woman, is she?"

"No."

"She'd be likely to go with you?"

"Yes, she'd go anywhere I chose, I guess."

"She must be the right sort."

There was a pause, and Jason struck suddenly at the thing that had been hanging over both of them like a shadow. "Out there, you'd be where your Ma couldn't put her nose in."

"Oh, I'm going away. . . . I'm not going to stay here."

Jason suddenly brightened. "Then come along with me. I'd even wait till you could get away. We ought to get better acquainted, Philip, and you'd like it out there." He laid a hand suddenly on Philip's arm. "I'll tell you something, if you promise not to tell your Ma . . . at least not till I'm gone."

He looked searchingly at Philip, who asked, "What is it?"

"You mustn't tell. You've got to promise."

"No, I won't tell."

"You've got brothers and sisters out in Australia!" Jason looked at him with an air of expectancy, but Philip only looked puzzled.

"What on earth do you mean by that, Pa?"

"You wouldn't be alone out there. You see I've got a family there too. . . . You'd have brothers and sisters there."

"But you're married to Ma."

"That's all right. I ain't a bigamist. I've just never been married to Dora—that's my other wife. She knows about Em. I told her everything. I guess she always liked me so much that not being married didn't matter."

The little man put his head on one side. At the thought of Dora his depression seemed to vanish. As for Philip, he simply stared, failing to live up to such an announcement. It neither surprised nor shocked him, for the whole thing seemed completely unreal, as if he were holding the fantastic conversation in a dream. It was the other thing that was real—the sight of the room in disarray with Mary's handkerchief laid on the table by the hand of Naomi . . . the memory of the sordid bed with the depression in the gray coverlet.

"You don't seem surprised," said his father.

"No. . . . No. . . . Nothing surprises me any more. I suppose if you wanted to have a family out there, it was all right. You can't expect a man to stop living." (He was right then: his father had had a woman out there.)

"But you see, Philip, they're your brothers and sisters . . . your father's children."

Philip made an effort. "How many of them are there?"

Jason's yellow waistcoat swelled with pride. "Three boys and two girls," he said. "Nobody can say I haven't done my part in helping the world along. All strapping big ones too. The youngest . . . Emma . . . is thirteen."

"Emma!"

"Yes. I called her after your Ma. I always liked the name, and I always liked your Ma too, when she's not having tantrums."

Suddenly Philip wanted to laugh. The desire arose from a strange mixture of pain and mirth. It was ridiculous.

"The others are Jason, Henry, Hector and Bernice.

It was Dora who named the others. Dora's a wonderful woman . . . like your Ma in a way, only Dora understands me."

There was a long, sudden silence, in which Philip thought, "If I'd only done as he did, everything would have been all right. He's happy and he's been free . . . always. I was weak and cowardly. I didn't do one thing or the other, and now there's no way out."

"You see what I mean," said Jason. "You'd have a home out there, and a family too. You wouldn't be going alone into a new country." He looked at his son wistfully. "You'd better come with me . . . woman or no woman."

"No, Pa . . . I can't. I've got to marry the woman, and I want to go to a new country . . . alone." His face was gray and drawn suddenly. "I've got to do it . . . it's the only thing."

"You'd better think it over, Philip."

"I've thought it over . . . I've been doing nothing else."

His father took up the tan derby. "And you won't tell your Ma, will you?"

"I won't tell her . . . ever. You needn't worry."

"You can tell her when I'm gone . . . I don't want to face her, that's all."

Jason went out, all depressed once more. Philip wasn't his boy at all. Emma had done something to him.

When he had gone, Philip sat down and began to laugh. He felt sick inside, and bruised. "Oh, my God! And I've got three brothers and two sisters in Australia! And that's where he got the accent. He got it from Dora!"

28

That night he sat with Mary in the Victorian drawing-room, planning their future. It was the first time he had ever entered the house, and he found the quiet, feminine sense of order in the big room soothing and pleasant, just as Emma had found it melancholy and depressing. But he hadn't come to her to be comforted and petted, as he had always done before: he was a different Philip, pathetic, and yet hard, kindly, yet cold in a way, and aloof. He did not speak of the stable, nor even of Naomi, and Mary, watching him, thought, "Perhaps I'm wrong. Perhaps after all he's been sensible and put all that behind him," and then, in the next moment, she saw him close his eyes suddenly. She knew what he was seeing . . . that room in the boarding-house where Naomi had died. "They ought never to have let him go there," she thought. "If any of them had any common sense, they wouldn't have let him do it." But she knew, too, that no one could have stopped him. He had gone because he saw it as his duty, a kind of penance: he was the sort who would never spare himself anything. . . .

And, reaching over, she touched his hand, but there was no response. After a time, he said, "It's all right, Mary. It's just a headache. I've been having them lately."

They couldn't marry and stay there in the Town with every eye watching them, waiting for some bit of scandal: but Philip seemed obsessed with the idea that they must be married at once. At first she thought it might be because he wanted her so much, and then she saw that it was for some other reason, which she could not discover.

She asked him why they must hurry, and he said, "Don't you want to be married? Don't you care any longer?"

"Of course I do, Philip. You ought to know that."

"Besides, I can't bear staying here any longer."

But even that, she felt, wasn't the real reason. She did not press him, and together they planned what they were to do. The lease on Mary's house was finished in a month, and she could go away with her sister-in-law, Rachel, and the two children, to Kentucky, where a sister of her mother's lived. And then, quietly, Philip could send the twins there, and come himself. He would bring old Molly to help care for them.

"Rachel loves children," said Mary, "and she'll never be separated from mine. She'd like two more in the household." (Only she wished they weren't Naomi's children . . . they would always be reminding him of Naomi. It seemed impossible to be rid of Naomi. The shadow of her was always there, coming between them.)

After a long silence, she said suddenly, "You *do* want to marry me, don't you, Philip?"

As he answered, it seemed to him that he came back from a great distance. "Marry you? Marry you? Why, of course I do. What have you been thinking of? What have I just been saying?"

"I don't want it to be because you think you have to . . . because of that night at the stable."

"No . . . no . . . of course not. I want to marry you. I couldn't think of *not* doing it. Where did you get such an idea?"

"I don't know . . . only you're so queer. It's as if I didn't make any difference any more . . . as if you could do without me."

For a moment he turned cross. "That's nonsense! And you know it. I can't help being like this . . . I'll be better later on."

"I don't know."

But he did not try to convince her. He simply sat staring into the shadows of the old room and at last he said, "And then when everything is settled, I want to go back to Africa . . . to Megambo."

"You can't do that, Philip . . . you mustn't. It would be like killing yourself. You can't go back where there's fever." She wanted to cry out wildly, desperately, against the vague, dark force, which she felt closing in about her.

"That's all nonsense," he said. "Doctors don't know everything. I shan't get the fever. I've got to go back. I want to go back there to paint . . . I've *got* to go back."

"You hated the place. You told me so."

"And you said once that I really liked it. You told me that some day I'd go back. Do you remember the day we were walking . . . a few days after I came home? You were right. I've got to go back. I'm like that queer Englishwoman."

"You won't go . . . leaving me alone."

"It wouldn't be for long . . . a year, maybe."

She did not answer him at once. "A year," she thought. "A year! But that's long enough. Too long. Anything could happen in a year. He might. . . ." Looking at him as he lay back in the old horsehair sofa, he became unbearably precious to her. She seemed to see him for the first time—the thin, drawn, tormented face, the dark skin, the high cheekbones, the thin lips, even the tired eyelids. He didn't know she was watching him. He wasn't perhaps even thinking of her. He looked young, like a boy . . . the way he had been long ago at twenty, when he was still hypnotized by Emma. She thought, "I can't lose him now just when we've a chance of being happy. I can't. I can't. He's mine . . . my Philip." He was free now of his mother, but he was still a captive.

She took his hand and pressed it against her cheek. "Philip, my Philip," she said. Opening his eyes, he looked at her for a moment lazily, and then smiled. It was the old shy smile she had seen on that solitary walk into the country. And then he said slowly what Naomi had once said— "I'm tired, Mary dear, that's all. . . ." She drew his head to her shoulder and began stroking it slowly. She thought, "It's odd. My grandmother would turn in her grave if she knew. Or maybe she'd understand. He's been mine always, since the beginning. I mean to keep him."

And yet she knew that he was in that very moment escaping her. She knew again the terrifying sensation of fighting some dark and shadowy thing which she could neither see nor feel nor touch.

"Philip," she said softly. "Philip."

"Yes."

"I'm going with you to Africa."

A little pause, and then— "You'd hate it there. You'd be miserable."

She saw suddenly that he had wanted to go alone, to hide himself away. She was hurt and she thought, "I can't let him do it. I've got to fight to save us both."

Aloud she said, "I wouldn't mind anything, Philip, but I've got to go with you. That's all I care about."

"There's the children."

"I've thought of that. I've thought of everything. We can leave them with Rachel and old Molly." She would make the trip a lark, a holiday. She would care for him every moment, and even see that he took the proper drugs. She would fight the fever herself. Nothing could touch him if she were there to protect him. She could put her own body and soul between him and death.

"You're sure you want to go, Mary?"

"Of course I'm sure. It's the only thing I want . . . never to be separated from you again. Nothing else makes any difference."

But this time she did not ask him whether he really wanted her. He smiled at her again. "A poor, weak fool like me doesn't deserve such a woman."

She kissed him, thinking, "Yes, my dear, you're poor and weak, and a bit of a fool, but it doesn't make any difference. Maybe that's only why I love you so much that it breaks my heart."

For a moment, it seemed to her that he again belonged to her, body and soul, as he had belonged to her on that terrible, beautiful night in the stable. She knew now. She understood that strange, sad happiness that always seemed to envelop the wicked Lily Shane.

29

When he told Emma the next day that he meant to marry Mary Conyngham, she turned suddenly white about the lips, and for once she was silent for a time before speaking. She must have seen that she had lost him forever, that she had lost even her grandchildren; but she had never yet surrendered weakly and she did not surrender now. She held her tongue, moved perhaps by the memory of Jason's, "You never learn anything, Em. You'd better leave the boy alone, if you ever expect to see him again."

She only said, "You might have waited a respectable time, so people wouldn't talk. Why, Naomi's hardly cold in her grave. You certainly don't owe her much, but. . . ."

"No one need know. We're going away. We'll keep it a secret if you like."

She softened a little. "Why couldn't you wait a little time?" (Mary might die or he might grow tired of her, if he would only wait.)

He looked at her steadily. "I've waited too long already, years too long."

"And now that your Pa's going back to Australia for a time, I'll be alone . . . I won't have anybody. It's hard when you're beginning to be old to find your life hasn't come to anything . . . all the struggle gone for nothing."

He saw that she was beginning to "work herself up" in the old fashion that she always used as a last resort. He knew the signs, and he didn't care any longer. She couldn't touch him that way. The trick had worn itself out, and he saw her with a strange, cruel clarity.

One thing, however, did soften him . . . "now that your Pa is going back to Australia for a time. . . ." She didn't know that she would never see Jason again.

"I'll come sometimes to visit you," he said. "You won't lose me."

"But it's not the same, Philip. When a girl marries, she still belongs to her mother, but when a boy marries, he is lost forever."

"But, Ma, I was married before."

"But that didn't count. Naomi didn't make any difference. She was always a sort of poor thing."

PART FOUR
THE JUNGLE

1

THEY made a part of the journey from the coast by the feeble half-finished railway that had only lately thrust its head like a serpent through the wilderness that had been untouched when Philip with Naomi and Swanson and Lady Millicent had made their way on foot to the coast. It was the end of the rainy season, before the coming of the burning heat, and Mary saw the country at its best, when it was still green and the earth still damp and pungent. The railroad came to an end abruptly, for no reason at all, in a clump of scrubby trees, and here they passed the second night in a shack shared by the East Indian guards. Long after nightfall, Mary heard the first roar of a lion— a strange, spasmodic, coughing sound, that came nearer and nearer until the frail wall of the shack trembled with the reverberation. Sitting up in bed, she fancied that she heard the beast circling the little shed. It came so near that she listened to the sound of its wheezing breath . . . a queer, brutal sound, that created a sudden vision of slobbering, ruthless jaws.

In the morning, she found the footprints of the beast in the damp earth, great toed prints pressed deep by the weight of the tawny body. And again the terror seized her, this time a terror less of the beast than of the dark thing for which he seemed to stand as a symbol. She knew as she stood looking down at the tracks in the earth that what had happened just before dawn was not a nightmare, but reality. It was part of this life which she was entering. Every day would be like this. She said nothing to Philip. She succeeded in behaving as if the night had been the most usual thing in the world. For she was aware that she must not disturb the peace that seemed to settle over him, slowly, with each mile that brought them nearer to Megambo and the brassy lake. He appeared no longer to be tired and troubled; yet he was not the old, gentle, dependent Philip she had always known. It was still a new one she had never seen before—a Philip who seemed still and quiet, who seemed at times to be looking far beyond the world that lay all about them. Twice she had discovered him thus staring across the scrub-covered plains, as if he were enchanted by the sense of vast emptiness.

She never shattered his moods by so much as a word, yet she was frightened, for at such times he seemed to withdraw far beyond her into a strange mystical world of his own where she had no part. Once she awakened in the night to find him sitting by the side of the fire, awake, looking up at the dome of cobalt sky powdered with stars. She lay there for a long time watching him. He turned toward her, and she closed her eyes quickly, pretending to be asleep. The old terror seized her that he was escaping her in an unearthly fashion that left her powerless.

On the fourth day, at the crest of a low hill covered with thorn-trees, Philip halted the little train of bearers, and said to her, "That ought to be the lake and Megambo." He pointed into the distance where the plain seemed to break up into a group of low hills covered with trees, and then far beyond to turn into the dark line of a real forest. At an immense distance, out of the heat, the mountains appeared like a mirage. She stared for a long time, and presently she saw that what at first she had believed to be only sky was in reality a vast lake. As she looked, it seemed in a way to come alive, to be striking the reflection of the sky from a surface made of metal. It was a dark, empty country, wild and faintly sinister in its stillness.

2

It was Swanson who saw them coming and went out to meet them on the edge of the forest. He had heard the news from a black runner on his way up the lake to join a party of German engineers who were bound inland. He was so changed that Philip looked at him for a moment with the air of a stranger. He was much thinner and had lost most of his hair. As if to compensate the loss, he had grown an immense sandy beard, which gave him the air of a comic monk. But the slow, china-blue eyes were the same, and the way of talking slowly, as if he were always afraid that his tongue would run faster than his dull brain.

Philip said, "This is my wife," and the shadow of Naomi suddenly fell on the three of them. "You got my letter?"

Poor Swanson had turned crimson, and stood awkwardly, holding his battered straw hat in his sausage-like hands. "No," he stammered. "No—what letter?"

For a moment there was a terrible silence. They both saw that he had expected Naomi. He had thought all the while that the woman he saw from afar off with the train of bearers that wound along the river was

Naomi . . . coming back. And it was true. She *had* come back. She had returned in the strangest way to take possession of them all. She was there in the stupid, puzzled eyes of Swanson, in the confusion of Mary, in the tragic silence of Philip.

It was Philip who spoke suddenly. "Naomi is dead!" And Mary thought bitterly, "She isn't dead! She isn't dead! This place belongs to her. This strange man wishes that I were Naomi."

"We've missed you," said Swanson dully.

"I'll tell you about it . . . later, when we're settled. Let's be moving on now."

"I'm glad you've come back. I got no letter from you; I only knew from the Germans who came through a week ago." Swanson had suddenly the air of a child who has forgotten the poem that he was to recite before a whole audience of people. He was aware, in his dull way, that he had blundered.

Philip said quickly, "I'm not coming back to work . . . at least not as a missionary. That's all finished."

"We never get any news out here," said Swanson humbly. "I didn't know."

"Are you alone?"

"No . . . there's a new man. Murchison . . . he's a preacher. He's doing Naomi's work."

(Naomi! Naomi! Naomi!)

"Let's go on now," said Philip. He shouted at the bearers an order to march, and as they walked, Philip said, "We passed a train of bearers in the distance yesterday . . . over beyond the Rocks of Kami. Who was it?"

For a moment Swanson was silent. He scratched his head. "Oh, that . . . that . . . it must have been

that queer Englishwoman's train . . . going back
alone."

They were entering the borders of the real forest,
where the moist earth was covered by a tangle of vines
and a pattern of light and dark. Phillip asked,
"Why . . . alone?"

"She died three days ago . . . of the fever.
Murchison would have sent her away if she hadn't
been sick. She abused missionaries. She said we were
spoiling her country."

"Yes . . . she thought it belonged to her."

The shadows grew thicker and thicker all about
them. They walked in silence, save for the occasional
chatter of a monkey.

"It was the third time she'd been back," said
Swanson.

"She must have been quite old."

"About sixty, maybe. She told Murchison to stop
praying over her. 'Stop slobbering over me,' is what
she said."

"Yes . . . she *would* say that. Where did you bury
her?"

"Down the lake . . . by the lagoon."

By the lagoon . . . the spot where Philip had come
upon the black women carrying water from the lake.
It was a beautiful spot, a quiet place to rest.

"She asked to be buried there. She liked the place."

They walked in silence until suddenly through the
trees and the tangle of vines the glittering lake became
visible, and a moment later the clearing on the low
hill where Philip had once fought back the ravenous
jungle. There was no trace of the old mission that
had been burned; there were two new huts, larger than

the old, built by the patient Swanson of mud and of stones dragged up from the river-bed in dry season.

Mary, watching Philip, knew what he was seeing. Naomi . . . Naomi. The place belonged to her in a strange, inexplicable fashion. She saw suddenly that Naomi perhaps belonged in a place like this with a stupid man like Swanson . . . a man who was all faith, too stupid even to have doubts.

On a platform before one of the huts a strange figure sat before a table reading aloud in the native tongue some long harangue which was repeated after him by ten or a dozen black girls who sat swaying monotonously to the rhythm of their own voices. The sound was droning and monotonous, like the sound of a hive of bees.

"That's Murchison," said Swanson. The figure was dressed in a black suit like an undertaker, with a high white celluloid collar gaping about a reedlike neck, which it no longer fitted. On his head was a stiff straw hat, yellowed with age. He wore steel-rimmed spectacles that in the heat had slipped well down upon a long nose.

"He's dressed up to greet you," said Swanson.

The black girls, all save one or two, had ceased their buzzing and were staring now with pokes and giggles at the newly arrived procession. The Reverend Mr. Murchison halted the two dutiful girls who were going mechanically on with their lesson, and stepped down from his throne. He was an ugly little man with a sour expression.

He shook hands and to Mary he said, "I suppose you'll want to take back your girls. I've been teaching them while you were away. We've made a good deal of progress, I guess. . . ."

There was a silence and Mary said:

"But I'm not Naomi . . . Naomi is dead."

The Reverend Mr. Murchison passed lightly over his error. "Like true children of God," he said, "let us kneel here in the dust and humbly thank Him for having brought you safely through a perilous journey."

The little man flopped duly to his knees, followed by Swanson. Mary waited, watching Philip, and then she saw him kneel along with the others. He didn't protest. He knelt and bowed his head. She knew suddenly why he was doing this—because it would have pleased Naomi. Then she knelt, too, with the old fear in her heart. She was afraid, because he was praying. . . . He kept slipping further and further. . . .

"O Just and Almighty God," said the dry, flat voice of the withered Mr. Murchison, "we thank Thee for having brought these poor humble travelers safely through their perilous journey. . . ." Swanson knelt dumbly, his head bowed. It was the gnatlike Mr. Murchison who ruled the mission. But it was the meek Swanson who was the servant of God. Mary saw all at once the vast and immeasurable difference.

3

Philip made no effort to paint. The box containing his things lay forgotten in a dark corner of the hut, and for three days he went out to spend hours wandering alone along the shores of the tepid lake. Mary only waited, fighting a queer unnatural jealousy of the ghost that walked with him. And on the fourth night she was awakened by his voice saying, "Mary, I feel ill. I'm afraid I've caught the fever again." It was a voice peaceful and full of apology.

By noon the fever had taken possession of his thin body, and by evening he lay still and unconscious. For three days and three nights Mary sat beside him, while Swanson fumbled with his medicines, and kept saying in his kind, clumsy way, "He'll be all right now. You mustn't fret. Why, he's strong as an ox. I've seen him like this before." She sat by the bed, bathing Philip's thin face, touching his head gently with her hand. In her weariness she deceived herself, thinking at times, "He's cooler now. It will pass," but in the end she always knew the bitter truth—that the fever hadn't passed. It was always there, burning, burning, burning the little life that remained.

Sometimes in his delirium he talked of Lady Millicent and Swanson, but nearly always of Naomi. She was always there, as if she, too, stayed by the side of the crude bed . . . watching.

In the middle of the fourth night, when Swanson had come in to look at him, Philip stirred slowly, and opened his eyes. For a moment he looked about him with a bewildered look in the burning blue eyes, and then he reached out weakly, and took her hand. "Mary," he said, "my Mary . . . always mine since the beginning."

He asked her to get a pencil and a block of paper out of his box, and then he said, "I want you to write something for me. I'll tell you what it is. . . ." When she returned, he lay silent for a time, and then he said, "It's this, Mary. Listen. . . . Write. . . . I think it ought to go like this. . . . 'Whatever happens, after my death, I mean that my children, Philip and Naomi . . . whom I had by my first wife, Naomi Potts, are never to be left in the care of my mother, Emma Downes.' " He hesitated for a moment, and then weakly murmured, " 'The same is my wish with regard to any child who may be born after my death . . . of my second wife, Mary Conyngham.' " Again he paused. " 'This is my express wish.' " He beckoned with his eyes to Swanson. "Raise me up," he said. "Here, Mary, give me the pencil and the paper." She held the drawing-block for him while the thin, brown hand wrote painfully the words "Philip Downes."

The pencil dropped to the floor. "Now, Swanson . . . you must sign it as witness. . . ." Swanson laid him back gently and then wrote his own name and went quietly out.

As his grotesque figure shut out from the doorway the blue of the African night, she knelt beside him, and, pressing the dry, hot hands against her cheek, she cried out, "But you're not going to die, Philip. . . . You're not going to die! I won't let you!" She would hold him by her own will. Anything was possible in this strange, terrifying world by the lake.

"No . . . Mary . . . I'm not going to die. I only wanted to make certain."

The room grew still, and all at once she found herself praying. Her lips did not move, but she was praying. She was ashamed to have Philip hear her, and she was ashamed, too, before God that she should turn to Him only when she had desperate need. But none of these things made any difference. In her terror and anguish she prayed. God would hear her. He would know and understand if he were a good God.

Then suddenly she felt his hand relax ever so little, gently, and she said softly, "Philip! Philip!"

After a long silence, he said, "Yes . . . Mary," and pressed her hand feebly. "I'm here."

"Philip . . . I think there is to be a child. . . . You must live on his account."

"I'm glad, Mary . . . I mean to live. I mean to live."

She fell to praying again, and again she felt the thin hand relax. This time it slipped slowly from her cheek.

"Philip! Philip!"

He did not answer, and again she called, "Philip! Philip!"

His eyes were closed, but he still breathed. She began to pray once more, pressing her body close to his. She never knew how long she knelt there, but presently she knew that the thin, brown hands were no longer hot. The fever had gone out of them, and she thought suddenly, "The thing has passed, and he is safe." But the coolness turned slowly to a strange dead chill. She raised her head and looked at him. He seemed asleep, but he was so still. She touched his face, and the head fell a little to one side. The mouth opened. And then she knew. . . .

Without a sound, she slipped to the dusty earth beside the cot. She tasted the earth with her lips, but she did not even raise her head.

When she came out of the hut to find Swanson, it was still dark, although a faint rim of light had begun to show above the surface of the lake. Near the opening in the barricade, the night fire had burned to a glowing pile of embers. For a long time she stood there beneath the stars, listening to the mysterious sounds of the African night, on the very spot where Philip had once stood, half-naked, listening to the sound of the drums, lost in a strange, savage delight at the discovery of being alive and young and a man. And at last there came to her the feeling that she was not alone, but surrounded by the creatures who filled all the night with their sense of life. She was not alone, for Naomi was there, too. This strange world belonged to Naomi. She herself was only an intruder.

A sound of birds churring in the darkness roused her, and she went off to find Swanson. He was asleep in his hut and he wakened slowly, clumsily. For once, understanding without being told, he rose and followed her.

As the gray turned to rose above the lake, and the sounds of the waking forest grew more distinct, she knelt by the side of the cot while Swanson prayed, and slowly she came to understand that in his simplicity he was a good man, akin in his selfless simplicity, to the wild things in the gloomy forest that surrounded them. She understood, too, that Philip had meant to die thus, that he had come here to the spot where death was certain. But she saw, too, that he had really died long ago, on the night that had followed their happiness in the room above the stable. She didn't hate Naomi: she had never hated her.

The morning light began to filter in through the doorway, and the spaces below the thatching. She stirred and took up the drawing-block on which Philip had written his name. No, it was not Naomi that she hated. . . .

Two days later they buried him beneath the acacia not far from the fresh grave of the battered old Lady Millicent, on the spot where once, for the first time, he had known a blinding intimation of what life might be. He had known it again afterward—once as he stood in the moonlight listening to the drums, and again, on the day the wicked Lily Shane came to the stable; and then at last on the night he returned to find Mary waiting in the darkness.

It was the simple Swanson who read the service, because Mary wished it; for the Reverend Mr. Murchison made her think of Christians like Emma Downes and her brother, Elmer Niman. . . . It was the Reverend Mr. Murchison who would be the first Bishop of East Africa.

4

When Emma returned home one night from the restaurant to find a letter from Madagascar addressed in a strange handwriting, she knew what had happened. For a long time, she sat at the dining-room table, staring at the letter, for the sight of it threw her into one of those rare moods when for a moment she gave herself over to reflection and so came unbearably near to seeing herself. She had known all along that it was certain to happen, yet the knowledge had not prepared her in any way. It seemed as hard to bear as if he had been killed suddenly by some terrible accident in the Mills.

He had not told her he was returning to Megambo until he had gone, when it was too late for her to act; and now she knew that he had died without ever seeing the letter she had sent, as it were, into space, to follow him in time to turn him back. He had died, she saw, without even knowing at all she had written, begging him not to be so hard, to think of her as his mother who was willing to sacrifice everything for his happiness. She would (she had written) forgive Mary, and try her best to behave toward her as if Mary were her own daughter. What more could she have done? To forgive Mary who had stolen him from her?

As she sat there the dull pain of a hopeless loneliness took possession of her. Here she was, at fifty, beginning for the first time to feel tired and in need of companionship, and she had no one—not even her own grandchildren. It was cruel, she told herself, to have suffered as she had suffered, with no reward but this—to end life alone after struggling for so long, always bent upon doing the right thing. Surely she had lived as God meant her to live, a Christian life filled with sacrifice to individuals and duty. Surely no one since Job had been so bitterly tried . . . no husband . . . no son . . . alone.

And presently her blunt, strong fingers tore open the envelope, and she read the letter. It was brief, almost like a cablegram . . . a few lines which told her what she already knew, that Philip, her little boy, was dead. The sight of the word "dead" and the name "Mary Downes" signed at the end, filled her with a sudden wave of bitterness that swept away all her sorrow. It was Mary who had stolen him from her like a thief. What could be more sinful than to steal from a mother a son for whom she had sacrificed her whole life? It was Mary who had destroyed him in the end, by filling his head with strange ideas, and leading him back to Africa. She was finished now with Mary. She would like to see Mary dead. And some day (perhaps it had happened already) Mary would receive the wandering letter and read, "I will even forgive Mary and try to treat her as if she were my own daughter." Then perhaps for a moment she would feel remorse over what she had done.

The letter lay crumpled in her work-stained hand. She began suddenly to weep, falling forward and burying her head in her arms beneath the glow of the gasdome, painted with wild-roses. She had suffered too long. . . . She kept seeing Philip as a little boy. . . .

After midnight, when she had ceased to weep, she rose, and, turning out the light, went up the creaking stairs of the home she had made her own by the labor of her own hands . . . the house (she thought bitterly) she had meant for Philip. She had done everything for his sake.

Alone in her own room, she thought, "I must not give in. I must go on. God will in the end reward me." The old spirit began to claim her.

She put on mourning (a thing her conscience had not permitted her to do when Naomi died), and in the Town people said, "Poor Emma Downes! She has had almost too much to bear. It is a life like hers that makes you sometimes doubt God . . . a good woman like that deserves a better reward." She even had a letter from Moses Slade.

Only McTavish did not join in the pity. To him it seemed that the chain of her calamities was as inevitable as a Greek tragedy. It was not God, but Emma herself, who had created them. And he saw what the others did not, that Emma was by no means a broken woman.

And, after a time, she came even to create a certain glory out of Philip's death, for she found that people believed he had gone back to Megambo to take up his old work, and so had gone back to certain death and martyrdom. She did not disillusion them: it could not, surely, be wrong to let them believe that her Philip was a martyr. Philip, who must now be with God, would understand. And, sitting in church, she knew that people about her thought of him as her martyred son. He had not lived to be Bishop of East Africa, but he had died a martyr. . . .

There remained, however, one more blow. Two months after Philip's death, she received a second letter, in a strange handwriting, this time from Australia. As she opened it, there fell out a photograph on a picture postcard. It was the photograph of seven people, all of them strangers save Jason, who sat in the middle of the front row beside a large, rather coarse and plain woman, whose hand rested on his shoulder. At the bottom was written: *"Upper row: Jason, Henry, Hector. Lower row: Bernice, old Jason, self and Emma."*

It was "self and Emma" which startled her. Who was "self," and who was "Emma"?

She read:

"Dear Madam:

"I am writing because I knew you would be interested in the details of Jason's death. . . ."

(Jason's death! Jason dead!)

"He died a month ago on board ship coming home. . . ."

(Coming home! What did it mean—coming home? This house was Jason's home!)

"He died from a fall down some steps. I guess he had been taking a drop too much. You know how Jason was. And he hit his head where he had fallen once before. You remember the scar he had. Well, that's where he hit himself. He didn't ever become conscious again, and died two days later.

"I know you will be wondering about the postcard. Well, it is me and Jason and our five children. No, Jason was no bigamist. We was never married. He came to my father's ranch looking for work twenty-four years ago. The eldest, Jason, is twenty-two come Michaelmas. He wasn't much good as a worker, but he was good company and the ranch was a lonely place, so Pa kept him on. He told such good stories. And the following spring—I was eighteen then, but developed like a woman of twenty-five, he seduced me. I guess I wanted to be seduced. You know what a

way Jason had with women. My only complaint against him as a husband was that it was hard to keep him in order. Well, when Pa found out that I was in the family way, he was hoppin' mad, and I didn't care, because I was off my nut about Jason. Pa said he had to marry me, and Jason said he couldn't, because he already had a wife. So then when Pa had cooled down a bit, he said we was all to go to Sydney, and pretend we was married there, and if Jason ever deserted me he'd go after him with a gun and shoot him. The way it was about here then, it didn't make much difference if you was married or not. It was kind of wild. So we pretended we was married because Pa was a believer and a Primitive Methodist.

"Well, at the time Pa died, we had four children, and he left everything to me, I being his only child, and heir. Emma was born after he died. Maybe you'll think it was funny about her name. It was Jason who wanted to call her Emma. He said he'd like to because it made him think of old times. I said it was all the same to me, though I wanted to call her Opal.

"Jason must have told you that he was rich and owned a lot of land. He was always a liar. Well, it ain't true. He didn't own a square foot of land, and he never made a ha'penny in all the time he was my husband. I even gave him the money to go back to America to see you. He wanted to go so bad I couldn't say no to him. I guess he was curious about that son of his in America, and maybe he wanted to see you, too. I just wanted you to know this, so you wouldn't think there was any money coming to you or your son.

"I always speak of him as my husband. He may have been married to you, but he was really mine. He

was happy out here and I need never to reproach my-
self for anything I did while he was alive. He always
belonged to me and as I've often told him, before
he passed away, that counts for more than all the
banns and marriage certificates in the world. That's
why I didn't mind his paying you a brief visit. I
KNEW he'd come back to me.

"Well, I can't think of any more that ought to be
said. He often spoke of you kindly. The worst he
ever said was, 'Em had an unfortunate temperament.'
I think that was how he put it. He was embalmed on
ship, and at his funeral looked very natural. He was
a remarkable young-looking man for his age. Well,
I will stop now.

"Yours respectively,

"Dora Downes.

"(Mrs. Jason Downes.)

"Postscriptum. The picture is good of all except
me and Emma. I never did photograph well. It was a
thing Jason always said—that photographs never did
me justice."

When she had finished reading, Emma took up the
postcard and looked again at the three strapping sons
and the two robust daughters, but her chief interest
lay in the figure of Dora Downes (Mrs. Jason
Downes!) She was a healthy, rather plain woman,
with an enormous shelflike bosom on which her fat
double chin appeared to rest. Beside her, Jason appeared, small and dapper and insignificant, like a male
spider beside the female who devours her mate after
he has filled Nature's demands.

"She must have been plain always," thought Emma. "She's really a repulsive woman."

Then she rose and, going into the kitchen, lifted an iron plate from the stove, and thrust into the coals the letter and the picture postcard, sending them the way of that other letter left by Jason twenty-seven years earlier.

One thing in the letter she could not forget—"*I knew he'd come back to me.*"

It was a little more than a year later that Moses Slade and Emma Downes were married quietly in Washington, but not so quietly that Sunday newspapers did not have pictures of the bride and bridegroom taken outside the church. They had come together again, through the strangest circumstances, for Moses, still unmarried, had found himself suddenly involved with Mamie Rhodes, who Emma had once said "did something to men." He was, in fact, so involved that blackmail or the ruin of a career seemed the only way out . . . the only way save marriage with some woman so prominent and so respectable as to suffocate any doubts regarding his breach of morality. "And what woman," he had asked himself, "fitted such a rôle as well as Emma Downes, who was now a widow . . . a *real* widow whose troublesome son was dead." He saw with his politician's eye all the protection she could give him as a prominent figure, known for her moral strictness and respectability, pitied for the trials she had borne with such Christian fortitude. Such a woman, people (voters) would say, could not marry him if the stories about Mamie Rhodes were true.

So he had gone to Emma and, confessing everything, thrown himself upon her mercy. For five days she kept him in doubt, and terror, lest she refuse, and in the end she accepted, but only at a price . . . that it should remain, as she expressed it, "a marriage in name only."

In the end, she subdued even Moses Slade. It was in reality Emma who sat in his seat in the House of Representatives. It was Emma who cast his votes. She became, in a small way, a national figure, concerned always with moralities and reforms. She came into a full flowering as chairman or member of a dozen committees and movements against whisky and cigarettes, and for Sunday closing. She made speaking tours, when she was received by palpitating ladies who labored in vain to sap the robust vitality of their country. There were times when her progress became a marvel of triumph. She was known as a splendid speaker.

But the apotheosis of her glory was reached in the war, when she offered her services as a speaker to right and to left—to aid recruiting, or Y.M.C.A. funds, to attack Bolshevism and denounce the barbarous Huns. She had a marvelous speech which began on a quavering note: "I had a son of my own once, but he gave his life as a martyr in Africa, fighting the good fight for God and home and Christian faith, even as all our boys are fighting to-day against a whole race, a whole nation bent upon spreading murder and destruction across the face of God's bright earth. (Cheers.) If my son were alive to-day, he would be over there, on the rim of the world (cheers), etc., etc."

It was in making this speech that she wore herself out. The end came on a wet, chill night in Kansas

City, when, speaking on behalf of the Y.M.C.A., she was taken with a chill. Moses Slade came from Washington to be at her bedside, and so was there at the end to tell her that "she'd given her life as much as any soldier who fell in Flanders Field."

She was buried in the Town, alone, for the grave of her husband was in Australia, and that of her son beside a tepid lake in East Africa. The funeral service, in the enthusiasm of the war, became a sort of public festival, done to the titanic accompaniment of the Mills, which pounded now as they had never done before, to heap up piles of shells in the dead, abandoned park of Shane's Castle. It was an end which she would have liked. The new preacher, more sanctimonious but less moving than the Reverend Castor, made a high-flown and flowery funeral oration. He did it skilfully, though it was a difficult thing to speak of her trials and still not raise the ghosts of Naomi and the Reverend Castor. But the ghosts were there: they troubled the minds of every member of the congregation.

In conclusion, he said in a voice rich with enthusiasm, "She never lost her faith through trials more numerous than are the lot of most. She gave her son to God and her own life to this great cause which is so near to the heart of us all. She was brave and courageous, and generous and tolerant, but she fought always for the right like a good soldier. She never had any doubts. She was, in brief, all that is meant when our hearts lead us to say of some one, 'She was a good woman. . . .'"

It was in the following year that the Town bought the Castle from Lily Shane who had never returned to it since the night of the riot. The Town demolished the place and even dug away the hill itself to make a site for the new railway station. When the wreckers attacked the stable they found a room whose walls were covered with pencil sketches. By the window stood a half-finished painting black with soot and dust. On the table there was a coffee-pot, several soiled plates, and a fragment of something which turned out to be bread. Nearby beneath a layer of soot lay a woman's handkerchief of fine linen marked with the initials M.C.; one of the workmen took it home to his wife. The other things—the sketches and the painting—were thrown into a heap and burned on the very spot where eight years before there had been another fire in the snow.

THE END